# THOMAS ANNELY

*A Story Inspired by Real People and Real Events*

by Fred and Mary Marzocchi

Visit our website at
www.StillwaterPress.com
for more information.

First Stillwater River Publications Edition.
ISBN: HC: 978-1-963296-98-3
PB: 978-1-963296-99-0
Library of Congress Control Number: 2024920103

1 2 3 4 5 6 7 8 9 10
Written by Fred and Mary Marzocchi.
Cover illustration by Fred Marzocchi.
Published by Stillwater River Publications,
West Warwick, RI, USA.

Names: Marzocchi, Fred and Mary, author.
Title: Thomas Annely : a story inspired by real people and real events / by Fred and Mary Marzocchi.
Description: First Stillwater River Publications edition. | West Warwick, RI, USA : Stillwater River
    Publications, [2024]
Identifiers: ISBN: 978-1-963296-98-3 (hardcover) | 978-1-963296-99-0 (paperback) | LCCN:
    2024920103
Subjects: LCSH: Annely, Thomas--Fiction. | Gunsmiths--United States--History--18th century--
    Fiction. | Firearms--Fiction. | Revolutionaries--United States--History--18th century--Fic-
    tion. | Patriotism--Fiction. | United States--History--Revolution, 1775-1783--Fiction. |
    LCGFT: Historical fiction. | Biographical fiction.
Classification: LCC: PS3613.A79246 T46 2024 | DDC: 813/.6--dc23

The cover art and design elements throughout the book were created by Fred Marzocchi. The illustration depicting Thomas Annely on the front cover was from the artist's imagination on how he envisioned Thomas to look.

*To see more of Fred's art please visit: fredmarzocchi.com*

# NOTE TO READER

Believe it or not, this story was told to me by an original American Made 18th Century Flintlock Musket.

In 1963, I purchased a flintlock musket from an antique gun collector in Bellingham, Massachusetts. The collector had two muskets for sale; one was a beautiful British Brown Bess, in very good condition, the other was an American made musket. The American made musket was not in as good condition as the Brown Bess, but it was totally original. What made it really special was the maker himself, Thomas Annely, had etched his name onto the flintlock plate.

I just had to buy it and have kept the musket hanging over my fireplace for all these years. I love this musket as much as I love my country and all of its history.

Many years later, I decided to research the name, Thomas Annely, more aggressively. I shared with my wife Mary what I had discovered, and she was as compelled as I was to look even further into the Annely family name.

What we found was that Thomas Annely, his sister Elizabeth and other members of the Annely family played an important part in the building of our country. They not only witnessed historical events, but risked their lives for our new country's fight for freedom.

-Fred Marzocchi

THOMAS ANNELY

# CHAPTER I

**KING GEORGE II**
Actual Portrait

'Tis the 5th day of August, in the year of our Lord, 1751, when I, Thomas Annely, stepped outside of my family home and made my way to our small gunsmith shop in Bristol, England. A light rain had begun to fall as I hurried along the cobblestone streets of the portside city.

I could hear in the distance the familiar sounds of gulls squawking and the tinkering of the tall ship's masts. As a boy, I sat along the harborside, watching the merchant ships set sail to faraway lands. I would imagine myself aboard one of the mighty ships, fighting off pirates with my trusted musket and shooting them square between the eyes. "Aye, there would be no better shot than I!" I would exclaim. Now that I am older, I still reminisce about the days of my youth.

I continued my walk down Small Street, where our gunmaking shop has been for nearly forty years. Many an Annely learned the fine craftsmanship of gunmaking in that well-worn shop. I crossed the street, approached the heavy oak door, and paused to straighten the weathered sign. I ran my fingers over the engraved gold lettering, "Gun Endeavors," the new name I chose after I was left to manage the workshop myself.

As I entered through the heavy door, the familiar smells of linseed oil and fresh-cut wood filled my nostrils. I paused to look around the dusty shop and felt a pang of nostalgia for the days I worked alongside my brothers. I could almost hear their voices and the day-to-day sounds of gunmaking coming through the silence. The empty bench before me had only one pistol, ready to be assembled. It pained me to know that the business was indeed dying. "I am a gunmaker, not a salesman or a bookkeeper," I shouted out to myself, frustrated at being left to mind the shop without the aid of my family.

My memories of always being by my father's side, watching him as he worked, filled my heart. He was a master gunsmith and much to my mother's chagrin, I spent more days here, learning from him, than I did schooling.

He would let me work the bellows some days while he tended to the fire in the forge. I loved the sounds of the iron rods softening in the crackling fire. His strong arm hammered, again and again, the molten iron against the anvil. "Mind yourself, Thomas," he would warn as sparks flew around me. I would watch him in awe and hoped, someday, to be as fine a gunsmith as he.

As fate would have it, my father passed away suddenly when I was only a mere lad. My poor mum, a brave woman, did all she could to keep the business afloat. "There'll be no more schooling, lads; now you need to work," she stated firmly. My older brothers Edward, Richard, and I worked hard for our mum and survived well enough until my brothers left for America.

My brother Richard was the first to voyage to the new land. He established a workshop building muskets in New York, while accumulating a small fortune as a merchant of goods from all around the world. Like so many, he ventured out to be a part of the new world and had become quite wealthy in America. He would travel back to Bristol on many occasions.

Soon after, my sister Elizabeth joined him in America. Unwed and with no dowry, she left our homeland with the hopes of a better life for herself and was a great help to our brother Richard.

The workshop Richard established in America grew by leaps and bounds, and he was in need of an apprentice. His business associates in Bristol recommended that he take along a young man named Francis Lewis, who was the son of a prominent family from Wales. As a young lad, Francis suffered a great misfortune; both of his parents died unexpectedly, leaving him alone with no siblings. Fortunately, he was raised by a wealthy aunt who saw that Francis was well-educated. When he came of age, he inherited his family properties, which he wisely sold to purchase merchandise. Francis was quite intelligent for a man of only twenty-one years of age and was eager to set sail to bring his goods to America.

It was obvious that Richard and Francis were cut from the same cloth and worked well together. As the years passed, their business grew tremendously and became a great success.

On September 6th of the year 1743, we received terrible news from America. Sadly, my brother Richard was stricken with dysentery and died within days. The Lord took him from this world too soon and in the prime of his success. Our dear mother had lost her secondborn without even a glance at his face once more.

In my brother Richard's will, he had bequeathed his spacious countryside estate, Whitestone to Elizabeth. "'Tis a magnificent home, made from the pure white stone it sits upon, high on the hill overlooking the bay waters of New York," she wrote.

To my surprise, my brother left me his townhouse in New York City. My good brother must have felt he needed to repay me for a debt I had paid on his behalf back in Bristol. It was very generous of him, and I am grateful knowing I would have a home in New York City if I ever desired to go to America.

My sister Elizabeth became very close to Francis Lewis and soon they were married. It seemed natural that the two would marry, for I sensed their love for each other in her letters.

As far as my brother Edward was concerned, he found it extraordinary that Richard did not mention himself nor our mother in his will. This raised strong doubts in his mind about the authenticity of the will Elizabeth and Francis sent him. Upon the advice of his New York attorney, the honorable William Kempe, he suggested he come to America to settle our brother's estate. Soon after, Edward voyaged to New York City with his wife Eva and two young sons.

Once in America, Edward met with Elizabeth and Francis, and after much deliberation, all parties agreed that Edward would take over Richard's business in New York City. Francis Lewis would continue handling all the foreign trades at sea. Thus began a new life for Edward and his family. As the years passed, Edward and Francis managed to find harmony working together despite any differences they may have had.

It was well past supper time as I walked along the dark alleyways to my home. My mum had grown accustomed to me working late hours and was grateful I was doing my best to keep the family business going. My dear, sweet Mother; I would be hard-pressed to find such a special and tender lady as she.

When I entered our humble home, I saw my mother sitting near the warmth of the hearth, spinning yarn. The aroma of the hare stew kept warm over the smoldering fire made me realize how hungry I was.

"Thomas, is that you?" she called out as she spun. "Yes, Mum." I replied, bending down to kiss her cheek.

She rose to get me my usual tankard of ale and filled my bowl with the savory, warm stew. I tucked into it like a ravenous beast. She sat silently across from me with her hands folded as if praying.

"Your brother Bernard has been anxious to see you; he is upstairs reading and writing as always," she said as she rose and cleared the table.

I hurried and finished the last bites of the delicious stew. "Goodnight, Mum; I will go up to see him now," I said, anxious to hear what my brother had to say. "Goodnight, son, and do not let those business worries keep you from a good night's rest," she replied.

Bernard, my older brother, fancied himself a scholar. His love of books often infuriated our father, for he had high hopes of all his sons following him in the gunsmith trade. If not for Bernard, our business would have surely gone under sooner. The royalties he received from his published book helped keep us afloat.

Bernard was in bed in our shared room, with a candle burning on his side table. His nose was deep inside some profound book, lost in its story. He closed the book and sat up to face me. "Good evening, Thomas. I know 'tis late, but I need to speak with you."

"Aye, Bernard, I fear I know what you are about to say," I sighed.

Bernard spoke softly, in his cool and calm manner, "Thomas, we are experiencing a very depressing time. The people feel King George II is paying more attention to the American colonies than our own country.

Regarding our business, I reviewed the financials with my banker and he has advised me not to invest any more money. We should declare bankruptcy, for there is not enough revenue to pay our expenses," he said remorsefully.

"Bernard, I have tried my best. 'Tis just too difficult without Edward here, and now there's hardly enough work to earn a day's pay."

"Thomas, you must not feel any remorse; no one has been as dedicated as you to keeping our family business going. What will you do? Gunsmithing is your passion?"

I proceeded to tell Bernard about a letter I received from our brother Edward. "Edward has grand ideas of building up the business and wrote that my gunsmithing skills are much needed."

"Well, Thomas, perhaps 'tis time you went and joined Edward and our sister Elizabeth in America?" Bernard implied.

Suddenly, my heart beat faster as the reality of it all sank in. "Aye, Bernard, it has been my dream to keep the family business going, but it seems I have little choice but to take Edward's offer. 'Tis the only way I will be able to repay my debt to you and send money to Mum," I replied with despair.

Bernard paused and let out a deep breath. "Thomas, 'tis not what I wanted to happen either, but it seems to be the wisest choice now. I suspect Edward needs a trusted brother to be working beside him. We both know the business of Richard's estate left a sour taste in his mouth and has made him a very suspicious man. Have you mentioned anything to our mother about going to work for Edward in America?"

"No, not yet, but you know our mum; she senses it, for sure."

"She's a wise woman, no doubt. Try to get some rest, and we will talk to her in the morning," replied Bernard as he blew out the candle and closed his eyes to sleep.

I could not fathom leaving my beloved England, where I was born. Nor did I want to leave my dear mum and Bernard to fend for themselves. Yet, deep down inside, I knew my gunmaking days here in Bristol were coming to an end.

It was a restless night, worrying about telling my mum I was leaving. Bernard woke first, and I followed, weary from my lack of sleep, as I stumbled to breakfast.

"Good morning, Thomas; come and break your fast," she greeted. "Tea is fine for now, Mum," I said as I joined Bernard at the table.

As usual, my mum was the first to rise and was always tending to the hearth, preparing the meals for the day. I never appreciated my mother more than today, knowing how much I would miss her. She sat beside us, sensing I had something to say and spoke bluntly, "Get on with it, Thomas. Tell me what's on your mind."

I broke the news to her about the business going bankrupt and explained to her that I did all I could not to let this happen. Bernard chimed in, agreeing with all that I said. "I did my best, Mum," I said sheepishly.

She reached out and grasped my hands, staring directly into my eyes. "Thomas, I know how hard you have tried. You have become a master gunmaker like your father; God rest his soul. He would have been very proud of you." Her words touched me deeply and filled my heart with pride.

I then told her about Edward wanting me to join him in America and how the new world needed experienced gunmakers. I could see she was trying to hide her despair about another one of her children going off to America.

It was evident to her that I had made up my mind, and after much conversation, she agreed it would be the wisest choice. "I trust your judgment, son," she said as she rose and returned to cooking.

7

I spoke softly, "Thank you for understanding." She turned around, her eyes moist with tears. "If you are determined to go, then I give you my blessing. However, you must promise me one thing. When you arrive in America, teach them how to build a proper musket."

We both smiled, and I replied, "I will, Mum; I'll teach them the Annely way."

I planned to leave on the first of September, so it was time to pack up all my belongings. My brother Bernard, always quick with ways to make money, came into our room carrying a small package wrapped up in strings. "Thomas, I have a tip on how you can earn some extra money in America," he said as he handed me the package. "Inside are a few British newspapers for you to take with you. I have heard that news from the homeland is quite popular amongst the colonists. When you reach America, the lads who work for the local gazettes will give you five to six times more than what I paid for these. You'll earn a few shillings, enough to get yourself a proper meal with some money left over, compliments of me," he said with a wink and a smile.

I tilted my head back and laughed, "Thank you kindly, brother. I am certain I will need a good meal after the voyage, and a few shillings will come in handy, too."

I spent the rest of the week finishing the little work I had left to complete and closing up the gunshop. Now, it was time for me to leave my old family gun shop for what may be the very last time. I gathered all my tools, turned, and locked the door behind me. I paused and glanced once more at our sign, Gun Endeavors, wondering what would happen to the old shop.

With great sadness, I left behind the business my father had built. Yet, with great expectations, I looked forward to what my future would bring.

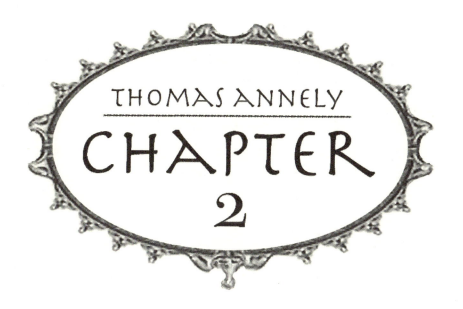

THOMAS ANNELY

# CHAPTER 2

Today is the day I will embark on my journey to America. I woke up before the first light, not able to sleep with all the excitement to come. I sat in bed and gazed at my brother Bernard, sleeping soundly beside me. I would miss my kind brother and all the days we shared.

I went downstairs, surprised to see my best shirt and breeches lying neatly over the chair by the hearth. My favorite leather boots were polished up beautifully on the floor next to the chair. A tear came to my eye, realizing my dear mum had stayed up into the night preparing them for me. I heard soft steps behind me as I turned to see my mum standing there with a warm smile. It left me with a lasting impression of her in my mind. I went over and held her in a long embrace. She softly said, "I will miss you, my son." I choked on my words as I replied, "I will miss you, Mum."

We spent the wee hours loading up my trunk with the gifts she had made. "Please, Mum, leave some room for my belongings," I teased. I knew how hard she worked, making her healing salves and scented soaps for the elders and sewing clothes for the young ones. She handed me a handsome leather pack with a thick strap to wrap around my waist. "Mind your papers and money, and keep them close to you at all times," she warned. I hugged her and promised to write when I arrived in America. I was grateful she had decided not to see me off at the harbor, sparing us both any more tears. Deep inside my heart, I feared that I would never see my sweet mother again.

The sea was graciously calm on this warm September morning. The familiar smell of the fresh salty air steadied my rattled nerves as Bernard and I arrived at the harbor on the Bristol Channel. The harbor was bustling with merchant ships preparing to sail for the New World. I could see my boat, *The Voyager*, being loaded up at the pier with all the goods for America. "Well, Bernard, soon I will be part of the goods on this great ship," I said, trying to make light of the moment. Bernard patted me on my back and replied, "It will be a lucky day in America to have such a fine lad as yourself set foot on its land." I put my arm around Bernard and gave him a parting hug. "I will write as soon as I can," I yelled, rushing up the ramp as the ship's bell rang.

I walked aboard the massive vessel, feeling excitement and trepidation for the journey ahead. Ever mindful of the monies Edward lent me, I had purchased the least expensive ticket in steerage.

The ship's purser examined my papers and took my ticket. "Mr. Annely, you can see your family off from the main deck. Afterward, the crew will show you to your bunk. The ship hand will take your trunk to storage," he said flatly. I watched as the heavy-set crewman effortlessly lifted my trunk and placed it on his shoulder. "Follow me," he said gruffly. He pointed to the main deck as I hurried along to keep up with his pace. "Go there and say your goodbyes, then you can follow the others down below," he shouted, whisking my trunk away.

I pushed and shoved to the edge of the deck and saw Bernard looking up and about, trying to find me. I waved as I enthusiastically shouted out his name. We were waving and smiling, doing our best to appear optimistic, when deep inside, we both felt quite solemn.

The loud bell rang out, signaling it was time to leave the deck so all the hands could do their work to prepare the mighty ship. Soon, the massive sails caught the wind, and we were off. I leaned against the wall as I tried not to lose my balance, following the others down the narrow, steep stairs into the ship's dark and dismal lower deck. "Mind your heads and keep moving," the head Steward shouted amongst the loudness.

The sunny September morning turned into a gloomy day below deck. Everyone was scrambling amongst loud shouts and fighting over who would have the best bunk. I quickly jumped up and grabbed one of the end bunks. The passengers were filing in, so I knew I wouldn't have this row to myself for long. "Hey Mate, will you give me a hand?" an older gent called up to me. I reached down and helped pull him up next to me. "Thank you, son," he said, crawling over to his space.

Clutching my pack to my waist, I watched passengers climb up into each row of the narrow bunks. It was already feeling a bit stuffy, and no hatches were open to let the fresh sea air in. Each passenger was assigned one set of eating tools, a small tin canister, and a thin blanket with a straw-filled pillow. "Dinner will be at 1:00 sharp," the head Steward announced loudly. Observing the size of the tin canister, I knew the servings would be meager.

I lay back against the rough burlap that covered my bunk. The swaying ship made my stomach queasy, and my head was aching. I reached into my pack and took out a piece of ginger my mum had given me. The salty sweetness tasted good and eased my stomach.

I offered a piece to my bunkmate. "Such a kind gesture, son, much obliged," he said with a toothless grin. Thick creases lined his sun-weathered face, typical of a sailor who had spent many a day at sea. I smiled and introduced myself: "My name is Thomas."

"Pleased to meet you, son. My name is Howard, but you can call me Howie," he replied as I shook his rough, calloused hand.

We made small talk until the dinner bell let out its loud clang. There was such a commotion, with passengers rushing to get their portion of food. The improper behavior, especially of the men, seemed so barbaric. They were pushing in front of the women and children for a meager bowl of lukewarm soup and stale bread.

Soon, I found myself scrambling to fill my pail with whatever gruel they were serving. Thankfully, tucked away in my pack were bits of salted beef and cheese my mum had packed for me. I had to mind it well, or some hungry rat would snatch it away while I was sleeping.

The days passed, and I had not grown accustomed to the dampness of the sleeping quarters. My only relief was my daily walks on the main deck. The fresh, salty breeze cleared my nostrils from the stench of the stale air below.

One day, when Howie and I returned from our walk, we found our berth occupied by a large, burly man. "Begging your pardon, Sir, " I called up, "you seem to be in the wrong berth." The man with arms as big as tree trunks looked down angrily and snapped, "Who says so?"

"We say so!" Howie piped up boldly.

The brute hung his legs over the side of the bunk and jumped down, standing with his face to mine. His breath nearly knocked me over with the smell of stale tobacco. "Well, my little fine fellas, I dare ya's to make me move."

I needed to think fast on my feet before he knocked me off them. "Now listen, my good man, I will not fight you. You are double the size of my friend and me. Back home, we would settle this with pistols," I said.

"You ain't suggesting a duel, are you boy?" he replied. "No, Sir, I propose we have a target shootout," I said.

His face broke out in a mischievous grin. "Ha, and you think you have a better eye than me, do ya? We will see about that; I've been shooting before you were born!" he exclaimed as he stumbled up the ladder to the main deck.

I looked over at Howie, who was surprised by my bravado. "I hope the captain goes along with this one, lad," he said with a wink.

To my luck, the captain was as annoyed with this bullish fellow as we were and gladly agreed to oblige my request. "This man has cast a thorn in too many sides. I heard you are a gunsmith, but how's your shooting, son?" the captain questioned. "Well, Sir, you will find that most gunsmiths shoot fairly well," I replied, humbly. "Can I trouble you to have one of the crewmen take me to my trunk so I may retrieve my pistols?" I asked.

"No need, my boy; I have a good pair in my cabin, and it will be much fairer to you both. My man will fetch them for you," he replied. "Thank you kindly, Sir; I am much obliged," I said as I shook his hand.

A small crowd gathered to see what the spectacle was about. "Well, are we gettin' on with this or what?" shouted the brute. The Captain walked up to the man and said, "Settle down, Finnegan, or I'll be puttin' you to the plank. We'll handle this fair and square, and the best shot will get the bunk. You hear me?" he said sternly.

"Fetch me my dueling pistols and deck of cards!" yelled the captain to his first mate. Taking the ace of spades out of his deck of cards, he walked over to the main mast and ordered his crewman to nail the card against it. He stepped back 20 paces, turned around, and said, "This is where you'll be shooting from," he announced loudly for all to hear. "He who gets it closest to the spade in the center will be the victor and reap the reward," he shouted.

The first mate loaded one musket ball in each of the impressive pistols, made from fine maple wood with alabaster finishing on the handles. I nodded in admiration to the captain as the mate handed me the fine pistol.

The brute they called Finnegan turned and said, "You may have the honors, my boy." The crowd of passengers moved in on the excitement, watching anxiously with high hopes of some good entertainment. I calculated the movement of the ship and the wind over my left shoulder, hoping to get the right results. I aimed the pistol, cocked back the hammer and gently pulled the trigger and fired. The loud burst of the gun, exploding the lead ball from the barrel, startled the onlookers as it traveled through the air to its target.

The captain ran over to the mast, pulled off the card, and stuck his finger through the hole where the ball had penetrated. "Bullseye, dead center!" he shouted, holding it high for all to see.

Cheers and whistles erupted from the spectators, and Howie joined in the excitement. To my surprise, the big brute walked over to me and said, "Well, my boy, I'm not even going to try to outshoot you! The berth is yours, son." He extended his hand and said, "My name is Pat Finnegan, and that is the best shot I have ever seen!"

"Why, thank you, Sir. My name is Thomas Annely," I said, shaking his hand firmly.

The captain came over and congratulated me. "You put the "Old Finn" in his place, a regular Davie you are, fought Goliath and won!" he exclaimed with a hardy laugh. "My pistol has never been fired so accurately. You sure are a fine shooter, son," he said, slapping me on my back. "Tonight, you and your bunkmate will dine in my cabin!"

That evening, Howie and I ate better than we had since we left home. Sitting at the Captain's table and eating a proper meal of cod fish, buttered potatoes, and boiled carrots tasted delicious. The captain, amazed at my shooting ability, inquired, "So, tell me, lad, where does a gunmaker learn to shoot like that?" his words slurring from too much wine. "I learned from my father, who was a master gunsmith. Every musket or pistol we made, we would take it out in the field and prove that all was working properly. It was one of my fondest memories of my father," I said emotionally.

The wine was loosening my lips, so I knew it was time for Howie and me to retire. I stood up, tapping Howie, who was starting to nod off, "Thank you kindly, Captain, for this wonderful meal; it has been a most pleasurable evening." The captain stood and shook my hand. "My pleasure, Tom. It has been a most enjoyable evening for the crew and me. I have never seen such a truer shot than yourself," he remarked. Howie thanked the captain and the crew as he stumbled out to the main deck.

We left the comfort of the captain's quarters and headed back down to the confinement of our bunks. I could hear Old Finnegan sound asleep two rows down, snoring loudly, one large arm hanging off the side of the bunk. "He won't be messing with you again," observed Howie as we crawled up to our berth. With our bellies full and the spirit of the wine still lingering, we felt sure we would get a good night's sleep.

Unfortunately, the night was not as restful as we had hoped. A strong wind and rainstorm was passing, and the ship swayed heavily amongst the mighty waves of the Atlantic.

The sound of the crew running around and tending to the sails on the deck above was deafening. "Don't ya worry, son; the crew will keep her steady," Howie assured me. All the passengers were awake now, huddled together in their bunks. Except for an occasional whimper of a child, they all remained surprisingly calm. After all these days at sea, they had faith in the good Captain and his crew.

Some of the elders had taken ill, and their family members tended to them as best as they could. Howie kept my mind occupied and amused with the stories of his years in the Royal Navy. "Be mindful of the ladies in the city, boy," he would tease, "they are not the wee wallflowers they pretend to be," he said with a hardy laugh. Years at sea had taken their toll on the old salt, yet he was as agile as a man twice younger.

The sea was quieting down now, and the morning sun was peeking through the cracks of the hatches. We were all weary from the lack of sleep yet glad the night and the frightful storm were over. I joined the others on the floor and tried to ease the young ones' minds by participating in their games. Hide and seek was their favorite, even though there was hardly a spot to hide on the crowded ship.

Some days, I thought the dreadful journey would never end. The nights were long, and the sounds of the others' discomfort did not aid in a good night's sleep. At these times, I would long for home, thinking about the days of my youth. The only thing that kept me going were my thoughts about the new world and the adventures ahead. I soon drifted off to the lull of the swaying ship.

"Tommy my boy, wake up; 'tis land ahead!" Howie shouted as he shook me from my half-slumber. I sat up quickly and banged my head on the low beam above. "Sorry mate, didn't mean to startle you," said Howie. "No mind, Howie!" I replied as I jumped down from the bunk. Howie was right behind me, as quick as a mouse. Soon, the others followed to see what was for most of us, our first look at the new world.

We gathered on the crowded main deck, standing shoulder to shoulder. It was then I saw, through a thick veil of fog, my first glance of America. Our ship had docked, and I could see the crew rolling up the sails and securing the lines of the massive ship.

On the bow of the ship stood the Chaplain calling for silence, as he said a solemn prayer for the five unfortunate souls who lost their lives on the voyage. Five of the crewmen stood beside him, armed with pistols. A shot was fired in the air as the Chaplain called each name. I folded my hands in prayer to thank our Almighty Lord for my good fortune.

Howie was up ahead, with his sack upon his back, ready to go down the ramp and head for shore. I will miss my new friend and will never forget his kindness to this unseasoned lad. He glanced back and tipped his dusty old cap as he rushed off the ship. The Stewards were yelling out our names, checking off lists, and lining us up. "Be sure to take all your belongings you brought in the hole!" the head Steward shouted. A hole it was indeed, I thought to myself.

The fog was clearing, and I could see the busy harbor of New York ahead. Shuffling behind all the other passengers to disembark, I glanced up at the old ship that had taken me safely to America and said a silent thank you.

Passengers, some of whom I recognized, were greeted by loved ones waiting anxiously for their safe arrival. I secretly wished Edward awaited me, but that was not our plan. I insisted, and he agreed, that it would be best if I took some time to acclimate myself after the weary voyage.

As I stepped off the ramp unsteadily a young lad looking for newspapers from England greeted me. Bernard was right again! I smiled as the lad paid me quite handsomely for my small stack of newspapers. I looked forward to my free meal and having some extra shillings in my pocket.

"I see you made it to shore, mate," I looked up to see the familiar face of my bunkmate, Howie. "What are you doing here?" I asked, puzzled that he was not long gone by now. "I picked myself up a side job unloading all your trunks and such," he said. I was amazed at the strength of this man who was much older than I. "You are going to work for me someday, Howie," I stated.

He let out a bellowing laugh as I wobbled over to him on my weak legs. "I've no doubt you will make a fine Master, but now you need a cold drink." He waved me over to a cart where a very stout, jolly fellow was filling mug after mug of cold ale to the weary, thirsty patrons. Never had a mug of ale tasted so good as I gulped it down to the last drop.

Howie had made his way back to the dock to greet the boats carrying several trunks from storage. I sat down on a hardened tree trunk and checked my pouch to see if all was in good order. The few pounds I managed to save were safe deep inside.

I took in the fresh sea air and looked at all the sights around me. Several ships were arriving, packed full of all sorts of goods, along with more weary travelers from all over the world. Sitting here, I felt oddly at home in this new world, with its salty sea air and rocky shoreline. Everything around me was reminiscent of my beloved Bristol, only newer. As weary as I was, I was flush with excitement and restless to be moving along.

I could see Howie and the crew lining up the trunks along the portside as I stood up slowly, feeling lightheaded from the brew. Amongst the sea of trunks, I finally saw mine with the name Annely carved on the side. If it wasn't for Bernard carving my initials on all the sides of the trunk, I may not have recognized it.

Howie was at the shore, loading the boats with goods returning to England. Lacking the strength to go back down, I yelled to him, but the winds took my voice, and he never turned around. I was sad that I could not say a proper goodbye to my new friend.

Horsemen with carriages waited portside to take the weary passengers to their destinations. Too weak to make my way on foot, I waved to the first available carriage. "Blackinton Inn, Sir," I said to the driver as he stepped down and loaded my trunk in the back of the carriage. He tipped his hat and welcomed me aboard. "Fine establishment, Sir. You will be quite comfortable there," he replied as he climbed back aboard.

With a shake of the reins, he steered his obedient mare through the streets of New York. I was grateful for the peaceful ride as I took in the sights of the busy city around me. The horse's trot nearly lulled me to sleep as we traveled the crushed seashell streets.

"Here we are, Sir," he said, slowing the carriage to a halt. He jumped down to carry my trunk in for me. "'tis part of my service, Sir," he said with a smile. "Thank you kindly; I will be sure to ride with you again," I said, following him into the Inn. I paid him for his services with a bit extra, one of the many things Edward had taught me in his letter.

The innkeeper and his wife, a pleasant older couple, greeted me. Their warm smiles made me feel at home. "Welcome, Mr. Annely. You must be weary from your journey. Please follow me to your room; I believe you will find it comfortable. Dinner will be served promptly at 6:00. My wife has made some delicious stew with baked biscuits," he rattled off, escorting me down the long hallway.

It was a lovely room, warm and inviting, especially for this worn-out traveler. A tray with freshly brewed tea and warm scones sat on the side table. A mahogany washstand with fresh linen and soap stood in the corner. "Sir, there is some warm water in the basin. Please ring the bell in the hall if you need anything." I thanked him profusely for his kindness. "My pleasure, Mr. Annely; I will let you settle in," he said, closing the door behind him.

I felt like a pauper who had become King! I devoured the fresh scones and gulped down with the warm, sweetened tea. I quickly removed my dirty clothes and threw them in my sack for washing.

I was too tired for a formal bath, so I washed myself in the warm water. I slipped into my nightshirt, laid on the soft feather bed, and fell fast asleep. I never did get to enjoy Mrs. Blackinton's stew.

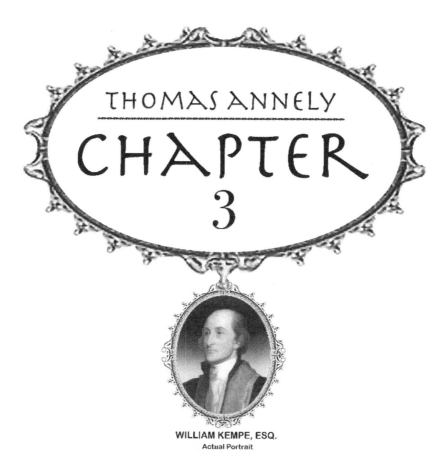

# THOMAS ANNELY

# CHAPTER 3

**WILLIAM KEMPE, ESQ.**
Actual Portrait

It had been a fortnight since that unforgettable voyage at sea, and still, my legs were wobbly, and my stomach was weak. If it was not for the dried beef and aged cheese my Mum had packed for me, I most likely would have starved on the journey. I promised myself not to travel in steerage when I returned to England.

Now that I was well-rested, I was eager to see my brother Edward, and my sister Elizabeth. Edward had kindly arranged for me to stay at the Blackinton's Inn. They have been most welcoming, making me feel much at home. The cooking did not match my Mum's, but it provided me with the nourishment I needed.

I woke up early this morning with much anticipation. Today was the day I would finally see my brother Edward and meet with the lawyer to settle my ownership of Richard's townhouse. In the few years since Edward has been in America, he did very well for himself. As members of some very exclusive gentlemen's clubs, Edward and his wife Eva often socialized with wealthy British Aristocrats. My nephews, young Edward and Joseph have private tutors at their home in the city.

Sipping my tankard of ale, I anxiously awaited Edward's arrival. A wide smile crossed my face as I turned to see Edward entering the tavern. He appeared every bit of a city gentleman, dressed handsomely from head to toe. Tall, with the same olive skin as our father, he looked more Mediterranean than English. His brown hair was pulled back with a tail of curls at the base of his neck under a felt-cocked hat. Unlike my brother, with my slight build and light complexion, I appeared every bit that of an Englishman. Only the same brown hair made us resemble each other.

When he saw me, he sped over and wrapped his arms around me. "Thomas, 'tis so good to see you, my brother."

"Edward, you are looking well!" I replied as we embraced each other fondly. "And you as well, my young brother, although you are a wee bit thin and could use a visit with my tailor," he chuckled.

Edward quickly called over to Mr. Blackinton to seat us at his finest table. The innkeeper nearly fell over as he rushed to accommodate my well-heeled brother's needs. Over the hearty dinner we talked about Eva and the boys and all the goings-on in their lives.

Edward changed the subject to discuss our forthcoming meeting, "Thomas, I have already written to my lawyer, William Kempe. He has been looking into the property at Whitestone, which I feel belongs to all of us, Annelys. Before we meet with the honorable Mr. Kempe, I want you to know I feel no ill will against Richard leaving you his New York townhouse. What perplexed me was that Richard did not consider me, nor our dear Mother, in his will. After all, 'twas I who saw to our mother's wellbeing since our father's unfortunate death. It seems obvious to me that the very clever Francis Lewis has duped us," he expressed, surprising me with his words.

I did not want to believe what he was saying was true. I heard Francis Lewis was a good and honorable businessman. I would have to keep my opinions to myself to save face with both sides.

"Incidentally, Thomas, I will take you to see our sister on Sunday for our nephew's baptism. She is beside herself with excitement to see you," Edward said as he sipped his ale. "She is not the skinny little lass we grew up with but quite the lady in her white castle and all her fineries," he remarked bitterly.

Edward suddenly glanced at his fine gold timepiece, "Time to go, my boy!" he exclaimed, beckoning the innkeeper over. "Put it on my bill, good man," he boasted as he threw a few shillings on the table.

Outside, Edward's elegant black coach and driver were waiting, "Hurry along, Thomas, or we will be late for our meeting," he shouted. We quickly climbed into the carriage and rode swiftly to his lawyer's office.

Our meeting with Mr. Kempe went more smoothly than I had anticipated. I was relieved that Edward kept the meeting brief and did not bring up his concerns about the Whitestone property. I wanted to avoid coming between Edward and Elizabeth in this matter. After I signed all the paperwork and exchanged keys, we stood up and shook hands. Mr. Kempe, in his pleasant manner, welcomed me to the city. He handed me one of his handsome calling cards, promising to call on him if I needed his advice. We said our goodbyes and bounded down the stairs to Edward's waiting carriage.

Clearly, in a hurry, Edward instructed his driver to take us immediately to Richard's townhouse, "I apologize, Thomas, but I won't be able to show you inside. I have some pressing issues to take care of at the shop. The Inn is two blocks to the North. Any fine gentleman can direct you back after you have seen your new home. I will pick you up Sunday morning to take you to Whitestone," he said in one breath as I exited his carriage. I hadn't a minute to thank him as he whisked the driver ahead in his shiny, black carriage down the road.

I stood at the bottom of the stairs, looking up at the impressive two-story home before me. When I reached the top of the stairs, a brass lion head affixed to the black oak door greeted me. Fumbling with the heavy key, I unlocked the door and entered the foyer. Long shadows of late afternoon sunlight illuminated my way through the home where my brother Richard once lived. The house was richly decorated in warm colors with mahogany furniture in each room, ideally suited for a bachelor gentleman.

I lit a candle and entered the master bedroom at the end of the hallway. In the center of the room stood a mahogany four-poster bed with carvings of lions on each post. A wash basin sat on a matching mahogany table with an oriental-style chamber pot under the bed. I recognized a small writing desk in the corner, the same one Richard had back home in Bristol. In the corner of the room sat a wooden-framed bathtub lined with copper, fit for royalty. I imagined Richard purchased the tub on one of his many trips abroad.

Upstairs were two smaller, equally inviting bedrooms with overstuffed beds and fine furnishings. Never had I imagined I would live amongst such luxury!

The next day, I packed my meager belongings at Blackinton's Inn and moved into Richard's townhouse. I felt so fortunate and grateful to my generous brother for leaving me his handsome home in the city.

Sunday arrived, and I woke up extra early, anxious to see my sister Elizabeth and to finally meet her husband, Francis. Elizabeth gave birth to a healthy baby boy while I sailed to America. I looked forward to the joyous day of my nephew's blessed event. I was surprised Edward agreed to come today, considering his strained relationship with Francis and Elizabeth. Nonetheless, I was happy we would all be together.

I could see Edward's carriage, gleaming in the morning sunlight, waiting on the street below. I grabbed my sack with gifts our Mum had made for the children, locked the door, and flew down the stairs. My breath was labored as I climbed into the carriage.

Inside was my sister-in-law Eva, looking as lovely as I remembered. My nephews, young Edward and Joseph, were dressed in their finest attire. They sat stoically with little expression on their faces. "Eva, 'tis so lovely to see you, and look at how my nephews have grown!" I exclaimed. "We have also looked forward to seeing you, Thomas," she replied stiffly.

We had little conversation on our ride to Whitestone, so I turned my attention to the scenery along the way. We traveled through the crowded city streets, ferried over the East River, and bumped along the countryside roads. The leaves of the trees were in full bloom with the rich colors of autumn.

How wise it was for Richard to have a home in the city and one in the country. I must admit, I was very impressed with this city they called New York.

Having made this trip many times, Edward seemed unmoved as he read his daily news. At the bend of the road, Edward pushed his spectacles to the bridge of his nose and pointed to a magnificent estate. "There it is, Thomas. That is Whitestone." Edward said with a broad smile.

I looked up in awe. All that Elizabeth had said in her letters could not describe the sheer beauty of it. The house of pure white stone stood majestically on top of a hill, surrounded by tall trees and acres of land. Across the way, I could see horses and sheep nibbling the rich, green grass. I strained my neck to see the smaller dwellings in the back. I could hardly wait to see more.

As we rode up the long, winding entryway to the estate, the driver slowed his mare to a trot. Between the two stately white columns stood Elizabeth, with babe in arms. My little niece, Ann, clung shyly to her mother's side.

No longer the girl I remembered, Elizabeth had become a lovely young woman. Her long auburn hair was blowing in the gentle bay breezes, and her cheeks glowed with the last rays of summer.

As I exited the carriage, Elizabeth handed her children over to her young negro servant and came running, arms outstretched, to greet me. "Thomas, I thought I might never lay eyes on you again; oh, how I have missed you!" she exclaimed as we embraced each other lovingly.

"'Tis a fine day, Elizabeth; I have missed you so. How lovely you are; motherhood becomes you. And what a remarkable home you have," I expressed, holding her tightly. She turned and greeted Edward, Eva, and the boys. "Good day to you all; thank you for bringing Thomas here," she said as she led us into the foyer of her spacious home.

Edward excused himself and took his boys to walk the grounds out back. The dutiful wife, Eva, did not acknowledge Elizabeth or fawn over the children. Instead, she chose to remain with her husband and followed him outside.

Elizabeth disregarded their rudeness and carried on with our joyful reunion. "Thomas, meet your niece Ann and your nephew Frannie," she said enthusiastically, handing the half-asleep infant into my arms.

"Awe, Elizabeth, what a fine baby boy you have here," I said, gently kissing the soft forehead of my new nephew. "And what a pretty little lady you are," I said, addressing my flaxen-haired niece.

"Please come sit, Thomas; I have something to ask of you," said Elizabeth, leading me to the settee in the hallway. I sat beside her, holding

Francis Jr., as he slept soundly in my arms. "Francis and I would like you to be the Godfather for young Francis," she expressed, smiling from ear to ear. I looked down at my sleeping nephew and proudly replied, "It will be quite the honor to be the Godfather of this little fellow, dear sister."

I could hear footsteps coming down the stairway from the second floor. "Well, hello there," came the bellowing voice of Elizabeth's husband, Francis. "I see you have met my darling Annie and my namesake."

I handed the babe over to Elizabeth's waiting arms and stood to greet my brother-in-law, Francis. "I'm pleased to meet you, Sir. You have a lovely daughter and a very fine son," I replied, shaking his hand.

"'Tis very kind of you to say, Thomas, and I am glad to meet you finally. Elizabeth has been very eager to see you. Please, call me Fran." He kissed my sister on the cheek, causing her to blush. "Francis, love, Thomas has agreed to be Frannie's Godfather," Elizabeth cheerfully expressed.

"That is wonderful. I thank you, dear boy, come and have a bit of brandy to celebrate."

"Oh, Frannie, must you whisk him away so soon?" Elizabeth exclaimed. "Come now, Lizzy," as he affectionately called her. "You go freshen up; I'll only keep him for a minute."

I followed Francis to his study, an impressive room with deep burgundy walls shelved with rows of books. We sat across one another in comfortable leather chairs as he handed me a fine, crystal snifter filled with the rich, brown liquor. "Here's to your arrival in America and your good health," he toasted as we clinked our glasses. I thanked him for his sentiment and drank the most welcomed drink down.

I liked Francis Lewis from the first time I heard his bellowing voice. He was a man's man and had a charismatic way about himself. My father always said, "Your gut and a firm handshake are the best judgments of a man." He was confident in his manner, which I thought was needed for a man who makes his living in trade.

A quiet knock was at the door, and a meek, finely dressed negro man spoke humbly, "Beggin your pardon, Sir, the Mistress says 'tis time for church. Shall I bring up the carriage?" he questioned. "Come in, Kingsley. I would like you to meet the Mistress's brother, Thomas Annely, all the way here from England," he boasted. "Most glad to meet you, Sir," he said, extending his hand to shake mine.

I was impressed by the kindly manner Francis bestowed upon his servant. "'Tis nice to meet you, Kingsley, and please, call me Thomas," I replied. He smiled as he turned and went on about his duties. "Well, I guess we best be going; we don't want to keep the Minister waiting," Francis quipped as he led the way.

The grand house was so impressive, nothing like I had ever seen, yet I felt at ease in this man's presence. I stopped to gaze at the stately portraits in the hallway. One was of Elizabeth, capturing her youthful beauty and soft brown eyes. The other of Francis, with a strong jawline and a stern expression, was quite the contrast to the pleasant man I had just met.

As we went outside, Elizabeth was waiting with her servant girl, holding young Francis, who looked angelic in his white baptismal dress. Elizabeth astounded me with her natural beauty, dressed as finely as any of the aristocratic women I had observed in the city.

Standing next to Elizabeth was an attractive, older woman dressed very properly. "Thomas, I would like you to meet Mrs. Hannah Beard. She has graciously accepted to be Francis Jr.'s Godmother," said Elizabeth as I walked up to meet her.

Elizabeth mentioned in her letters that Mrs. Beard was our brother Richard's assistant. "Pleased to make your acquaintance, Mrs. Beard." I made a slight bow before assisting the ladies onto their carriage.

"Time to go, Thomas," Edward called out, waiting by his carriage with his family in tow. I jumped aboard and off we rode to the church.

We arrived at a quaint countryside chapel with a small steeple above it. Mrs. Beard and I stood beside Elizabeth and Francis at the altar, surrounding the baptismal tub. We glowed with pride as Mrs. Beard held young Francis in her arms while the minister prayed and poured holy water across his forehead. He let out a soft cry but soon relaxed when he was placed back into Elizabeth's loving arms. The ceremony ended, and we all rode back to Whitestone, where a delicious meal awaited to celebrate the blessed occasion.

Seated next to Mrs. Beard, I found her a pleasant and interesting conversationalist. She immediately put me at ease as she spoke all about Whitestone. "This is where I first met your brother Richard. He was a fine gentleman and had a wonderful sense of humor. I was his assistant and tended to all his business matters," she remarked proudly. "Richard spoke of you often, Thomas; he would boast on how you would be as fine a gunsmith as your father one day," she expressed. "'Tis a great compliment, Mrs. Beard," I replied humbly. "Oh please, call me Hannah; Mrs. Beard sounds like an old schoolmarm," she said with an infectious laugh. As the conversation continued, I sensed that she had great affection for my dearly departed brother, Richard. Perhaps even more than she let on to be.

After the delicious dinner, Elizabeth called me over, "Come with me, Thomas; I would like to show you around the grounds," she said, hooking arms with mine.

Walking through the parlor, I noticed a familiar-looking musket above the mantle. I leaned in for a closer look when Elizabeth said solemnly, "That was Richard's musket; it was the one our father made for him when he was a boy." I stood admiring the musket and recalled Richard packing the gun in his crate when he left for America. "'Tis remarkable; I would have known our father's craftsmanship anywhere," I said. "I would like to give it to you, Thomas," she said sweetly. "Oh no, Elizabeth, I'd be honored to have it, but you must keep this for young Francis," I replied. "Perhaps you are right, Thomas," she agreed, tucking her arm closer to my side as we went outside on the veranda.

We paused and took in the scene of the bay below, breathing in the fresh salt air. "I'm so glad you are here, Thomas. I stand here often, thinking of Mum, Bernard, and you back home in Bristol."

It was a magnificent spot, with breathtaking views and wide open spaces for hunting and fishing. I noticed a small cemetery plot on the hill overlooking the bay. "Is that where Richard is laid to rest?" I asked solemnly. "Yes, let's go visit," she said, leading me over.

As we entered the low gate, a pure white granite stone bearing Richard's epitaph stood regally, facing the bay. In the shadow of his stone lay the graves of Elizabeth's first two children, who died at birth, with their names carved into small white stone markers. It pained her to look upon them, so I remained silent, paying reverence. My dear sister remains cheerful and strong, despite all the tragedies she has endured. As we headed back to the house, I grew concerned, "I must hurry, or I may lose my ride," I said. "Oh, Thomas, stay the week with us," Elizabeth pleaded. "I would love that, Elizabeth, but I will start in the shop tomorrow. I cannot wait to start working again; I miss every aspect of building guns. I promise you, I will come visit as often as possible," I assured her as I gave her a parting hug.

Edward, Eva, and the boys were saying their goodbyes when we walked up, "I'll be right with you, Edward," I shouted. I hurried off to bid farewell to Francis and their guests. "You are a welcome addition to the family," Francis exclaimed as we shook hands goodbye.

Aboard Edward's carriage, we traveled in silence until I spoke up, "'Twas a lovely day, and what a feast," I exclaimed, clutching my stomach.

"Aye, a bit much if you ask me," said Edward, unbuttoning his overcoat.

"I enjoyed meeting Hannah, too. She must have been a great help to Richard," I remarked.

"Oh, Hannah, she is still in love with our dearly departed brother Richard," Edward shot back rather cruelly. "He left her quite comfortable, with a home on the estate and plenty of pounds to go with it."

Eva remained silent, nodding her head in agreement. I was starting to dislike this side of Edward. It seemed Eva may be the culprit behind his crude actions. She most likely has grandiose ideas about becoming a refined lady, and her sense of entitlement was poisoning my brother's reasoning.

"I am looking forward to getting back to work with you, Edward," I said, hoping the change of subject would bring forth a more positive side to my brother. "Thomas, your abilities to build muskets and pistols will be advantageous for both of us in this country. Just wait, you will see," he replied, making me excited to start my new venture.

The ride back to the city was uneventful and quiet, which I preferred after the busy day. When I returned home, I collapsed on the bed and fell fast asleep.

Monday morning came too soon. I woke up worn and tired from our pleasant Sunday. Edward would expect me early, so I dressed quickly and flew out the door.

The crisp morning air invigorated my senses as I walked the city streets towards the workshop. I shall never forget how free I felt in this new world, where every man could make his own way. It was my first taste of American freedom.

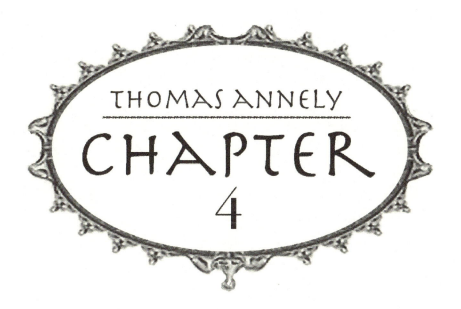

THOMAS ANNELY

# CHAPTER 4

F ive years have passed since I came to this great city of New York. Working alongside Edward and Francis has developed into a harmonious and successful venture for all of us. Francis is a fierce negotiator, an expert haggler for getting the lowest prices on the goods he purchases from all across the Atlantic. Edward, the master marketer, sells the goods at the Fly Market, down by the docks, and makes an excellent profit. And I, the English gunsmith, manage the lads in the workshop, building and repairing some of the finest guns for the local patrons.

The demand for more goods from foreign countries has made Edward and Francis very wealthy men. To my delight, Edward put aside his differences with Francis, and they carried on successfully as partners. I would not consider them the best of friends, but they suit each other well in their trade business.

My sister Elizabeth gave birth to a healthy boy they named Morgan. I would spend Sundays with her and the children to keep them amused while Francis was away at sea. She was a great support to her husband, but spent many a lonely day without him.

Alas, with every great country, there will always be war, and this new country was no different. The ongoing hostilities between France and Great Britain had found its way to the new colonies. And, as with every conflict, came new opportunities for business.

It was unbearably hot, so I opened the doors and windows to Edward's shop. It provided little relief from the muggy August heat. I stood outside the doorway and wiped the sweat off the back of my neck.

The two apprentices we brought on board were loading up our large cart with supplies for Francis to deliver up north. I could hear the sounds of horse hoofs on the cobblestone street and turned to see Francis. He rode high in the saddle, accompanied by an Indian, on magnificent golden horses. "Good morning, Francis; you look like old King George himself up on that grand steed," I joked. Francis laughed as he and his guide dismounted off of the majestic beasts.

Francis spoke to his guide in his native Wales language, which the Indian guide remarkably understood. "Thomas, this is Nootau." said Francis, introducing me to his Indian guide. He raised his hand to greet me, and I smiled and did the same in response.

They will be traveling today to deliver the goods way up north. It was wise of Francis to take a tribesman to act as a pathfinder along the way. With his leather-bound notebook in hand, Francis jumped aboard the cart and noted each package in his book. Nootau stood still, waiting for Francis to finish his inspection.

"Thomas, would you be so kind as to show Nootau to the stables, where we may keep our horses until our return?" Francis asked. "Why, of course," I said while Nootau followed me, guiding the horses.

I felt awkward, having never been in the company of an Indian before. I was quite impressed with the sight of him and wished I could speak his language. His brown skin, the color of the rich soil of England, glistened from the blazing sun. He wore little: a tan loincloth with tight leggings and a bright red sash around his waist. He carried a tomahawk decorated with brightly colored feathers. A flintlock musket hung from his shoulder. His long, black hair was adorned with what looked to be eagle feathers. A beaded leather strap with a silver pendant of an eagle hung down upon his hairless chest. I imagined the eagle had great significance for him and his people. He caught my eye, pointed at the eagle, and said in perfect English, "Strong, proud." I nodded and repeated, "Yes, the eagle is strong and proud." He smiled and exposed yellowed teeth, most likely from their fondness for smoking.

I envied Francis, for he was living the most exciting of lives. I, on the other hand, was only a gunsmith, a simple man in comparison. I secretly wished I could travel with them for what would be another one of Francis's exciting adventures.

"'Tis all here, Thomas. Good job, my man," said Francis, shaking my hand. "I will watch over Elizabeth and the children while you are gone," I reassured him. "Many thanks, Thomas; 'tis much appreciated."

They climbed aboard the wagon and went on their way as my new Indian friend raised his hand in the traditional Indian salute. I raised my hand as I watched the cart wobble along the uneven street. Back in the workshop, I was feeling a little low, as I always did, when Francis would leave.

It was too hot to use the forge today, so I took to tasks that required less effort. As the work day was coming to a close, Edward came in through the door. "Good afternoon, brother, 'tis a hot one today! Did Francis come by to pick up the goods?" he questioned. "Yes, he had an Indian guide with him as well. The men had the cart all packed, and they left early this morning. Where are they heading?" I inquired. "They are delivering uniforms and armaments for the British troops at Fort Oswego," Edward said as he slipped into his office.

As the weeks passed, we became quite concerned. Francis was long overdue for his return, and we had not heard a word from him.

Then, one day, Edward rushed into the workshop, calling out to me, "Thomas, please come into my office straight away. I'm afraid I have some terrible news!" I hurried in and sat down, anxious to hear what Edward had to say.

"Thomas, I have been told that the French and their Indian allies attacked Fort Oswego; at the time, Francis delivered the supplies. The word is that many have been killed, including the commanding officer. I am sorry to say that Nootau, his guide, was one of the dead. All they know about Francis is that he is missing. My source has told me 'tis quite possible he may have been captured and taken to France as a prisoner of war," Edward said, with one long breath.

It was indeed terrible news, and I dreaded having to explain this to Elizabeth. I saddled up and swiftly rode to Whitestone, feeling despair deep inside. I did not want to deliver this horrible news to my sister. She nearly fainted in my arms when I told her that Francis had most likely been captured and taken to France as a prisoner. I never mentioned a word of how brutal an attack it was or how many were killed. All I could offer her was our assurance that Edward and I would do everything in our power to bring her husband back home to her.

With Francis gone, Edward and I had to find a new balance to keep our business in good working order. Edward split his time between managing the trade relations that Francis had established and selling the goods at the Fly Market. I kept my nose to the grindstone, working hard to keep up with the supply of guns that were in high demand due to this nasty French and Indian War.

Months turned into years, and the war with France continued. Within that time, Edward received word from a reliable source that our dear brother-in-law Francis was, indeed, being held prisoner in France. We were deeply relieved to know that Francis was alive, yet frustrated that the French would not release him. Elizabeth wrote numerous letters to the authorities in France, attempting to find the location of her husband, but received no response. However, we never gave up on our diligent pursuit of finding him.

I spent as much time as possible with Elizabeth to comfort her and the children through the long, lonely years without her loving Francis.

# THOMAS ANNELY

# CHAPTER 5

**BENJAMIN FRANKLIN**
Actual Portrait

The ten years since I have been in America has been very productive, and I have grown more confident in my gunmaking skills. My brother Edward is one to reckon with at times, yet he and I are very compatible in our work ethic. What is most important to me is that I can now send a substantial amount of money to my mother and Bernard each month.

With Francis away in prison, Edward has continued trading at sea. When he is home, he spends his days at the Fly Market, selling the goods to the local patrons. I do what I do best, and that is gunmaking. Another week has begun, and today, my nephew Edward, who prefers to be called Ward, will start his apprenticeship. Gunmaking is in the Annely blood, and I am proud that my nephew Ward will follow in our footsteps. I hope to be as patient a teacher to my nephew as my father was to me.

As I approached the workshop, I noticed my young nephew puffing away on a clay pipe, smoke billowing over his head. "Ward, does your father know you smoke a pipe?" I questioned.

He rudely blew the smoke my way, "Not really, my father doesn't seem to care what I do," quipped Ward.

I grabbed the pipe from his hand and snapped it with my fingers. I sensed this coddled young man needed some strong guidance. "You don't have time for this; now come inside."

Much work needed to be done today, and I would not let my nephew's spoiled attitude deter me from training him properly. The British gunsmiths, known for their meticulous attention to detail, make some of the finest quality muskets in the world. My father taught me this craftsmanship, and I was determined to teach Ward the Annely way.

"Ward, you will be my right hand. Do you know what that means?"

He replied, puzzled. "I think so."

"Listen to what I say and closely observe what I do nephew, and you will learn the Annely family trade of gunsmithing, the right way. I tell all my apprentices that the lock is the most important part of building a superior musket. It must be strong, durable, and efficient in every way, and that is just the beginning. Weight and size are also important, especially to the soldier who has to carry it."

As the days went by, Ward developed a genuine interest in gunmaking. He quickly memorized all the steps in making a proper musket. I became quite impressed with the turnaround in my young nephew and was grateful for the help he was providing. He and the other lads in the shop worked well together. The gunshop was buzzing with business, and nothing made me happier.

One day, I heard squabbling outside the workshop and went to see what all the noise was about. Ward was chasing away a young lad, no more than ten years of age, who was begging for a job. He was a sight to be seen, with ragged clothes on his back and tousled blond hair to his shoulders. I overheard Ward shouting at the young lad, "Not you again; we keep telling you we have no work for you. Go on your way, you little bastard!"

Day after day, the lad would return, pleading for work, and the men would continue telling him to move along. They laughed amongst themselves at how defiant this young boy was.

As I watched him walk out the door, his head slumped to his shoulders, I remarked to the men, "He's a determined little fellow. I will give him that." Suddenly, we heard a loud clammer coming from outside. Ward and I quickly ran to the door and saw the young boy in a scuffle with another boy.

A much bigger lad was pummeling the boy with his fists, yelling, "This is my street; you need to be leaving, you little urchin!"

The little fellow punched back as he shouted, "This is my street now, you bloody bloke!"

Ward and I rushed out and pulled the boys apart as they swung their arms about. The bigger lad ran like the wind down the street, frightened by our presence.

"What is going on here?" I questioned the persistent lad sternly as Ward held him by his arm.

"That bloke says this is his street, Sir," said the scruffy lad, trying to catch his breath.

"Come in here and settle down, son," I ordered as Ward led him into the shop. The men were snickering amongst themselves about how feisty the boy was. "Alright, men, never mind the lad," said Ward as they turned around and carried on with their work.

I sat the lad down by the hearth, where my kettle of tea was warming, and some cornbread was on the table beside it. "Here, have a spot
of tea and a bite to eat," I offered. He was famished and devoured every
bit of the bread while slurping down the tea, wiping the crumbs off his
mouth with his raggy sleeve.

"Thank you kindly, Sir; I have to go now," he yelled as he headed
towards the door to leave.

"Hold up there, boy. What is your name?" I called out to him.

He swung around and said rather proudly, "I don't know my proper
name, Sir, but they call me Chip. My father would always say I was a
"Chip off the old Block," so he took to calling me Chip."

"And where would your father be now, Chip?" I asked, curious what
sort of a man could leave such a young lad alone.

"My Pa died right after my Mum, and they is together now," he said
with a sorrowful look.

"And who is minding you?" I questioned.

"No one, Sir, I mind myself," he said proudly, holding his chest high.

I paused, impressed by the boy's courage, as my eyes examined him
up and down. I responded straight away, feeling confident that this
young boy might prove to be a good little helper. "Meet me here early
tomorrow morning Chip, and we will see what I can do. Ask for me,
Thomas Annely."

He grabbed my hand and gave it a hardy shake before running off
with a wide smile on his face.

As I entered the workshop the following day, Ward rushed over to
me, flustered, "Uncle, that little beggar is here again, asking to see Sir
Thomas".

I let out a slight chuckle, "Ah, I see he showed up on time," I replied
as Ward looked on with confusion.

The boy looked much cleaner than the day before, even with the same shabby clothes. "Chip, 'tis a good sign that you are here, bright and early. Come along with me," I said for all the men to hear.

I brought Chip around the shop and introduced him to Ward and the rest of the men. I could see by the surprised look in their eyes that they were wondering what the young boy was doing here. One piped up and remarked, "Mind your belongings; this little bloke might steal them when you turn your back!" I turned my head sharply and gave him a hard stare, "Sorry, Sir, just a joke. I didn't mean any harm," he apologized and quickly returned to his work.

"Look, Chip, you are now considered the low man on the totem pole. That means you do whatever the other lads tell you to do."

"Yes, Sir Thomas, I will," replied Chip humbly as I handed him the broom.

"You must always keep the floor clean. It will be up to you to prove you are worthy of more wages. Until then, I will give you food and a few pence if you do a good job," I said sternly.

"We all have to start from the bottom and work our way up," I advised.

"I will do my very best to make you proud of me, Sir Thomas," he replied, getting to work straight away.

THOMAS ANNELY

# CHAPTER
## 6

After the sudden death of King George II, his grandson, King George III, was crowned to become the new ruler of England. The young King made us all stand up and heed what he was imposing upon the colonies. King George II did not pay much mind to the colonists, provided he had a hand in appointing the governing officials. The elder King was satisfied with the laws that the colonies had put in place. But now, the times were changing; this new King had other ideas and was determined to make his mark. He boldly sent out a proclamation that adhered to every pole and building in the city, calling for *"all good subjects to help put down the rebellion."*

The Brits may have won the war against the French and their Indian allies, but the war cost them greatly, and Britain was in dire financial straits. The changes that would come next ignited the flames inside many a man's belly. The colonists were becoming more eager to fight for their independence and freedom.

It was becoming increasingly difficult to pay yourself a decent wage, let alone pay your help. The new regime had placed British soldiers all about town. They would harass the local traders and force them to pay more taxes on their wares sold. I could not help but agree with these good people that this was unfair and unjust treatment.

I had hoped now that the war with France was over, we would have long-lasting peace, and Francis would be back home with Elizabeth. Yet it seemed neither of my wishes would be granted, for our new King was raising havoc, and our dear Francis had still not returned.

Sunday arrived, and I set off on horseback to visit Elizabeth and the family. When I approached Whitestone, Kingsley was there, as usual, to greet me. "Good morning, Mr. Thomas; I hope you had a pleasant ride. You go along; the Mistress is excited to see you," said Kingsley as he took my horse to the stables.

I sprinted up the marble steps and into the entryway as Elizabeth called, "Come in, Thomas. I am down the hall in the green room." I walked down the long hallway and entered the garden room full of women. "Ladies, this is my brother Thomas, who I have told you about. He is the master gunsmith at E&T Annely Gunsmiths here in New York," she announced proudly.

The long table they sat around was covered with various fabrics of deep blue wool, fine linen, rolls of white canvas, and trimmings of gold and red. The ladies were handsomely dressed in their Sunday finery. Elizabeth sensed my discomfort and led me out to the hallway. "Sorry, Thomas, for overwhelming you. The ladies and I started this sewing circle a while back, and it has brought me great comfort with Francis away. We are like sisters," she expressed.

"That is wonderful, Elizabeth; if you beg my pardon, I think I will join the children outside," I replied, anxious to remove myself from the attention of all the ladies. I walked by the portrait of Francis and paused to look at his face; how I missed my jovial brother-in-law. I prayed to the good Lord that he would rejoin us soon. Even after all these years, none of us had lost our faith that he would return safely someday.

Looking out the paneglass window, I saw the children playing in the yard. I envied their youthful exuberance as they chased each other around. I went outside to join them, and young Francis shouted, "Uncle Thomas is here!" They all encircled me, jumping up and down with joy. I smiled and embraced all three as their young faces beamed excitedly. It made me happy to know my presence brought them joy, for the years without their father, left them with an emptiness I could never fill. It saddened me that Morgan barely remembered his father. However, Elizabeth kept him vivid in their minds by telling them all the stories of their father's exciting adventures. One could not deny that their father led a most remarkable life.

Elizabeth's servant, Phoebe, came to retrieve us for dinner. After Elizabeth's lady friends said their goodbyes, she told me that Francis's business acquaintance, Gifford Dally, and his wife would join us.

"Why don't you go into Francis's study and pour yourself a brandy? I am certain you could use one after being attacked by my band of Indians," Elizabeth said, referring to her wayward children in jest. I laughed at her remark, "Yes, sister, I did fear for my scalp for a moment." She smiled, knowing how much I loved spending time with them.

As I relaxed in the comfort of Francis's study, sipping my brandy, I heard a slight knock upon the door. When I opened it, a tall, distinguished-looking gentleman was standing there. "Good day, Mr. Annely; I heard I could get a fine glass of brandy in this room," he said, making me laugh with his pleasant manner. "Why, of course, you must be Mr. Dally. 'Tis good to meet you, Sir. Please call me Thomas," I replied, pouring him a generous glass of brandy.

"Good to meet you as well. Please, call me Gifford." He paused to sip the rich liquor. "Now, this is a fine brandy," he remarked before continuing our conversation. "I understand you and your brother, Edward, own the establishment of E&T Annely Gunsmiths in New York City. The word is you make some of the finest muskets and pistols this side of the Atlantic," he declared, making me proud.

"'Tis excellent to hear that, Sir; we Annelys take great pride in our work," I replied humbly.

"I am somewhat of a collector of guns myself. I am particularly fond of the flintlock pistols; perhaps I will commission you to make me a set someday," expressed Mr. Dally.

I nodded and replied, "I would like that very much, Sir." I was impressed with this fine gentleman and looked forward to getting to know more about him.

"I see you two have met," said Elizabeth, poking her head into the study. "Come along, my good men, dinner is ready," she announced.

The dining room table was nicely arranged with exotic flowers in brightly colored pots. I was pleased to see Mrs. Hannah Beard, waving her gloved hand my way. Elizabeth called out to me as I entered the room, "Oh Thomas, you have met Mr. Dally. Please come meet Mrs. Anne Dally," she said enthusiastically.

I made a slight bow. "Please to meet you," I said as Mrs. Dally smiled pleasantly. I took my place at the table, sitting next to Hannah. We exchanged pleasantries as we enjoyed another delicious meal at Elizabeth's table.

During the meal, I listened intently to Gifford and Anne Dally as they spoke proudly of their daughter.

"Sarah will be tutoring Elizabeth's children to speak French," said Mrs. Dally, smiling with pride.

"Maybe, in the future, the French will come to their senses and become our allies," said Gifford boldly, referencing, no doubt, to Francis's imprisonment.

Mr. Dally rose up from the table, tapping his fork against his glass. "May I have everyone's attention?"

We all quieted down, as we waited to hear what he had to say.

Mr. Dally continued, "My dear friends and family, I want you all to take a moment to acknowledge my good friend, Francis. When he traveled to Fort Oswego that fateful day, he had no concern for his own safety. All that was on his mind was that he needed to attend to our British troops by ensuring they were outfitted well, in uniforms and arms. Here's to Francis for his courage and his strength of character. I am sure these strong traits he possesses will see him through this ordeal, and he will come back to us soon," he toasted. We all lifted our glasses in unison to our brave Francis, wherever he was.

Elizabeth spoke softly of her devotion to her imprisoned husband, "With our dear Lord as my witness, I shall continue to be his lady in waiting till he is returned safely to me, no matter how long it may take," she expressed, lowering her head to hide her tears.

I remained silent, for my words could not add any greater encouragement than what had already been said. I would not let any thoughts of doubt run through my mind as I remained strong in my conviction that Francis would return someday.

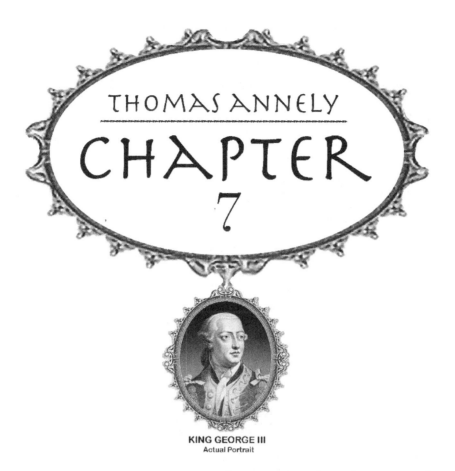

THOMAS ANNELY

# CHAPTER 7

**KING GEORGE III**
Actual Portrait

A strong rainstorm was making its way through New York City, flooding the streets and overflowing all the rivers. A lone rider on horseback was struggling through the blinding fog. The heavy rain bore down hard, soaking the horse and rider as they trudged along the muddy path. When he finally arrived at his destination, he dismounted his horse, walked up to the door, and banged loudly with the brass knocker. He pulled up the collar of his heavy cloak and tipped his hat down to shelter himself from the rain.

The man overheard a female voice coming from within. "Kingsley, who in heaven's name could be out in this bad weather? Please go see who is at the door."

"Yes, Ma'am," Kingsley replied with apprehension as he slowly opened the door. A man, dripping wet with rain, stood staring up at him. Kingsley squinted his eyes and suddenly realized the man before him was his master, Francis Lewis.

Without saying a word, he wrapped his arms around Francis and pulled him into the house. "My man Kingsley, 'tis so good to see you again," replied Francis, holding on to him. Kingsley quickly helped his master remove his wet cloak.

Elizabeth entered the foyer and paused in disbelief, barely recognizing her husband standing there, seven years older. Rushing to his side, she fell into his arms, nearly knocking him over. She paid no mind to his wet clothes or the scratchy beard on his face as they embraced in one another's arms. They clung together, not wanting to let go, tears flowing freely from their eyes. Kingsley stood there, watching the happy reunion as his dark brown eyes pooled with tears. The broad smile on his face said it all. Her man was back with her, and at that moment, no words needed to be said.

Upon hearing the clatter, Francis Jr., Ann, and Morgan came running into the foyer with Phoebe chasing behind them. "Father, Father," they all shouted with glee as they ran to his side, welcoming his long-awaited embrace. "Oh, my children, how you have grown," said Francis as he clutched onto them, tears streaming down his face.

"Kingsley, take care of the Master's horse," said Elizabeth as she guided her husband to sit in the parlor. Francis paused and looked about, taking in the sight of his family and home. "My dear, I have missed you and the children so much; you cannot know the agony I have suffered. I was not even allowed to write to you," he said with labored breath. "I know only too well, my love. I have also suffered greatly, not knowing if you were alive or dead," she said, sitting down beside him, not want-ing to leave his side. The children sat on the floor, encircling around them, as their faces beamed with happiness.

Elizabeth called out to Phoebe, who was waiting nervously in the hallway, "Phoebe, please bring some warm water up to my bedroom and see the children to their beds," she said to her obedient servant.

"Oh, Mother, we want to stay with Father," protested Ann. "Now, children, your father is very weary from his long journey, and he needs his rest," said Elizabeth, bringing frowns to their faces. "Do not be sad, my loves; he misses you all greatly; tomorrow morning, we shall have the grandest of times together again," she said reassuringly. One by one, they embraced their father warmly and kissed him goodnight.

Elizabeth led Francis up the stairs to their bed chamber, removing his wet, dirty clothes as she helped him climb into the welcoming bath. She gently washed the years of grime off his weathered skin and care-fully tended to the sores covering his body. As he relaxed, nearly drifting off from the soothing waters, she clipped away at his long hair and shaved the beard off his face. Kingsley returned to help her lift his weak body from the tub as they placed him on the soft bed, covering him with heavy blankets. He spoke little, but the smile on his worn face told Eliz-abeth how grateful he was to be back home. "There, my love, you look much more like yourself," she remarked, leaving her thoughts to herself of how much thinner and older Francis appeared. He fell fast asleep be-fore having anything to eat or drink. As she watched his chest rise and fall with each breath, she whispered prayers of gratitude to the good Lord for bringing him back home.

As Francis slept, Elizabeth immediately went to her desk and penned a letter to me.

*Dearest Thomas,*

*I have wonderful news to share with you! Our beloved Francis has come home! He is worn, thin, and in much need of a long rest. All things considered, he seems quite healthy. I don't know how he made his way back to us, but he is here, and that is all that matters to me.*

*Please share this good news with our brother Edward, and as soon as Francis is feeling up to it, we will all get together to celebrate his homecoming!*

*Fondly, your delighted sister, Elizabeth*

A fortnight had passed, and Francis was already regaining his strength and usual vigor. Finally, I received the invitation I was anxiously awaiting; Elizabeth had invited us all to Whitestone on Sunday to celebrate Francis's homecoming.

When the day arrived, I set off early in the morning on my trusted mare, excited to see my dear brother-in-law.

When I rode up to Whitestone, Kingsley greeted me as usual. The expression on his face was much more relaxed than it had been in years. "Good to see you, Mr. Thomas. All is wonderful here now that we have the Master home with us again," he said, grinning from ear to ear. I smiled at their devoted manservant, "Kingsley, we are all very grateful to you and how you watched over Elizabeth and the children while Francis was gone. You are a good man," I said, patting him on the back. "'Tis my pleasure, Sir; the Mistress and Master are like family to me. They are out in the back, enjoying a walk in this fine weather," he said before bringing my mare to the stables.

I walked to the grounds out back and stopped short to take in the sight of them. In the distance, Elizabeth and Francis walked hand in hand with their three children following closely behind. Seeing them all together again brought a peaceful feeling to my heart.

Francis Jr. noticed me from afar and came running, "Uncle Thomas!" he called out as I walked to join them. He grabbed my hand and led me over to his father. Francis and I grabbed hold of each other, "'Tis so good to see you, Thomas; I have missed you!" I placed my hand upon his shoulder and replied, "Aye Fran, 'tis so good to have you back, and you are looking very well, my friend. I hope you don't mind me coming early, but I could not wait to see you."

Elizabeth came between us and locked her arm on Francis's and the other around mine, "My two favorite men, here together again," she expressed, smiling, guiding us back to the house. Their happiness was infectious, and I could feel all the strain from the last seven years floating away.

It felt like nothing had changed when Francis invited me into his study for our usual glass of brandy. This time, he had much more to discuss with me as he sat in his comfortable leather chair with a pensive expression on his face. "Thomas, I have had a lot of time to think. Hell, I've had seven years!" he said with an awkward chuckle. "When I was holed up in that wretched prison, my only solace was knowing that you were watching over Elizabeth and the children." I reached over and placed my hand over his, "'Tis the least I could do, Sir; you know I am always here for you and Elizabeth."

He leaned back in his chair, his eyes cast downward as he took a long breath. When he spoke, his words came tumbling out as if he held them in for the seven years he was gone.

"Well, Thomas, it all started at Fort Oswego. We had just unloaded all the supplies when suddenly we heard gunfire, and an arrow came swiftly through the air, striking poor Nootau right in his chest. It killed him instantly. A troop of French regulars then rushed upon us with their Indian allies, who took almost thirty of us as prisoners."

"They tied our hands behind our backs and made us trudge down rough paths of untamed wilderness all the way to Montreal, brutally killing any man who fought back. They hung their bloody scalps on their hips in plain sight, making us fear for our lives. Along the way, one of the Indian captors took a liking to me because I could speak their language. When we reached Canada, my Indian friend pleaded with the French to release me, but they would have no part in it. They shoved me on a ship with the other prisoners and sent me off to France."

"The guards forced us down the dingy hole of the ship. Unfortunately, some of the prisoners did not survive the rough voyage. We finally made it to France, with only a few of us left. An old, rickety wagon took us to what appeared to be an old stone fort."

He continued as I remained silent, captivated by his words. "The guard shoved me into a stone-cold cell with only one small, barred window. I could see the sunset every evening, so I knew my window was facing west, towards all of you in America."

"The floor was so filthy that I feared catching some dreaded disease. Once in a while, the guard would throw a bucket of water onto the floor in a poor attempt to clean the cell. All it did was leave a huge puddle for the rats to drink from. The food they were feeding us was tasteless, but after a while, I looked forward to the awful gruel."

"They kept us isolated from one another, each in our wretched cell, except for our morning chores, when we were allowed outside to clean the prison yard. We prisoners were mostly fellow Brits, a few Africans, and some were French. I would listen to the guards' conversation to learn some of their language."

"There were days I thought I would surely go mad. They treated us no better than the common rat that infested our cells, beating us if we did not obey their every demand. The only thing that kept me alive was my thoughts of Elizabeth and the children. It was the most horrible of experiences, one I would not wish upon my worst enemy."

"One day, as I was lying on the cold hard floor, a guard opened the door to my cell and announced loudly that my day had come, the war was over, and I was free to leave. I did not believe what he was saying was true, for after all the years I spent in that awful cell, I truly believed it was where I would die."

"Five of us left the prison that day and were dropped off in a small fishing village by the sea. The little bit of French I had learned served me well with the people in the village. I received food and lodging in exchange for doing odd jobs and found extra work along the docks with the local fishermen. You cannot imagine this tired old man's relief when I finally saved enough francs to buy passage back to America. It felt wonderful to be out in the open sea, breathing in the fresh salt air. When the ship finally docked in New York harbor, I walked down the ramp, threw myself to the ground, and kissed the land I love!"

"In the seven years I was imprisoned, I realized two things that I shall never take for granted again: how much I love the freedom of my country and how much I love my wife, Elizabeth."

I sat there, mesmerized by his harrowing story and amazed by the resilience of this remarkable man. Francis leaned into me and said softly, "Do not tell Elizabeth what I have told you. I will tell her in good time, but I am not ready yet." he asked. "Of course, Fran, you have my word," I assured him. I felt honored that he confided in me; I could not imagine living through such a nightmare and holding all those dreaded memories inside.

Inside the foyer, Elizabeth waited by the front door to greet Edward and Eva. When they arrived, she watched as her brother's long legs exited out of the carriage. He reached for Eva's petite gloved hand and helped her down while her nephews followed out behind them. How lovely and elegant they all looked to Elizabeth, who had not seen her brother Edward nor his family for quite some time.

"Elizabeth, 'tis so good to see you, dear sister," Edward said as he embraced her. Eva grasped Elizabeth's hands and told her how happy she was for her while her sons kissed their aunt on her cheek before swiftly running off to join their cousins.

"'Tis so good to see you all," said Elizabeth as they entered the foyer together. Edward paused and turned to face her, "Elizabeth, we are so grateful that Francis is home, safe and sound. Now, tell me, where is that old man of yours?" remarked Edward, looking about the house. "Francis is with Thomas in his study, having their usual brandies, for old times' sake," replied Elizabeth. "That sounds like a good place to be," said Edward as he excused himself to join them.

Edward came into the study and greeted Francis warmly, "Francis, everyone at our shop has missed you so. 'Tis so good to have you back!" he exclaimed. "'Tis so very good to be back and to see you as well, Edward. You have been so generous. I will never forget the years you supported Elizabeth while I was in prison."

"I cannot imagine what you must have gone through, old boy, but I must say you are looking very well in spite of it," said Edward in astonishment at how strong Francis appeared. Francis smiled and patted Edward on his back, "Someday, I will tell you all I went through, but for now, I would rather feast on that delicious meal I smell cooking." We had a hardy laugh as we followed him to the dining room.

The meal we shared seemed all the more delicious, and the wine that poured so generously around the table was even sweeter now that we were all together again.

After dinner, Edward and I joined Francis outside for a long-awaited cigar. Francis let out a long puff of smoke and exclaimed, "It has been far too long since I enjoyed a smoke with my dear friends." Kingsley came out carrying a tray with snifters of brandy upon it. "Oh my, can it get any better than this? The perfect ending to a perfect meal." he boasted, sipping the rich brandy down. Edward and I lifted our glasses to him, "Here's to you, Francis, and may you enjoy good health and prosperity for the rest of your life," toasted Edward.

"I want you both to know that I plan on returning to work very soon," Francis boldly announced. Excited to hear this news, Edward spoke first, "'Tis good to hear, Fran. We have eagerly awaited your return. Lord knows it has not been easy for me to fill your shoes. However, I want you to rest up and take all the time you need. When you are ready, I will meet you at the workshop and bring you up-to-speed on our business." Edward pulled out an envelope from his breast pocket, "In the meantime, here is some money, which I am certain you and Elizabeth could use right now. Rest assured, there is more money to come. I have kept it in a safe place for your homecoming," Edward replied.

"'Edward, you are a loyal partner and a generous brother-in-law. I look forward to getting back to business; the sooner, the better!" Francis exclaimed with his usual vigor.

I marveled at my brother-in-law's fortitude. He had lost seven years of his life but was determined to live his remaining years with purpose and duty to his country.

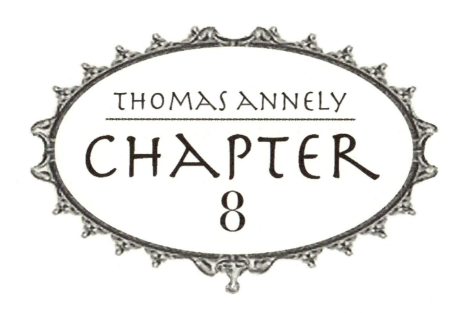

# THOMAS ANNELY

# CHAPTER
8

I t has been three years since Francis returned from his long imprisonment. To have Francis back with Edward and myself, working together again, has been wonderful. As I made my way to the workshop, I paused and took a deep breath of the fresh air of spring. The still-hardened ground sprouted signs of life with little shoots of green.

I hurried along as usual, even though I knew Ward and the boys would be at the shop bright and early. Chip had proven reliable so far, showing up early each day. What he lacked in work experience, he made up for with sheer determination.

I received a message from Mr. Dally expressing his desire to come by today to tour the workshop. I hoped he would bring his daughter Sarah along. Elizabeth spoke of her often, and I was curious to meet her.

I was enjoying my walk as my mind wandered back to Bristol and the pleasant mornings along the Avon River. Not so long ago, I dreamed of coming to this great land. However, the unrest in the city threatened the peaceful existence I had enjoyed since coming here.

Suddenly, men shouting in the distance awakened me from my morning stupor. The Liberty Boys, as they were called, were putting up another one of those bloody poles in defiance against the British. I did not know what they thought they would accomplish with the Brits keeping a tight rein on the city. At times I felt the desire to join their cause, but I felt an even stronger desire to keep myself from being hung from a tree.

As I approached the workshop, I could see two richly dressed gentlemen I did not recognize leaving our workshop. The taller fellow was a formidable-looking man with an angular jaw that jutted beyond his nose. His steely eyes gave a sinister stare as he glanced back my way as if he was sending me a warning. The portly one, most likely his manservant, hurried along, attempting to keep up with his long-legged master. I watched him ride off in his carriage, with a cloud of dust following him.

I quickened my step, entered the workshop, and found Ward standing behind the front counter. "Who were those two gentlemen?" I inquired.

"The taller one's name is Edmund Fox, and he's a real nasty fellow, I might add. He came in rather angry, looking for my father, and when I said he was not here, he pounded his fist on the counter. He left his calling card and ordered me to give it to my father immediately," he said, clearly shaken by the intimidating encounter.

"Mind things here, Ward. I will go speak to your father about this," I said as I headed out the back door to Edward's home. Edward was home resting, recuperating from his last voyage to the West Indies. We had unloaded large wooden kegs off the ship when he returned. I never questioned Edward about what was in those kegs, for his business at sea was not my concern.

I knocked on the door, and Edward's manservant, Charles, answered. "Good mornin', Master Thomas, come in," he said as he ushered me into the sitting area.

Edward's home, which was next door to the workshop, was not nearly as spacious as Elizabeth's but equally impressive. Candles burning brightly inside crystal-cut sconces illuminated the richness of the dark paneled walls.

Edward entered the room, wearing a long robe and holding a delicate teacup. "Thomas, my boy, what brings you here so early?" he asked as he sat in his usual chair. "Charles, bring my brother some tea," he shouted to his servant.

"Nay Edward, thank you kindly, but there is no time for tea now. An imposing man came in to see you this morning, berating your son with his rudeness," I said, placing Edmund Fox's calling card in front of him.

Edward paused in silence as he glanced at the card; a frown formed upon his face.

"Do you know this man? He caused quite a stir, demanding to speak with you," I asked, growing frustrated.

Edward stood and walked over to the window, turning his back to me as he spoke. "Yes, I've known this man for a long time. Edmund Fox and his wife are acquaintances of ours, and they are both devoted British loyalists. Do not be concerned, my fine brother. I will talk to him," he replied.

I stood up, clearly understanding that this conversation was over and that my brother was not going to confide in me. "Well, Edward, remember, if there is anything I can do, I am here if you need me."

I quickly left and rushed down the stairs to the workshop. I wanted to prepare for Mr. Dally's visit. He was expected any time now.

"Boys, tidy up a bit. We have guests arriving soon," I barked.

"Straight away, lads, you heard Master Annely," said Ward.

Ward was becoming my "right hand" and a master gunsmith. Edward could have witnessed this if he had come into the shop more often.

I could hear a carriage pulling up out front and I went quickly to the door to greet them. I was pleased to see Mr. Dally with a young lady, whom I assumed was his daughter Sarah, exiting his carriage. I held the door open for them, "Good morning, 'tis a pleasure to have you both here today," I said, welcoming them into the workshop.

I could see the lads sneaking glances at the young lady and muttering to each other. I understood why, for she was even lovelier than Elizabeth had described.

Her chestnut brown hair was pulled back in a tight knot, revealing a milky white neck. The emerald-colored dress she wore emphasized her exotic green eyes. Her soft smile and friendly manner made her even more alluring. This beautiful young lady must have a long line of admirers, I thought to myself. I barely heard Mr. Dally when he introduced her to me, "Thomas, I would like you to meet my daughter, Sarah." I stared into her eyes as I replied, "'Tis a pleasure to meet you, Miss Dally." Sarah returned the sentiment, smiling at me sweetly.

As I showed them around the workshop, Mr. Dally listened intently. I explained the system I had put in place to produce arms more efficiently. Sarah seemed equally impressed as well.

I approached Ward and introduced him, "This is my nephew, Ward Annely, Edward's eldest son. He is our shop foreman and does a fine job," I boasted. Ward shook hands with Mr. Dally and smiled at Sarah as they politely greeted each other.

"This is an outstanding establishment that you and Edward have here," remarked Mr. Dally. "Thank you, Sir, and I have not forgotten my promise to build you a fine pair of pistols someday," I replied.

"Why, thank you, Thomas. Judging from what I have seen here today, I am certain they will be the best pistols I will ever own. Now, I have other business to attend to in town. Would you mind keeping my daughter amused while I am gone? You can use my carriage if you like. I am in need of a walk, and the weather is quite agreeable," stated Mr. Dally.

"Of course, Sir, that is if your daughter doesn't mind, " I replied humbly. Sarah smiled at me warmly, and I knew I had my answer.

Mr. Dally quickly exited the shop, promising to be back before sundown. I secretly wished he would take longer than expected.

I instructed Ward to take over for the rest of the day as Sarah and I ventured out to the city for what I knew would be a most pleasant afternoon.

"Mr. Annely, it is such a beautiful day. Do you mind walking?"

"I don't mind at all, Miss Dally. I prefer it. Please, call me Thomas."

"Only if you will call me Sarah," she replied, smiling at me.

I directed their driver to wait at the stables out back. "You may water your horse if you like," I told him. "Much obliged, Sir," he replied as he tipped his hat and rode off.

Sarah tucked her tiny, gloved hand inside the crook of my right elbow as I proudly escorted her around the town. Passersby nodded and tipped their hats at this lovely lady I had on my arm.

"Oh, look at this quaint French Bistro," Sarah remarked. The owner, a short, mustached gentleman, was sweeping the front entranceway. The man smiled and said in his native tongue, *"Entrez, s'il vous plait?"*

*"Bonjour, Sir, table pour deux s'il vous plaît,"* Sarah replied in fluent French.

*"Oui,* you lovely couple," he remarked. The owner was quite taken with Sarah as he sat us at one of his finest tables.

"Do you mind if I order, Thomas?" she asked. "Oh, please do, as long as you don't surprise me with frog legs," I replied jokingly. "Actually, Thomas, cuisses de grenouille is very delicious."

"I must say, when you say it in French, it does sound appetizing," I replied with a chuckle.

Sarah ordered a tray of delicious cheeses and a loaf of heavy-crusted bread. She enjoyed a richly colored red wine while I had my ale. "Sorry, Sarah, I never had a taste for wine," I commented, hoping she didn't find me too unsophisticated.

"Now tell me, where does an Irish lass learn to speak French?" I inquired playfully. "Well, Thomas, first of all, I am an American and very proud of it. I was born here and lived my whole life in New Jersey. My father was born in Ireland, and my mother in France. She often spoke to me in French when I was a child, so I learned it rather quickly. I love the language. It is so romantic," she said as she sighed.

"I agree, and you speak it very well," I replied. "Thank you, Thomas. I have enjoyed teaching Elizabeth's children French. How about you? Can I teach you French?" I laughed, "I'm afraid I would butcher the language you love." We shared a laugh before continuing our conversation.

"Tell me, Thomas, where were you born?"

I paused before responding, recollecting my homeland, "I was born in England, in a seaport town called Bristol. "Tis quite nice, being near the sea."

Sarah's lips turned up in a smile. "Oh yes, I have heard how lovely Bristol is; you must miss it so," she said softly.

Her deep, green eyes captivated me. The mere sight of her took my breath away. I gathered my thoughts and replied a bit awkwardly, "Ah, yes, although the city here is much like Bristol, with the port and all. I hope to return someday, but I have grown fond of the people and their freedom here."

"Well, as long as your King does not ruin it for us all," she said, surprising me with her reply. I paused, pondering how to respond to her comment.

"Aye, George III is quite different from his grandfather. I'm sure things will get better soon." I quickly replied, keeping my comments brief, for it was far too risky to air your opinions in public these days.

Sarah suddenly turned quiet as she realized I was avoiding the subject. I was sure she thought I was a coward for not having a more profound opinion.

Before making any further comments on this subject, I suggested, "Perhaps we should head back now; I would not want to keep your father waiting."

As we stood to leave, I saw my sister-in-law Eva sitting with her maid Maggie at a table behind us, sipping her wine. She gave me a wry smile as if she thought I knew she was there all the while. "Eva, I did not see you sitting there. Otherwise, I would have asked you to join us," I remarked, shocked at seeing her there. "That's quite alright, Thomas; I rather enjoy my quiet time here," she said with her usual stiffness. I led Sarah to her table to introduce her, "I would like you to meet Miss Sarah Dally; she tutors Elizabeth's children."

She gave Sarah a curt smile and said rudely, "Do you teach them how to dislike our King?" Sarah's face flushed red as she tried to justify her comment, "Oh no, of course not! It's only the many taxes he is implementing that I am not fond of," she shot back.

"Thomas dear, you need to teach your lovely friend here about how good we British are," she quipped as she stormed out the door, her maid rushing behind her.

Sarah was clearly upset, and for good reason. My sister-in-law Eva is quiet as a snake and attacks when you least expect it. This confrontation with Eva was not good. I don't know Eva well, but I know of her type. She won't let this one rest, and of that, I was sure.

"I'm sorry, Sarah, she was rude, and her behavior towards you was uncalled for. I will deal with her," I said, attempting to change the dark mood that had taken over our pleasant afternoon.

Eva was standing outside the bistro, fuming because her carriage was late. She was angry and needed to speak with Edward right away. Her driver came speeding up, apologizing for making her wait. "Never mind, just take me home," she demanded.

Eva rushed into her home and threw her coat and hat into Maggie's arms. She charged into Edward's study. He was sitting at his desk, reading his mid-day messages. "Eva, you startled me, dear. Are you well?" he inquired. "No, Edward, I am not," she said rudely. "You need to talk with that brother of yours," ordered Eva, her hands planted firmly upon her hips.

"You mean Thomas?" he questioned.

"Why, of course, Thomas, do you have any other brother here?"

"Eva, please sit down. You need to get a hold of yourself, dear. I cannot imagine what my good brother could have done to upset you."

"'Tis that woman he is consorting with, Sarah Dally," she retorted.

"Who?" he inquired.

"Oh, Edward, don't be so naive. She's a rather pretty girl. I am certain you know full well who she is."

Edward spun around in his chair, looking Eva directly in the eye. "All right, Eva. You have my full attention now. Who in heaven's name is this Sarah Dally you are speaking of," he replied, frustrated by her demeanor.

Eva stamped her foot loudly, "Oh Edward, come now, surely you know her father, that traitor Gifford Dally?"

Edward paused and placed his finger to his temple, "Ah yes, I do know of him, a very prominent merchant from New Jersey, am I correct? What makes you think he's a traitor, woman?" he shot back sternly.

Eva stormed out with Edward trailing behind her. "Clearly, Edward, you have forgotten what our good friends, the Fox's, told us about the Dally's. They are traitors to King George!" she shouted, slamming her sitting room door in Edward's face.

Sarah remained silent as we walked back to the workshop. The mood had shifted from light to heavy, and all my attempts at pleasantries were replied with only a nod and a polite smile.

Sarah's father was waiting in his carriage at the front of the shop. "There you two are," he called out from the window of his carriage. "I trust you both enjoyed your afternoon stroll?" I smiled at him as I helped Sarah board the carriage. "I hope to see you again soon, Sarah," I said meekly. "Thank you, Thomas, for a pleasant time," she replied, with none of the warmth she had bestowed on me earlier.

"Good day to you, Sir. I hope your business dealings went well," I said politely to Mr. Dally. "Why yes, Thomas, it was a very productive day. It was kind of you to keep my daughter company. She surely would have been bored coming along with me. Good day to you, young man," he said with a broad smile as his driver whipped the reins, and they were gone.

I stood there, watching the carriage ride off, angered by the cruelty these times brought out in people. I would not let one woman's petty ways ruin my chance of happiness.

My brother is married to a cold, vindictive woman. I never interfered with my brother's personal life, but this time, I had no choice; I had to say something to Edward.

THOMAS ANNELY

# CHAPTER
## 9

**FRANCIS LEWIS**
Actual Portrait

va woke up late, as usual, most likely from too many nightcaps the evening before. She immediately started barking orders to her well-worn help, "Maggie, where's my coffee," she shouted. Eva was British down to her bones, yet she had nothing but disdain for the taste of tea.

This evening, Edward, Eva, and Ward were to attend a formal dinner at Edmund Fox's residence for General Gage. My nephew Ward, being of the proper age, was forced by his doting mother to attend.

"Can't I stay home with Joseph," he pleaded with his mother.

"Edward, my son, you must attend these affairs if you expect to marry well. Now hurry along and have Charles get you dressed."

My brother Edward had no desire to dine with Edmund Fox; he only agreed to attend to satisfy his pretentious wife. However, along with General Gage, many high officials in the British army would attend tonight. It would do him no harm to be seen in the company of these influential men.

"Charles, be sure Edward and young Edward's shirts and breeches are pressed and their shoes are polished," she ordered. "Yes, ma'am," said Charles obediently.

"And has my dress arrived?" "Yes, ma'am, came early this mornin'," said Maggie. "Well, 'tis about time," she ranted, heading to her dressing table.

Brushing her thinning black hair, Eva frowned in her smoky mirror, observing the fine creases beginning to form around her eyes. She reminded herself that she was still attractive and would not be outdone by the dull British wives of her husband's acquaintants.

Eva applied thick, white makeup, concealing any imperfections on her face. Her cheeks were reddened with plum, and her eyes were lined with dark kohl, which brought out the color of her deep, blue eyes. Her long black hair was tied up in a tight knot upon her head, with ringlets of curls cascading around her face. Maggie tightened the laces on her corset, accenting her tiny waist, "Tighter, Maggie," she ordered. Her face winced as Maggie pulled tighter, making her bust protrude, exposing her milky white skin. She stepped into her satin petticoat while Maggie fastened the laces and helped her slip into her long gown.

Eva looked exquisite. The lavender–blue hue of her dress accented the porcelain tone of her skin. White lace was stitched into the sleeves, extending beyond her petite hands. She smiled at her reflection in her mirror, wondering if she made the right choice wearing blue. She would not want the loyalist ladies gossiping that she may be sending a silent message. "Maggie, tell Charles to make sure my husband wears his coat with the red embroidering," she ordered.

Edward and Ward waited patiently for Eva to make her appearance. She took Edward's breath away when she entered the room. Despite her arrogant ways, she was still a beautiful woman.

"Mother, you look lovely," Ward expressed. Edward reached for Eva's hand and kissed it. "Yes, dear, you truly do," he agreed.

"You both look very handsome," she remarked as Ward escorted her down to the waiting carriage. She was pleased to see that they were both wearing hints of red embroidery on their decorative waistcoats.

The entryway to the home of Edmund Fox was lavishly decorated for the evening, with brightly plumed Ostrich feathers placed in large, ornate vases. Inside the grand parlor, elegantly dressed women in various colored gowns and elaborate wigs gathered. The men were handsomely dressed, with fancy embroidered coats and starched breeches with silk stockings. They were all fiercely loyal to the crown and brimming with excitement to meet the General.

Eva greeted Mr. & Mrs. Fox with the charms she reserved for only those she thought worthy before mingling with all the others.

Ward was amazed by the sights around him and pleasantly surprised at how lovely the Fox's daughter Amelia was. Dressed in pale pink, she looked like a delicate flower with golden curls falling past her bare shoulders. She smiled sweetly as she greeted all the guests. He prayed she was not a loyalist like all the others here.

Impeccably dressed waiters, holding trays of elegant long-stemmed glasses, served the guests pink champagne. Ward, sipping the sour liquid, smiled politely, even though he disliked the taste immensely.

Suddenly, the chatter in the room quieted down when the British General Gage, dressed in full military uniform entered and stood for his formal introduction. "My guests, may I introduce, The Honourable General Thomas Gage and Mrs. Margaret Gage," announced Edmund Fox. Gage was the Commander in Chief of all the British forces and had his headquarters in New York. He was flanked by two red-coated uniformed British soldiers guarding the couple.

The guests flocked around, excited to speak with the General. They were all waiting anxiously for updates on all the happenings up north.

All the guests moved into the green room, which was filled with various lush, exotic plants. The full moon lit the room, beaming in through the vaulted glass ceiling. Several chairs filled the space, along with a podium for the guest of honor to speak.

The elegant guests filled the room with color as they sat at their assigned seats, with the Annelys seated in the back. Eva, insulted by the seating arrangements, urged the servant to find them better seats. Embarrassed by his wife, Edward rebutted her remark and said to the man-servant, "These will be fine. Please sit down, dear." Eva's face flushed, and Edward knew she would not take kindly to him tonight.

The General took his place at the podium, looking upon the esteemed guests who held him in the highest regard. "Firstly, I wish to extend my gratitude to Mr. & Mrs. Fox for sharing their lovely home with all of us." The guests clapped as Edmund Fox and his wife, seated in the front row with Mrs. Gage, beamed with pride.

The General said firmly, "My dear friends, I am sure you are quite aware of the unruly behavior of these ragtags who call themselves the Sons of Liberty."

"As civilized citizens and loyal subjects to our good King George, we must do our part to stop these rebels. They are more inclined to draw from the government's dole than to earn an honest wage. How else do they have so much time to loiter on the streets, stirring up trouble and terrorizing the good, loyal people of this city," he said, pounding his fist on the podium.

"We cannot add fuel to the fire by supplying arms to the commoners known not to be loyal to our King. Every loyal citizen must report any suspicious behavior of anyone who is blatantly a traitor!"

"Our British troops need your monetary support more than ever. The barracks the men are living in are not sufficient enough, and they are in great need of better lodging, food, and supplies. We must help our men in arms so they may continue to protect the good people of this great city of New York!"

There were countless yeas from the devoted loyalists in agreement as the General went on with his rant. Edward sat silently, observing the fever rising within the small group. Eva chimed in with the rest, and Edward was disgusted by her actions. Eva glared at Edward with an evil look. He did not recognize the woman his wife had become.

Edward's stoic behavior did not go unnoticed. Edmund Fox kept his sly eyes on all his guests during the speech.

The guests clapped enthusiastically as the General concluded his speech. They all moved to the dining room, where a large feast awaited them.

Edmund stood back, waiting for all the guests to exit, and looked sternly at Edward as they walked past him. "Edmund, it was a wonderfully motivated speech by General Gage," piped up Eva. "Why yes, Eva, and one we should not take lightly," he replied, keeping his eyes on Edward.

Edward had to admit that Mrs. Fox outdid herself with the lavish dinner she presented. The guests enjoyed several choices of meat, oysters on the half-shell, whole roasted fish, freshly baked bread, and much more. The conversation around the table, spurred by the General's spirited speech, was quite lively. Edward would have enjoyed the rousing conversation if it weren't for the unpleasant Edmund Fox at the table.

The women moved to the main hall and were seated on comfortable cushioned settees. A musical quartet played, entertaining the high society ladies while they swished the air with their delicate lace fans. The men, with their overstuffed bellies, loosened their waistcoats and went outside on the porch. The smoke of the fine imported cigars encircled their heads while they drank generous snifters of brandy and debated amongst themselves the news of the day.

Edward was doing his best to mingle with the men. He looked to his left and saw Edmund Fox approaching him. "Edward, follow me to my study; I need to talk with you," he insisted, leading the way.

Seeing his father being pulled away, Ward followed them, shielding himself to the side so he would not be seen. As he approached the study, he stood quietly, listening to what was being said behind the door.

Inside Edmund Fox's study, Edward glanced around at the exotic animal heads that adorned each corner of the room. A large mahogany cabinet housed an impressive collection of weaponry, including various muskets, knives, and pistols.

The flag of Britain hung from a free-standing pole behind Edmund Fox's massive desk.

Edmund walked over to the mantel, taking down his early model Brown Bess musket. "Now, this is a finely made musket, wouldn't you say, Edward?" he questioned, gently holding it in his hands. "Yes, very fine, Edmund. They have always been my favorite."

Edmund placed the musket back over the mantel and walked over to face Edward. He stood taller than Edward, and with his steely eyes, he could be quite intimidating.

"Edward, I must get to the point here; you seemed uninterested in the General's speech, am I correct?" he questioned.

"No, Edmund, I was listening to every word he said," Edward replied.

"Well, do you agree with him?" Edmund asked firmly.

"Yes, but not totally. The colonists are already paying surplus taxes for the Upper Barracks. The good General expects these humble colonists to pay even more taxes when they can barely afford to take care of their own? I suppose he wants me to freely supply the British troops with all the arms they need?"

"Yes, Edward, does your Annely blood not run red? Would you prefer to be loyal to these rebels who are against our King?" he said angrily.

"I prefer to stay out of this conflict and be neutral, Edmund."

"There is no such thing as neutral Edward; you are either with our King or against him," he threatened. "I wouldn't want to see you or your family going down the wrong path. And you would be wise to warn your younger brother Thomas to mind himself, too. I think you both have been greatly influenced by your traitor brother-in-law, Francis Lewis."

Edward was fuming, yet he knew there was no reasoning with the likes of Edmund Fox.

"Remember what I am telling you, Edward. If you know what is good for you, you will make the right choice," he said, storming out of the study.

Edmund Fox has the King's arm so far up his arse, 'tis no wonder he walks ramrod straight, Edward thought to himself as he followed him out to join the other guests.

Ward, concealed behind a door, overheard the whole conversation. Suddenly, he felt a tap on his shoulder. Startled, he turned to see

Amelia. "Ward, here you are. Why aren't you mingling with the guests?" she questioned. Ward thought quickly and replied, "I apologize, Amelia. I was looking for your father to make his acquaintance."

"I am sure my father is somewhere enjoying a fine cigar with the general; I believe you owe me a dance?" she said with a coy smile.

Ward was angered by Edmund Fox, making his father appear as a puppet on his strings. As he led Amelia in the waltz, he wondered how the crude Edmund Fox could have such a lovely daughter.

By the end of the evening, young Amelia sought out Ward over all the other young men to dance with. To Eva's delight, it was clear that the two had a mutual attraction for each other, and she would make sure they would meet again.

She rather liked the young Amelia. With her father's money, she could have chosen the first stud who came along to plant his seed in her. Most women settled into the dull existence of being a wife and mother. It was clear to Eva that Amelia had higher aspirations from her station in life, and she felt she would be the perfect companion for young Edward.

Eva wandered off looking for her husband, only to find him sitting outside on the veranda, alone, with a drink in his hand. "Edward, go get your son. The guests are leaving, and I don't want to be seen lingering," she barked.

They spoke little of the evening as they rode home in their carriage. "I trust you had a good time, son?" Edward inquired. "Yes, Father, it was a lovely evening," he replied, never looking his father in the eye.

As they arrived home, Charles greeted them and helped Eva down from the carriage. Eva, never saying a word to either of them, tossed off her heels and retired to her bedroom for the night.

Edward went to his study with his favorite brandy in hand. He knew the thought of a good night's sleep was futile.

Ward went for a walk in the cool night air to get his thoughts in order. He wondered why his father acted cowardly and did not stand up for himself against Edmund Fox.

## THOMAS ANNELY

# CHAPTER 10

I left early for work this morning, knowing that Ward would be late and I would need to open up for the men. I wasn't particularly anxious to hear how the evening went. I, myself, would never want to attend a dinner party with the likes of those sophisticated folks, and I was sure Ward felt the same. Although, I heard Edmund Fox has a lovely young daughter, which certainly would have made the night more bearable for him.

I was anxious to hear what Ward thought about Edmund Fox. He is known as one of the wealthiest men in town, and his business dealings with the British have been less than admirable.

I hoped to see Edward at the workshop today, for I had much to discuss with him. I needed to address my sister-in-law Eva's alliance with Edmund Fox.

Chip was prompt as always, sitting on the stoop of the shop's entryway. He was becoming a fine little apprentice, and the men had taken a real liking to the young lad. I had grown particularly fond of him as well. I often wondered where the boy went off to at night, knowing he had no family to speak of. I made a point to invite Chip to supper this evening to learn more about him.

Half past the hour, Ward came in and immediately went to work, inspecting the new shipment of wood we received. To my surprise, Edward followed shortly after and headed straight into his office without even a greeting.

Later in the morning, Edward popped his head out of his office and called me, "Thomas, can I see you for a moment, please?"

"Yes, of course, Edward," I replied.

I entered Edward's office and found him sitting at his desk surrounded by piles of paperwork. It had only been a week since I last saw him, yet his face had grown pale and tired looking.

"Come in, Thomas; I will not bore you with the details of last evening, but I did not have a wonderful time at Edmund Fox's dinner. I swear Fox is the devil himself. For some reason, my lovely wife, Eva, worships the ground he walks on," he ranted. "I need to review all the ledgers of our current orders along with the names of the purchasers. 'Tis just a matter of time before Edmund Fox comes marching in here, demanding to see our records."

The sweat was building up under my collar. "Edward, who is this Fox fellow who thinks he has the right to our records?" I questioned.

"Thomas, he's a man you don't want to be on the wrong side of. He is in deep with the British officers," warned Edward.

I hesitated, realizing this was not the ideal time to talk to Edward, but I could no longer contain myself.

"Edward, I need to talk to you about Eva," I blurted out.

Edward looked at me straight on, "Thomas, if this is about that Sarah Dally girl, Eva has told me all about her. She is clearly jealous of this young woman, and I am sure her thoughts are misguided. Nevertheless, I recommend you take heed of this warning. The Dallys are known sympathizers of the rebels, and anyone seen in their company will be viewed as such. You need to be careful, dear brother. The redcoats are ruthless. They would just as soon see you hang if they had one inclination that you are not a loyalist. Especially you, being a gunsmith. They are watching us, brother!" he warned.

I stood up in defiance of my brother's words: "I will not be told whom I can socialize with. 'Tis why I came to America in the first place! This is not just about Sarah Dally; Eva has gone too far. I am concerned her alliance with Edmund Fox may cause us great harm."

Edward let out a long breath, "Thomas, please sit down. There is no freedom here anymore. If you choose not to follow the King, his henchmen will hang you. As far as my dear wife, do not be concerned; I have talked to her about minding her own business. Now, please, go get my ledgers."

I had to hide my anger as I went to retrieve the ledgers for Edward. I realized I could no longer confide in my brother about my concerns, for it was obvious he was worn down by it all. On Sunday, I would see Francis, and hopefully I would find a kindred soul from whom I could seek some good advice.

A chilly rain had begun to fall as the men and I closed the shop for the day. "Mind your heads; 'tis a wet one out there," I said as they filed one by one out the door.

I stopped Chip and invited him to supper, and to my surprise, he gladly accepted. As we made our way to the Inn, I hoped the Blackintons would not mind me bringing a young lad to their fine establishment. I was quickly put at ease when we were greeted by the ever-joyful Mr. Blackinton.

"Good evening, Thomas, and who might your little friend be?" he said. "Why, my good Sir, this is my new apprentice, Chip. He will be joining me for supper tonight."

Mrs. Blackinton came out of the kitchen with her usual pleasantries and fussed over the boy. "Thomas, who is this handsome young lad you have with you this evening?"

I introduced Chip to Mrs. Blackinton as she led us to one of her best tables next to the warm fireplace. Chip was transfixed as the blaze of the fire caught his stare. I sensed he had not felt the warmth of human compassion nor a roaring fire for quite some time.

I ordered two bowls of beef stew with warm bread, and Mrs. Blackinton laughed. "You'll have none of that. This evening, you'll be having roast beef with Yorkshire pudding," she replied boldly.

"Aye, he's a darlin' boy, Thomas," remarked Mrs. Blackinton as she hurried back to prepare our meals. I recalled how sad I felt for the Blackintons when I heard they lost their only son to yellow fever.

We finished the delicious meal and were about to leave when Mrs. Blackinton called out to us, "Hold on, Thomas. I have something for young Chip." She handed Chip a package wrapped in burlap and tied with a thick rope. "These should fit you right fine," she said, smiling warmly.

Chip unraveled the package, and inside was a new pair of breeches, two fine linen undershirts, a heavy woolen overcoat, and a pair of leather shoes. A wide smile crossed Chip's face, "Thank you kindly, ma'am," he replied humbly. "This is very generous of you, Mrs. Blackinton," I said as her eyes welled with tears. I sensed these were clothes that belonged to their late son. "A handsome lad as Master Chip here deserves some proper clothing," she remarked. Chip warmed her heart when he hugged her goodbye.

As we stood outside the Inn, contemplating which direction to go, I looked down at Chip and asked him the question that had us all curious, "Where do you live, Chip?" He raised his hand to point and replied, "Why just around the bend here, Sir."

He led me down a dark alleyway. The sounds and the smells were frightening to a grown man; I could not fathom how a young boy could live here. The rain had begun to fall harder when we stopped at a pile of crates tucked under a stairwell, covered with ragged clothes.

"Chip, is this where you sleep?" I remarked, appalled by the sight of it. "Yes, Sir, don't worry, I am used to it," he replied. "Now Chip, 'tis a rainy, damp night; I want you to come stay with me, son," I said sternly. "Are you sure, Sir? I'll manage just fine."

"I will not take no for an answer. Pack up your belongings and come along," I insisted. I shielded myself from the rain while he gathered his things. "Follow me, Chip," I muttered as I led the way to my flat. "Thank you kindly, Sir," Chip said. He rushed up, clutching his bundles, and walked quickly beside me.

I was glad I insisted that Chip stay with me. It was unhealthy for the lad to sleep out on a night like this or any other night. Not everyone who comes to this great land has such good fortune as I. For some, it's a struggle to survive. Chip had experienced great misfortune in his young life, but this lad was a survivor. It was time I gave back some of my good fortune to someone who needed it badly.

# THOMAS ANNELY

# CHAPTER II

**ELIZABETH ANNELY LEWIS**
Actual Portrait

C hip did stay with me that cold rainy night, and to my delight, he agreed to live with me for a while. He was a welcome addition to my empty home and insisted he would earn his keep by helping me tend to the house.

He was out the door most mornings before I even had my tea. I could not be more proud of the fine young man he was becoming.

Today was Sunday. As usual, I would go to Whitestone, but today, I would bring Chip along. He is the same age as my nephew Morgan, and I thought they might become good friends.

I had purchased a one-horse carriage for Chip and me to travel to work together. It was not as grand as Edward's, but it suited me just fine.

I hoped Sarah would be at Whitestone today so I could make amends after our unpleasant conversation with Eva. I needed to speak to Francis, but seeing the fair Sarah would also do me a world of good.

Riding along, I could hear the church bells ringing, calling all the faithful to prayer. It made me think of St. Stephens, back home in Bristol, and the years I spent attending mass there.

As we rode past the old church, two British soldiers suddenly forced us to an abrupt stop. I looked over at Chip with confusion as the soldiers ordered us to get down from my carriage.

"May I inquire what this is about?" I asked. "What is your name, Sir, and where are you going?" said the soldier, ignoring my question.

"I wasn't aware that I needed to alert anyone of my whereabouts," I stated boldly.

"Sir, your name and destination, or I will take you forcibly to the barracks for further questioning," he ordered.

"My name is Thomas Annely, and I am going to visit my sister out of town," I replied reluctantly.

"And the boy with you?"

"He is my live-in apprentice joining me for the day." The other soldier walked around my carriage without any explanation, searching for something. He gave a nod of his head and said to the other soldier, "All clear, they can go." They hopped on their horses and departed as quickly as they appeared.

I glanced back at the church and saw a group of curious onlookers watching. Through the crowd, I could see steely eyes glaring directly at me. It was Edmund Fox, standing tall amongst all the churchgoers. My instincts told me, without a doubt, that he had a hand in this British encounter.

As we climbed back aboard my carriage, Chip was shaken. I patted him on the knee and tried to ease the boy's mind. "Do not concern yourself, son; 'tis just a sign of the times."

We rode in silence all the way to see Elizabeth. My thoughts went to how I would confront the authorities on this uncalled-for action, but I assumed my grievances would fall on deaf ears. This made me even more anxious to talk to Francis straight away.

As we arrived at Whitestone, Elizabeth greeted us warmly and was delighted to meet Chip. "You run along out back; the boys are waiting there for you," she said, smiling at the lad and making him feel at home.

I pulled my sister in for a hug and held onto her gently, "I am so sorry, dear sister." Elizabeth had suffered another miscarriage, and I could see the sadness in her eyes for the little one she lost. "Alas, Thomas, the doctor says I am all done childbearing," she said softly. "Aye, Sister, you and Francis have three wonderful children, and Francis is blessed to have you," I said to comfort her.

I looked behind her to see if anyone was joining us for the day. "Sarah will arrive here later for dinner, in case you were wondering," she remarked after catching me sneaking glances into the foyer.

"It will be pleasant to see her again. Is Fran in his study?" I quickly changed the subject before my sister could drill me on the attractions of the fairer sex.

"Yes, Thomas, 'tis always business with you men. Don't be late for dinner; it will be served sharply at 1:00," she said with a smile. My sister's resilience amazed me, as she always maintained her sunny disposition, no matter what was bestowed upon her.

I went by the parlor, stopping only once to admire my brother Richard's musket hanging over the mantel. I could hear Richard's voice from when I was just a wee lad, making me swear I would not touch it. I smiled at the memory as I went around the corner to see Francis.

I knocked lightly on the door. "Oh Thomas, my boy, good to see you again," said Francis, with his usual boisterous voice. "I see a fine-looking young lad out there playing with Morgan. Would that be your Chip?" he questioned. "Why yes, Sir, and he is turning out to be a fine helper in the shop," I stated proudly.

"With a master like you, Thomas, no better guidance could be given."

"I appreciate your confidence in me, Sir, but today I am in need of your guidance."

Francis walked over and securely closed the door to the study. "Have a seat, Thomas. How can I be of help to you, my friend?"

I immediately felt relief, having such a kind soul as Francis, to tell my troubles to. "Fran, there is much going on in the city that has me perplexed. My brother Edward has not been himself lately and seems to be under a great deal of stress. He does not look well, and I am growing concerned."

Francis listened intently with genuine concern, "Have you confronted him about the cause of his stress?"

"Nay, he has made it clear that he does not want to concern me with his troubles, but I have a notion that I know who the culprit is," I replied boldly.

Francis leaned in, speaking softly, "And who may this culprit be, perhaps his bitch of a wife, if you pardon my expression."

"Aye, no doubt she is part of the problem, but I fear this gentleman named Edmund Fox is to blame. Why, just today, as we passed by a church on our way here, I was accosted by two British soldiers. They demanded I tell them my name and where I was going. One soldier threatened to detain me if I did not comply. They were looking for something but, naturally, found nothing. All the while, Edmund Fox was watching from behind on the church grounds. This is the second time I have seen this man, once leaving the workshop after he harassed Ward, and now today, pestering me."

Francis faced me as he spoke, "Thomas, this Edmund Fox is not too fond of me either," he replied, making me understand that he was well aware of the man. "I am afraid your intuition about this fellow is correct. His name suits him well, for he is the slyest fox of them all. Don't let his loyalty to the King fool you; he is more worried about losing the wealth he has amassed. He was a poor boy from Liverpool, born to a whore for a mother. He stole away on a sailing ship to America when he was a young lad and managed to stay out of the workhouses by doing dirty deeds for the British elites. Fox has done well for himself; I will give him that, but not with an honest day of work. He is a bloodhound for the British, always searching for anyone who is not loyal to King George."

"Fran, I cannot convince my brother to confide in me, so I am at a loss for how to help him. I do not know why this fellow is harassing my fine brother and now me."

Francis paused to light up his cigar and continued on, "Thomas, beware, this man has a reputation for being a superior marksman and a duelist. He has killed more than his share of Patriots who he considered traitors. He is ruthless and will stop at nothing until he controls every merchant in the city, especially gunsmiths like yourself. I am sure I will be next on his list. The soldiers were most likely paid a hefty sum by him to search your carriage to see if you were hiding any weapons. Contrary to what this buffoon believes, he is nothing but a pawn to these British Officers he calls friends, and someday he will get what is coming to him!"

I had never heard my mild-mannered brother-in-law speak so fervently, and nothing could have prepared me for what he would say next.

Francis stood up, walked over to his study door, opened it slightly, and looked left and right into the hallway. He closed the door firmly and turned the latch to lock it. Sitting down, facing me, he pulled his chair close to mine and said, "Thomas, what I am about to tell you cannot leave this room. Do I have your strict confidence?"

I hesitated for a moment, bracing myself for what I was about to hear: "Of course, Fran. I will keep whatever you say to myself."

"Thomas, I am sure you have heard about the Sons of Liberty?" he questioned cautiously.

"I have heard about the troubles they have been stirring up in the city," I replied, curious where this conversation was going.

"Thomas, the extreme taxation imposed by King George III is strangling all the good people of these colonies. It started with the bloody stamp act, which, thankfully, with the aid of good old Benjamin Franklin, they were forced to repeal. Now those clever bastards put in place the Declaratory Act, giving them the right to tax us any damn way they please! How far will they go before they take away all of our democracies?"

"Gifford Dally and I have become part of the founding members of the Sons of Liberty in New York. 'Tis not all a group of radical young men as they would lead you to believe. In fact, we are a diverse group of businessmen with one goal: to end the tyranny being brought on by this King. To repeat a phrase that is not said enough, *No taxation without representation*," he said in one long breath. "Thomas, we could use a good man like yourself. Can we count on you to join us?" he pleaded.

I hesitated, trying to compose my thoughts before speaking. "Fran, my good man, what you are saying is treason; if you are found out, the Brits will hang you," I said with genuine concern.

"'Tis a chance we are all taking, son," he said as he stood and walked over to the window, gazing at the children playing. He turned to face me and said softly, "If we do not do this, what kind of future will our children have? They would never have the freedoms we have come to take for granted in this fine new world."

I stood up and walked over to him. "But what of Elizabeth? If you are caught, what will become of her?"

He replied, shocking me with his words, "Your dear sister, my Lizzy, is just as devoted to this cause as I am. She has formed a group called "The Daughters of Liberty." That group of lovely ladies who meet here in their Sunday best are all "daughters of liberty." They are brave women, Thomas, especially your sister. You should be right proud of her."

"And Sarah, is she part of this group of Elizabeth's? Is she a "daughter of liberty," too?" I asked with trepidation.

"I will let Miss Sarah answer you on that; the Dallys are expected here for dinner."

"Thomas, with your abilities as a gunsmith, we would like to call on you to help our cause. Is this agreeable with you?"

"I need some time, Fran. I am sure you understand. Please be assured that you can trust this conversation will go no further than these four walls."

We shook hands, and Francis placed his hand on my shoulder, "Thomas, Edward would never tell you this, but you Annely brothers may have a price on your heads. That is why those soldiers approached you. I can protect you, brother, but you need to trust me. Please do not hesitate too long, for I fear it may be too late," he warned.

Francis heard a light knock upon the door and opened it to find Kingsley standing humbly, "Mr. Lewis, the Mistress sent me to fetch you and Mr. Thomas for dinner."

"Fine, Kingsley, we will be right there, and I want the children to join us in the dining room," said Francis.

"Yes, Sir, the Mistress has it all arranged," he replied.

"I want to spend some time with the children and meet your Chip before I leave for Philadelphia."

As we entered the dining room, seated beside Elizabeth were Mr. & Mrs. Dally and their daughter, Sarah, with the children sitting opposite. I noticed neither Hannah nor Ann was present.

"Good to see you again, Thomas," piped up Mrs. Dally. "'Tis a pleasure to see you all again," I said as I sat beside Chip. Sarah nodded her head and lowered her eyes from my stare.

"Excuse me, where would Ann be?" asked Francis.

"Oh Francis, I told you Ann will be dining today with her dear friend Miss Margaret. You know, William and Mary Robertson's daughter?" replied Elizabeth.

Francis Jr. chuckled and remarked, "Dear friend indeed, 'tis Miss Margaret's brother George, who she is dear about."

"Mind your manners there, Frannie. There will be no telling of tales at this table," reprimanded Elizabeth. "Sorry, Mum, I didn't mean anything by it," he responded apologetically.

"Good God, family, let us eat and not bore our guests with trivial quibbling," said Francis, winking at Elizabeth.

I was grateful for the idle chatter; it helped keep my mind off my conversation with Francis. As pleasant as the meal was, I barely ate; all I wanted to do was talk with Sarah.

"Another delicious home-cooked meal, dear Patty has outdone herself," remarked Francis, complimenting the cook. Everyone nodded in agreement while Mr. Dally patted his full stomach.

"Now, men, join me in my study for some after-dinner brandy," said Francis as he rose from the table. "Beg your pardon, Sir, do you mind if I pass? I would like to spend some time with Miss Sarah," I expressed to Francis. "Why certainly, Thomas," he replied with a slight grin.

"Mr. Dally, would you mind if I escorted Sarah for a walk around the grounds?"

"No, Thomas, not at all, that is if Sarah doesn't mind," he said, glancing at his daughter for her approval. "I would like that, Thomas," replied Sarah, flashing her green eyes my way. "Excuse me, Elizabeth and Mother, I will be joining Thomas for a walk," she said politely.

Elizabeth and Anne smiled; they agreed that Thomas and Sarah made a lovely pair and had high hopes for the young couple.

The warmth of the sunshine felt so welcoming, and the crispness in the air was invigorating. Sarah placed her hand in the crook of my arm as I led her out to the grounds.

Sarah paused and looked at me with softened eyes, "Thomas, I want to apologize for my behavior at the bistro. The wine made me giddy, and I spoke far too much," she said, lowering her eyes in shame.

I placed my hands on her delicate chin and lifted her face to mine, "Sarah, dear, you have nothing to be sorry about. You were right about what you said, and I don't care what my sister-in-law thinks," I said as I leaned in and kissed her lovely lips.

She smiled at me sweetly, lifting her gloved hand and sweeping my hair away from my eyes. "I believe you are stealing my heart, Thomas Annely," she said softly.

"No, Miss Sarah Dally, 'tis you who have stolen mine." We stood there, staring into one another's eyes. I embraced her with my arms and lifted her off the ground. She laughed with delight as I spun her around before gently placing her back on her feet.

"Sarah, I hope that unpleasant meeting at the Bistro won't deter you from visiting me in New York," I asked.

"Thomas, I would like nothing more than to spend another lovely afternoon with you, but I am afraid I will not be coming to the city," she said reluctantly. "It is not a place for us Dallys to be right now. My father has advised me against it. I suggest you leave that city too, Thomas."

I turned to face the bay and took a deep breath, taking in all this girl, whom I was falling deeply in love with, had to say.

"Sarah, I want nothing more than to be with you, but I need time. My brother needs me more now than ever."

"I know, Thomas, I understand, but for your sake please heed what I say."

We both stood silent, staring out to the bay. I placed my arm around her shoulder and said warmly, "Until we meet again, you will be in my mind and heart."

Chip chatted all the ride home about how he could not wait to visit Whitestone again. I smiled at the lad, but my mind wandered back to all Francis and Sarah said. I was falling in love with this woman and wanted to make her a part of my life, but at what cost? Would I have to betray my English heritage and brother to be with the woman I love?

I knew I wasn't being truthful to myself. I didn't like what the Brits were doing any more than any other colonist. I realized I knew where I stood; I stood with the Americans.

# THOMAS ANNELY
# CHAPTER 12

Autumn in New York, and its pleasant weather, is my favorite time to spend by the portside. Breathing in the crisp air of the sea invigorated my lungs. It nourished my soul and gave me strength to face another day in these troubled times.

There would be no turning back for this man who voyaged here not so long ago. As discouraged as I was feeling, I had no regrets about coming to America. I knew I was facing a crucial turning point in this new world, and yet, as strange as it might seem, I was excited about this next chapter in my life.

Today, I would have to face Edward, the brother who gave me my start in this new land, and tell him about my alliance with the cause. I knew it would tear him apart.

Edward, ever faithful, would never go against his beloved England. What he did not understand was that this fight for our rights was not about England, but rather about a King, who wanted total control over the colonies.

These good, civilized people have lived and prospered in harmony with the mother country for many years. They have their own set of rules by which they live; they do not need the strong arm of Britain to govern them. The added taxation that this King demands is pure tyranny. The Brits would just as soon lead these people to poverty than watch them prosper.

Edward, worn out from lack of sleep, stumbled into the workshop and headed for his office. He paused, looking around the half-empty workspace that was once bustling with business. "Good day, Father," said Ward as his father passed him by. "Hmm, yes, good day, boys," Edward said as he closed the door to his office. Ward, having grown accustomed to his father's lack of attention, shrugged his shoulders and went back to work.

Edward sat down in his well-worn leather chair, staring at the mounds of paperwork on his desk. He grabbed his sales ledgers, put his elbow on the table, and held his chin as he scanned the pages. Slamming the book shut, he spoke to himself. "How am I supposed to tell these fine people I cannot fulfill their orders? And how in God's name do I know who is a loyalist and who is a rebel?" he sighed.

Ward knocked lightly on his father's office door, "Excuse me, Father, Mr. Edmund Fox is here to see you."

Edward let out a frustrated breath and replied, "Send him in, son."

Edmund Fox brushed Ward aside, forcing his way into Edward's office.

Struggling to remain calm, Edward said, "Have a seat, Edmund, and what can I do for you this morning?"

"I am here to find out exactly who you are selling your arms to," he inquired sternly.

"Edmund, I told you, I have no alliance with either side; I am simply trying to keep my business intact through these times. Here are my ledgers. Tell me, Sir, can you decipher which of my customers are loyal to the King?"

Edmund grabbed the ledgers from Edward's hands, "I will tell you," he said.

Anger built up in Edward as he sat there watching Edmund look through his ledgers. Suddenly, Edward grabbed the ledger from his hand and said, "Enough, Edmund, you have no right to examine my books. Please get out of my office!"

Edmund glared at him, "You are questioning my authority? Did you not hear the orders from General Gage that anyone who aids these rebels will be considered a traitor? Edward, this is my last warning, you must stop selling guns to these sons of bitches, or you won't be selling guns at all! Be wise, Edward. All I have to do is alert the British that you are not complying with the King's orders, and you will be out of business!"

"Furthermore, I am well aware that your brother Thomas has been consorting with known rebels. As for Lewis, that brother-in-law of yours, he had better watch his back, too. He is getting closer to a hangman's noose, more than he knows!" he shouted as he slammed the door behind him.

The pressure was mounting for Edward. He felt caught in the middle and had no desire to get involved.

Edward poked his head out of his office, looking around, "Ward, send your Uncle Thomas into my office as soon as he arrives," he ordered, closing his office door.

Walking up to the workshop, I thought I saw Edmund Fox riding away in his carriage. Whenever that man came calling, it was not good.

"Good day, boys," I said as I entered. The shop hands had been reduced to Ward, Chip, and another lad. "Good morning, Uncle Thomas. My father is in his office and needs to see you at once," announced Ward before I even took off my cloak.

I knocked lightly and entered Edward's office. My brother was sitting at his desk, shuffling nervously through his papers.

"Good day, Edward; I believe you wanted to see me?"

"Yes, Thomas, please sit down," he said anxiously.

It was difficult for me to see my once-strong brother Edward appear so weak. He looked nothing like the man I first saw when I arrived in America. The well-groomed, confident businessman had been replaced with a slouched-over, disheveled, tired man.

"'Tis time, Edward, for you to tell me what is going on with this Fox fellow."

Edward sat upright and responded boldly, "Edmund Fox is a true loyalist and as cruel as they come. He has high aspirations and will do anything to obtain his lofty goals. 'Tis you, Thomas, that I am deeply concerned about. You're treading in deep waters, my brother, by the company you have been keeping. The Brits are watching and 'tis not safe for you here anymore. You need to get away from the city, perhaps go back to England for a while, until things calm down around here."

I stood and replied boldly, "I am not afraid of this Edmund Fox fellow."

"Aye Thomas, it goes much beyond him; 'tis the long arm of the King that has reigned down on this city. Don't believe these rebels who think we can fight it; we can only step aside."

"Edward, I appreciate your concern for me and will heed what you say, but I will not return to England. I am an American now," I said, leaving no doubt about my loyalties. I turned and left his office, not allowing him to respond.

I finished my tasks for the day and grabbed my cloak and hat. I walked over to my nephew Ward and patted him on the back. "You are doing a fine job, son. Keep up the good work," I said solemnly. Chip was standing there, looking at me, sensing something was wrong. "Chip, we will be leaving now. Come along," I said.

We rode back to my townhouse in silence. As we entered, Chip said, "Thomas, Sir, what is troubling you?"

I pulled off my shoes to warm my feet by the hearth, "Pour us both an ale, son, and we'll have a talk."

Chip sat across from me, sipping his ale with apprehension on his face. "Is this all about that bully who came to see Sir Edward today?" he questioned.

"Aye, Chip, you are right about him being a bully, though there is much more going on right now. 'Tis not safe here anymore, and we need to get out of this Tory city of New York."

Chip looked forlorn, "All I have ever known is New York City," he said nervously.

"I know, son, and you can come back one day, but I want you to come with me for now. Do not breathe a word of this to anyone for your safety and mine."

I reached over and put my hand on Chip's shoulder, "Are you with me on this, son?" I questioned. "Yes, Sir," he said, staring me in the eye.

Chip excused himself and went off to bed. I stretched my aching back and stumbled off to my bed, falling fast asleep from the exhausting events of the day.

The morning sun streamed through my window, waking me from my slumber. Chip was already up, tending to the fire and preparing our morning meal. "Good morning, Chip; I hope you slept well, son."

"Fine, Sir," he replied. I sat down and watched Chip move with ease around the hearth, preparing our morning meal. Oh, the blissfulness of youth, I thought to myself, yet I sensed the poor boy was growing up too fast with all that had been put upon him.

"Chip, we will remain working at the shop until I make other arrangements. As I said, do not mention a word of our plans with anyone, not even Ward," I warned. "Yes, Sir Thomas," Chip replied, feeling uneasy.

We left for work at the usual early morning hour, with Chip minding the reins of my carriage. As we approached the workshop, I could see the candles casting light outside the window of Edward's office.

Entering the workshop, Chip went immediately to his work as if it were any other day. I knocked on Edward's door. "Come in," he said, prompting me to enter. "Good day, Edward. I hope the morning finds you well."

With no response to my greeting, Edward spoke bluntly, "Thomas, sit down; we have much to discuss. Have you come to any conclusions about our discussion yesterday?" he questioned.

"Why, yes, I am taking your advice, Edward, and I have some ideas for what I want to accomplish. I am considering starting a new business in New Jersey."

"Aye, Thomas, I would prefer you return to England."

"Brother, fear not for me, for I am following my heart's choice. I respect and appreciate your genuine concern, yet I cannot go back. I will not step aside; rather, I will do my part to preserve the freedom of this great new world," I replied proudly.

Edward opened his desk drawer and handed me an overstuffed envelope, "Thomas, I see you have made your choice. Take this for you and Chip."

I peeked inside the envelope and gasped, "Edward, dear brother, this looks like a year's wage here; I cannot take all this money."

"Yes, it is Thomas, and you must take it; you deserve much more," he replied sincerely. "I am humbled and much obliged, Edward. Chip and I will be working as usual until we leave, and I have alerted him not to mention a word of our plans, even to Ward." Edward nodded and said, "I will explain to my son when the time is right."

Edward walked me out of his office, placing his hand on my shoulder, "Thomas, you know this is not what I wanted to happen, and I look forward to the day when we brothers can work together again."

"And I, too, brother," I replied, grasping his hand.

As I walked back to my desk, I wondered what would become of my brother Edward. I was more concerned for him than I was for myself.

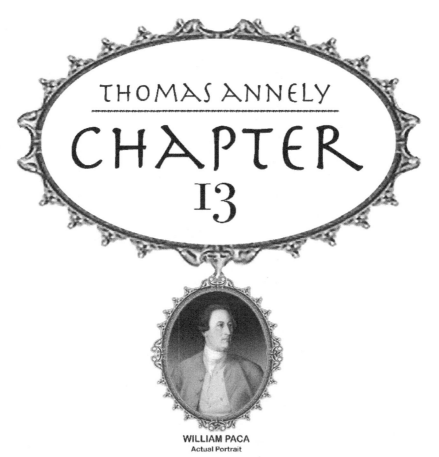

# THOMAS ANNELY

# CHAPTER 13

**WILLIAM PACA**
Actual Portrait

Sunday had arrived, and as usual, Chip and I headed to Whitestone to visit Elizabeth and her family. I hoped Francis had returned from Philadelphia, for I needed to speak with him. I was glad to receive word from Sarah that she would be there later.

As we arrived at Whitestone, Phoebe, Elizabeth's young servant girl, greeted us and led the way into the main foyer.

Elizabeth was her usual cheerful self, busy preparing her dining room for today's dinner. Chip ran off to find Morgan, who promised to take him hunting. I excused myself to speak with Francis, who was thankfully at home in his study. "Good day, Sir," I said, greeting Francis. "Come in, Thomas. 'Tis good to see you, my brother."

I went straight into my rant, "Fran, I need to speak with you privately." Francis, sensing the urgency in my voice, closed the door behind me as we took our seats in his leather-backed chairs.

"Everything you warned me about is becoming true. Edward has advised me to leave the city. He feels it is no longer safe for me to be there. I am being watched by the British because of my alliance with you and the Dallys. I will not stand by and let them take from me all I have worked so hard for. I have made my decision to be a part of your cause and serve you in any way you see fit," I said with fortitude.

Francis slid his chair closer to mine and patted me on the knee. "'Tis wonderful to hear, Thomas. Your great ability as a master armorer will be paramount for our cause."

"Incidentally, how is your brother, Edward?" he inquired.

"Alas, Fran, Edward is not good; he is beside himself with worry," I replied solemnly.

"I am deeply disappointed in my brother's position. He feels he should remain neutral."

"Aye, Thomas, do not be too harsh on your brother. Edward is torn, like so many of our fellow Englishmen. You should know that he sent several barrels of gunpowder over the river to New Jersey. Perhaps your brother is not so willing to 'step aside' as he says," said Francis.

"I did not know this, Francis," I said sheepishly. "I had delivered the barrels to the port but I had no idea who they were for. He never confides in me."

"Thomas, your brother Edward can be a stubborn man. I suppose his lack of making you his confidant is his way of protecting you. I am sure you have noticed Edward has nothing but disdain for me. He has it somewhere in his close-minded head that I took advantage of your brother Richard's passing for my own fortune. I assure you there is no validity to his thinking. Richard was very pleased when I asked his permission to marry Elizabeth. She and I fell madly in love long before Richard took ill. We were both by his side when your dear brother passed. He was weak, but his message was clear: he wanted Elizabeth and Hannah to live at Whitestone and never go without. Richard and I were not only business partners but the dearest of friends. His passing was one of the saddest days of my life," he said as he stood and poured us both a brandy. "Let us drink to his memory," he said, clinking his glass with mine.

Beaming with pride, he said, "From this day forward, we are joined together as brothers-in-arms, devoted to ending the tyranny that threatens our liberty. Now, let's go join the others in the dining room," said Francis.

There were only five of us today because my niece Ann was at her girlfriend Margaret's house. Annoyed by his daughter's absence, Francis said, "Ann is not joining us again?" he lamented.

"Francis, do you not recall how wonderful young love can be? She is smitten with Margaret's brother George," said Elizabeth.

I spoke up and inquired about Hannah: "I have not seen Mrs. Hannah for a while. Is she not well?"

"She is fine as a fiddle, off tending to her elderly sister in Virginia. I hope to see her back for the holiday," replied Elizabeth.

"I am glad to hear she is well, but I miss her company," I replied.

We finished another delicious meal that Patty, their cook, had prepared. Her cooking skills would rival any of the taverns in the city.

"Everything was delicious as always, Elizabeth. Pardon me, please; I want to check on the boys before Sarah arrives."

"Oh, those boys," sighed Elizabeth, "They better not bring me another squirrel," she said, scrunching up her nose.

I laughed and assured her I would make them leave the nasty rodents behind for the scavengers to eat.

I walked outside and took a deep breath of the crisp fall air. It would soon be winter, and I needed to enjoy the pleasant weather before the frigid cold and dampness arrived.

The boys were walking up the bank, dragging a deer behind them. "Good work, boys; it looks like venison stew will be on the menu this week," I said with a smile. "He's a six-pointer, fine job, boys. You better bring it to Kingsley to prepare it for us all."

"Thomas, there you are," I turned to see Sarah walking towards me. "Oh my, what do we have here," she said, observing the deer they had killed.

I playfully covered Sarah's eyes and whisked her away from the unpleasant sight. "Come along, Sarah. A pretty lady should never have to view such a sight," I exclaimed. "Nor smell it," said Sarah as we walked away laughing.

The boys hurried along, eager to share their hunting stories with the others.

I put my arm around Sarah and pulled her close, "Now you, my dear, are a most pleasant sight. I have missed you," I said, kissing her cheek. Sarah smiled warmly and replied, "And I have missed you too, Thomas."

I led Sarah over to the wooden bench and wrapped my arms around her, blocking the chill of the cool breeze coming off the bay.

As we sat silently, enjoying the view, I turned and said, "Sarah, you will be pleased to hear that I will be leaving the city soon." She turned and wrapped her arms around my neck, "Oh, Thomas, I am so glad you have decided to leave," she said, holding me tightly. She released her arms and sat back, "I could not be happier, Thomas, but why now? What has happened?"

"I have been planning it for a while. I could not bear being without you any longer." I stood looking down at her, "Yet, I could not, in good conscience, leave my brother during his time of need. Ironically, Edward is the one who is insisting I leave. He has grown quite concerned for my safety. The Brits have been keeping a watchful eye on all of us, Annelys. No doubt my sister-in-law Eva had a hand in that," I said with frustration.

Sarah stood up and wrapped her arms around my waist, "Your brother is being wise, Thomas. These times will only get worse before they get better. I need you here with me," she said, squeezing me tightly.

"Sarah, the British sympathizers are getting desperate. I fear for my brother, and I hope he leaves the city as well. I have spoken with Francis, and he will help me to find a place for Chip and me to work and live."

Sarah grew silent and looked away towards the bay. "What is wrong, love?" I inquired while turning her shoulders to face me.

"I rather hoped you would be looking for a place for you and me, Thomas."

"Of course, Sarah, I want all three of us to be together. Chip is a grand lad; I had hoped he could stay with us for a while."

"Oh, Thomas, I am quite fond of Chip, but I was hoping we would have a place of our own."

"And we shall, Sarah, but I cannot leave Chip behind; if you knew what the lad endured in his young life, you would understand."

Sarah sat beside me, taking my hand in hers, "Tell me, Thomas. I want to understand."

"Alas, Sarah, Chip was a scrappy, young lad when he came begging for a job from us. You had to see the sight of him; one could tell the boy was living on the streets. He was a proud one, though, and it took one cold, rainy night to finally convince him to get off the streets and stay with me."

"Chip was very melancholy that evening, and I asked him what was troubling him. He broke down, with tears in his eyes, and told me every time it rained, it made him very sad. I asked him if he had any kinfolk, and he told me he could barely recall his Mum, except for the sound of her voice singing him to sleep. She died when he was very young, and his father was so distraught he took to drinking heavily."

Sarah's eyes softened, "How awful for the boy."

"Yes, 'tis a sad story; Chip was right proud of his father despite their bad fortune. He boasted about how he taught him the ways of the streets. His father told him that when a well-heeled couple walks by, Chip should compliment them on how handsome they looked, bow and tip his hat, and hold that position for a wee bit. The people would be so charmed by Chip that they would throw a shilling or two into the hat."

"His father would laugh and boast that he was a lover. A lover of ale and wine, it seems, because most of the money they begged for was squandered away on drink."

"One exceptionally cold and snowy night, they needed to seek shelter indoors. All his father could find was an old wooden hay shed to sleep in. Chip remembers his father trying to keep him warm by wrapping him inside his long green coat. The warmth from his father's body was so comforting that he fell fast asleep. When he woke the next morning, his father's body was stone cold. He tried to wake him but realized his father had passed away while he slept."

"The poor lad was crying when he told me his story, so I wrapped my arms around him to comfort him. I told him he was not alone anymore and could stay with me as long as he wanted. When I was a boy and my father died, I had my Mum and my siblings to grieve with me. Chip had no one, so he lived on the streets until I finally convinced him to stay with me."

Sarah cried, "How tragic for the boy and how selfish of me to think only about myself."

"No, Sarah, the last thing Chip wants is our sympathy. I had hoped that you and I could give him a real family he could call his own. Besides, he is coming of age, and before you know it, he will be moving on to make his way in the world."

Sarah snuggled beside me and put her head on my shoulder, "Thomas, you are an extraordinary man. Chip and I are lucky to have you."

"I will be the lucky one, Miss Sarah Dally, when you become Mrs. Sarah Annely." I kissed her softly on her full red lips, feeling the warmth of our love as she embraced me, welcoming my kiss.

I reluctantly pulled myself away, "I think 'tis time I spoke to your father."

We smiled at one another as we kissed once more.

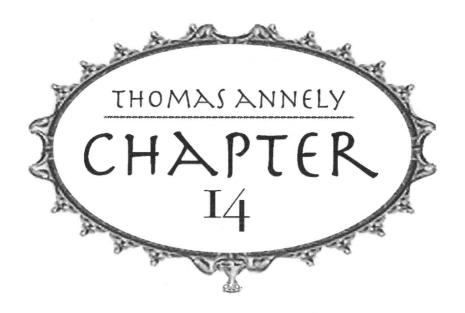

THOMAS ANNELY

# CHAPTER 14

**M**y nephew Ward would frequent the local pubs and listen to the lively discussions of the disgruntled colonists. Their passionate conversations about how the new laws violated their rights made him want to stand up and fight with them. Yet, Ward's true passion was for gun making. The Annely blood ran deep within him. He was more skilled as a gunmaker than fighting.

Ward sensed the business was failing. The tyrant Edmund Fox paid one too many visits, and he was doing his best to wear Edward down. My brother was too proud to ask for help or confide in any of us. I could see the hurt in my nephew's eyes when his father would not ask for his opinion about anything.

Ward would take his time getting home each night, hoping his mother would have had her usual nightcaps and be sound asleep. He did not want to get a tongue-lashing for being out late.

As he walked up to the entryway of his home, he could see the lantern burning in his father's study. When he entered the door, their manservant Charles ushered him in, "Good Evening, Master Edward. Your father would like to see you before you retire."

Ward removed his coat and gloves, handed them to Charles, and walked to his father's study. He knocked lightly and called in, "Father, do you wish to see me?"

"Yes, Ward, come in and sit, son. I have something important to discuss with you."

Ward sat down, anxious to hear this news that his father urgently needed to share.

Edward lit his cigar and sipped his brandy, pausing before telling Ward what he needed to say.

"Son, 'tis not safe here any longer for your Uncle Thomas, so I have advised him to leave New York. His acquaintances with the Dally woman and your Uncle Francis have raised suspicions that he may be sympathizing with the rebels. Quite frankly, he has put us in a dangerous situation," said Edward soberly.

"Father, I have heard about the Dally's involvement with the cause, but Uncle Francis, too?" questioned Ward.

"Yes, son, the word is that your Uncle Francis is aiding the Sons of Liberty, a group of men who are causing havoc with the British authority and are against our King. Whether this is true or not is neither here nor there. If the loyalists have the slightest inclination that you are not on the side of the crown, they will have your neck," warned Edward.

"How will we survive and work in the shop without Uncle Thomas? What will happen to Chip? Will he also be leaving?" Ward inquired anxiously.

"Now, Ward, I started this business without your uncle, and I shall do it again," Edward said confidently. "I would imagine your Uncle

Thomas will take Chip with him; after all, he has become like a son to him."

Ward felt his whole world was crashing in on him, and his blood began to boil with anger, "These bloody loyalists are causing all the problems. Why don't they go back to England and leave us the hell alone!"

"Son, calm yourself; these are your fellow Englishmen you are referring to; you must take care with your words," cautioned Edward. "We need to keep our heads down, and soon this will be over. Now go to bed, son, and we will talk more about this tomorrow," said Edward, ending his conversation abruptly, leaving Ward in a state of discontent.

Ward was furious, but he knew it was fruitless to argue with his father. Once again, he felt dismissed like a small child. He did not believe his father was naive or a coward, yet it was apparent he had been beaten down by the heavy hand of Edmund Fox. Ward knew, contrary to his father's beliefs, he could never bury his head in the sand and ignore what was happening all around him.

Unbeknownst to Ward, his mother was wide awake in her sitting room, eavesdropping on her firstborn's entire conversation with his father. She was not surprised that her weak husband could not choose a side. What angered her the most were the words her son had spoken. She sensed he believed in what the rebels were doing and feared he would join an alliance with them.

Eva, true to her loyalist ways, knew what she had to do. She would go to the one man who could convince her son to stay true to King George, and that man was Edmund Fox.

# THOMAS ANNELY

# CHAPTER 15

**GENERAL WILLIAM HOWE**
Actual Portrait

How right my brother Edward was in convincing me to leave New York City, where loyalists were watching on every corner. My fellow Englishmen would not take my departure from the King too kindly. My dear brother Edward has, once again, made the just decision for me. As always, I have heeded his advice.

Regretfully, this would be my last week working with Edward, and I needed to square things with my nephew Ward. He was right to be mad at me for not foretelling him about us leaving. I was not too happy about it either, but I had no choice.

As if nothing had changed, Chip had taken the carriage and headed to work bright and early. The winter chill was bitter as I wrapped my scarf around my face. A light snow had begun to fall, making me regret walking this morning. To my relief, Chip came around the corner with our carriage and pulled in on the reins to halt the steed.

"How about a ride, Sir," Chip said as I climbed aboard the carriage. I tipped my hat and said, "Much obliged, son, 'tis a bitter one today, for sure."

I entered the workshop with my usual greeting, only to receive a cold reply from Ward. "Morning," he said as he went about his business.

I found Edward in his office, toiling over the books. "Come in, Thomas," he said, gazing up over his spectacles resting on the bridge of his nose.

"Good morning, Edward, 'tis good to see you, brother," I said.

Edward took off his spectacles and laid them down on the open ledger. "'Tis good to see you as well, Thomas," he replied.

Our conversation paused as we sat, taking in the sight of each other. "You know, Thomas, this is not what I wanted."

"Neither did I, Edward. These times leave us little choice. Even though I'm afraid I have to disagree with your opinion of neutrality, I will always regard you with respect and gratitude for all you have done for me," I said sincerely.

Edward gave me a somber smile and thanked me for my kind words. He put his spectacles on and went back to reading his ledgers. I did not take his abruptness personally, for I have grown accustomed to my brother's ways through the years.

I left his office and went back to fetch Ward. I found him working over the forge, sparks flying as he pounded the molten metal with the strength of his forceful arm. I stood watching him, reflecting on how much he looked like the grandfather he never knew. My father would have been so proud that his grandson was becoming a master gunsmith and keeping the Annely tradition alive.

After he had finished working the forge, I approached him and said, "Ward, please come join me for a spot of tea; I need to talk to you."

Ward reluctantly walked over, sat down by the hearth, and poured himself a cup of tea. "Ward, you must realize leaving is not something Chip nor I want to do, but we have no other option. I wanted to tell you sooner, but involving you in any of this could be dangerous for you. What you don't know can't hurt you. Do you understand?"

"Well, what I didn't know hurt me plenty, Uncle."

"Ward, I sincerely apologize. You are right; I should have told you."

Hearing our conversation, Edward walked out of his office and spoke bluntly to his son, "Ward, do not be upset with your uncle. 'Twas I who told him not to say anything to you. I am your father, and 'tis my place to tell you."

"Father, you could have confided in me sooner; I am not a child anymore!"

"Do not be insolent, son. We will discuss this at home," Edward replied as he returned to his office, shutting the door behind him.

Ward was fuming, "Look how he runs back into his office. He thinks he can hide in there, and everything will go away!"

I hesitated to respond, not wanting to fuel this fire burning in my nephew.

"Ward, your father believes he can stay neutral and everything will be fine. I only pray that he is right. You must stand by him during these times, but I will not be far away if you need me."

Ward looked at me sadly and said, "I will miss you and Chip so very much."

There was little more for me to say, so I returned to my area and packed up some of the tools I had brought from the homeland. Chip continued his usual routine and helped Ward finish the work for the day. It troubled me to know that these two fine lads will no longer work together.

I have nothing but contempt for Edmund Fox. This terrible man is trying to destroy the Annely family.

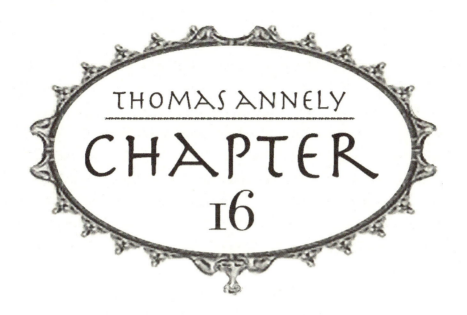

THOMAS ANNELY

# CHAPTER 16

The time had come for Chip and me to leave and make our new start. Elizabethtown, New Jersey, was to become my new home and workplace, where I would establish my gun shop, and I was looking forward to the challenge.

It was a bittersweet day, for I was forced to leave the place I have called home for some time now. It was unfair, I thought, feeling a wee bit sorry for myself. Yet, all along the thirteen colonies, brave men and women were making even greater sacrifices than I.

I was not ready to let go of my townhouse yet, so selling it would have to wait. Leaving made me feel disloyal to the memory of my dear departed brother Richard, who had bequeathed his New York home to me.

I had packed most of my belongings in old crates that Howie had supplied me. He had partnered with another seafaring fellow, and the two had become quite successful in running a ferry service across the

Hudson. I entrusted Howie with my belongings, for no one knew the waterways better than the "Old Salt," as I affectionately called him.

We ferried over the Hudson and rode through the picturesque countryside to our new home and workshop. I was more than satisfied with the two-story brick house that Francis had found for me. The ground floor is wide open with solid wood floor planks that will serve as a fine new gunmaking shop. Upstairs is a spacious living area with two bedrooms and an extra room for Chip. Sarah assured me that once we were married, she would add her "women's touch" to beautify the place.

Francis strategically chose New Jersey, with its central location between New York and Philadelphia. He was eager for me to get my workshop in order, for the time had come for me to start producing arms for what was about to come.

Although I would miss my life in New York City, I looked forward to the next chapter in my life and where it would take me.

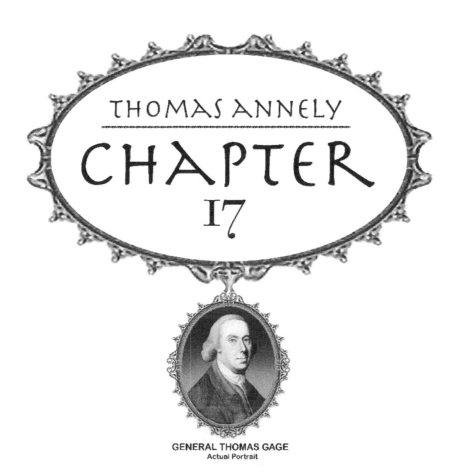

# THOMAS ANNELY

# CHAPTER 17

GENERAL THOMAS GAGE
Actual Portrait

Edmund Fox was furious. He was convinced that E&T Gunsmiths was producing arms that would end up in the hands of the rebels.

"Edward Annely, the proprietor of E&T Gunsmiths, is a weak man," Edmund told the British Officer. "He cannot decide which side he wants to be on. He pays no mind to the orders from our King and goes about his gunmaking business, selling arms to whomever. It is time we put a stop to this anarchy and teach him a lesson."

"I understand, Sir. It will be done," replied the dutiful officer.

Two days later, in the stillness of a brisk winter's night, four British soldiers dressed in civilian clothes traveled with a team and wagon along the deserted city streets. They spoke little, focusing only on the task at hand and staying warm against the bitter wind. The moonless night was so dark all they could see was their breath, frozen in the chilly air.

Not to alert anyone of their presence, the soldier at the reins kept the team at a slow trot. When they arrived at the Annely's workshop, one soldier stood guard while the other three, using the butt of their guns, broke the lock and entered through the back door.

Once in, the mayhem began. The soldiers grabbed the neatly stacked boxes of gun parts off the shelves, threw them to the floor, and stamped on them, breaking them into bits. The fresh wood stocks were smashed to pieces against the stone hearth and thrown onto the smoldering fire lingering in the fireplace. Tin cans, full of linseed oil and stain, were tipped over, causing them to drip all over the workbench and onto the floor.

The destruction continued as they ransacked Edward's office. Breaking the lock to his safe box, they split it open and stole all the money inside. Desk drawers were recklessly emptied, with papers strewn all over the room. Following strict orders, one of the soldiers grabbed Edward's ledgers and stashed them in his sack.

They proceeded to the back room, where the finished muskets and pistols were shelved. They took every one of them, carrying as many muskets as their arms could hold to the wagon waiting outside. They paused to admire the finely made pistols before stuffing them inside the waistband of their breeches. Barrels of gunpowder were lifted and loaded into the back of the wagon.

The gun stocks burning on the smoldering wood chips began to take hold, and soon, a roaring fire filled the fireplace. "Time to go," warned the soldier standing guard as they all jumped into the wagon, throwing their sacks beside them. They swiftly galloped off, unseen.

Edward, as usual, had fallen asleep in his easy chair. He woke up suddenly when his servant Charles knocked lightly on his study door.

"Mr. Edward?" he called in after opening the door a crack. "Yes, Charles?" said Edward drowsily.

"I am sorry to wake you, Sir, but I believe someone left the fire burning in your workshop. I can see the brightness through my window," said Charles.

Still, in a half-asleep stupor, Edward was baffled as he went and looked out the side window facing his shop. Charles was right; he could see the fireplace burning brightly. Frustrated, Edward assumed Ward forgot to douse the fire before leaving. He begrudgingly threw on his breeches and overcoat. "Sir, I can do this for you," offered Charles. "No, Charles, I will take care of it. Please wake Ward and tell him to meet me in the workshop."

Edward walked out into the chilly night air, carrying a lantern to light his way. "How can Ward forget the number one rule that he has known since he was a young lad," he muttered angrily under his frozen breath as he made his way down to the workshop.

Edward grew angry when he found the latch on the back entrance had broken off, leaving the door wide open. He lifted his lantern and immediately noticed someone had broken into the shop. He quickly pushed open the door, hung his lantern on the nearest hook, and saw a stream of linseed oil leaking dangerously close to the roaring fire.

He rushed in, taking care not to slip on the greasy oil, and threw the bucket of water he had kept by the hearth onto the fire. As the fire started to diminish, Edward looked around in shock at the ransacked mess that was once his orderly workshop. They had stolen all his inventory.

After being roused by Charles from bed, Ward threw his overcoat over his nightshirt and flew barefooted down the back stairs to the workshop. He remembered lowering the fire, so he expected the worst. He rushed into the door, slipping and nearly falling on his backside.

"Father, what in heaven's name happened here?" he shouted as he saw his father sitting on a stool with his head in his hands.

"'Tis all gone. They ruined everything. And they took all our fine muskets and pistols," Edward responded, his anger draining him of any strength he had left.

"There is little we can do here now, son. It will have to wait till morning," Edward said weakly. They snuffed out the remaining fire and attempted to secure the door shut. Ward grabbed the lantern and led his father back up the stairway to their home.

Everyone in the household was up now, waiting anxiously by the door. Edward entered his home with his head hung low. Eva greeted him with young Joseph by her side. She gasped at the sight of young Edward with his bare feet. "Maggie, go fetch some woolen socks, and Ward, go warm yourself by the fire," she ordered.

"What has happened?" Eva questioned Edward. "Robbers have ransacked the workshop. Everything is gone, Eva." Joseph rushed to his father, wrapping his arms around his waist. "Oh, Father!" he exclaimed, tears burning in his eyes.

"'Tis alright, son. Go join your brother in the study," said Edward, attempting to comfort his young son.

Eva took pity on her husband, "Charles, bring my husband some brandy into our bed chambers and warm some milk for the boys. Edward, come with me." She led her husband to their bed and helped him slide under the heavy quilt. He did not seek comfort from Eva, for too many hurtful words had passed upon her lips, and he could not envision kissing them again. He rolled on his side and fell into a fitful night's sleep.

Eva lay awake, livid with Edmund Fox. She knew he was to blame for this. Remorse came over her, knowing she was also to blame. This disaster may have been avoided if she had not aired her grievances about her husband's indecisiveness to Edmund. What began as a delightful distraction became a dangerous liaison between her and Edmund Fox. Secretly, they would meet in the darkened back room of Fraunces Tavern. Hidden away, they shared passionate embraces as they proclaimed their mutual affection for one another. "How foolish of me," she thought as she realized what she had done. She was clearly being hoodwinked by the clever Mr. Fox.

Although she had scant affection left for her husband, she no longer felt the burning desire to berate him into being a loyalist. From now on, she will stay far away from Edmund Fox.

The following day, Edward woke up with a clarity that he had not felt in a long time. The events of the evening made him realize that he had been fooling himself, thinking that he could remain neutral with no consequences. His gunmaking business was ruined, and there was no point in fighting against the Brits and the likes of Edmund Fox.

Skipping his morning meal, Edward dressed quickly to report the vandalism to the authorities. He instructed Ward, "Leave it all be for now son, until I have the authorities properly inspect the damage."

Before he left, he sat down and penned two messages, one to his lawyer and the other to me. Edward instructed his manservant Charles to deliver one of the messages to his lawyer in town and to post the other to me in New Jersey.

Edward had his driver take him directly to the headquarters of the British authorities. Edmund Fox was in so deep with them that he had little confidence they would offer him much aid. Nevertheless, he had to follow the protocol and file a report to see if he was entitled to any compensation.

The stoic officers told Edward they would inspect the property within the week. "My good sirs, I would like to clean up my workshop.

Can you not come sooner? I need to get my business back in working order as soon as possible," pleaded Edward.

"I will handle this," said a voice from behind that he immediately recognized as Edmund Fox. Edward turned and saw him standing there with a sly smirk on his face. It took all Edward's strength to restrain himself from strangling the man. "What seems to be the problem?" Edmund questioned, his nonchalant tone irritating Edward even more.

Edward remained cool. He knew the game Edmund Fox was playing, and he would not join in. "Alas, Edmund, vandals broke into my workshop last evening, and they stole and burned all my goods," he replied, pretending to play into Edmund's hand.

"'Tis a shame, Edward. I will see to it that these officers inspect your property at once and report back to me with their findings. I'm sure the British will apprehend the dirty Yankee rebels that are responsible."

"I am much obliged, Edmund. However, I would prefer they send the report directly to my lawyer," Edward replied.

Edmund grabbed Edward's arm, "Edward, your insolence is wearing my patience. How dare you embarrass me before the men and contradict my orders!"

"Edmund, it was not my intention. I simply want to streamline the process and get my business back up and running."

"Ha, Edward, I wish you luck with that," he said flippantly as he turned and left as quickly as he had appeared.

Edward was done dealing with Edmund Fox and all he stood for. He would leave the matter of the ransacking of his workshop in the hands of his capable lawyer. He decided right then that it was time for him to leave. He could not remain in America and fight for a cause for which he had no passion.

It was time he returned to England for a while, or at least until things settled down here. Perhaps he would take Joseph. It would be good for him to spend time with his grandmother and Uncle Bernard.

Back home, he went into the bed chambers and checked in on Eva, who was finally sleeping soundly. She was tossing and turning during the night, so he was not surprised to find her still asleep.

As he stood, looking down upon her, he remembered how happy they were before they came to America. The joys of being a mother and a wife wore off quickly with Eva when her desire to become a woman of distinction changed her completely. She fancied herself to be a real aristocratic lady, and once she set her sights on that, there was no turning back.

It was time for Edward to gather his family to tell them of his plans.

THOMAS ANNELY

# CHAPTER 18

**M**y brother Edward wrote to me with the horrible news about the ransacking of his workshop. I felt deeply for my brother, for not only had they stolen all his goods but had taken away from him all that he had built in America. I had hoped, perhaps a bit naively, that with all Edward's connections he would have been protected. I sensed Edmund Fox was to blame. That bastard saw to it that the British made my brother their target.

Edward decided to return to England until the unrest in America was over. He could not stay in a country without any belief in its cause. Eva would not sail back with him, for she had no desire to return to the life she had before. He knew she relished her high society life and would continue even without him here. Edward blamed himself, knowing that his dedication to his business had led him to neglect his wife.

Young Joseph was eager to travel with his father, but Ward had no desire to leave America. It was decided he would stay behind to mind his mother and oversee his father's merchant business. Ward would be the loyal son and obey his father's wishes, but his plans were to spend the rest of his life with Amelia Fox.

At first, Eva wanted Joseph to stay behind with her until Edward convinced her otherwise. "Eva, if the turmoil that is happening in Boston comes to New York City, you know they will take any available male, young or old, to fight; whether it be British or American."

Eva's defiant expression softened and took on a look of fear. If her youngest were to be taken away from her, she would rather it be by the hand of his father than have her son's life be put in grave danger. Her fears of Ward joining the Sons of Liberty already haunted her nighttime dreams.

Edward sat alone in his study and wept silently so no one could hear. Deep down in his gut, feelings of anger and doubt were gnawing away at him. "Why did I allow myself to be intimidated by Fox? Why did I not fight back?" he questioned himself in despair.

Edward shrugged off his sorrowful thoughts and wiped his damp eyes against his sleeve. He stood tall and looked out his window to the silent street below. Leaving America was the only option for a man who chose to remain neutral. If he stayed, he would have to choose between the British and the Americans, and he had no desire to cause harm to either side.

Upon receiving word that Edward was leaving, Elizabeth arranged to visit her brother at his home in the city. She would brush aside their differences and brave the cold, wintry weather to bid him farewell.

"Kingsley, please have the carriage ready at first light. I am going to visit my brother, Edward," she instructed her manservant. Ever mindful of his Mistress's welfare, he inquired, "Will Master Morgan be joining you?"

"No, I will be fine; Morgan is still in Philly with his father," she replied curtly. "Then I'll be going with you, Ma'am," he replied, swiftly returning to his chores, leaving her no chance to rebuttal his remark.

Elizabeth and Kingsley arrived at the East River ferry just as the morning fog lifted. She was grateful for the heavy woolen blankets that Kingsley had packed, for the cold air sent a chill down to her bones.

The river was smooth despite the winter weather as the flatboat took them over quickly. They disembarked and headed up to Edward's house, stopping only once for poor old Kingsley to use the public backhouse to relieve himself. He hesitated, not wanting to be seen, for negro men were not allowed to use the public facilities.

"Oh, hogwash," said Elizabeth to Kingsley. "You go ahead; anyone who bothers you will get the butt of my gun," she replied, lifting the heavy blanket to reveal a pistol she had hidden underneath. Kingsley smiled and remarked, "Mrs. Lewis, I swear, you are braver than a pack of wolves." He held the highest respect for this bold woman and would gladly serve her till the good Lord called him home.

Edward, surprised by his sister Elizabeth's visit, greeted her with a warm embrace. He instructed Kingsley to take the horse and carriage to the stable.

"'Tis good of you to see me before I leave, Elizabeth. Come in and warm yourself by the fire," he said, holding her arm as he led her into Eva's sitting room. As always, a tray of warm biscuits and a pot of steaming tea were waiting by the hearth. "This is lovely, Edward, much appreciated with the cold chill in the air," she replied as she poured herself a cup of tea. "Where are Eva and the boys?"

"They will be down shortly. I asked them to provide us with some time alone, for I have much to talk to you about, Sister," replied Edward.

"Alas, Edward, Thomas told Francis and me about the ransacking of your workshop. I am deeply sorry, dear brother," said Elizabeth sincerely.

"Elizabeth, I appreciate your kind thoughts, but I fear 'tis only the beginning of what the British have in store for us. I am very concerned for you and Thomas. Your alliance with the rebels, Patriots, or whatever they call themselves, is dangerous. The British authorities have all of us, Annelys, on watch, as well as Francis. Undoubtedly, they have placed a price on your husband's head. I care for your safety and would prefer you all return to England."

Elizabeth felt her brother was acting out of fear. She had no respect for a cowardly man, for she was fearless. "Edward, after what these British loyalists have done to you, does that not raise your desire to fight back? What example would we show our children if we all retreated to England, with our tails between our backsides?" Elizabeth said boldly.

Edward's face reddened as he spoke loudly, "Elizabeth, you have not changed. Your boldness will lead to your demise. I suggest you heed my advice, stay out of men's work, and mind your homefront for your children's sake."

Eva walked in after hearing Edward's remark, "Why, Edward, that is no way to speak to your sister. I apologize for my husband's rudeness, Elizabeth. I am certain it comes from a genuine concern for you," she replied with a sincerity Elizabeth did not recognize. While she appreciated her sister-in-law's defense against her brother's arrogance, she knew she could not trust her.

Elizabeth did not want to continue where this conversation was going and quickly changed her tone, "Edward, I did not come here today to have ill words with you. I came to wish you a safe journey and ask if you would be so kind as to give these gifts I brought to Mum and Bernard. I am envious that you will be with them soon. I miss them so much."

Edward's tone softened as he spoke, "Thank you, dear sister, and I apologize if my words upset you. I am your older brother and care deeply for your safety," he said sincerely. "I will gladly give your gifts to Mum and Bernard. It will bring them great joy when I tell them what a lovely woman you have become," he said, bringing a warm smile to Elizabeth's face.

Joseph came bouncing into the room, "Aunt Elizabeth, I am going to England," he said with youthful exuberance. Elizabeth wiped her tears and hugged her young nephew, "I am so happy for you, dear nephew; I only wish I could join you."

Edward walked Elizabeth to the bottom of the stairway where Kingsley was waiting with the carriage. "I am sorry, brother. I have too bold a tongue," she said, holding back tears. "Aye, sister, while I fear for you, I am the proudest of brothers to have such a remarkable sister. Godspeed to you and Francis," he said fondly. "I will watch over Eva and Ward while you are gone. Safe travels, my brother," she said as they embraced and bid each other a fond goodbye.

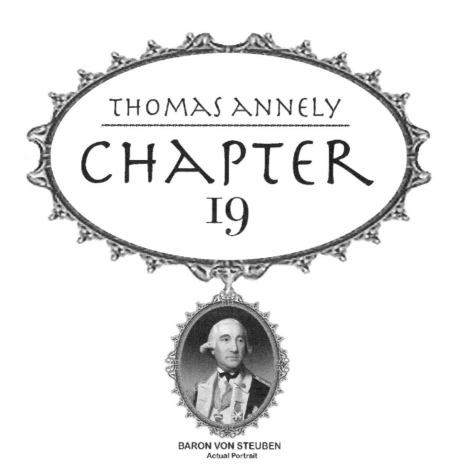

THOMAS ANNELY

# CHAPTER 19

**BARON VON STEUBEN**
Actual Portrait

Now that his father had left for England, Ward felt free to approach Edmund Fox for his permission to court his lovely daughter Amelia.

Ward was well aware of the bad blood between his father and Edmund Fox and suspected that Fox had caused his father's troubles. Still, it did not deter him from falling hard for the fair Amelia.

Ward and Amelia would meet secretly whenever they could steal away.

"Amelia, I am weary of these clandestine meetings we must endure."

"Alas, Ward, I too, am tired of being unable to be with you in public," sighed Amelia.

"I am going to speak with your father," said Ward daringly. "No, Ward, you know how my father feels. He will never accept an Annely into our family."

"My mother would certainly accept you in our family; she is more than eager to have a daughter-in-law of your class," he said, annoying her.

"Don't refer to me that way Ward; you know how much that angers me. I am my own woman, and if I have to leave my family and its wealth behind, so be it."

Ward pulled her close, biting her earlobe, "You are a feisty one, my dear," he teased. "Oh, Ward, I swear you enjoy making me angry and playing with my emotions," she said, pulling herself away from him.

He wrapped his arm around her slender waist and slid her next to him. "Amelia, I know you do not agree, but we, Annelys, are honorable. I must ask your father's permission to court you."

"Ward, you know he won't agree to let you court me," she said boldly.

"Amelia, I have to try to do the noble thing, for your sake and mine."

"It's getting late. I need to return home soon before my mother becomes suspicious," Amelia said.

Ward and Amelia stood embraced in a long, passionate kiss. Amelia spoke breathlessly, "I will see you soon, my darling," she replied as she covered her head with the hood of her cloak and hurried home.

Ward stood there, still feeling the warmth of their embrace, watching her fade into the darkness. He was angry that he could not properly walk her home, and begrudgingly went on his way.

Back home, Ward paced the floor of his bedroom. What was on his mind could not wait until morning. It was half past the eighth hour, but he was certain Mr. Fox would still be awake.

He threw on his overcoat and his fine leather gloves and quietly slipped out the door. He hurried along the empty streets to the Fox's residence.

When he reached their home, he paused briefly to catch his breath. He was relieved to see lanterns were burning in the foyer. He pounded firmly with the door knocker of pure silver, shaped like a fox's head.

A tall thin negro man answered the door, "Good evening, young sir. How can I help you?"

"I am here to see Mr. Edmund Fox," Ward said firmly. "Whom shall I say is calling?" he questioned.

"Tell him Edward Annely, Jr. is here to see him."

"Please, sit here while I ask Mr. Fox if he will see you."

Ward watched the servant walk down the long hallway to Edmund's study. Though not decorated as lavishly as the night of the party, it was quite impressive with its massive Greek statues aligning the way.

"Excuse me, sir, a young man named Edward Annely, Jr. is here to see you."

Edmund was surprised and asked his servant, "What on earth is the boy doing here at this late hour?" He was not amused. However, his curiosity got the better of him, and he instructed his manservant to send him in.

He brought Ward into the study, where Edmund was sitting behind his massive desk, his hands folded under his chin.

"Good evening, Mr. Fox. I apologize for the late hour, but I need to discuss an urgent matter with you."

Edmund stood up tall, striking an imposing figure, as he walked around and looked down at Ward, "And what might this urgent matter be, young man, that could not wait until the morning?"

"Mr. Fox, I came here to ask your permission to court your daughter, Amelia."

"Ha, and what makes you think the son of a traitor is worthy of my daughter!"

"Mr. Fox, my father is not a traitor; you have no right to call him that. He merely wished not to choose a side in this country's political dispute. He is an honest businessman and did not deserve all that happened to him. Because of what my father went through the last few weeks, he became distraught and depressed which forced him to retreat to England to recuperate."

"What's this you say, your father has left? Why, that is the wisest choice the man has ever made," Edmund replied rudely.

Edmund's eyes filled with anger as he lashed out at Ward. "You are a fool, son, if you think I would ever permit my daughter to court an Annely. And you are an even bigger fool if you thought we were going to let your father, a traitor, keep making guns and selling them to the rebels. He got what he deserved," he blurted out as he gulped down his brandy.

Ward was fuming. Edmund Fox outright admitted he was responsible for ransacking his father's workshop and made it very clear that he would never let Ward court Amelia.

Ward's anger became uncontrollable as he approached Edmund Fox, took out one of his leather gloves, and slapped him hard across the face.

Edmund was startled and laughed off Ward's slap, "You must be joking, son, you don't really want to challenge me to a duel. Do you not know my reputation? Go home, boy. Your mother Eva would not approve of this." he said, turning his back to Ward.

Edmund Fox's cocky response angered Ward even more. He took his other glove out of his pocket and threw it forcefully, hitting Edmund in the back of his head. Edmund snapped his head around and glared at Ward, his eyes flaring red, "Now you have taken this too far, boy. If it's a duel you want, then it is a duel you shall get! Make your arrangements with your seconds, and I will meet you at Weehawken any time you prefer. The less Annelys in this world the better!" he shouted.

Amelia could hear loud voices coming out of her father's study. She feared it was Ward, holding to his promise to confront her father.

She threw on her robe, hurried down the stairs and saw Ward storming out of her father's study. "Ward!" she cried out, trembling. He glanced back at her, his face flush with anger, pausing to speak to her when Edmund followed him out of his study.

"You do not speak to my daughter, now or ever," he commanded as Ward turned and bolted out the door.

Amelia stood frozen, tears streaming down her cheeks as she watched Ward leave. Her father approached her and yelled angrily from the base of the stairs, "You want to court this young fool? A son of a traitor and a coward himself? He's just like his father; they would rather side with the rebels than be loyal to our king. You will never see him again; I'll see to it!"

Amelia turned and ran back up to her bedroom, throwing herself on her bed sobbing. All her fears were coming true. And now, the man she was falling in love with left without even speaking to her.

Hearing all the commotion, Amelia's mother, Emily, called down to Edmund from the top of the stairs. "Edmund, what on heaven's earth is going on?"

"Go ask your daughter what is going on!" said Edmund as he returned to his study and slammed the door.

Emily entered Amelia's bedroom and found her sobbing on her bed. "Amelia dear, are you alright?"

Emily sat on the side of the bed and placed her hand on Amelia's back, "Why are you quarreling with your father? What is troubling you, dear?" she questioned softly. Amelia was no longer a child, yet Emily yearned to hold her to soothe her tears away.

Amelia sat up, wiping the tears from her eyes and wrapped her arms around her mother. "Oh Mother, how can you love a man who is so cruel," she said, shocking her mother. "Why Amelia, what makes you say such things? That is no way for you to talk about your father; he loves you so much."

"I don't believe he is capable of loving anyone, Mother," Amelia said, burying her head back in her pillow.

"Stop that child, do not talk about your father like this!" she scolded.

"Oh, Mother, must you be so naive? Father is a bully, and you know it. I hate him! Ward was only asking if he could court me, but Father has clearly refused!"

"That is enough, child. You are being the cruel one now! Your father is doing what he thinks is best for you. Now, try to go to sleep, and we will discuss this in the morning," she said, rushing out of the room and closing the door behind her.

Ward ran like the wind all the way home. The cool air calmed his rattled nerves as the realization of what he had done settled in. Edmund Fox was not a man to be challenged. Killing came easy to him.

Every man that Ward relied on was away and he certainly could not confide in his mother. All she would care about was that he ruined his prospects to be with Amelia. As he reached his home, he went into the stable and saddled up one of the horses. He jumped on and rode straight down to the river's edge to see his Uncle Thomas's old friend, Howie.

Along with his ferry service, Howie had built an Inn aptly named "Ye Olde Salt by the Sea" with a tavern and a few rooms for overnight stays.

It was late when Ward entered the empty tavern, startling Sam Blackinton, who was busy wiping down the bar. Sam and Mary Blackinton came to work for Howie, after the British confiscated their Inn and their beautiful home. The kind couple lost all they had and were told never to return.

Sam, surprised, said, "Ward, what brings you here at this hour?"

"Good evening, Mr. Blackinton; I was hoping to find Howie here?" he inquired without further explanation.

"Have a seat son, and I will go fetch Howie," he replied, rushing back to find him.

Ward went behind the bar and snuck a nip of brandy for himself. The pain of the warm liquid burning down his throat was his just reward for the reckless way he had behaved with Edmund Fox.

Howie came out, surprised to see the lad who seldom frequented his establishment, "Ward, my boy, what brings you here at this hour?" he asked, pouring two nips of brandy.

"I'm afraid I raised the hair on the neck of that bastard, Edmund Fox," Ward replied, gulping his second nip of brandy, which went down much smoother than the first.

"Alas son, you should not be messing with the likes of him. The man is pure evil, and no good will surely come of it."

Ward bowed his head in shame, feeling remorse for what he had done. "I'm afraid 'tis too late, Howie; I challenged him to a duel," he said meekly.

Howie put his hand on Ward's shoulder, "Aye son, you've got yourself in a right pickle. Best you be talkin' to your Uncle Thomas. Go home now, get yourself a good night's rest, and I'll take you to

Whitestone in the morning light. 'Tis Sunday, and with any luck, your uncle will be visiting your Aunt Elizabeth."

Ward heeded Howie's advice and hurried back home, where Charles was waiting to tend to his horse. "Master Edward, go inside, 'tis too cold out here," he insisted.

Ward entered quietly not to disturb his mother, who was reading in her sitting room with her usual nightcap by her side.

"Edward?" she called out to him. He reluctantly turned around, entered his mother's den, and bent down to kiss her cheek. "Good evening, Mother. Sorry to disturb you. I will be retiring now, and I suggest you do the same," he said before heading to his room.

"Not so fast, young man," she replied sternly. "I hope you have been out with Amelia and not drinking with the other lads at the pub."

"Aye, Mother, I was with Amelia; I cannot keep anything from you," he said, forcing a smile as he quickly retreated to his room.

Exhausted, he threw off his clothes and fell into bed, hoping he could quiet his anxious thoughts and get some sleep.

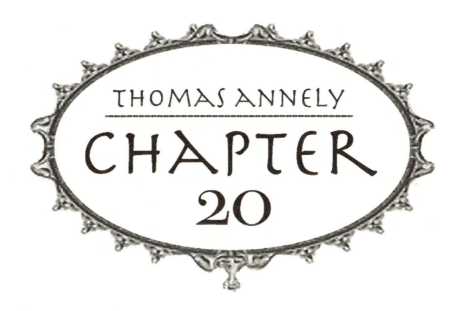

THOMAS ANNELY

# CHAPTER 20

**W**ard rose early Sunday morning while his mother slept soundly in her bedroom. He quickly threw on his woolen cloak and left word with his manservant. "Charles, tell my mother I have gone to Whitestone to visit my Aunt Elizabeth for a few days," he instructed as he dashed out the door. As planned, Howie was there bright and early, waiting with his horse and carriage. Together, they traveled along to Whitestone as quickly as they could.

Feeling remorse for his behavior, Ward wished he had sailed with his father to England. He would rather brave the high seas than look down the barrel of Edmund Fox's pistol. He told himself he could use some schooling in good old-fashioned British manners.

Elizabeth was looking forward to my Sunday visit and was surprised that our nephew Ward had arrived unexpectedly with Howie. She walked out to the foyer to greet them. "Ward, what a pleasant surprise to see you both," she said as her voice quivered, fearing he had brought bad tidings. She braced herself and asked timidly, "Is everyone alright?"

"Aye, Aunt, we are all well. I apologize for coming unexpectedly, but I need to speak with Uncle Thomas urgently," Ward said anxiously.

Seeing the vulnerable look on her young nephew's face, she spoke gently, "What is it, Ward? You know you can confide in me."

"Dear Aunt, I do not want to trouble you, but I have made a terrible blunder, and I need to discuss it with Uncle," he said, leaving her in the dark.

Elizabeth suspected her young nephew's boldness had gotten him in some sort of trouble, and he was in deep, over his head. "I understand. When your uncle arrives, I will see to it that he speaks to you straight away. Have a seat in the parlor, and I will have Phoebe bring you a drink," she said, leaving him alone with Howie.

Phoebe was waiting at the door for our arrival, "Good day, Master Thomas and Master Chip. The mistress is waiting on you and needs to see you right away!" she exclaimed.

I was anxious to hear what Elizabeth needed to see me about, so I bounded up the stairs, with Chip following behind. Elizabeth greeted us in the foyer with a look of concern: "Thomas, I am so glad you are here, and you as well, Chip." Without greeting my sister properly, I spoke out, "Elizabeth, Phoebe said you needed to see me straight away. Is everyone alright?"

"Everyone is fine, Thomas, but Ward is here with Howie. I'm afraid our nephew may have done something foolish. He is waiting to speak with you in the parlor," she said, her voice trailing as she led the way.

I entered the room. There sat Ward, with his head in his hands, being consoled by Howie. "Thomas, 'tis good to see you, my friend. Your nephew is in need of your good guidance. I'll be leaving you two alone," said Howie, walking out of the room. "I'll be waiting for you out here, Sir," Chip said respectfully, following Howie out.

"Ward, what has happened?" I gently inquired. Ward went into his rant, telling me about his encounter with Edmund Fox. "I simply went there out of respect, to ask for his permission to court his daughter. He berated me and told me I was no good for her. Worst of all, he insulted my father. He admitted that he was responsible for having the workshop ransacked! He drove me to it, Uncle. He made me so angry that I slapped him hard across his face with my glove!"

"You challenged Edmund Fox to a duel, son?" I questioned, disbelieving this clever lad could be so foolish.

Ward sat up straight with his chest puffed out, "He was so arrogant, treating me like a child. He laughed at me at first, but then I threw my other glove and hit the bastard right off the back of his head!"

I sat silently, contemplating my choice of words carefully. "Ward, you have insulted this man. A man who is clearly beyond you in his skill with a pistol. Whatever made you think that you could win a duel with this man? A duel with him could mean your death, and I won't have my brother losing his son. You must go there and apologize."

Ward stood up, sweat dripping down his face, "I will not. He doesn't deserve my apology!"

"What is that you say, Ward? 'Tis time you listened to me, son. We will go to the city tonight and meet with Edmund Fox to resolve this matter in a more diplomatic way. If he agrees to accept your apology, then you will do so with your bloody tail between your legs. Have I made myself clear?" I asked firmly, poking my finger into Ward's chest.

"I'm sorry, Uncle Thomas, I have come to my senses; I will do what you say," Ward replied humbly, humiliated by his actions.

I went over to Howie, who was waiting in the foyer with Chip. I placed my hand upon his shoulder, "Thank you, dear friend, 'twas wise of you to bring my nephew here. I will be returning to the city tonight to speak with Edmund Fox. I hope to get him to call off this foolish duel Ward got himself into."

Howie stood up and patted me on the back, "'Tis good of you, Thomas. The lad is lucky to have an uncle such as you. He is in your good hands now, so I'll head back if you don't mind. Godspeed, my friend."

After seeing Howie off, I went to see Elizabeth, who was beside herself with worry. When I told her what Ward had done, she placed her hand over her heart and cried out, "Oh my dear Lord, Edmund Fox will kill him!"

"Dear sister, do not concern yourself. I will be going back to the city to make amends with this Fox fellow," I replied, hoping to make her believe I could change this man's mind.

Elizabeth, wise beyond her years, faced me and said, "Be careful, Thomas; Edmund Fox has it in for all of us, Annelys. You will need to be as clever as a fox to snare this one," she warned. "I hope our nephew appreciates what you are trying to do for him."

Although Elizabeth was disappointed that I had to leave, we both knew this was something I had to do. Ward, Chip, and I climbed aboard my carriage and went to New York City to hunt down the fox.

# THOMAS ANNELY

# CHAPTER 21

**THOMAS PAINE**
Actual Portrait

When we arrived at my townhouse, Chip went to work, preparing the fire and heating the stew Elizabeth had packed for us. I could not eat. Even the aroma of beef did not tempt me. I needed to settle this travesty between Ward and Edmund Fox straight away.

Ward, looking forlorn, said, "I appreciate what you are about to do for me, Uncle, but I can't see that bastard again. He will never allow me in his house." I did not react to his remark. The boy did not need to feel any less of a man than he already did. Instead, I carried on with my strict instructions for how the day would go. "Ward, here's the plan; we will head to Edmund Fox's house now, and you will wait in the carriage.

When the time is right, I will have you come in to make your amends and apologize to Edmund Fox."

With Ward at my side, I rode off, confident I could convince this man to see things my way. The night had fallen by the time we arrived at Edmund Fox's regal residence in the wealthy part of the city. His home was as intimidating as the man: a solid red brick, two-story structure with a gabled roof and two massive chimneys. A slight chill went up my neck at the thought of showing up unannounced at this man's house. I instructed Ward to wait at the carriage out front while I walked up the brick-laid pathway to the entranceway. The shiny, silver fox knocker on the massive door glared at me with dark, malevolent eyes.

Ward waited nervously outside, looking up at the lantern burning in Amelia's bedroom. It took everything in his power not to bound up those stairs and steal her away.

I rapped two or three times until finally, the door creaked open, and a nicely dressed negro man greeted me, "May I help you, Sir?" I removed my dusty hat and said, "My name is Thomas Annely. I apologize for visiting without an invitation, but I must speak with Mr. Fox immediately," I said confidently.

He led me into the foyer and instructed, "Wait here, Sir, and I will inform you if my master will see you."

I watched him walk up the long stairway and knock on what looked like a bedroom door. "Come in, Matty," said Fox. "Sir, a fellow downstairs is rather anxious to see you and said he must speak to you at once. His name is Thomas Annely."

Annoyed by my visit, Fox angrily replied to his servant , "Please, Matty, tell me this is untrue. Is this not another one of those bastard Annelys coming to see me uninvited? Alright, bring the bloody rebel into my study, and I will be right down."

As time passed, I anxiously waited until his servant finally returned. "The Master will reluctantly see you now, Mr. Annely," he announced rather snootily as he escorted me into the study.

Entering the impressive room, his vast collection of guns displayed in a decorative mahogany cabinet caught my eye. Framed trophy plaques for excellence in marksmanship hung upon the paneled walls. Suddenly, the door swung open; I turned to see Edmund Fox standing there, regally dressed in a velvet blue robe with a devilish look in his eyes.

He walked over and glared down at me with a sinister stare. I tilted my head upward, attempting to make eye contact with this tall man. "Good evening, Mr. Fox. My name is Thomas Annely," I said, extending my hand.

He refused to shake my hand and spoke out sharply, "What is so important for you to come here uninvited and disturb me this evening? Is this a trait amongst all you ill-mannered Annelys?"

"Sir, we have a dilemma regarding a duel you made with my young nephew. I consider that plenty of a reason to call on you."

"Mr. Annely, I did not challenge your nephew. The foolish boy challenged me."

"I understand, Sir, but he is just a young man out of his mind in love with your daughter. He is sincerely sorry and would like to apologize for his inappropriate behavior."

"Where is this nephew of yours now?" he inquired.

"He is waiting outside in my carriage and is eager to express his apologies to you, Sir," I replied.

"It seems your nephew is a coward; otherwise, he would have pleaded for his life himself," Fox remarked.

"I assure you, Mr. Fox, my nephew is not a coward. He is staying outside because I asked him to wait until you and I reached an agreement."

"So what exactly do you want me to agree upon, Mr. Annely?"

"I want you to accept my nephew's apology and reconsider this foolish duel," I replied.

"Well, Mr. Annely, I will do nothing of the sort. The duel will go on as planned."

"What kind of man are you? Do you not have any compassion at all?"

I questioned boldly, with anger building up inside me.

Edmund Fox came closer, his hot breath spewing onto my face as he poked his bony finger into my chest, "You, Sir, have plenty of nerve, coming to my home, begging for your nephew's life. You, Annelys, are all traitors to our King and have been supplying arms to the rebels who are destroying this country. You call yourself an Englishman, yet you persist in building guns to kill other Englishmen. I am wise to you, Annelys, and your treasonous ways!"

I took in a deep breath, barely holding my composure from his insulting remark, "Mr. Fox, this is America, and here we have the right and the freedom to build arms for anyone we choose. You, Sir, have no right tarnishing our good Annely name by calling us traitors!"

Edmund Fox paused before responding, placing his hand upon his chin. He glared at me slyly, "You are bold with your words, Mr. Annely. I wonder if you are as brave with your actions. I will consider what you ask of me, but only under my conditions."

"And what would they be, Sir?"

Suddenly, he lifted his hand and slapped me hard across my face, "There, Mr. Annely, I challenge you to a duel, and your nephew Ward will be next! What do you have to say about that? Do you accept my challenge, or are you a coward like the rest of the Annely family?" he shouted with fire in his eyes.

With the sting of his slap lingering on my face, I looked him square in the eye and said, "Mr. Fox, I will indeed accept your challenge."

"Then be prepared to die, you stupid fool! I will make the arrangements with my seconds and they will contact you with the time and place. I suggest you start making your funeral arrangements. Now, Matty, show this fool out!"

Angrily, I picked up my hat and briskly walked out. I was ashamed that I had let that man intimidate me into doing what he wanted.

Ward was stunned when I jumped up on the carriage, shook the reins, and rode off quickly without saying a word. He remained quiet, staring at my profile, waiting for me to say something. "Ward, we will talk about this when we get to my townhouse," I said, too angry to speak further.

Back at my townhouse, I stormed up the stairs as Ward brought the horse and carriage to the stable. Chip rose quickly from his seat in front of the hearth, anxious to hear what happened. I lifted my hand to him, "I can't speak about this now, Chip. Please go to your bedroom, and we will talk in the morning."

Ward came rushing in the side door. "Uncle, what happened?" he asked nervously. "Ward, all I will say is that my plan did not work. Go to bed; I need time to think." Ward lowered his head and reluctantly went off to the bedroom.

I poured myself a brandy and stared at the smoldering fire, needing the time to make some sense of what just happened in the home of Edmund Fox. The conniving Mr. Fox managed to challenge not one but two Annelys to a duel.

What I set out to accomplish this evening turned right around on me. I should have listened more closely to my sister Elizabeth when she warned that I would have to be more clever to snare this fox. It was foolhardy of me to think that he would listen to reason.

Edmund Fox has a deep-rooted hate for all of us, Annelys. The sooner he can rid us of this world, the happier he will be. He considers all of us Annelys traitors. I do not want him to believe we are cowards.

I knew my only choice was to keep my word and follow through with this challenge to a duel.

THOMAS ANNELY

# CHAPTER 22

I t was the first of February, and the weather in New Jersey was bleak
and cold, portraying my exact feelings at the time. I regrettably
received word from Edmund Fox's second that the duel would take
place at dawn on the sixth of February. I got myself into this horrid situation and would now have to find a way to deal with it. Telling Sarah
about this would be a feat unto itself, so I decided it best not to mention
it to her at all.

I had left Ward back in New York City with a stern warning to stay
away from Amelia Fox and not to tell anyone, especially his mother, of
the impending duel. I could see the fear in his eyes when I advised him
to sharpen his shooting skills because if Edmund Fox were to kill me,
Ward would most certainly be next.

My first instinct was to hide my nephew away under the protection
of his mother. But I knew that if Ward were to become a man, he would
have to witness the errors of his ways. He, along with Chip, would serve
as my seconds.

This unfortunate event was to present itself off the shores of the Hudson, on the popular dueling grounds of Weehawken. Many a man had met his fate on this wooded ledge below the Palisade Cliff. The British Army was well aware of the area but mostly turned a blind eye to these sorts of events. I knew Mr. Fox had many duels there, so this would not be a new experience for him.

I had to consider the worst-case scenario, so I put all my affairs in order and wrote down my wishes for what would happen to my houses and the gunshop if I did not return.

It was a cold, dark morning when the dreaded day came upon us. Chip and I boarded my carriage as the sun struggled to show itself amongst the heavy cloud covering.

I managed to remain calm, even though anger was burning inside at this Edmund Fox fellow. He put me in a most unfortunate position when all I was trying to do was prevent an unnecessary duel between him and my young nephew. We rode solemnly to meet Howie and Ward on the Jersey side of the Hudson River.

Dressed in our best attire, we traveled in silence down a rough dirt road to our destination. Chip's jaw was tense with fear for what he was about to witness. The brave lad never spoke a word and rode on like a loyal soldier going off to battle on my behalf.

Deep in thought, I wondered what the fates would bestow upon me today. Was I a fool to accept this duel with a madman? And one who finds great pleasure in spilling another man's blood? I, unlike Fox, have never even aimed a gun at another man, let alone kill one. Yet, I was ready to face this Fox fellow because of my love for my brother's son.

Ward had lied to his mother and told her he would be attending business in Boston for the next few days. Instead, he and Howie anxiously waited at the river's edge for our arrival at Weehawken. Two oarsmen and a doctor accompanied them inside the boat.

We tied up our horse and carriage and walked over to the banks, where they were waiting. Howie looked directly into my eyes and grasped my hand. "Thomas, Edmund Fox has met his match today. Godspeed, my friend." I shook Howie's hand and thanked him for his encouraging words. The doctor gave me a reassuring nod of his head and expressed that he would wait on the boat, for he could not be a witness to the duel.

Up a ways, a longboat was tied at the shore, with Edmund Fox's men waiting to take him back to New York after the duel. Chip and Ward followed me up the ledge, where we saw Fox and three other gentlemen, dressed impeccably, waiting for us. One of the men stepped aside from the others and introduced himself as the referee. The lads stood beside me as we were formally introduced to Edmund Fox's seconds.

The referee took his place to begin, "Gentleman, before we commence, I must remind both of you that this duel could result in your death. Is there any possible way that we may resolve this duel?"

Edmund Fox boldly replied, "My answer is no, and allow me to explain why. This man, Thomas Annely, is a traitor to all Englishmen. He and his brother Edward are building arms and selling them to the bloody, rebel bastards to kill all those who are loyal to our good King George III. I am a loyal subject of our King and feel it is my responsibility to kill this traitor!"

Chip shouted out, "This man is a liar! What he is saying is not true!"

"Young man, you best shut your mouth, or I will see to it that you will die along with him!" Fox warned.

"Mr. Fox, I have heard enough. Let's get on with this duel!" I replied sternly.

The referee stepped between us and called for our attention, "Mr. Fox, I know how familiar you are with the art of dueling with pistols.

However, being Mr. Annely's first duel, I will explain the rules on his behalf."

"Both of you will stand back-to-back, with your pistol in your hand, barrels pointing up. I will begin the count of one and ask you both to take a step forward. I will continue counting, and after I reach the count of ten, you will turn around and be obliged to fire at your opponent. Please listen carefully to what I am about to say; if either of you fires before the count of ten, you will be disqualified and declared a coward. Your opponent then has the right to fire his remaining shot, and you must stand and wait for it."

The referee opened a mahogany case, revealing two ornately decorated dueling pistols. "Mr. Annely, you have been challenged by Mr. Fox to this duel, so therefore, you are first to select the pistol of your choice," he declared. I took a deep breath, reached into the case, and picked out the pistol closest to me. Fox abruptly grabbed the remaining pistol, nearly knocking the case out of the referee's hands.

As advised by the referee, we both checked our pistols to ensure they were loaded properly.

"Gentlemen, take your position back-to-back and cock your weapon. Please take one step after each number is shouted out."

"I will now begin the count."

One…two…three…four…five…six…seven…eight…nine…ten"

At the count of ten, I took the last step and turned around. I aimed my pistol directly at my opponent and fired. I heard a large blast as if both of us had fired at the same time. Suddenly, I felt an intense pain in my left shoulder. The strike was so powerful it spun me around like a windmill. I fell, with my face smashing into the dirt. As I lay there, with my pistol still clutched in my hand, I could hear Chip's voice shouting, "Thomas, Thomas, you've been shot!"

I dropped my gun and grabbed my shoulder, which was throbbing in pain and bleeding badly. Chip yanked off his neckerchief and wrapped it around my shoulder to stop the bleeding, reassuring me, "You'll be alright, Sir, you'll be alright."

Chip and Ward gently lifted me to my feet. I felt weak and dizzy as I looked with blurred vision to where Fox was last standing. Squinting my eyes, I saw a body lying flat on the ground, with two men standing over it.

The lads walked me over on my unsteady legs to where the body lay. There was Edmund Fox, with blood flowing out of a large hole bored right through the middle of his forehead.

I suddenly realized I had killed a man for the first time in my life. Edmund Fox was no more.

Ward nervously yelled out, "Let's go, we need to get you to the doctor, quickly!" he exclaimed, as blood seeped down my arm through the makeshift bandage.

The lads held onto me as we stumbled down the bank to the Jersey shoreline. Howie rushed to my side and remarked, "I heard you shot that bastard right between the eyes. You sure have the eye of the hawk, my boy." The doctor immediately tended to my wounds as they helped me into the boat. I winced at the excruciating pain from my shoulder to the bruise on my face. "Hurry, men, we must get this man over the Hudson; he is bleeding badly," the doctor ordered.

As I lay on the boat's bench, I could see dark silhouettes of men carrying Edmund Fox's body, like pallbearers, over to his boat.

In my foggy haze, I could hear Chip whispering to Ward that he overheard one of Fox's seconds proclaim, "I have seen many a duel, but never before such an accurate shot as I saw today."

Upon hearing those words, I did not feel any pride at all. I felt terrible for having to kill this man. If I survive this day, I know it will be one I will never forget.

Dazed and disoriented, all I could hear was the rapid swish of the oars as we crossed over the Hudson and the doctor's voice calling out, "Stay awake, Mr. Annely. We are almost there!"

Crouched down beside me, the doctor pressed a cloth against my wounded shoulder and shook me whenever I would drift off. I clenched my teeth from the throbbing pain that penetrated my shoulder, fighting off the feeling to black out. The chilly spray of the water hitting my face helped me stay awake as the oarsmen rowed as fast as they could.

Finally, we reached the river's edge, and the men dragged the longboat to shore. Chip and Ward lifted and carried me into Howie's Inn. With one sweep of his strong arm, Howie cleared off a large dining room table, instructing the men to lay me down on it.

Drifting in and out of consciousness, I could feel the throbbing pain of the lead ball deep inside my skin. I heard the muffled sounds of the doctor yelling, "Bring those lanterns here, closer, closer!"

I turned my eyes away from the bright lights beaming over my head while Ward and Chip held me down. The doctor ripped open my shirt, exposing my wound; I felt the sharp sting of the alcohol as he poured it all over my shoulder. I winced in pain when his knife dug into my skin and removed the lead ball that was deep within my muscle. I was relieved to hear the clang of the metal ball being thrown into the tin pan. What seemed like hours was only minutes as the men hovered over me, watching the doctor close up my wound. "You're a lucky man, Mr. Annely. The ball hit you square in the flesh and did not penetrate bone. You'll be mighty sore for a while, but you will be fine," the doctor said reassuringly.

Howie yelled, "Sam, bring some more whiskey over here!" My mouth was so dry I could barely speak as I forced myself up to sip the strong liquor. Chip and Ward gently pushed me back down onto the table. "Go easy, son; you need to rest now." the doctor ordered. "I'll keep a watch on him, Doc, don't you worry," Howie said assuredly. The lads helped me to a room Mary had prepared inside the Inn. I tossed and turned all night from the constant, throbbing pain. As uncomfortable as I felt, I was grateful to be alive.

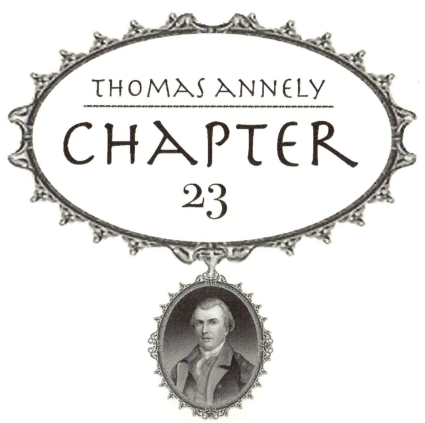

THOMAS ANNELY

# CHAPTER 23

**GENERAL NATHANAEL GREENE**
Actual Portrait

Ward would not leave my side as he sat, watching me as I slept. Chip was sleeping soundly in an overstuffed chair in the corner of the room. Ward's mind would not let him rest. The reality of the day's events was too much for him to bear. He buried his head into his hands, muffling the sounds of his despair from the guilt he was feeling. I woke and turned to see my nephew suffering beside me. "Ward," I whispered in a barely audible voice. Ward dropped his hands from his face, "Uncle, I am so sorry for everything," he blurted out.

"I know, son, I know. 'Tis time for you to go home and tell your mother everything."

"No, Uncle, I can't leave you!" he cried.

"I'm alright now, and I have Chip to care for me. Go home, son," I said as I drifted off back to sleep.

Ward rushed out of the Inn, jumped on his horse, and galloped off to his home, trying to hold back the tears.

Eva was wide awake, pacing the floor, waiting for her son to arrive home. She expected him back days ago and was growing quite concerned. She was accustomed to Ward working long hours for his father's business, but he was gone much longer than expected this time. Her faithful maid, Maggie, waited by her side. "Don't worry, Missus Eva, Master Edward will be back soon," she said, attempting to calm her.

Eva poured herself a generous snifter of her husband's brandy and sipped it slowly, hoping to steady her nerves. Ward's absence was filling her exhausted mind with worry.

The sound of horse hooves on the cobblestone pavement made her heart jump as she rushed to the entryway and flung open the front door.

There was Ward, staggering up the stairs in blood-stained clothing, gasping to catch his breath.

Eva wrapped her arm around his waist and led him into the foyer, "Oh dear, Ward, you are covered in blood! What happened?"

"Mother, this is not my blood; 'tis the blood of Uncle Thomas," he muttered as he slumped down onto the side chair.

Eva was bewildered, "What does your Uncle Thomas have to do with this?"

Ward stood on weakened legs and shouted, "Mother, you have a fool for a son. A few weeks ago, I went to see Mr. Fox for his permission to court Amelia. He said I was crazy if I thought he would let me be with Amelia. He also insulted Father and called all of us Annelys traitors. He made my blood boil, and I lost all control. I foolishly struck him with my glove and challenged him to a duel. Then I ran scared, like a dog with my tail between my legs, straight to Uncle Thomas." Eva sat quietly, allowing her son to rant.

"Uncle Thomas planned to see Edmund Fox and reason with him to call off the duel. But no, sir, Fox would not agree. He ended up challenging Uncle Thomas to a duel and promised to kill me next! Don't you see, Mother, because of my stupidity, Uncle Thomas was shot!"

"Oh, dear God, poor Thomas," Eva exclaimed.

"No mother, not poor Uncle Thomas, poor Edmund Fox. Being the marksman Uncle Thomas is, he shot Edmund Fox right between the eyes!"

"Oh my God, Ward, Thomas killed Edmund Fox?"

"Yes, Mother, Uncle had no choice. It was either him or Fox."

Eva felt faint and placed her hand on her chest, trying to catch her breath. So many emotions were running through her mind as the tears flowed freely from her eyes.

"Are you weeping for that bastard? Are you still in love with that man?"

Eva slapped Ward across the face, "Ward, I feel nothing for Edmund Fox. What I am feeling is relief that you are alive and so very thankful for what your brave Uncle Thomas did for you."

"I am sorry, Mother. I should not have said that." Ward wept, putting his head on her lap. Eva stroked her son's head, comforting him: "'Tis alright, son; 'tis all over now. We both must be strong, for who knows what the future has in store for us."

Eva had Charles help Ward to his bedroom, "Put his blood-stained clothes to the fire, Charles; I never want to see them again," she ordered.

Eva sat on the edge of Ward's bed, "'Twas a terrible day, Mother. When I saw Uncle Thomas lying there bleeding, I didn't know what to do. It should have been me," he said with anguish.

His words cut straight through her heart, "Ward, where is Thomas now, and is he well?" Ward sighed, "You know I can't tell you his whereabouts, but I will tell you the doctor said he thinks he will recover from his wounds."

Eva sighed in relief, "I am forever grateful to him and I would like to tell him so. I don't expect you to believe me after all I have done, but you can trust me not to tell anybody about your Uncle Thomas."

Although Ward loved his mother, he was suspicious of her sincerity. Seeing the doubt on her son's face, Eva knew she had a long road ahead to win back the trust and affection of her family.

She could see her son drifting off, "You sleep now, my darling. We will talk more in the morning," she said softly. She watched his face relax as he finally fell asleep. Eva shuddered at the thought that this day could have had another outcome.

She remembered when she was enamored by Edmund Fox, and now she felt nothing but hate for him. She longed for her husband's warm embrace to help ease her feelings of despair. His absence made her realize how much she truly loved him and how foolish she was to let her faithful husband slip away. Exhausted, she threw herself on the sofa and let the tears flow. Her thoughts turned to remorse, "I am a fool; I am to blame for everything. I made this happen," she repeated over and over again.

She pledged to herself that from this day forward, her love for her husband and family would come first. After all these years, she finally realized being a part of the Annely family was a blessing.

THOMAS ANNELY

# CHAPTER 24

I woke, half-dazed, realizing I was still in New York City at Howie's Inn. I struggled to sit up while Chip rushed to my side. "Thomas, please lie back. The doc gave me strict orders to keep you still."

I reluctantly laid back, grabbing his forearm, "Chip, go get Howie; I need to get out of here," I pleaded as the obedient lad rushed out the door.

As much as my shoulder throbbed, it was unsafe for me to be in the city. I was anxious to get home, but I knew I wasn't well enough for that long of a trip. Thankfully, I had good, reliable men working at my gunshop in New Jersey.

Howie came in with a big grin on his face. "Aye Thomas, what's this, I hear? You want to get up and leave?"

"Howie, you know 'tis not safe for me to be anywhere in this city. If the British find me here, it will put you all in harm's way."

"Thomas, relax now; you ain't well enough to travel."

"Then I will have Chip take me to Whitestone. 'Tis not too far to travel, and Elizabeth will tend to me. At least I will be out of the city."

Howie finally agreed but insisted we take his team and covered wagon to hide me from the British along the way.

Chip drove the team early in the morning, with me stowed away in the back. There was no time to send word to Elizabeth to tell her about our arrival or what had happened. The last time I saw Elizabeth, I told her I would try to negotiate peace between Ward and Edmund Fox.

When we arrived at Whitestone, Kingsley looked surprised to see a big covered wagon riding up with Chip alone at the reins. "Kingsley, Thomas is in the back, wounded. Please help me get him inside!" he shouted, bringing the team to a halt.

"Yes, Master Chip," replied Kingsley, hurrying to help me get down. As unsteady as I was, it felt good to be upright on my feet, feeling the blood flow return to my legs.

Phoebe was standing in the doorway, looking out at all the excitement. "Phoebe, please fetch Mrs. Elizabeth for me!" Chip called out to her.

Elizabeth, alarmed, rushed outside when she saw the men helping me up the stairs with my arm wrapped in bandages. "Thomas, what in heaven's name has happened?"

Chip spoke excitingly, on my behalf, "That evil man, Edmund Fox, challenged Thomas to a duel! Thomas got wounded badly, but Edmund Fox is dead. The doctor tended to Thomas at Howie's Inn, but he needed more time to heal, and we couldn't stay in the city."

Elizabeth sighed, "Dear God, are you alright, brother?" she asked. "Yes, Elizabeth, just a little tired and sore," I replied.

Elizabeth called out to her servants, "Phoebe, go fetch Mr. Francis and have him come down straight away; Kingsley, bring Thomas into the spare room."

"Thomas, I am so glad you came to stay with me," she expressed.

Francis came rushing down the stairs, following us into the room. "Lie down here, Thomas," he said, standing by the bed.

Elizabeth sat down beside me. "What happened, Thomas? How did you manage to get yourself in a duel with Edmund Fox?"

"The man gave me no choice. I now realize Edmund was trying to find a way of eliminating both of us."

"Thomas, it took great courage to go up against Edmund Fox. The man was a British loyalist who hated our family," replied Elizabeth.

"Poor Mr. Fox, it serves him right; he underestimated your ability to fire a pistol," boasted Francis.

"I didn't want to kill the man," I replied solemnly.

"Thomas, do I need to remind you of what that terrible man did to your family? Edmund Fox had a reputation for living by the gun; thus, he died by the gun. Remember, he challenged you to the duel, and any honorable man, like yourself, cannot refuse a duel," replied Francis.

"Perhaps you are right, Fran, but a civilized man must never feel good about killing another human being. I make guns to protect people."

"Wise words, Thomas. If only we could be assured that the men we are dealing with are civilized. Now, you must get yourself better; our country needs you," replied Francis as he left me to rest.

Elizabeth, my kind and loving sister, tended to me daily, helping me heal physically and mentally.

"Thomas, I hope you realize you saved Ward's life. If you had not done what you did, we would all be grieving for our nephew. Edmund Fox was not capable of listening to reason. You have rid this world of a madman, one that would have gone on and killed as many Annelys as he could."

I reached over and placed my hand upon hers, "Thank you, dear sister, for your words."

"Incidentally, Thomas, where is Ward? He should be here with you, showing his gratitude."

"I told Ward I would be alright and to go home to tell Eva all that had happened. 'Twas probably just as well; the lad was beside himself with guilt and fear. He needed the comfort of his mother."

"Well, I hope he has learned to mind his temper and stay amongst his kind," she said angrily, frustrated with our nephew's behavior.

I smiled sincerely at my sister, amused by her feisty ways. I would never say what I was thinking, but I believe I know where Ward inherited his boldness.

Being here with Elizabeth helped me greatly, and I started to feel more like myself. I walked outside to find Elizabeth and Francis enjoying the fresh air on their veranda. "Thomas, 'tis good to see you up and about, my man," said Francis as he poured me a cup of tea.

"Come sit. We have been wanting to talk with you," said Elizabeth. "Take heed, Thomas. She's about to talk your ear off," teased Francis.

"You hush now, Francis; there are some things my brother needs to know, and 'tis time we told him," she shot back, giving her husband a stern look.

"My Lizzy is right, as always, 'tis time we make you aware of what that Edmund Fox was all about," he replied.

I kept silent, curious to hear what they had to say.

"Thomas, that man did far more damage than you can imagine. If he were a dog, he would have been a bloodhound; once he was on your scent, there was no stopping him. He had his spies everywhere, and sorry to say, our sister-in-law Eva was one of them. He knew who was a rebel and a loyalist; and God help you if he crossed your path. He had a mission to rid the city of anyone who was not a loyalist by any means he saw fit. His pistol killed many of my lady friend's good husbands."

"What your sister is saying is all true, Thomas. I discovered he had a list of all our names and several other good people. Lord only knows what plans he had scheming until you, my dear brother-in-law, put an end to his reign. You helped out our cause immensely by getting rid of that man."

I sat there, absorbing what they were telling me. "I guess I had been naive, thinking this man only had it in for us, Annelys. The little time I spent with him made me realize, the man had no conscience," I replied.

Francis placed his hand upon my shoulder, locking eyes with mine, "Thomas, 'twas fate that you were there that day. For no one but you could have beat Edmund Fox at his own game. You are one of us, Thomas, a true American Patriot."

After a week of Elizabeth's good care, I felt well enough to return to New Jersey. As we said our goodbyes, I was happy to hear that Francis had plans to visit our workshop in Elizabethtown within the next few months. I embraced my sister, making a promise to come back again soon.

In the quiet of the dawn, Kingsley brought Howie's covered wagon around, and Chip and I said our goodbyes. When we arrived back at the Inn in the city, Howie had my horse and carriage waiting and managed to sneak us over the Hudson.

Chip insisted on taking the reins as we made our way back to our home in Elizabethtown. The lad had grown up so much, especially in the last week.

"Chip, a week ago, I asked you and Ward to be my seconds. At no time did either of you question what I asked of you. You just made it your duty to be beside me. I will never forget how much it meant to me."

"Sir, you are a hero to us. Nothing would have stopped us from being there. You must know we both love you. I think you are the bravest man I have ever met."

"Thank you, Chip, but enough of this; I need you to help me with an even bigger problem. How do I explain this whole ordeal to Sarah?"

"Sorry, Sir, you're on your own with that one."

We shared a hardy laugh as we made our way back home.

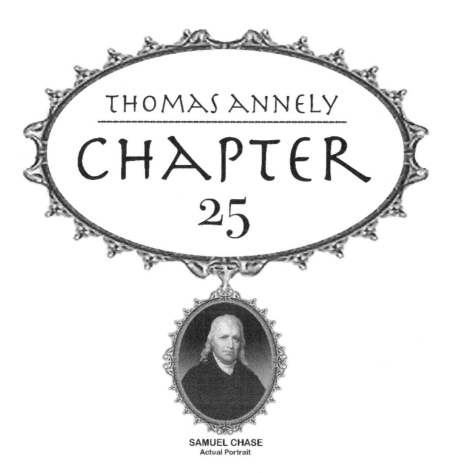

# THOMAS ANNELY

## CHAPTER 25

**SAMUEL CHASE**
Actual Portrait

Now that I am back home in Elizabethtown, all I can think of is seeing my sweet Sarah. I thought it was time I told her all about the duel and hoped she would forgive me for not telling her.

The terrible experience of being shot and coming close to death made me realize how precious life is. I knew I was deeply in love with Sarah, and now was the time to ask her to marry me. Sunday, I would visit her at her family's home and make a proper marriage proposal.

When I arrived on Sunday, Sarah was surprised by my unannounced visit. I pulled her into a warm embrace and told her how much I loved her. My outward show of affection made her uneasy, so she took my hand and led me to the veranda, sensing that I had something important to say.

I then told her about the duel and all the events that led up to it. She surprised me with her reaction. I was sure she would be angry, but instead, her only words were how proud she was of me and how happy she was that I was alive. She swung her arms around my neck and cried soft tears on my shoulder. I knew right there and then that I would love this woman forever.

I immediately went to see Mr. Dally and asked his permission for Sarah's hand in marriage. He graciously gave us his blessing and insisted we have the wedding here, at their lovely countryside estate.

When Elizabeth received my letter about our forthcoming marriage, she wrote back, telling us how happy she was and that she would be honored to make Sarah's wedding dress. Sarah was overjoyed because Elizabeth had handmade some of the finest dresses she had ever seen.

Although neither my brother Edward nor Francis could attend, I was pleased to have Chip as my best man. Kingsley would bring Elizabeth over from Whitestone, and Howie, Mary, and Ward would be there.

The day had arrived, and Sarah admired her reflection in the mirror as Elizabeth, beaming with pride, made the final adjustments to the wedding dress. Elizabeth had outdone herself. The dress was beautiful. The silky yellow fabric, with delicate weavings of green and gold, looked radiant against Sarah's warm complexion.

I was grateful to Mr. Dally for providing us with the proper attire. Neither Chip nor I were accustomed to wearing such fine clothing as we stood ramrod straight, unable to move in the stiff overcoats.

It was time to take our place in front of the minister. I nervously tugged to loosen the cravat around my neck as I awaited my beautiful bride-to-be.

The sight of Sarah descending graciously down the stairs, with Elizabeth by her side, will be one I shall never forget. Mr. Dally took her arm and led her to me at the makeshift altar. I could not imagine what I had done to deserve such a beautiful bride.

After the ceremony, the Dallys prepared a delicious feast with some of the finest wine I had ever tasted. Soon, we danced and sang old English and Irish ballads well into the evening. It was a wonderful day, one that I shall always be grateful to the Dallys for.

We were back in Elizabethtown, and my new bride, Sarah, was settling in, making our house a home. The lads and I had finally completed building my new gunmaking shop. Now, I'd be able to devote time to the making of my first sample musket. Most of the muskets used in battle are long, heavy, and awkward to carry. I wondered how ordinary men, with no formal training, learned to handle the weight of them.

Ever mindful that a soldier's musket is his constant companion, I was determined that my musket design would meet all the needs of the colonial soldier.

I prefer muskets that are shorter in overall length and have a stock lighter in weight, thus making it easier to handle and fire. I chose butternut walnut for the stock, a wood native only to America.

The clang of the iron pounding would be deafening to most men, but it was music to my ears. Chip finished welding the barrel, brushed off the residue, and began the arduous chore of boring the hole in the barrel. I left the heavy work for these strong, young lads to save my aging back.

I had commissioned Samuel Parker, a fellow gunsmith, to supply the brass furniture. Although the lads and I could have made all the brass parts ourselves, I decided to use Sam's excellent craftsmanship to expedite the making of my musket.

After carving out the stock, I dipped my clean rag into the warm linseed oil and smoothed it all over the wood, bringing out the grain's natural beauty.

Once the stock had dried, I assembled the musket for the first time, ensuring all the brass and iron furniture fit correctly. I must say, I was very pleased with the final results.

The next day, Chip and I took it outside for the first firing as the men watched, crammed together in anticipation, at the shop window.

I loaded it up, took my place 50 yards away from the target, and fired the first shot. It proved to fire perfectly, better than any other musket I have made. I kept stepping back, gradually adding distance, and still, I easily hit the target.

When I walked back into the shop, all the lads stood up and clapped, congratulating me on my accurate firing.

I stayed late into the evening, writing notes for my production plan. I had finally finished my new sample musket. It was perfect, with all the attributes I desired: a 69-caliber musket lighter than most, with a thin, sturdy stock, shorter in length with good balance, and easy to maintain. "You did good, Annely," I said, admiring my craftsmanship.

I carefully wrapped it in a thin linen cloth and put it away for safe-keeping. I received a letter from Francis stating that he would visit on Sunday. It was perfect timing; for now, my sample musket was complete, just in time for Francis's visit.

Weary from lack of sleep, I headed upstairs to join Sarah in our welcoming bed. She woke briefly and whispered, "I swear, Thomas Annely, you would rather sleep with that musket than your wife," she said affectionately. I kissed her cheek and replied, "Trust me, dear, my new musket, which I do love, is no match for my love for you."

As usual, sleep did not come easy as my mind rambled on. I needed to add the final touches to my musket. I slipped quietly out of bed, careful not to wake Sarah, lit a lantern, and carried it down to my workshop.

I placed the lantern on the workbench while I retrieved my musket. Securing it in the vice, I pounded my **TA** mark on the top of the barrel. With my hammer and chisel, I held my hand steady and inscribed **T. ANNELY** on the lock plate.

Now, my musket was complete, and I could finally rest. I quietly made my way back to my bed, next to the sweet warmth of my wife.

Sunday morning, Francis arrived with lots of news about what was happening up north. "Fran, 'tis so good to see you," I said warmly. "'Tis good to see you too, Thomas," he replied as we shook hands. "Sit by the hearth; you must be weary from your journey. Would you care for a drink?" I offered.

"No, not yet, Thomas, but I will take you up on that drink later. Right now, I am anxious to see your workshop and the new musket you have written about."

Francis looked around, impressed by what he saw, "Thomas, 'tis a fine job you and the lads have done. This shop you've built could not have come at a more appropriate time."

I led Francis to the counter and unwrapped my musket sample from the thin linen cover. "'Tis a beauty, Thomas," Francis remarked as he held the musket in his hands. "'Tis so light and the perfect length. How does she fire?"

"Let's go outside, and you shall see for yourself," I said proudly. I loaded up the musket to fire and handed it over to Francis. "Go on, my good man, have a go at it."

Francis raised the musket, held his breath, and fired, hitting the target ahead squarely. He reloaded and shot two more times, each time hitting the target. He smiled and exclaimed, "Amazing job, Thomas. You have outdone yourself! How soon can you produce more of these?"

"The lads and I are more than ready, Sir. Once we can secure some capital, I will load up with supplies."

"Thomas, you need not worry about money; I will give you all you need. You do what you do best and make these bloody fine muskets as quickly as possible!" he exclaimed. "This musket is just what our troops will need."

"Fran, my good man, I fear you will bankrupt yourself supporting me."

"Thomas, this new land and all its freedoms allowed me to make a great fortune. I owe a lot to you, Annelys, especially your dear brother Richard, for giving me my start. 'Tis my duty to fight the tyranny that threatens this young nation, and I will do all I can for this American cause. Elizabeth and I have agreed to use whatever monies we have to support the Patriots. With God's good graces on our side, we know he will always provide for us."

I smiled and placed my hand on Francis's shoulder, "Fran, there are no two finer people than you and my dear sister Elizabeth. God has blessed me to have you both in my life."

Chip had been eating mainly at the local tavern and rarely joined us for dinner. I was concerned about him spending too much time with the lads at the tavern and wondered what they were filling his head with. I made a mental note to myself to talk with the lad. He needs to know how much he is serving his country by being a gunsmith.

As we sat and enjoyed the light dinner Sarah had prepared for us, Francis told us the Brits had closed the Port of Boston, stopping all imports. "Naturally, the colonists are concerned that the New York port will be next," he warned.

"Do you really think that will happen, Fran?" I questioned with concern.

"Yes, Thomas, I do. That is why a group of prominent men have formed a committee to oppose these unfair acts from the King. I am the 51st member of this Committee of Fifty, making it the Committee of Fifty-One," he boasted proudly.

Sarah and I listened with genuine interest as Francis continued, "The Committee is asking all Patriotic Americans to refrain from buying imported goods. 'Tis necessary to let the British know we will not tolerate their high taxes."

"I am now in charge of procuring military supplies, including arms, for this impending war. Thomas, your expertise as a gunsmith is needed more now than ever. The seeds of war have been planted, and we must be ready when they sprout! Elizabeth and her "lady friends" are busy making clothing and uniforms for the colonists. They are preparing for the worst, and I suggest you and Sarah do the same. Now is the time to stock up on food and the like, for who knows what the bloody Tories will try to take from us."

It was a lot to take in at once, and I was grateful when Sarah changed the subject to a more personal tone. "How is your daughter Ann these days?" she inquired. "I have no daughter," Francis replied bluntly, surprising us both.

Sarah chuckled softly before responding, "Come now, Francis. You do indeed have a daughter, and a very beautiful one at that."

"Not anymore. Ann intends to marry that loyalist George Robertson against my wishes. Would you believe, of all things, he is a Captain with the British Navy?"

"I know it is not what you hoped for Ann, but there is no stopping young love. I pray you can all reconcile someday." Sarah said before excusing herself and retiring to our bedroom.

Francis and I stayed up late into the evening, enjoying our brandy and cigars. It was good to be in the company of Francis once more, who had become my closest confidant.

Our conversation shifted to a more serious note, "Fran, I'm still haunted by something Edmund Fox said to me before the duel. He accused me of making guns to kill our fellow Englishmen. I can't help but feel that there was a bit of truth to his words. When I came to America, I never imagined that I would be making muskets to go to war in this free land."

Francis spoke boldly, "Thomas, the British are no longer our allies and can not be thought of as such. We are Americans now, and the guns you make are to defend our freedom. You have become a hero amongst our fellow Patriots. As I have said, you and your brother were not the only men harassed by Edmund Fox. He was responsible for killing many good Englishmen and terrorizing anyone loyal to our cause. Believe me, Thomas, you made many people happy when they heard Edmund Fox was dead."

Once again, Francis's words of wisdom managed to get through my thick English skull. His keen perception and vast knowledge erased any doubts or fears that lingered in my mind.

Francis stood up, brandy in hand, and I did the same as we locked arms and repeated our solemn oath from many a fortnight ago,

"Brothers-in-arms, devoted to ending the tyranny threatening our liberty."

THOMAS ANNELY

# CHAPTER 26

It had been a long, difficult year for Ward. His irresponsible actions, which led to the death of Amelia's father, caused her to lose her love for him. Her grieving mother refused his many attempts to see Amelia and make amends. And his father's business was failing terribly due to the unsettling times.

Eva could see her son was in pain as she watched him pace about. He was still brooding over not being able to talk to Amelia.

"Edward, come here so we can talk," she called out from her sitting room.

Ward reluctantly joined her as she poured them both a glass of brandy. "Edward, I have something to tell you. Your father wrote that he wants me to join him in England," she said, surprising Ward.

"Really, Mother? Are you seriously thinking of going?"

"Yes, son, I miss your father immensely. I am hoping we can reconcile so we can be a true family again. Your father and I would like you to come as well. It would be nice for us all to be together."

Ward paused before responding to her request, "I can't, Mother; I need to be here."

"Son, do you still have hopes for Amelia?"

"I do not know, Mother. I have not seen or heard from her since this terrible thing happened. She has not responded to my letters," he said, hanging his head low.

"Ward, I know this is not what you want to hear, but you must leave her be. Your Uncle has killed her father, and in her eyes, you were the instigator. We all know, especially me, how evil Edmund Fox was. I am certain Amelia knows as well, deep down inside. However, she and her mother will always feel that the Annelys are to blame for her father's death."

His mother's words pained him, yet he knew she spoke the truth. As much as he longed for Amelia's warm embrace, he knew it was over.

Ward realized that Amelia's father's death was not his fault. It was Edmund Fox's hatred for the Annelys that sealed his fate.

Weeks passed, and Ward kept himself busy, helping his mother prepare for her journey back to England. Despite his mother's overbearing ways, he would miss her immensely. Yet, he was pleased she was reconciling with his father.

Bound for Bristol, Eva left with a heavy heart, for she would be leaving her firstborn son behind. She looked forward to the day, God willing, they would all be together again.

Ward's home was empty now, except for his faithful servants, Charles and Maggie. He was grateful for their company and the help they provided. Today was Sunday, their day off, and the house felt too quiet from their absence.

Ward sat in deafening silence, with only the occasional chime of the hallway clock. He wished he had gone to church with Charles and Maggie to find some peace.

As he sipped his tankard of ale, he heard a faint knock at the front door. He hesitated, thinking perhaps he heard incorrectly, when suddenly the clacking became louder and more rapid.

Ward went to the window, and all he could see through the pouring rain was a vague silhouette of someone standing there. He anxiously opened the door, disbelieving the sight before him. "Amelia, my love, come in out of the rain!" he cried as he held her arm and led her inside.

There she stood, with sadness in her eyes yet radiantly beautiful as ever. Ward caught his breath. "Amelia, I knew you would come. I am so happy to see you." He wrapped his arms around her and felt her body stiffen under his embrace. She lacked the usual warmth she had shown him in the past. He released his grasp as he escorted her into his father's study.

He removed her rain-soaked cloak from her delicate frame and placed it upon the chair behind him. They both sat, temporarily silent, gazing into one another's eyes. He reached across, grasping her hand. "Amelia, I have waited so long for this moment." Amelia lowered her gaze and spoke softly, "I had to see you, Ward. Even against my mother's wishes, I needed to speak with you in person."

Amelia raised her sorrowful eyes, "Ward, you must stop pursuing me; it is impossible for us to ever be together again."

"Amelia, what happened to the strong woman who proclaimed that she would never let her family rule her life?"

"Because of you, Ward, my father was killed. Did you expect me to ignore what you caused and carry on with our love affair like nothing ever happened?"

Ward paused, taking a deep breath before speaking, "Amelia, I was a fool, and believe me when I say I am truly sorry about what happened to your father. My Uncle did all he could to reason with him, but he would not agree to cancel the duel. Your father said that once he killed my uncle, he would come after me. He had it out for us, Annelys, and there was no changing his mind."

Amelia spoke up, raising her voice, "Ward, you are very much like my father was, stubborn and loyal to a fault. I told you nothing good would come of meeting with my father, yet you went ahead and did it anyway. It doesn't matter anymore. Your actions have ruined any future we may have had. I loved you very much, but you broke my heart, Ward Annely. My mother has decided to leave this dreadful city, and I will accompany her."

Ward felt the weight of her words upon his chest. He no longer recognized her as the woman he fell in love with, but it did not lessen the pain he felt deep in his heart.

Amelia stood and left him with these parting words, "Ward, I am torn between love and hate for you, but I truly wish only good things for you in the future."

She grabbed her cape, threw it over her shoulders, and left swiftly, crushing his hopes of ever having her back again. She was gone from his life forever this time, and it broke his heart to know he could never be with Amelia.

He felt his life was spiraling out of control, and more bad news was coming. His father had written to tell him he was selling the workshop. Ward was to use the money from the sale frugally for all living expenses.

Ward was determined to be the man he knew he was capable of being. He would not sit back and wallow in self-pity about what he had lost. He left his temper and foolish ways behind and made the just decision to go to the one person he admired the most, his Uncle Thomas.

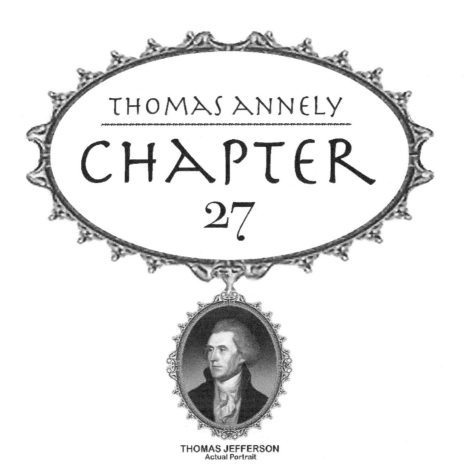

THOMAS ANNELY

# CHAPTER
## 27

**THOMAS JEFFERSON**
Actual Portrait

My gunshop is in good working order, and Chip is doing a fine job overseeing the men. True to his word, Francis secured our finances, with enough money to buy all the wood and parts we needed to start the production of my new musket design. Fortunately, I have a few very good gunmakers in my shop, and they are all Patriots for the American cause.

The men sat attentively while Chip and I explained the procedure that would enable us to produce many muskets in an orderly, timely manner. I developed this system while working with Edward at E&T, and it proved to be quite successful.

"Now, listen up, men! I will expect nothing less than top-notch work from each of you. Before each musket receives the Annely stamp of approval, it must be fully tested, inspected, and proven. We have our plan and our goal. Now, let's try to meet it for our country and our freedom!" I exclaimed.

Filled with inspiration, the men stood and cheered before quickly dispersing to get to the task at hand.

Ward was visiting today, and I planned to encourage him to stay. His master craftsmanship was much needed, and his natural ability as a leader would greatly help Chip and me. It would be good for him to get back to doing what he does best: gunsmithing.

I heard knocking, and Chip, excited to see Ward, dashed over to answer the door. "Ward, 'tis so good to see you!" exclaimed Chip as he wrapped his arm around Ward's shoulder, leading him into the work-shop.

Ward looked about and smiled as he inhaled the familiar smells of the fresh-cut wood, linseed oil, and the burning forge. I walked over and greeted my nephew warmly. "Ward, I am so glad you decided to come!" I exclaimed. "Good day, Uncle. 'Tis so good to see you as well. What a fine workshop you have here."

"Yes, 'tis a fine place, but we are missing one thing: you, my nephew." Ward's face flushed, "Aye, Uncle, 'tis kind of you to say, but I don't want you to feel obligated to take care of me."

"Quite the contrary, nephew, you belong here. Sorry to say this, but you are no merchant, and neither was I," I said in jest.

Ward laughed, "You are quite right, Uncle. My father had good in-tentions for me, but I feel more at home in a gunshop. Would you mind if I stay and watch you work for a spell?"

"Aren't you weary, son, after your journey over?" I inquired. "Not at all, Sir," said Ward as he removed his outer coat, rolled up his shirt sleeves, and followed me around the shop.

That evening, we all sat around the dining table, enjoying Sarah's delicious feast. "Thank you, Ward, for this delightful wine," said Sarah, sipping the rich, burgundy liquid.

"It came straight from the French bistro in the city," said Ward.

Sarah glanced my way and winked. "Yes, I remember it well. Your Uncle Thomas took me there, and I enjoyed it very much," she remarked kindly.

"By the way, Ward, how is your mother?" she inquired. "She is well, thank you. She has traveled back to England to be with my father and brother Joseph," replied Ward.

"I am sure you miss them greatly, but I am so glad that she has returned to your father and they are together," Sarah replied sincerely.

Ward confided in us about his visit from Amelia and said their relationship was over for good. Sarah and I noticed a substantial change in Ward's demeanor. He seemed much more confident with himself since the ordeal with Edmund Fox. It was clear that the unpleasant experience made a man out of him.

Ward and I sat by the fire, sipping our tankards of ale. "Uncle, I didn't realize how much I missed gunmaking until today. I would be honored to work for you under one condition. You must teach me how to be as good of a marksman as you are," remarked Ward.

"Yes, I will gladly teach you, Ward, for it will only make you a better prover of muskets."

Knowing Chip and Ward would be working together again was a wondrous feeling. I felt proud, knowing I would have the best gunmakers in the county working alongside me. I have trained both of them, and they are very aware of the quality of workmanship I demand.

My plan was in place and now was the time to act upon my promise to Francis to aid our country's cause.

THOMAS ANNELY

# CHAPTER 28

Elizabeth found herself alone, once again, at Whitestone. Francis was away, attending one of many Continental Congress meetings at Carpenter Hall in Philadelphia.

She walked down the long hallway and entered her brother Richard's favorite room. It's a grand room filled with the many treasures he acquired on his travels as a merchant at sea. Gazing out the window, she looked admiringly at the green, rolling hills that meandered down to the crystal blue waters. Her heart swelled at the beauty surrounding her, and she knew this was where she belonged, in her magnificent home at Whitestone.

Richard loved it here and expressed more than once that Whitestone was where he wished to be buried.

She felt Richard's presence all around her as she sat in his comfortable leather chair. Hanging above the pure white stone fireplace was the stoic portrait of her dearly departed brother. How she yearned to see his smiling face and hear his laughter once more. Richard had bestowed upon her many gifts; he instilled in her qualities that went far beyond material possessions. He taught her to be brave in the face of an adversary and to have courage in her convictions.

"This is where it all began, with you, my dear brother," she said out loud. "If not for you, none of us Annelys would be in America. You built this grand house from the abundance of white stone it sits upon for all of us to call home."

She was a young girl when she sailed with Richard to this great land that would soon be her home. How gentle Richard was, consoling her as she wept. It was her first trip abroad, and she was missing their mother so.

"Do not be frightened by the unknown, dear sister, for here you will grow to be a brave and dignified lady," he said, easing her fears and giving her hope for the future.

Before Richard built Whitestone, they lived in the townhouse Richard purchased, one block from the new workshop he established. She would join him every day at work, where he patiently taught her all the details of his business. When he would sail away on one of his many trade ventures at sea, she would be lonely without him. Upon his return, she would ride with Kingsley in the back of the wagon to the portside to help transport the many crates of newly purchased goods to the Fly Market. It was there that Elizabeth learned the delicate art of bartering, selling the much-needed wares to the eager colonists.

Hannah Beard was there from the beginning, managing Richard's office and minding the books. Elizabeth was very fond of Hannah. She was, to Elizabeth, a cross between an older sister and a true, sincere friend. Elizabeth was too young to realize that Hannah had a great affection for her brother Richard. She simply admired her devotion and dedication to her brother's business affairs. If she were more inquisitive or mature, perhaps she would have realized they were in love.

Every Sunday, they would ferry over the East River to the land Richard had purchased in the country. She recalled how nervous she was, afraid the horse and carriage would fall off the flatboat and they would surely drown in the river.

"I will build a grand estate on this land, Elizabeth, made out of this white stone we are standing upon," Richard boasted as he stamped his foot.

She loved it there, with the spectacular view of the bay below and the vast acres of lush green land. Being a gunsmith by trade, Richard taught her to shoot her very first musket. He would laugh his most infectious laugh when she would block her ears at the loud blast of the gun firing. "Be brave, Elizabeth; you must learn to shoot so you can fend for yourself. In this new land here, with a vast amount of uncivilized territories, you must be able to protect yourself and your family someday."

On one of Richard's trips abroad, he sailed back from England, bringing a fine young gentleman named Francis Lewis.

She remembered when she first laid eyes on the charming Francis Lewis from Wales, who, at the young age of twenty-one, was soon to be Richard's partner in his trade business.

Francis impressed her when he talked about his ambitious dreams for his future. Elizabeth was instantly smitten, and she sensed he felt the same. When Francis asked Richard's permission to court her, she was overjoyed when he enthusiastically gave his consent.

Their happiness was short-lived, for soon Richard's life would come to an abrupt end. How devastated they all were when Richard suddenly became gravely ill. Not even his family doctor would examine him, for he feared contracting his illness. Francis, Hannah, and Elizabeth would lovingly tend to him, wiping his forehead with a cool, damp cloth to ease his suffering. Even as he lay there dying, how generous and loving he was. In a weakened voice, he expressed his final wish that he would leave his beloved Whitestone to Elizabeth.

There have been times of sadness and great joy in this magnificent home. It was where she raised their three children and where the souls of four of her babes and Richard were buried. While Francis was away, she endured many years of loneliness and enjoyed many happy Sundays with Thomas's visits to ease her solitude. Speaking silently at Richard's portrait, she expressed, "This is where I will stay, my dear brother, till my dying day."

How she wished Richard was here, with his infinite abilities to guide us through these difficult times. She was sure he would be beside us, fighting against the injustices brought on by this unreasonable King.

She spoke out loud to the gentle eyes looking upon her, "If only you could see our brother Thomas. He reminds me so much of you, Richard, and now he is a master gunsmith and a brave Patriot. And what a fine wife he has in Sarah, a Daughter of Liberty herself, aiding the cause in any way she can. You would be right proud of me, Richard, for I am the leader of this group of patriotic ladies."

The fire burned bright, crackling and sparking, casting a soft glow around the room. Phoebe came in, relieving her of her sentimental thoughts, and announced, "Pardon me, ma'am. Your lady friends have arrived and are waiting in the green room."

"I will be there straight away, Phoebe," she said, pausing to glance once more at the face of her most loved brother.

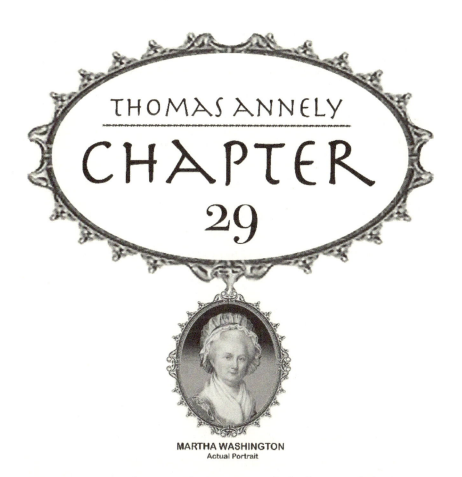

**THOMAS ANNELY**

# CHAPTER 29

**MARTHA WASHINGTON**
Actual Portrait

I t was amazing how much the men and I had accomplished in such a short time. I secured strong relationships with all the finest arms suppliers throughout the colonies, thus enabling us to speed up production by purchasing components from these other suppliers. With the time saved, we doubled our original expectations on the production of muskets.

Fighting had broken out in Massachusetts, and the Minutemen proved to the Brits they were not backwoods farmers but a force to be reckoned with. The revolution was no longer referred to as the impending war. It was happening, and soon, it would be here, in New Jersey.

Chip was outside in the proving area when he saw an elegant, black coach approaching in front of the workshop. A finely dressed coachman sat at the reins, with two armed escorts on horseback on each side.

Exiting the coach were three distinguished-looking gentlemen, along with Francis. The first gentleman wore no powdered wig despite his balding head. He walked very erect, attempting to appear taller than his short stature. The second gentleman was tall and thin and had the look of a dandy in his powdered wig and frills. The third gentleman had a rugged look about him and a stern expression on his face. Francis was very animated and talked excessively as he led the gentlemen to the main door of the workshop.

Chip rushed into the back entrance and excitedly whispered in my ear, "Thomas, Uncle Francis is here with three fancy men in a very fine coach." I was surprised by Francis's visit and overly curious about who the other gentlemen were. Chip followed me as I went to answer the door.

I opened the door, and Francis ushered the men in quickly to shield their identity from anyone passing by.

"Welcome, gentlemen, to my workshop. 'Tis good to see you, Francis, what a pleasant surprise."

"Good to see you too, Thomas. I apologize for the impromptu visit. These gentlemen are on their way to Boston and will drop me off at Whitestone. I thought it was an opportune time to show these fine gentlemen your operations here in Elizabethtown."

I took a deep breath and led these distinguished men into my disorderly office. Francis made the introductions, and Chip scrambled to find chairs for all to sit.

I recognized the shorter gentleman as John Adams, the prominent lawyer from Boston. The other two were John Hancock and Samuel Adams. All were delegates from Massachusetts, returning with Francis from the meeting of the First Continental Congress in Philadelphia.

I apologized for my untidy office when John Adams remarked, "Mr. Annely, a neat office is a sure sign of an unproductive man." We all had a hardy laugh, which helped ease my anxiety about meeting these prominent men.

John Adams, the more serious of the men, spoke, "Mr. Annely, our country is on the cusp of a new beginning, that will bring freedom for all generations. Francis has informed us of your skillfulness as a gunsmith and dedication to our cause. The fight for freedom has begun up north, and soon, our brothers in every colony will stand up with them. The colonies will need many muskets and pistols, now more than ever."

Samuel Adams addressed me directly, "Mr. Annely, let me be clear: everyone in this room knows what you have done to rid a British loyalist bastard from this earth. That made you a hero amongst Patriots."

"Hear, Hear," the gentlemen cried out.

"We need a man like you to take the bull by the horns of this monumental task," said Samuel.

"And I have the means to support you in this grand endeavor, Mr. Annely," boasted John Hancock.

I remained silent, feeling overwhelmed as I looked across the room at the four prominent men staring back at me. I sat up straight, regained my composure, and replied, "Gentlemen, I will do what you ask of me with all my heart and soul."

John Adams responded, "Mr. Annely, we sincerely thank you. We understand this is quite a challenge we have put upon you. Your blood may be that of an Englishman, but now you are a true American Patriot."

"Hear, Hear," the men replied in unison.

Francis stood, prompting the others to rise, "Thomas, would you be so kind as to show these men your fine workshop?"

As I led the men around, they nodded in approval of the production system I had in place, shaking hands and complimenting my workers on their fine job. The lads continued their work without knowing who these finely dressed men were.

"Gentlemen," I said, proudly introducing Ward and Chip, "These lads have been trained well and are both master gunsmiths. They manage the workshop quite well as long as I stay out of the way," I remarked as the men laughed.

"Excuse me, gentlemen," said the coachman, poking his head through the front door. "We must move along if you wish to reach Whitestone before dark." "Yes, we will be there straight away," replied Francis.

"I'm afraid we must be taking our leave now, Thomas," alerted Francis as we all shook hands and said our goodbyes.

"It has been an honor to meet you all," I said sincerely. "It has been our pleasure," replied John Adams as they exited to the awaiting coach.

Francis lingered behind, "Thomas, this has been a most productive meeting. I wish I could stay longer, but your sister Elizabeth expects my return tonight. I will catch holy hellfire for not warning her of my distinguished guests that I am bringing home," he chuckled.

"Aye, Francis, she will be overjoyed to meet these fine gentlemen. It will also be a pleasure for them as well to meet such a fine woman as our Elizabeth. Now go along, brother, lest you miss your ride," said Thomas.

"I will see you soon. Godspeed my brother, and give my love to Sarah," he said as he rushed out to join the others.

It was impressive to watch the fine coach, flanked by two guards, ride away, leaving a trail of dust behind them.

Standing beside me, Chip remarked, "Those gentlemen seem very impressed with you, Sir."

"Chip, I am very impressed with those gentlemen. They are putting their lives and fortunes on the line for our country."

THOMAS ANNELY

# CHAPTER
## 30

It was nearly nightfall before the men finally arrived at Whitestone. They were all weary from their long journey, yet still intended to move along to Boston until Francis convinced them otherwise. "Gentlemen, it would be my pleasure to have you stay here for the evening. I am certain your horses are in need of a good rest, as are you and your guards."

"This is quite kind of you, Francis, but we cannot impose upon your good wife," replied John Adams. "On the contrary, my good Sir, my wife will be more than pleased to enjoy some intellectual conversation as opposed to being in the company of her dull husband. I am sure a glass of wine, a nice supper, and a good night's sleep would suit you all." Smiles spread across their weary faces as they all agreed to stay.

As they disembarked from the coach, Samuel Adams remarked, "This is a spectacular home you have here, Francis."

"Thank you kindly, Sam. 'Tis quite pleasant here; I only wish I could spend more time at home," replied Francis.

Waiting by the entryway, Kingsley greeted Francis warmly, "Welcome home, Sir," he said as he nodded at the others. "Gentlemen, my fine man Kingsley will take care of the coach and horses and make sure your men have food and drink and a place to bed down."

"Yes, Sir, 'tis my pleasure," replied Kingsley.

"Welcome home, Master Francis," said Phoebe as they entered the foyer. "'Tis good to see you, Phoebe; please bring some refreshments for the gentlemen and alert the missus that I have arrived with guests."

"Yes, Sir," she said shyly, collecting their overcoats and hats, avoiding eye contact with the men.

The men, all equally impressed with Francis' fine home, relaxed in the comfort of his study, enjoying the most welcomed snifters filled with brandy.

Phoebe knocked lightly on Elizabeth's door. "Mrs. Elizabeth?" she called out. "Come in, Phoebe. Did Master Francis arrive home?"

"Yes, Ma'am, and he has three important-looking men with him. They came in a fancy black coach!" Phoebe exclaimed anxiously.

Oh dear, thought Elizabeth to herself, "Tell Francis I will be down shortly and alert Patty to prepare more food for our guests," she called out as she hurried to make herself presentable.

Elizabeth brushed her graying hair and tied it back in a tight knot against the nape of her neck, leaving ringlets of curls around her face. She slipped out of her dressing gown, powdered her face, and slipped on her favorite light blue dress. There, this will have to do, she thought to herself as she pinched her cheeks to add color. She went downstairs to join Francis and their distinguished guests, whomever they may be.

Francis greeted her with admiration as she descended the stairs, "Still lovely as ever, dear," he whispered, taking her hand.

"Gentlemen, I would like you to meet my wonderful wife, Mrs. Elizabeth Annely Lewis," he said, proudly introducing her.

Astounded by the prominent men before her, Elizabeth replied, "'Tis my great pleasure to have you all in my home. I only wish my sons were present to be in the company of such honorable men."

"Sirs, you may speak freely in front of my wife, for she is as fierce a Patriot as any of us. In fact, my wife has formed the New York assembly of the "Daughters of Liberty" right here at Whitestone," Francis said proudly.

Samuel bowed slightly and lifted Elizabeth's hand to kiss, "It is my honor to meet you, Mrs. Lewis. You are to be commended, my dear. With ladies on our side, we can make the Tories tremble."

Elizabeth smiled and said, "Samuel, I am flattered by your sentiment, and I am sure all Patriotic women will appreciate your kind words."

"Elizabeth, I brought the men to meet Thomas at his workshop today," said Francis.

"I speak for all of us, and we are quite impressed with your brother's operations. He will receive our highest recommendation when we meet with the Congress again," John Adams remarked.

"Thank you, John; I am proud of all my brothers, especially Thomas. He is quite special to me," she responded.

Francis addressed the men, "Let's eat. I am certain you all are as famished as I am," he remarked, leading them to the dining room.

Patty had outdone herself. It was wise of her to serve the hearty soup before the meal, for the men scarcely noticed how meager the meat serving was.

John Adams spoke first, patting his extended stomach. "Everything was delicious, and I am quite full." The others nodded their heads in agreement. "'Tis our pleasure," replied Francis.

Phoebe placed a tray of delicate cookies on the table and served the men tall glasses of richly flavored sherry.

As they enjoyed their dessert, John Adams inquired, "Mrs. Lewis, where are your sons?"

Elizabeth replied, "Young Francis manages our merchant shop in New York City, and Morgan, my youngest, is following in your footsteps, John. He is attending the College of New Jersey, studying to become a lawyer. I understand your profession can be quite daunting at times. I believe wholeheartedly that all men deserve a fair trial. Your decision to defend those British soldiers accused of murder in Boston was a bold one and sent a clear message to the mother country that we Americans are a civilized, rational people."

"Mrs. Lewis, I thank you for your deep, profound words. I only wish everyone understood as you do."

"On more than one occasion, he saved my neck as well," piped up John Hancock. "Yes, indeed I did," replied John Adams, prompting a chuckle amongst the others.

"Mr. Hancock, we are all very grateful for the monetary support and influence you bring to our fight for independence. Without generous donors such as yourself, we would have little chance to stand up to the strong arm of the British army," said Elizabeth.

"The choice was easy for me. How could I support the loyalist view when it would mean giving up what America stands for? I could not be idle and see my fellow Americans suffer under the rule of a King who will not listen to reason," replied John Hancock.

"Lord knows we have tried; it was never our intention to incite war, but unfortunately, it may come to that," said John Adams.

"Yet, this King has given us little choice, dear cousin. When a man is pushed to the breaking point, he must fight back," Samuel said boldly.

"Alas, cousin, while I commend your bravado, we must lead with our brains rather than our brawn. Our strength of strategic planning is our only chance to make an impact against what some believe is the strongest army in the world," replied John Adams.

Sam, clearly agitated by his cousin's remark, chose to remain silent rather than speak words he would never use in front of a lady.

Elizabeth relished the rousing banter amongst the men: "Samuel, while I understand your cousin's point of view, I have the same boldness in my blood as you. I am of the same mindset that we must stand up and fight to protect this new country of ours. We must begin with greatness, not fear, for ourselves and the generations to come."

In unison, the men lifted their glasses and made a toast to Elizabeth. "Hear, Hear! Truer words were never spoken," said Samuel.

"Now, I promised these men a good night's rest. I suggest we retire to our rooms before dawn breaks," Francis remarked.

Elizabeth and Francis, awake in their bed, were unable to sleep from the exciting evening. "You were wonderful as always, Lizzy. John Adams took me aside and bestowed upon you a great compliment. You reminded him of his Abigail; from what I heard, she is a remarkable woman."

Elizabeth smiled, leaned over, and kissed her husband's cheek. "'Tis an honor to be your wife, Francis. I am forever grateful for your love."

"Aye, Lizzy, you are heaven's gift to me," he said with genuine affection as they fell asleep, wrapped in each other's arms.

Dawn broke, and the men were already dressed and ready to resume their trip northbound. "On behalf of all of us, we are most grateful for your hospitality. Francis, you must bring your lovely wife to visit us in Boston soon. It would be a pity if your Elizabeth never got the chance to meet my Abigail," said John Adams.

Elizabeth vigorously shook the hands of all the men and wished them a safe journey home.

The coach was waiting. All were well-rested and eager to move forward. The two escorts took their positions, flanking the coach on both sides with the Coachman at the reins. One by one, the men boarded, waving their goodbyes as they sped off on their way to Boston.

# THOMAS ANNELY

# CHAPTER

# 31

**COLONEL MORGAN LEWIS**
Actual Portrait

I t's a joyous time in my life, for my lovely bride Sarah is with child. Despite all that has happened and all that is to come, a new Annely, with God's blessing, will enter this world soon.

Sarah looked even more beautiful to me, with the glow of forthcoming motherhood upon her face. I prayed each day that no bad fortune would come to her.

Today, we are going to Whitestone to tell Elizabeth and Francis the exciting news. While it is risky for me to travel to New York, the good news we are bringing makes it all worthwhile.

As we crossed the Hudson, I looked forward to seeing my good friend Howie again. Time had taken its toll on the old salt, so the young lads he hired now tended to the ferries. He spent most of his days greeting guests and minding the bar in his Inn. I was saddened when I heard that Sam Blackinton had passed on. He left his wife Mary a very lonely widow, and we feared she might surely die of a broken heart.

"Good morning, Howie," I called out as Sarah and I entered the Inn. "Thomas, my friend, so good to see you and Mrs. Sarah," he replied, leading us to our usual table. The smell of ham cooking drifted through the dining room, awakening my appetite. On the other hand, Sarah excused herself to go outside for air to relieve her queasy stomach.

"Good morning, Thomas," called out Mary. Her disposition remained sunny, with just a hint of the sparkle gone from her eyes.

"Good morning, Mary," I replied as I rose to embrace her. "I miss my good friend, Sam," I said with sympathy.

"Aye Thomas, 'tis heartbreaking for sure, but my day will come soon when I will join him. Where is your lovely bride, Sarah?" she questioned, shifting her thoughts away from her sadness.

"She went outside to get a bit of the good salty air. Would you be so kind as to bring her some warm milk and dry bread?"

A warm smile spread across Mary's face, "She wouldn't be carrying some extra weight now, would she?" she inquired instinctively. "Aye, Mary, there shall be no keeping of secrets with you about. I was waiting until I told Elizabeth, but I am sure she won't mind. 'Tis true, God willing, soon there will be another Annely in America."

"Praise be to God!" she exclaimed, grasping her hands in prayer. "Now eat up, Thomas; I'll be preparing something special for the expectant mother," she said as she hurried off.

Howie pulled up a chair and sat down beside me. "She cooks up a fine-looking feast," he remarked as he jabbed his fork into my plate of ham. "Help yourself, old man," I shot back as we both shared a laugh.

"Is your Missus feeling poorly?" he inquired. "She's fine, just a bit of an upset stomach," I replied. Howie's face broke out into a grin as he slapped me against the back. "Something tells me you'll be having a wee one soon." I smiled at my friend, glad our secret was out in the open.

As happy as I was to see Howie, I felt uneasy being back in the city. "Howie, what is the talk about town? Have the British been inquiring about me or any Annely?" I asked with trepidation.

"Not one word about you, Thomas, but I have heard a lot of the folks saying they were glad that the bastard, Mr. Fox, was gone. They don't give much thought to who done it; just glad he's done," said Howie, as he poured himself a cup of tea.

Sarah came inside and joined me at the table; her cheeks flushed from the fresh sea air. The dry toast relieved her morning sickness, and soon, we were heading to Whitestone. I was grateful that my good friends, Mary and Howie, had each other's company to comfort them through their aging years.

As we rode through the city, I could not believe how much it had changed. The streets were full of men, women, and children making their way about, bartering for the little goods that were available. Men shouted in protest at the soldiers in their bright redcoats, seated high upon their massive horses. The soldiers rode amongst the people, attempting, with little success, to subdue the chaos in the disorderly city.

We could not get over the East River fast enough, for all the noise and disruption was too much for either of us to bear.

Riding on the country roads, I slowed the horse to a gentle trot. We took in the lovely scenery and the fresh smells of the sea once more. "I never tire of this magnificent view, Thomas," Sarah said as she laid her head on my shoulder. Holding the reins with my left hand, I placed my arm around her, relishing our moment of pure contentment.

When we arrived at Whitestone, Kingsley was there to greet us. "Good day, Mr. Thomas and Mrs. Sarah," he said, approaching Sarah to help her disembark. "I have her, Kingsley," I snapped, quickly jumping down and rushing to her side. I must have startled the poor man. "Beg your pardon, Sir," said Kingsley, leaving me to tend to Sarah while he led the carriage out back.

"Thomas, I am not an invalid, and poor Kingsley, you treated him rudely!" Sarah scolded, annoyed with my actions. "I'm sorry, Sarah, I suppose 'tis a natural reaction for an expectant father. I will apologize to Kingsley, but you need to go inside and rest now." Angry with my authoritative manner, Sarah huffed and climbed up the stairway alone.

I dashed up the stairway and grabbed her arm. She spun around to face me, her vivid green eyes filled with anger. "Thomas, if this is how you will be treating me until this child is born, then I shall go live with my mother!" she exclaimed, tears brimming in her eyes.

"Sarah, dear, I am only trying to do my rightful duty as a husband and protect you," I said, holding her in my arms. "Oh, Thomas, must you be so overprotective? I won't break, love, trust me," she replied softly.

Phoebe, who overheard us bickering, greeted us nervously as we walked inside.

"Good day, Mr. Thomas and Mrs. Sarah; I will let the missus know you are here," she replied, quickly scurrying off to fetch Elizabeth.

Phoebe found Elizabeth reading in her quaint sitting room, sipping tea, "Beg your pardon, Mrs. Elizabeth; Mr. Thomas and Mrs. Sarah are here. You best be aware; I overheard them quarreling with each other."

Elizabeth laughed, "Oh, Phoebe, you must be exaggerating," she replied, smiling as she walked out to greet us.

"Thomas, Sarah, what a pleasant surprise; I am so glad you have come to visit," she said as they embraced. "You both look well, but you must be tired from your journey. Phoebe, bring Sarah and Thomas up to the spare room and prepare some warm water for them," ordered Elizabeth.

"Yes, Ma'am," replied Phoebe, leading the way to our room upstairs.

Once we were alone in the bedroom, I embraced Sarah, "Don't be cross with me, Sarah," I pleaded.

"Oh, Thomas, I could never stay mad at you," she said, holding me tight. "You were right, Thomas. I am in need of a rest. Please give my apologies to Elizabeth and tell her I will be down this evening."

Perhaps I needed a rest as well, but I was too anxious to talk to Francis. I freshened up and went downstairs to find Francis sitting at his desk in his study. I knocked lightly, "Good day, Francis." Francis looked up and grinned, "Thomas, come in and sit down; you're just the man I wanted to see."

Francis stood up, walked to his study door, and closed it behind me.

"Thomas, I have good news for you. The men were very impressed with you and your operations, particularly John Adams. You have been commissioned by the Committee of Safety to make muskets specifically for the militia. Your business will expand tenfold, for you will be supplying arms to New Jersey and the surrounding colonies as well."

"Congress has formed the new Continental army and unanimously appointed the honorable George Washington as our General. The man is quite impressive; his very presence in a room demands attention. He speaks little, yet what he does say resonates with us all. I strongly suggest you enlist in Washington's army to give you a better understanding of the needs of our troops."

I took a deep breath before responding, "Francis, this is a great honor you have bestowed upon me, and I would be extremely proud to be a member of General Washington's army."

"Thomas, 'tis a great task for sure, but I have the utmost confidence in you. You possess those rare, combined qualities of being a superior gunsmith and a great leader to your men."

We both stood, locked arms, and repeated our pledge, "Brothers in arms, devoted to ending the tyranny that threatens our liberty."

"Now, let's go join our ladies," Fran said as he led the way to the dining room.

As we entered the dining room, Elizabeth remarked, "Well, 'tis about time you men decided to join us." We chuckled as we took our seats next to our ladies. I was pleased to see Sarah back to her usual self, conversing with Elizabeth at the table.

My wife's beauty still took my breath away, and memories of the first time I saw her came flooding back to me. I stood beside her, placing my hand upon her shoulder. "Excuse me, Francis and Elizabeth; Sarah and I have something to share with you before we eat." They looked up with curious expressions, anxious to hear what we had to say.

"It seems America will welcome another Annely to its shores; Sarah is with child," I announced proudly. With tears brimming in her eyes, Sarah placed her hand on mine as I leaned down to kiss her cheek.

"Oh my, 'tis wonderful news. I am so happy for you both!" Elizabeth exclaimed, rushing over to embrace us.

Francis summoned Kingsley, "Go to our cellar and bring up a bottle of our finest champagne; 'tis time for a celebration!"

After our first drink of sparkling champagne, Elizabeth inquired, "Sarah, have you considered a name for your child?"

Sarah replied, "Yes, we have; if it's a boy, he will be named after my father, Gifford. If it is a girl, we wish to name her Elizabeth, after you, my dear sister."

Elizabeth's eyes brimmed with tears as she placed her hand over her heart. "I am deeply honored by your kind gesture; 'tis a lovely thought to have a niece with my namesake."

"I, for one, would like to see a little Thomas running around the grounds here," said Francis. "That's my Frannie, always wanting boys," replied Elizabeth, shaking her head.

"Well, perhaps we should have one of each," I joked as Sarah gave me a stern glance. "One healthy baby will be enough for me right now," she said, patting her stomach.

I was glad to be back here at Whitestone. Sarah was so comfortable being around Elizabeth, who had become like a true sister to her.

We relaxed around the table, enjoying life's simple pleasures, something we rarely found time for these days.

THOMAS ANNELY

# CHAPTER
## 32

I t was time to tell Ward and Chip about everything that had transpired in the past few weeks and my plans going forward. I called out into the workshop, asking them to come into my office.

"Have a seat, lads. I have some new developments that I need to discuss. You must be wondering who those distinguished gentlemen were who came to visit with your Uncle Francis."

Ward commented, "I believe I recognized the shorter man as John Adams, but I do not know the other two."

"Yes, Ward, he was John Adams. The others were John Hancock and Samuel Adams. They are all delegates from Massachusetts and members of the Continental Congress," I replied.

"Sam Adams!" yelled Chip. "He's a hero to the men at the tavern. He formed the Sons of Liberty in Boston!"

"That is true, Chip, but we must not breathe a word that these prominent men were here, especially to your friends at the tavern. You cannot be sure who to trust these days," I replied sternly.

My remark did not sit well with Chip, yet I was confident he understood the importance of keeping quiet.

"First, I want you both to know that these men were very impressed with what we have accomplished here. Francis told me that we have been recommended to General Washington, and he is eager for us to start supplying arms for the Continental Army."

Chip's eyes lit up as he poked Ward on his shoulder, "Fancy that, Ward. We'll be making muskets for General George Washington himself," he boasted proudly.

"Yes, lads, 'tis official; however, we will have to follow the strict guidelines of the newly formed Committee of Safety and make some minor adjustments to my original musket design."

"And, I have more surprising news to tell. Yesterday, I enlisted in the Continental Army and will serve as a master armorer for New Jersey." I announced as the lads looked at me in astonishment. "I will now supervise all the local gunsmiths, as well as others in the surrounding colonies."

Chip said, "I would like to join Washington's army, too!"

"Aye, Chip, I will be traveling a lot more now and will need you and Ward here to oversee things. Rest assured, both of you will be compensated for the extra responsibility you will take on. Can I count on you both?" I replied.

Ward enthusiastically responded, "Yes, of course, Uncle, this is exciting news!"

"And you, Chip?" I questioned. Chip lowered his eyes and responded meekly, "Yes, of course, Sir."

"You should both feel proud, for you will serve the cause in a much-needed way. Remember, what passed our lips today shall be kept between us. When we refer to what we have discussed, we will use the code words "The Big Push."

Exhausted from the long day, I went upstairs, hungry as a bear for Sarah's cooking. There she stood, my beauty, at the hearth stirring the stew. I approached her, wrapping my arms around her and patting the swell of her belly. "How is my love feeling today?" She turned to face me, her cheeks reddened from the warmth of the hearth, and kissed me. "I am fine, Thomas, and how was your day, dear?"

I gulped down the cool tankard of ale she had poured for me. "I told Ward and Chip that I joined the army and how we have been commissioned to make even more muskets. I need to discuss it more with Chip at supper. He didn't seem as enthusiastic about it as I had hoped."

"Oh, Thomas, Chip told me this morning that he would eat with his friends at the tavern tonight."

Feeling frustrated with the lad, I ranted, "Again? I am growing concerned about him spending all his free time there. I will need to talk to him when he comes home tonight. I fear he may be influenced by the lads at the tavern."

"He's not a boy anymore, Thomas. He has a right to make his own choices. Don't tell him how to spend his time when he's not working," she said sternly.

"Aye, Sarah, you are right. He's no longer the scrappy young lad he was before but he is still a young man who needs a grown man's guidance."

Sarah, averting my attention away from Chip, sat on my lap and ran her hand through my shaggy hair. "You're looking a wee bit scrappy yourself, Thomas Annely. It's time for me to give you a haircut," she teased, wrapping her arms around my neck. I was grateful for Sarah's diversion, which took my mind off my many thoughts.

I had not been forthright with Sarah. I did not tell her all the responsibilities of my new appointment as an armorer and how much traveling I would need to do. I will be meeting with quartermasters from each colony and proving all their muskets and pistols. It will be my responsibility to ensure that each musket is built to the proper standards before they are shipped to the troops.

My only peace of mind is knowing Chip and Ward will be nearby to manage the workshop and be there for Sarah while I am away.

Many a brave man has been led away from his family and home, and many a brave woman has proudly tended and protected her family without them. I must prepare Sarah and teach her how to fend for herself. I have told her a great deal about the making of muskets; now, I would have to teach her how to fire one.

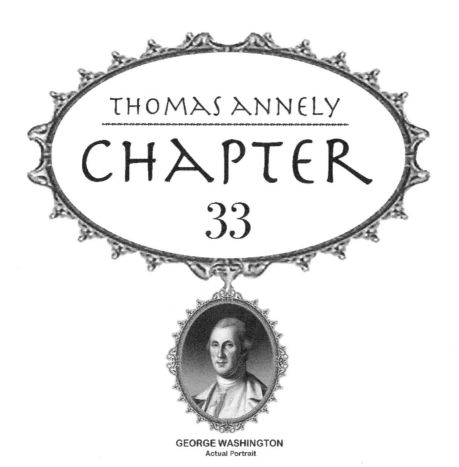

# THOMAS ANNELY

# CHAPTER

## 33

**GEORGE WASHINGTON**
Actual Portrait

The new year began bitterly cold. When I opened the window to observe the sky, a chilly blast blew in the brisk smell of winter. I could barely see the sun, peeking through the heavy clouds. I feared it might snow, so I knew I had to make haste to pick up the much-needed wood stock today.

Rushing down to my office, I hurried along, gathering my work order papers when one of the lads entered. "Sir, a letter arrived early this morning for you," he said, handing it to me. "The men and I have prepared your horses and wagon for your trip to Morristown. I hope the weather stays fair for you; they say a storm is coming."

I thanked the lad as I threw the letter upon my desk. I planned to read it when I returned, but then I noticed it was from my brother Edward in England. I had not heard from him for quite some time and was curious about what news he may have to share.

> *Dear Thomas,*
>
> *I write this letter to you with deep sadness. I regret to tell you that our dear Mother has passed away. 'Twas a peaceful death, for she never woke up from her deep slumber.*
>
> *She had been growing weaker in the past few weeks, but we did have a wonderful two days with her, with Bernard, Eva, and myself, recollecting all the years gone past.*
>
> *She spoke often about how happy she was for you and how eager she was to meet Sarah and her forthcoming grandchild. She was very proud of your success and how well you have done for yourself since you arrived in America.*
>
> *'Twas easy to feel her love for you and Elizabeth, and how much she missed you both. Of course, Bernard and I will see to it that our dear Mum has a proper burial. She will rest in the family plot next to Pa at St. Stephens church.*
>
> *I have enclosed a small lock of Mum's hair between the pages for you to keep in her memory.*
>
> *Godspeed, my brother, and may you find solace that our Mum had a good, long life and was dearly loved by us all.*
>
> *Love your faithful brother, Edward.*

I slumped down in my chair, holding my mother's lock of hair, feeling its softness between my fingers. I held back the tears, knowing it was God's time to take my mother back to him.

I walked slowly up the stairs to tell Sarah the news of my mother's passing. She rushed to me and wrapped her arms around my neck. "Oh Thomas, I am so sorry, love," she expressed. "Edward sent me a lock of my mother's hair. Can you please place this in our bible for safekeeping?" Sarah's eyes were filled with tears. "Of course, I will, Thomas," she said sweetly. "Come sit; I will fix you a cup of tea and something to eat."

"Thank you, love, but I must hurry along to Morristown. The men are in great need of more butternut wood to complete their work," I said. She wrapped a scarf around my neck. "Stay warm, Thomas, and get back to me as quickly as you can." She held me tightly, not wanting me to leave.

The frigid air hitting my face was what I needed to wake me from my sad thoughts. I was well on my way to Morristown, which was good because the weather was getting much more threatening.

I moved along quickly and arrived at the lumber yard an hour before schedule. The air was full of the fragrant smell of freshly cut wood as I loaded up the thick planks of butternut walnut onto the back of my wagon.

Although the weather had remained clear, the clouds were thickening, giving me cause for concern. Suddenly, the skies opened up, and a thick, heavy snow began to fall. I quickly paid the men for my order and got on my way as fast as possible.

The ride back to Elizabethtown was slow through the newly fallen snow. I felt a chill down to my bones as the snow and ice pelted against me. I wrapped my scarf under my cocked hat and tilted my head downward against the blustery wind. I threw a sheepskin over my shoulders to shroud myself from the cold and covered my hands with woolen gloves as I held onto the frozen reins. I could barely see the road ahead, but I dared not stop.

Suddenly, out of the silence, I heard a whimper. I pulled in on the reins to slow the horses and saw a dark silhouette in the snow. Concerned, I brought the team to a halt, grabbed my musket, and jumped down from the wagon. I struggled to get through the deep snow and was astounded by what I found. A woman with a large bundle of wood beside her was crying, almost completely buried in the snow. She was startled when she saw me but was too exhausted to rise. Wet snow clung to her hair and face, causing her to shiver.

I spoke softly, "Ma'am, do not be afraid; let me help you." She looked up at me with a confused expression, making me realize she did not understand.

I gently lifted her and carried the bundle of wood over to the wagon. I sat her on the bench beside me and covered her half-frozen limbs with my blanket.

She thanked me over and over again, in her native tongue, "Merci, Monsieur, Merci." I recognized the language as French, which, unfortunately, I knew very little of.

We rode slowly, her body trembling in the seat next to me. With her shaky hand, she pointed and said, "Monsieur, my home." I could see a small house up ahead, with smoke billowing from the chimney.

As we rode up the pathway to her home, a young lad came stumbling through the snow to greet us, "Mama!" he shouted with relief. The boy thanked me profusely as he helped me take her and the bundle of wood up to their home. "Make sure you get your mother by the fire and give her something hot to drink straight away," I instructed, grateful that the lad spoke English.

"My mother insisted on fetching some wood before the snow covered it. She told me to stay and watch my little sister inside. Please, Monsieur, come in and warm yourself," he offered.

"Thank you, kindly, but I need to get home myself before the snow deepens even more," I replied. The woman placed her cold hand on top of mine, smiled, and said, *"Que Dieu te Benisse."*

"She is saying, God Bless You," her son translated. I smiled back at the woman and said, in my native tongue, "God Bless You."

As I turned to leave, the young lad called out to me, "Monsieur, wait, you must tell me your name," he pleaded. "My name is Annely, Thomas Annely," I answered, puzzled by his request.

He stood, knee-deep in snow and said, "I will always remember the name of the man who saved my mother's life."

I was speechless at the young lad's parting words. I watched him as he helped his mother walk into their home. Through the window, I could see a little girl run and embrace her mother. Climbing aboard my wagon, I felt grateful to God that I was there to help this kind family.

When I reached Elizabethtown, my horses were trudging through at least two feet of snow. The wicked storm had made my return trip twice as long. Finally, I arrived, relieved to be back home. I dismantled the team from the wagon as the horses instinctively made their way into the barn. "Well done, old boys," I spoke, patting the snouts of the exhausted horses as I unhooked their harnesses and straps. With woolen blankets thrown upon their backs, they happily munched away on the fresh hay laid out for them. I stored the wagon securely inside the barn for the lads to empty in the morning.

Marching through the snow to the stairwell of my home, I was as exhausted and hungry as the horses. Chip, with a shovel in hand, came bounding down to greet me. "Thomas, Sir, you're home; I was not sure if you were going to be able to make it back!" he exclaimed. "Thank you, Chip, 'tis good to be back," I mumbled, too tired to speak.

Grateful to be home, I removed my wet cloak and boots and warmed myself by the roaring fire. The house was filled with the enticing smell of the hare stew warming on the hearth. I plopped my weary self down at the table while Chip served me a bowl of the warm stew and filled my mug with ale. He joined me at the table, watching me devour the hearty stew.

"Thomas, I was sorry to hear about your mother. I could have picked up the wood or at least gone with you to help."

I swallowed my food and took a sip of ale before speaking, "Aye, Chip, 'twas a sad day for sure, but the ride did me a bit of good. Keep that in mind, son, whenever you are troubled. Sometimes, you need a wee bit of time by yourself to sort things out. Besides, it would not have been wise of me to take away my best gunsmith," I said, arousing a smile from him.

The bedroom door flung open, and Sarah rushed out, "Thomas, you are home!" she exclaimed, greeting me warmly with a hug. Chip blushed and excused himself, "I will leave you two alone; I'm off to bed."

"Goodnight, Chip," we said in unison, smiling at the lad's innocence.

Sarah sat on my lap, and I wrapped my arms around her. "How is my best girl doing this evening?" I said teasingly.

"What do you mean, best girl? I better be your only girl," she responded coyly. "This girl will become an old woman soon if you keep me up late worrying, as you did tonight."

Sarah smiled sweetly, her green eyes sparkling in the glow of the candlelight. "Thomas, my love, this has been a difficult day for you. Now let's go to bed."

We lay in bed, wrapped in each other's arms; her warmth never felt so welcoming as tonight. As weary as I was, my mind would not let go of the vision of that poor woman stranded in the snow. I felt certain my mum had reached down from the heavens and put me in the right place at the right time to save that kind French woman. The thought of it gave me peace as I fell into a dreamless sleep.

THOMAS ANNELY

# CHAPTER 34

**B**ack home in Elizabethtown, the gunshop was bustling with business, and the men were working around the clock. I thought it was time to give them a proper night off.

"Men, you've all worked hard enough, 'tis time to call it a day! Go home and get a good night's rest, for tomorrow is another day. I will need you all here, ready to go, in the morning," I shouted into the workshop.

The exhausted men yelped a collective cheer, happy to be able to go home early for a change. They quickly stopped what they were working on and practically ran out the door.

Ward and Chip finished their work and locked up the shop securely. "I could use a drink, Ward. Why don't you join me at Buckhead's tonight? The drinks are on me," offered Chip. Ward hesitated for a moment before replying, "You know, a cold drink sounds good right about now."

They walked briskly to the stable, fetched their horses, and rode off like the wind. Chip yelled to Ward, over the sounds of the horses' hooves hitting the hard dirt, "I bet I will beat you to Buckheads." Ward laughed out loud, "We shall see, Chip, my boy," as he dug in his heels to speed up the horse.

Ward had to admit that it felt good to be out in the fresh night air, racing Chip with his surefooted steed. It had been a long time since Ward had gone out with the boys, and he was looking forward to some rousing conversation. A pint of ale sounded mighty good, too.

They arrived in town with Chip in the lead, "Looks like you'll be buying me a drink!" he shouted as they stabled their horses.

They walked to the tavern down the crowded street, bustling with people. Pretty young ladies, escorted by their protective mothers, smiled timidly at the lads as they passed by. Chip poked Ward in the shoulder, "I think the one in pink fancied you, Ward." Ward shoved Chip back, "Oh go on, I am done with women." Chip let out a hardy laugh and replied, "I highly doubt that, cousin."

When they arrived at the tavern, they heard laughter and boisterous voices singing barroom ballads through the heavy wooden door. Inside the tavern, the atmosphere was intoxicating, filling the lads with excitement for the evening ahead.

A voice behind the bar yelled, "Hey, Chip, good to see you, my boy!" Chip, smiling broadly, put his arm around Ward's shoulder and introduced him to the owner. "Buck, I'd like you to meet my cousin, Ward. I finally convinced him to join me at your fine establishment."

"Pleased to make your acquaintance, Ward," he said, pouring two foaming tankards of ale. "The first ones are on me, lads," the barkeeper boasted as he slid the tankards across the bar.

"Thank you kindly, Sir; 'tis a pleasure to be here," said Ward, as he tipped his tankard to the barkeeper and remarked, "Chip, you never lose! Now you are getting two free drinks, you lucky bastard!"

They stood, sipping the cold, refreshing ale, taking in all the sights around them. "I can see why you like it here," said Ward, noticing the pretty barmaid pouring drinks for the men. "Don't get an eye for Sally; she's my girl," joked Chip as they laughed. "Come, let's go meet my mates," he said, leading Ward to his usual table.

Chip introduced his closest friends, their eyes sparkling from too much ale. "This big fella' is Billy, the owner's son. Don't mess with him, or he will throw you out on your ear." Billy raised his fist in good nature as they roared with laughter. "Jimmy is the foreman at the Ironworks in town, and Charlie works on his father's farm."

One by one, the rest of the men introduced themselves to Ward. "Pleased to meet you all," said Ward, shaking many a hand at the table.

"Sally, bring some more ale over here for me and the boys!" Billy yelled out across the room.

Jimmy piped up, "Hey mates, have you heard the news from Boston? Our brave General Washington has kicked the whole, damn British fleet straight out of Boston harbor!"

"Hear! Hear!" the men shouted out in response, lifting their tankards.

"If the Brits are thinking about coming down here, we'll be ready for the bloody blokes. We Jersey boys will teach them a thing or two!" Billy spoke out boldly, guzzling down his ale.

"They thought they had us licked at Bunker Hill and then Concord, but our General showed 'em. He's a bold one, for sure," said Jimmy.

Ward observed the excitement in Chip's eyes as he listened intently.

"Jimmy, how did General Washington manage to run the bloody Brits out of Boston?" Chip asked.

"This Knox fella and his men trudged through the heavy snow, hauling over fifty cannons from Fort Ticonderoga all the way to Boston. Late at night, while the lobsterbacks were sleeping, General Washington had his men position those cannons high on a hill, pointing directly at all the British ships below. He sent a mighty clear message: either move those bloody ships, or we will blow them out of the water! The Brits couldn't sail off fast enough!" Jimmy exclaimed as the men let out a cheer.

Jimmy leaned in for only the men to hear and whispered, "You can bet the good General will be coming here next. We'll be ready to join him and blast the hell out of those lobsterbacks!"

With each drink of ale, the men's voices grew louder, traveling clear across the tavern. They clinked their tankards and shouted, "Freedom and Liberty for all!"

"Quiet down, you damn rebels!" shouted the voice of a drunken patron at the bar. "I beg your pardon, Sir; who are you calling rebels?" responded Jimmy.

The man stood up, stumbling over with his tankard of ale, spilling his drink along the way, "You bunch of mollycoddled Americans, livin' off the crown. Well, now it's time you paid your share!" his words slurring, in his drunken stupor.

Chip stood up and shouted, "Why don't you go back to England and kiss King George's ass!" Ward grabbed Chip's arm to hold him back, "Chip, don't let the words of a drunken fool get you riled; sit down, cousin."

"Drunken fool! You damn Yankees got a helluva nerve, calling me a drunken fool!" he shouted back.

Ward stood up, "Sir, to begin with, I am an Englishman, just like you. I expect to be treated with respect," he replied, putting the man in his place.

"Respect, you say? I'll show you respect!" The drunk lifted his arm and threw a punch with the tankard still in his hand. He narrowly missed Chip's skull as he stumbled, falling over the table and onto the floor. Billy rushed over, picked up the drunken man by the collar and punched him square in the face. Another man charged at Billy, grabbing and kicking him repeatedly, while more Englishmen, eager to get their hands on a rebel, joined in the fight.

Before they knew it, a brawl broke out amongst all the men in the tavern, shouting and punching each other. Shards of wood flew about as the rowdy men picked up stools and cracked them over each other's backs. Swinging their fists in wild punches, they fell onto the tables, breaking them apart all over the floor. Ward grabbed Chip and shouted over the rumble, "Let's get out of here!"

Chip followed Ward, but not before stopping and getting one good kick into the drunkard's side, "That's what you get, you bloody Tory!" Ward pulled Chip by his sleeve, "Come on, Chip, let's get the hell out of here!"

Ward and Chip ran like the dickens down to the stables, jumped onto their horses, and galloped out of town. Chip let out a rebel yell, "We showed them, didn't we, Ward?"

"Chip, be quiet. The whole town could be chasing after us," warned Ward.

"Let 'em come! I'll fight those Tory bastards anywhere, anytime. Wait till Washington gets here; I'll be right there, fighting beside him. We will show them whose country this is!" Chip shouted in his drunken daze.

Ward realized that coming with Chip tonight may have been a bad idea after all. Yet, he had to admit to himself; it had been a long time since he had such an exhilarating night. Ward hoped it was the liquor talking when Chip said he wanted to fight next to Washington. Ward feared for the lad, but he could not help but admire Chip, for he had more courage in his body than any one of his rowdy mates.

They finally reached Ward's home and brought the horses out back. Chip dunked his head in the water barrel, gulping down the dirty water. "Chip, that's the horse's water!" Ward yelled out. Chip laughed as he fell down to the ground. "I am as dry as a desert!" he exclaimed.

Ward picked up Chip and threw him in the barrel. "There, now you are as wet as a flounder," attempting to sober Chip up with the cold water.

"What's all that noise down there?" Ward's landlady shouted from the window above. "Sorry to disturb you, Mrs. Spenser. 'Tis only me; we'll be settling down now," Ward replied. "Quiet down, Chip; otherwise, I'll lose my flat," whispered Ward. "Sorry mate, I'm better now," replied Chip. "Come along, Chip, let's get you inside and warmed up."

Chip and Ward tiptoed up the stairs into Ward's flat. "I'll grab you some towels. Now get out of those wet clothes and go sit by the fire," Ward commanded.

Chip warmed himself by the fire, drinking the hot tea Ward poured for him. "Eat something; it will help your head," said Ward as he served Chip some cheese and crusty bread.

Chip wolfed down the food and wiped his mouth, "Much obliged, Ward, sorry I acted like an ass. You won't tell Thomas anything, will you?" he pleaded. Ward tapped Chip on his knee, "Come on now, cousin, you know me better than that. Besides, Uncle would have my head if anything happened to you," Ward replied, smiling. "Now, let's get some sleep. I promised Uncle Thomas I would have you ship-shape and ready to work early in the morning."

The next morning, the lads woke with achy heads from too much ale. They rode their horses much slower than the night before, on their way back to the workshop. They greeted their workmates, filing back in for another full day of work.

"You lads have a rough night?" questioned one of the men.

Chip replied, "What makes you say that?"

"The word is all over town that Buckheads Tavern has been shut down. There was a brawl last night, and the constable came in and arrested poor old Buck. I thought you both were going there last night?" he questioned.

"No, we changed our minds. Now get to work; we have lots to get done today," Ward replied, quickly changing the subject.

Although the lad doubted Ward, he knew enough to keep his mouth shut if he wanted to keep his job.

I had arrived early at the shop, and word was spreading fast about the excitement at the tavern. I was none too pleased to learn that Ward and Chip may have been involved, so I immediately called Ward into my office.

Ward came in with a humble expression: "Good morning, Uncle Thomas; how can I help you?"

"Ward, were you and Chip involved in that ruckus at Buckheads last night?" I questioned angrily.

"What's that you say, Sir?" replied Ward, testing my patience. "Don't be insolent, son; I know you both were there. Chip did not come home last night; he must have stayed at your place."

"Yes, Uncle, he did stay with me," Ward replied, his head hanging low.

"Ward, don't you understand? I am responsible for you and Chip, and the three of us solemnly promised to be fully committed to the cause.

I can't have my two top men acting like uncivilized rebels, adding fuel to the fire. In the future, I expect better decisions from both of you. This matter is over for now; get to work; we have much to complete today."

Ward felt foolish but all the wiser, having fully understood my bold words. He realized that if he wanted to be respected, he needed to earn it. Ward was determined to become the man that he yearned to be, one that he, himself, could be proud of.

**PORTRAIT OF ELIZABETH ANNELY LEWIS circa 1750**
Actual portrait of Thomas's sister, Elizabeth capturing her youthful beauty. She has been recognized by the "Daughters of the Revolution" for her dedication to the American cause.

> *E & T ANNELY GUNSMITHS A large assortment of guns & pistols, all Tower proof, also some birding guns with bayonets in their butts for gentlemen's use and guns with bayonets fit either for military use or fowling - long pieces for shooting geese, ducks, etc. Right sort of Indian guns with gun barrels and locks of all sorts. We make guns and pistols as any gentleman shall like and do all things belonging to the gunsmith's trade. New York Mercury, 7th of March 1760*

## ADVERTISEMENT IN THE NEW YORK MERCURY

DATED MARCH 7th 1760 for Edward and Thomas Annely's gunshop named E & T Annely Gunsmiths.

## ELIZABETH ANNELY LEWIS 1976
## COMMEMORATIVE PEWTER MEDAL

Franklin Mint issued a series of medallions commemorating the great women of the Revolutionary War era who played an important role in our fight against Royalist forces. The series of medallions was commissioned by the Daughters of the American Revolution (DAR) and solicited by the Franklin Mint.

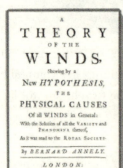

### EARLY 18th CENTURY BOOK
### TITLED
### *A THEORY OF THE WINDS*

Authored by Thomas's brother Bernard Annely for the Royal Scientific Society of England.

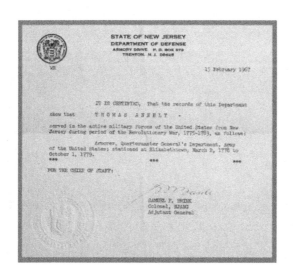

## ACTUAL WAR RECORD OF THOMAS ANNELY

when he served under General George Washington during the period of the Revolutionary War, 1775 - 1783. Provided by the State of New Jersey, Department of Defense.

## HANDWRITTEN LETTER BY EDWARD ANNELY

to his lawyer, William Kempe Esq, on August 22, 1754, discussing his concerns about his brother Richard's estate.

**CLOSE UP OF HAND INSCRIBED SIGNATURE, "T. ANNELY"**
As it appears on the lockplate of my Thomas Annely musket.

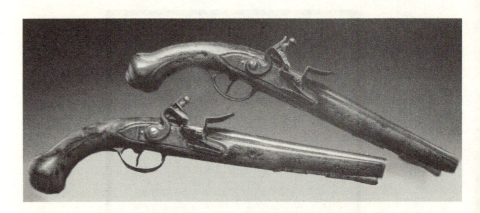

**A PAIR OF AMERICAN FLINTLOCK PISTOLS
BY THOMAS ANNELY**
Made in America between 1770 -1777. Underside stamped with a "TA" car-
touche for maker, Thomas Annely. *Owned by a Private Collector.*

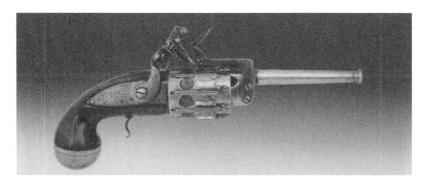

## SNAPHANCE REVOLVER – ANNELY PATTERN –
## 18th CENTURY

Early example of a revolver pistol, inscribed "T. ANNELY" on the lock plate. *Owned by a Private Collector.*

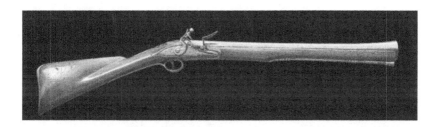

## STEEL BARRELLED FLINTLOCK BLUNDERBUSS
## BY T. ANNELY

Made by Thomas Annely, late 18th century. Annely's "TA" cartouche appears on the gun along with engraved "T. ANNELY" on the lock plate. *Owned by a Private Collector.*

## MY AMERICAN-MADE, 18th CENTURY
## THOMAS ANNELY FLINTLOCK MUSKET

The barrel is stamped "TA", and "T. ANNELY" is inscribed on the lock plate. The letter "A" is stamped on the steel ramrod head.

*Property of Fred Marzocchi*

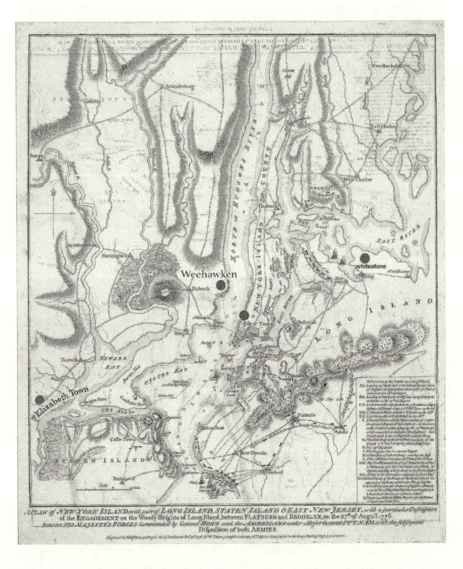

**1776 MAP OF NEW YORK AND NEW JERSEY**

Includes Weehawken, Whitestone, New York City, and Elizabethtown, where Thomas Annely and his family lived and worked. It also illustrates the site of the Battle of Brooklyn.

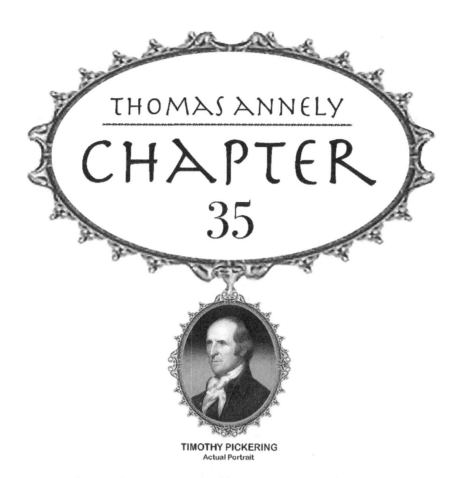

THOMAS ANNELY

# CHAPTER
## 35

**TIMOTHY PICKERING**
Actual Portrait

T he word spread like wildfire throughout the counties that General George Washington had liberated Boston and was now on his way southward. The Continental Army forged ahead, determined to free New York of the British troops as they had done for Boston.

As he and his troops marched through the cities and countryside of Rhode Island and Connecticut, they were greeted warmly by crowds of people wishing them well. They shouted words of gratitude to the man they considered their savior. Their accolades meant so much to General Washington. He needed all their support for the arduous war ahead.

I felt proud, knowing that we were providing his army with the muskets they needed so desperately. I prayed God would give me the strength to keep up with the demands of Congress and the Committee of Safety. I was blessed with the good fortune to have two fine young men, Ward and Chip, by my side, especially during these challenging times.

The day was pleasant, with the scent of promise in the air. The days were growing closer to the arrival of our firstborn child, so Sarah went to stay with her mother. As much as I missed her, I knew she would be more comfortable there, especially when I was expected to travel so much.

Chip and I were once again living alone, fending for ourselves. As I stumbled out of my lonely bed, I was surprised to see the hearth of my fireplace was cold, with only the lingering smoldering ash from the night before. I had grown accustomed to Chip rising early and preparing the hearth and our morning meal. I was tempted to wake Chip, but he had worked late through the evening, so I let him rest.

I lit the hearth and placed the kettle to boil as I washed and dressed for work. The house was eerily silent as I drank my tea alone and scoffed down some crusty old bread before heading down to my workshop.

Ward was there, bright and early as always, supervising the men and keeping them on task. My nephew impressed me more each day with his abilities as a leader and his talents as a gunmaker. "Good morning, Uncle; where is that cousin of mine?" Ward called out.

Even though not one drop of blood matched between them, it pleased me that Ward referred to Chip as his cousin.

"Chip must be worn out to the bone, for the lad is still sleeping," I replied.

Ward looked as perplexed as I felt. For all the time we have known Chip, he was always an early riser rather than one to sleep late. Ward shrugged his shoulders and went back to minding the shop.

The morning lingered, and still, there was no sight of Chip. Concerned he may be ill, I walked up the stairs to my home to check on the lad.

When I entered the kitchen, Chip was nowhere to be seen. I knocked lightly on his bedroom door a few times, with no reply. I opened the door slowly and was astonished to see the bed was empty and neatly made. I rushed in, looking around the room, until my eyes came upon a letter addressed to me on his bedside table.

As I sat down on the side of the bed, it felt like my blood was draining from my body. I reluctantly opened the letter and read the words I dreaded.

*Dear Thomas,*

*I know what I am about to tell you will not be easy for you to hear. My buddy Jimmy and I, along with some of the other lads from the tavern, have decided to join Washington's army in New York.*

*You know how much I always believed in the cause, and now 'tis my turn to do my part. I hope you can be proud of me, as I am of myself, knowing I will serve under General George Washington.*

*'Tis a difficult letter for me to write, for I do not want to leave you, the man who has taught me everything in life. You are a father, a brother, and a hero to me. I love you for eve-rything you have done for me.*

*'Tis our responsibility to have our own musket and knife when we enlist. I had no choice but to borrow yours that was hung over the fireplace. I know how much you love your*

*musket, and I promise I will return it to you as soon as pos-
sible. Having your musket by my side will comfort me as I
do my duty for my country.*

*Please give my love to Sarah, and I hope you and Ward
can forgive me for leaving this way.*

*I love you, Father, and I know you will wish me good
luck.*

*Your loving son, Chip.*

A lump formed in my throat as I struggled to hold in my emotions. I walked through my living room and stared at the empty space above my mantel.

I closed my eyes and softly prayed, "Dear Lord, I ask that you keep your faithful servant Chip in your good graces, and my trusted musket serves him well and keeps him safe."

I openly wept for the boy I have loved as a son. Wiping my tears, I felt an immense sense of pride, swelling in my chest. The lad is a true American Patriot, of which any father would be proud. What hurt me the most was that I never had the chance to wish him well and tell him how proud I was of him.

I turned to make my way back to the workshop when I was startled by a voice. "Uncle Thomas, is Chip alright?" Ward asked, standing in the doorway with a look of genuine concern on his face.

"Come and sit down, Ward; I need you to read this," I replied, handing him Chip's letter.

After reading the letter, Ward let out a sigh. "Uncle Thomas, the other night when we left the tavern, Chip said something about wanting to fight the Brits. I thought it was just the liquor talking, but now, in hindsight, I see that he meant it," he said, feeling remorseful.

"Ward, do not blame yourself, for I sensed it as well. I had hoped, knowing how much we needed him at the shop, would have kept him here longer."

"Uncle, I don't think anything could have stopped Chip once he set his mind to it."

"Aye, Ward, you know the lad well; all we can do now is carry on and pray that he stays out of harm's way."

Ward stood up and touched my shoulder, "Uncle, I promise you, I will be here for you always."

With sorrow in my eyes, I smiled weakly at my nephew, grateful for his kind sentiment. "Ward, you are now my right arm, and we are one. I am confident that you will carry out all that we must do."

"Yes, Uncle, do not be concerned. The men and I will take care of things here. It will not be easy without Chip, but I am up for the challenge."

"Thank you, nephew. I have no doubt about your abilities."

I followed Ward back down to the workshop. It seemed unreal to me when, just yesterday, I was thanking my lucky stars for having Ward and Chip by my side.

Sitting at my desk, I was so engrossed in my thoughts that I hardly noticed one of the lads knocking on my office door. "Excuse me, Sir. This boy here has an urgent message for you," he said as he led the messenger into my office.

"Mr. Thomas Annely?" the boy questioned. "Yes, I am he," I replied.

"I have a letter for you from Mr. Gifford Dally."

I fumbled nervously to find a shilling in my pocket and gave it to the young lad. "Thank you, Sir," he replied, handing me the letter and taking his leave.

I anxiously ripped open the letter from my father-in-law, telling me that Sarah was in labor and I was to come as soon as possible. I needed to put my worries of Chip aside and make haste to get to Sarah.

I called Ward into my office. "Ward, I have just received word that Sarah will give birth any time now. 'Tis not the best time for me to leave, but I must go to Sarah," I exclaimed.

"Uncle, this is wonderful news; Godspeed to you and Sarah. I will handle things here while you are gone. One of the boys will get your carriage ready straight away," Ward said reassuringly.

I rushed upstairs, stuffed some clothing in my overnight sack, snuffed out the fire, and locked up. I flew down the stairs where my carriage was waiting, jumped aboard, and rode off as fast as my horse would take me.

As I rode the rough paths to Sarah's parents' home, every young man along the way reminded me of Chip. They proudly marched forward, carrying muskets and sacks upon their backs. Just like our Chip, they were off to join Washington's army. I could not help but feel proud of these courageous young lads, and a part of me wished I could join them. I scanned their faces, hoping to see Chip among them, but he was not there.

I quickened my pace, telling myself I needed to shake off these thoughts and focus on getting to Sarah. I did not want to miss the birth of my firstborn.

When I arrived at my in-laws' country estate, I could see my father-in-law, Gifford, standing there, puffing away on his clay pipe. I halted the horse and dismounted my carriage to greet him, "Good afternoon, Sir. Is everything alright?" I questioned nervously. My father-in-law's expressionless face did nothing to ease my worried mind. He placed his hand upon my back, "Go on, son, Anne is with Sarah in the bedroom downstairs."

As I entered their home, I hesitated for a moment, taking in a deep breath to steady myself. I slowly walked into the bedroom and saw my mother-in-law, Anne, sitting on a chair at Sarah's bedside. In the dimly lit room, I could barely see Sarah lying in bed, perched up against the pillows, her face flushed red, with tears in her eyes. I rushed over to her, surprising Anne, as she stood and faced me, "Thomas, thank goodness you are here. Sit down, son," she said as she left us alone.

I sat and took Sarah's hand in mine, "Love, are you well?" "Oh, Thomas, I am more than well," she said, tears streaming down her reddened face. She pulled down her quilted blanket, revealing the most beautiful baby upon her breast. "Meet your new son, Thomas," she whispered, lifting the swaddled babe and placing him in my arms. Warm tears ran down my face as I kissed the forehead of my new son. I kissed Sarah and whispered how much I loved her.

At that moment, all the world's troubles melted away as I held my little boy and looked upon my lovely wife. I thanked the Good Lord for my most treasured blessings, Sarah and my newborn son, Gifford.

I thought it best to wait until the ride home to tell Sarah about Chip leaving, for I wanted nothing to spoil our moment of joy.

# THOMAS ANNELY

# CHAPTER
## 36

What an unbelievable sight it was to behold, as I was told by many who saw hundreds of British warships coming over the horizon. The mighty ships of war, in full mast, sailed into the New York harbor, leaving hardly any room for the smaller boats to pass by. Thousands of highly skilled British and Hessian troops unloaded onto the docks, crowding the streets of New York City. There were plenty of British loyalists cheering as the troops disembarked.

The British had visions of glory, confident this bold move would put an end to Washington and his ragtag army. They were sure that the rebel colonists would lay down their arms and, once again, bow down to their King George III.

I feared for my brothers-in-arms, who would have to face the powerful British forces. New Jersey was spared, for now, but I knew it was just a matter of time before the fight would make its way here.

My in-laws, Gifford and Anne Dally, arranged a large gathering at their country estate for our son's baptism celebration. At our request, Francis and Elizabeth graciously accepted to be the Godparents to our son, Gifford. It was not an opportune time to travel, especially for Francis, but nothing would keep us from this joyous family event. We would all have to be vigilant and mindful of our surroundings.

I woke up early from the cries of my young son being bathed in preparation for his special day.

With Francis traveling from Philadelphia, Elizabeth rode with Kingsley and Phoebe from Whitestone to our home. She brought the baptismal dress that young Francis wore at his baptism. I cringed at the thought of my son wearing a frilly dress, but Elizabeth insisted. "'Tis a gift from our mother from many years ago. She made me promise that my babes would be blessed wearing it. 'Tis the same dress we all wore, including you, my dear brother." I chuckled at the thought of it. As frilly as the dress was, I felt honored to have my son wear this precious gift from our mother.

We rode to the chapel dressed in our Sunday finery, with young Gifford looking angelic in his mother's arms. Kingsley and Phoebe, thankful to be part of the holy event, followed us in Elizabeth's carriage. Elizabeth was delighted to ride with us and fawned over our son all the way there. Sarah and I were beside ourselves with happiness for having our dear Elizabeth with us once more.

We were excited when Francis arrived. We watched as he exited the stately carriage, flanked by two guards. The men stood rigid by his side, watching intently for his safety. Elizabeth could not contain herself and ran off to greet her husband with a warm embrace. "Lizzy, I have missed you, my love," exclaimed Francis. "Come see the lovely babe," said Elizabeth as she led him over to us. "Aye, he's a lovely lad for sure," expressed

Francis. "My goodness, Thomas, what a strong grip he has," he replied, laughing, as my boy grabbed his finger tight.

It was a wondrous feeling to be together again. I only wished Chip was here to join us.

The tranquil setting of the small church, surrounded by trees blooming with white flowers, filled my soul with peace. I stood proudly at the altar as Elizabeth, with Francis at her side, held our precious son. The priest gently poured the holy water over his forehead and recited the blessing. Only the birth of our son could surpass the joyful feeling Sarah and I had in our hearts.

After the service, we traveled to the Dally's residence, where a feast fit for a king awaited us. For a moment, it felt as if time had stood still. For here we were, seated together once more. I was pleased to see Ward there, even though none of his cousins could attend. I was certain he was happy to be amongst family, just the same.

Mr. Dally clinked his glass to make a toast, "Good afternoon, my friends and family," he said, directing his smile to Sarah and me. "It is our pleasure to have you all here for the sacred blessing of our grandson, my namesake, Gifford Annely. May our Good Lord bless him and be beside him always." With glasses lifted, we all responded, "Amen."

Francis stood, glass held high, "And may the Lord keep our brave men safe, especially our sons, Morgan and Chip." Everyone responded once more, "Hear, hear, Amen."

Words of sentiment turned to the sound of silverware chiming against the delicate china while we enjoyed the delicious meal.

Mr. Dally, addressing Elizabeth, asked, "How was your ride from New York to New Jersey, Elizabeth? Did you encounter any British soldiers along the way?"

"Thankfully, no, Gifford. But, I have seen the tips of the mighty masts sailing up the bay," Elizabeth responded.

"Alas, there is a mighty storm brewing out there, and 'tis best to stay out of its way," warned Francis. "Now Francis, do not be putting the fear of God in us all. We must stand in the way and fight the storm," boasted Elizabeth.

"Hear! Hear!" we all replied with laughter as we raised our glasses to our brave Elizabeth.

"Elizabeth, what has become of your daughter Ann and Young Francis? We were surprised they could not be here today," inquired Mrs. Dally.

Elizabeth squeezed Francis's hand, as his face flushed red, "Yes, 'tis a shame, Ann has become engaged to a British Captain in the Royal Navy, and Francis Jr. married the daughter of a Tory. They have left us little choice but to separate from them," Elizabeth answered solemnly. Mrs. Dally remained silent when she realized she had touched upon a delicate subject.

"Francis, what news do you bring us from your friends in Congress?" asked Mr. Dally.

"Gifford, I am sure you realize I am sworn to secrecy. However, I can assure you that these great men are as united as we are in our quest for freedom," replied Francis.

"And what of General Washington? I have heard that Congress is giving him trouble. Is he up for the task?" inquired Mr. Dally.

"I truly believe he is the only man capable of leading this army. There is no stronger force than a man who guides his life by his own principles. He is so unlike the other generals, whose egos need constant stroking. I only wish we had more like General Washington," replied Francis.

We all nodded in agreement while clinking our glasses.

I was anxious to speak with Francis alone, for I had much to discuss with him. Foremost in my mind was Elizabeth. The enemy had reached the shores of New York. Once the fighting begins, Elizabeth will be in the fray of it and I am concerned for her safety.

The delightful day ended far too soon, leaving little time for private conversations. I was glad to hear that Elizabeth and Francis would stay with us for a few days, allowing us time to speak. Exhausted from the busy day, we all went directly to bed when we arrived at my home. The only one who did not sleep well was young Gifford, who woke us all up with his midnight cries.

Francis and Elizabeth, woken by the cries, wrapped their arms around each other. "I have missed your warmth, Lizzy. Too many lonely nights have passed without you, my love," lamented Francis. "I as well, Frannie," Elizabeth replied, snuggling closer to his body.

"Come with me to Philadelphia, Lizzy. I need you there with me, dear. The British are coming in full force to the city, and Whitestone could be in the middle of it all!" exclaimed Francis.

"Francis, we have had this conversation too many times. I will not leave Whitestone to be overrun with British regulars. When this is all over, we will be together again at Whitestone." Francis unwrapped his arms and rolled over, turning his back to her. "Come now, Fran. We have so few precious moments together; let us not quarrel." Francis turned and embraced her in his arms, their passion for each other overwhelming them.

Monday morning arrived too quickly, as I reluctantly left my warm bed to begin my workday. Elizabeth was up, bright and early, tending to the hearth. The smell of freshly baked biscuits filled the house, tantalizing my senses despite the feast I devoured on Sunday.

"Good morning, Sister, you are up bright and early," I remarked, biting into one of the warm biscuits. "Good morning, Thomas. Not too loud; I do not want to wake Sarah. I remember how exhausted I was when my babes were so young." I placed my hand on Elizabeth's shoulder, "'Tis kind of you, sister. We are so pleased to have you here."

"And I, as well, Thomas; I cannot wait to coddle my little nephew," she said, smiling.

"Perhaps I can convince you to stay for a while?" I asked gingerly. Elizabeth turned to me sharply and placed her hands on her hips, "Not you too, Thomas! Did General Francis drill you in what to say?" she questioned sternly. "Elizabeth, please sit; you are not being rational. As strong as you are, one woman cannot fight the whole damn British army. Fran has informed me that there could be battle engagements anywhere in New York." Elizabeth responded with defiance, "That is all the more I need to stay. Whitestone would be an ideal refuge for Washington and his troops."

Elizabeth reached over and placed her hand on top of mine, "Thomas, dear brother, I appreciate your concern. Please try to understand. I cannot abandon Whitestone. 'Tis where our dear brother Richard is buried along with four of my children."

"Elizabeth, no one is asking you to abandon Whitestone, only until all this is over," I pleaded. "Thomas, can't you see? If I leave Whitestone, the British will take it over for sure. I cannot let that happen. I am sorry, Thomas, but this subject is closed," she said boldly.

I stood up, looking directly into her eyes, "Elizabeth, I respect your determination, but you must respect mine. You mean too much to me, sister. With Fran away, 'tis my intention as a brother to watch over you and keep you out of harm's way. I want to hear from you often to ensure you are safe, or I will insist you come to live with me."

Elizabeth gave me a warm embrace, "Thank you, dear brother. I will not cause you any worry, and I will be sure to write to you frequently."

"Are you leaving already, Elizabeth?" said Sarah, coming into the room with little Gifford in her arms. "Oh no, not yet, dear sister. Now let me have that adorable nephew of mine," said Elizabeth, taking him from Sarah's arms.

Sarah leaned in and kissed my cheek. "Thomas, your son has a ferocious appetite. I will get nothing done until he's weaned," she said, bringing a laugh out of all of us. "I slept so late. What kind of hostess makes their guests do the cooking?"

"Nonsense, Sarah. You must be exhausted. I remember those days only too well," said Elizabeth, rocking my son in her arms.

"Excuse me, ladies, I am off to the workshop. Tell Fran to come down to my office whenever he is ready." I gave Sarah a peck on the cheek, "You girls have a wonderful day!" I exclaimed.

Ward was early as usual, and my workshop was bustling with activity. "Good morning, Ward," I called out. "Good morning, Uncle Thomas. I had a wonderful time yesterday," he replied. "Yes, it was a grand day. By the way, your Uncle Francis is staying with me for a few days; he'll be down soon for a visit."

"Yes, Sir, that will be nice; I will have the men tidy up," said Ward.

A short time later, sitting at my desk, I heard the men greeting Francis. I walked over to my door and called him into my office, offering him the seat across from me. "Thomas, I am glad we have this time to talk; things are heating up out there. I will need you to provide me with an updated report on how many muskets we can expect and when."

"Why certainly, Fran. As a matter of fact, I am working on that now. I will have the list ready for you before you leave."

"That would be grand, Thomas. General Washington is calling for more and more arms for the hundreds of young men who are enlisting. While they are full of vigor for the cause, nearly all of them are lacking in the proper equipment."

"We will do all that we can. I will bring on even more men if necessary. You can rely on me, Fran," I replied.

"Thank you, Thomas, that is music to my ears. I will be sure to relay your message to the General. I have already told him about the great effort you and your men have put into this cause." My face flushed with pride at the thought of General Washington hearing my name.

"On a more tender note, contrary to what we wished for, I cannot convince your sister to leave Whitestone," he said, lowering his head.

"I know, I have also failed to convince her. Rest assured, Fran, I will do everything in my power to watch over her," I replied sincerely.

"Kingsley will be coming Wednesday to take her back. I cannot bear to think of her at Whitestone alone," said Francis solemnly.

I replied, "Do not underestimate Kingsley. He is a good man and very devoted to our dear Elizabeth. He is brave as well."

Francis looked up, contemplating his thoughts. "You know Thomas, you are right. Kingsley can be our go-between. 'Tis unsafe for either one of us to be in New York. I will see that he keeps a close watch over her," he said as we stood and shook hands.

A light rain had begun to fall on the day Elizabeth and Francis would leave and go their separate ways. It was as if heaven knew the sadness in our hearts, for there was no guarantee that we would see each other again, especially during these times. Kingsley and Phoebe had arrived as planned, bringing a large trunk filled with Phoebe's belongings and hand-me-downs for young Gifford.

Elizabeth greeted her faithful servants with the same kindness she bestowed on us all. "Good to see you both. Come in from the rain," she said.

"What is all this, Elizabeth?" Sarah questioned.

"Phoebe has agreed to stay to help you with young Gifford," replied Elizabeth.

"Oh no, dear sister, I cannot take Phoebe away from you!" Sarah exclaimed.

"'Tis only me at Whitestone now; Kingsley and Patty will be sufficient. Phoebe was wonderful with my babies, and she is delighted to be watching over young Gifford," said Elizabeth. "Besides, Phoebe is scared to death of all the ships and the men she has seen in the harbor. She will feel much safer here," she whispered to Sarah.

Sarah's eyes softened, "She is most welcome here, Elizabeth, and I am so grateful," she said, embracing her. "Young Gifford will miss your welcoming arms, dear sister."

"And I will miss him greatly," Elizabeth said, bending down to kiss the forehead of the sleeping babe.

Sarah's eyes were brimming with tears. "Do not be saddened, my dear sister; we will all be together again at Whitestone. Our men, with providence on their side, will prevail, and soon we will be free Americans." Elizabeth said proudly.

We said our tearful goodbyes as they climbed aboard their carriages. "Godspeed," I whispered as I watched them ride away.

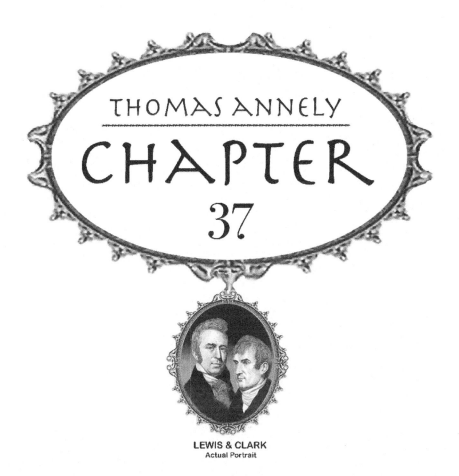

THOMAS ANNELY

# CHAPTER
## 37

**LEWIS & CLARK**
Actual Portrait

The heat of the summer was making it difficult to work the forge, and there were so many more musket barrels that Ward needed to make. He felt overwhelmed, yet Ward knew he was doing more for the cause as a gunmaker than fighting on the battlefield.

Days like today made him realize how much he missed Chip, not only for his help in the workshop but for the laughs they would share. He thought for sure he would have heard from him by now.

He made up his mind that he would visit Buckheads Tavern to see if anyone there had heard anything from Chip. As he rode his horse along the same path he and Chip had followed, he laughed at the memory of it all. He hoped that Sally, the pretty barmaid, was still working there. Perhaps she had heard from at least one of the lads that went to war.

Walking into the tavern, Ward was surprised to see how empty it was. Only a few older men sat around the table, drinking ale and pondering over the local gazette. It was a vast difference from the liveliness he recalled when he and Chip were there.

Buck was not tending the bar; his son Billy was in his place. Ward walked over and sat on a bar stool. "Hey Mate, ain't you Chip's cousin?" Billy called out.

"Why yes, I am Ward, and you are Billy, correct?"

"Yes, I am; good to see you, mate. What can I get you?"

"A pint of your coldest ale will do just fine."

Ward turned the stool around and saw a girl who looked like Sally in the distance, serving drinks to some men seated at a table. He spun the stool back around and faced Billy at the bar. "Where is Buck?" Ward questioned.

"Right about the time the lads had decided to join the army, my father had a stroke that left him unable to work. I would have joined the army with them, but I could not leave my sister Sally running this place alone."

"Sally, is your sister?" questioned Ward.

"Yes, she and I are now running the tavern together," replied Billy.

"Billy, have you heard anything from Chip or the other lads?" Ward questioned.

"No, I haven't, but maybe my sister Sally has heard something. Those lads were all smitten with her. She has had many admirers, but she won't leave our Pa for no one. She is loyal as the day is long," Billy remarked, handing me a newspaper. "Here, Ward, this is the most recent

New York Gazette. Read this article; it'll get your blood stirring," he said, laying the center page open on top of the bar.

Ward took the paper and moved to one of the tables to read it. Billy had piqued his interest in what this article was all about.

The article had excerpts from a book called "Common Sense," written by a fellow Englishman, Thomas Paine. As Ward read on, Paine's words went straight to his heart, swifter than the cut of a sword. Plainly written, so all could understand, he clearly expressed what we were all feeling. Ward felt that his words would turn loyalists into patriots and make any man want to rise and fight to keep his independence.

Ward laid the paper on the table and sipped his ale while Paine's words echoed throughout his head. These are the words that will inspire a nation, he thought to himself. For the first time, Ward felt genuinely confident that America would win this war.

"Can I get you some more ale, Sir?" came a sweet voice, breaking Ward out of his thoughts. Ward looked up at Sally, who was even lovelier than he recalled. Her crystal blue eyes sparkled as she smiled down at him.

"I see you have read the words of Thomas Paine. Remarkable man," she commented, pouring more ale into Ward's tankard.

Ward opened his mouth, stumbling on his words, "Yes, truly remarkable. Nice to see you again. My name is Ward. I was here with my cousin Chip a while back."

"Oh yes, I do remember you here with Chip. I miss the lad. Have you heard from him?" she questioned. "No, I was hoping that perhaps you had."

Sally sat at Ward's table, "I have not heard from any of the lads, althhough I did hear the soldiers are not permitted to write to their friends or family to preserve secrecy from the British. I pray they are all safe," she expressed. "By the way, in case you have forgotten, my name is Sally.

If you need anything, let me know," she said as she rose to attend to the other patrons, leaving Ward spellbound.

Ward could not take his eyes off her as he watched her move about the tavern. Somehow, this girl had found her way into his bruised heart, something he thought would never heal.

"Why don't you stop looking at her like a puppy dog and go over and talk to her? " said Billy, coming up from behind, surprising Ward. Ward laughed, "Was I that obvious, Billy?" "Oh yeah, lad, you're as smitten as all the others; good luck, my friend; you'll need it," Billy said, patting Ward on his back.

Ward mustered up his courage and walked over to where Sally was seated, counting the tabs for the day. Sally looked up at Ward standing over her, "Can I get you something, Ward?" she questioned.

Ward sat, going over the words he wanted to say in his head before he finally spoke, "Sally, I would like to take you to dinner on Sunday. Would that be agreeable with you?"

Sally smiled and said, "I don't fraternize with the patrons, but Chip once mentioned that you were a fine gunsmith. I will join you for dinner, Ward, under one condition," she replied coyly. "And what would that be, Sally?"

"You will have to teach me how to shoot." Ward laughed and replied, "It would be my pleasure."

Ward was filled with emotions as he rode home that evening. Saddened that he left, not knowing any more about Chip's whereabouts than he did before. Yet, excited at the thought of seeing Sally on Sunday. He wondered what others would think about him courting a barmaid. Indeed, they would think he was like all the others, tempted by her delicate beauty. He quickly shrugged off those thoughts, for deep inside, he truly felt something for this girl. He sensed a quality about her in the way she carried herself.

A feeling of warmth flushed over him, for he wanted nothing more than to spend time with this girl and to get to know all about her.

Their first Sunday became one of many Sundays that Ward would spend with Sally. As it turned out, Sally came from a very wealthy family. Her father, Buck, not only owned the tavern in town but many other properties around the colonies. Sally had shown a great aptitude for business from a very young age, prompting her father to agree that she should be educated properly. She went to live with a family relation in Virginia, where she was schooled throughout her formative years. Unfortunately, Sally's mother died young, leaving Buck a lonely widower with a daughter and three young boys to raise.

Sally had no choice but to abandon her dreams of becoming a teacher and return home to tend to her younger brothers and father. "I made that choice freely, Ward. I was grieving so much for my mother; my only solace was tending to the young lads," she recalled, with sadness in her eyes. "I did my best to care for them all, but the two younger ones were stricken with the fever, leaving only Billy and myself." Ward wrapped his arm around Sally's shoulder, consoling her as she wept from the memories. "You are an amazing woman, Sally. Your family is fortunate to have you," said Ward, holding her tightly in his arms.

Sally wiped the tears from her eyes and looked up at Ward. "You are the kindest man I have ever known, and I think I am falling in love with you," she said, their lips meeting in a passionate kiss.

"Sally, I feel the same way," he whispered as their lips met once more, with even more passion.

Ward could not believe his good fortune in finding the girl of his dreams. When he thought about the months he spent lamenting over Amelia, he never dreamed he would ever find happiness again.

Ward realized that what he felt for Amelia was simple infatuation. Now he knew how real love felt.

THOMAS ANNELY

# CHAPTER 38

America was in the midst of a war with Britain to fight for its independence, and I was very concerned for my brother-in-law Francis's welfare. I had not heard from him for quite some time and hoped all was well. I was filled with anxiety, and the strain of all that was expected of me was overwhelming. I needed the calmness of my workshop, doing what I like to do best to ease my frustrations.

I grabbed my cutting tools from the drawer, placed a piece of the fresh walnut stock onto my worktable, and sanded it to a smooth finish. Picking out my favorite carving tool, I whittled away into the hardened wood. My hands worked instinctively, carving intricate details with the edge of my chisel. It was the perfect remedy to clear my mind of everything troubling me.

The unrest amongst some of the people of the colonies made me wonder if it would ever be possible to win this war for our freedom, especially in New York City. The people of this city are dangerously divided in their political views. There are the wealthy who have no desire for change for fear of losing their fortunes. Some sympathized with the British and would never go against the crown. Others were afraid and hid their heads in the sand rather than fight for their freedom.

I am thankful to God that most colonists strongly believe in the cause. Like my brave son Chip, hundreds of young men are lining up to join the Continental Army, willing to give their lives for their country's freedom. These are the men General Washington needs now, more than ever.

As I was putting away my tools, I could hear the sounds of a horse and rider pulling up to my door. The young rider delivered a timely message from my brother-in-law Francis with exciting news from Philadelphia. Attached to Francis's letter was the front page of the Pennsylvania Post, printed with the newly written resolution from Congress, aptly named 'The Declaration of Independence'. This document, sent from Congress directly to King George III, left no doubt of their intentions to separate from the mother country.

These particular words affected me deeply as I read on.

> *"When in the course of human events it becomes necessary for one people to dissolve the political bands which have connected them with another, and to assume, among the powers of the earth, the separate and equal station to which the laws of nature and of nature's God entitle them, a decent respect to the opinions of mankind requires that they should declare the causes which impel them to the separation."*
>
> *"They are endowed by their Creator with certain unalienable Rights, that among these are Life, Liberty and the pursuit of Happiness."*

We, the American colonists, needed this vital document to ignite our souls. The clear, concise words gave us a deeper understanding of what we were fighting for. There will be no turning back now; we must carry on to become our own independent nation.

Francis is one of the fifty-six men who bravely signed their names to this Declaration of Independence. It was a bold move, one that will surely put a bounty on the heads of all these daring men.

As proud as I am of the bravery of my dear brother-in-law, Fran, it did not stop me from growing even more concerned for my sister's welfare. With Francis's signature on this declaration, he publicly announced his undeniable devotion to the cause. Beyond any doubt, I fear he has placed himself and my sister Elizabeth in harm's way.

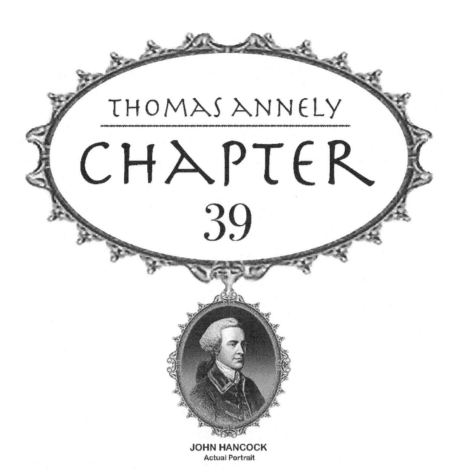

**THOMAS ANNELY**

# CHAPTER 39

**JOHN HANCOCK**
Actual Portrait

Elizabeth was home at her beloved Whitestone, with her faithful servant Kingsley by her side, contemplating a plan to protect herself and Whitestone. A messenger delivered a package from Francis. Enclosed was a copy of the Pennsylvania Post, with the Declaration of Independence printed within. She was quite proud of her husband's signature on this important document, alongside all the other prominent men. Reading the inspirational words, gave her more determination to go on firmly believing in the cause.

"Kingsley, I was told by Francis and my brother Thomas that Whitestone may be in the crosshairs of a major battle between the British and American armies. 'Tis just the two of us now, Kingsley. I had hoped my sons could come to our aid, but that is not possible. Morgan is now stationed up north and cannot leave his post. Francis Jr. shies away from us. Especially now that he has married Elizabeth Ludlow, the daughter of a prominent British loyalist, against our wishes."

"We must gather our most valuable items and hide them in the vault in the cellar. I will have Patty pack up some salted beef and some of the vegetables and fruits we preserved to place in there as well."

Elizabeth placed a small lock box on the table and explained its contents to Kingsley. "Enclosed in this box are monies and some of my fine jewelry. If anything should happen to me, I want you to keep what is in this box and use it as you see fit."

Kingsley listened intently, with a solemn expression upon his face. "'Tis kind of you, Mrs. Elizabeth, to put your trust in me."

Elizabeth placed her hand upon Kingsley, "You deserve it; you have been very faithful to both Francis and myself for all these years."

After they secured all her valuables inside the vault, Elizabeth continued with her instructions: "From now on, we must inspect all doors and windows and ensure the locks are working properly. Gather all our firearms and keep them loaded by each entryway. We must do all we can to protect ourselves and Whitestone against the British Army."

Elizabeth did not want to alarm her servants any more than they already were, so she decided not to tell them about the Declaration of Independence that Francis had signed. She knew the British would consider any signer a traitor. Francis was already being watched, but now he indeed has a price upon his head.

The days were long and lonely for Elizabeth. Her meetings with the *Daughters of Liberty* are now restricted. It was far too risky for the women to be found in the Lewis household. She missed the camaraderie of all her lady friends, working together and doing all they could for the cause. She carried on with sewing clothes for the men, along with helping Patty make vats of stew for any American soldier in need of a meal.

Patty was happy once more, singing one of her native songs from Jamaica as she tended to the cooking. Elizabeth was relaxing in her sitting room when she heard a slight knock upon the door. Kingsley was out tending to the animals, so she rose to see who was there.

As she slowly opened the front door, she was surprised and delighted to see her daughter, Ann, standing there. "Ann, my love, what a pleasant surprise! Come inside," exclaimed Elizabeth with joy. Ann embraced her mother, "Oh, Mother, I just had to see you. I know Father would not like me being here, but I could not stay away," she exclaimed, tears welling in her eyes. "Your father is away, but I think you are mistaken; he would love to see you."

Elizabeth looked out to see Ann's driver waiting by the entryway. "Tell your driver to bring his carriage out back."

"Not necessary, Mother; I will instruct him to leave and come back for me in a few days if you don't mind," said Ann. "Of course, I do not mind. I would love for you to stay longer," Elizabeth expressed as Ann waved her driver to move on.

Elizabeth wrapped her arm around Ann's petite shoulder and led her into the sitting room. She poured her daughter a generous cup of tea, "Tell me, dear, what brings you here today?" Ann held out her delicate hand, displaying her wedding bands on her finger. "Mother, George, and I were married last month." Elizabeth embraced her daughter, letting go of her feelings against her daughter's choice for a husband. "I am so happy for you, darling; I only wish I could have been there to see the beautiful bride."

"I, as well, Mother. I cried the whole night before, missing you so. It was a simple ceremony, only the two of us and the witnesses. I hope to have a formal wedding someday, with you there to share our day."

"And we will celebrate joyfully, here at our beautiful Whitestone, with your father giving you away, as it should be," Elizabeth sincerely said.

"'Tis a wonderful dream, Mother, but I don't think Father will ever forgive me now that I have married against his wishes. I am sorry, Mother, for disappointing you and Father so, but I couldn't help but fall in love with George. I hope someday you and Father will get to know him, to see for yourself what a wonderful man he is."

"Ann, I know all about the power of love, but this new country needs your devotion as well. You are an American, and if you want your children to enjoy the same freedoms you had growing up here, you must fight against this tyranny that has been forced upon us. You are young; you have your whole life in front of you. Don't you want to live here as a free American?" exclaimed Elizabeth.

Ann lowered her head, softly responding to her words, "Mother, the other reason I came was to tell you George and I will be leaving for England. 'Tis where we have chosen to raise our family. I was hoping you would come with us. 'Tis not safe here for you, or Father, anymore."

Elizabeth was stunned, her eyes filled with tears, "'Tis thoughtful of you, dear, but you know I could never leave Whitestone. 'Twas a promise I made to myself when your Uncle Richard passed. 'Tis where I will spend whatever days the good Lord has left for me, with your father beside me," she replied, grasping Ann's hands.

They spent the rest of the day, arms wrapped around each other's waists, walking the grounds. They reminisced about the days gone by and how much they enjoyed every moment. "You are the best mother," Ann said sincerely. She squeezed her mother tighter as they walked. They retired for the evening, feeling content to have these special moments together again.

The next morning, everyone rose early to a lovely, sunny day. "Oh, how I missed Patty's meals," exclaimed Ann as she sat with Elizabeth at the dining table. Patty brought a large tray of boiled eggs, cheeses, and fresh scones. "'Tis so good to have you here again, Miss Ann. I made your favorite scones to put some meat on you," Patty expressed. "'Tis Mrs. Ann now," Elizabeth piped up. Patty smiled from ear to ear, "Well, eat up now. You need to prepare for childbearing!"

After their delicious meal, Ann and Elizabeth went out to the veranda. They sipped their tea while enjoying the fresh breeze wafting up from the water.

The time had come for Ann to take her leave, and Elizabeth's heart was weighing heavy. She thought back on how sad she felt when she said goodbye to her mother in England. Elizabeth was determined to be as brave as her mother was and not let Ann see her pain searing through her heart.

Ann's carriage and driver arrived early and patiently waited outside. Elizabeth walked her only daughter down the stairs to the carriage door. Mother and Daughter held each other tightly, not wanting to let go.

Suddenly, Ann grasped one of her mother's hands and placed something inside her palm, closing Elizabeth's fingers around it. Ann entered the carriage, trying to hold her composure as she demanded her driver to move along swiftly. The driver whipped the horses and galloped away.

As the carriage faded into the distance, Elizabeth looked down at her clenched hand. She slowly unfolded her fingers to reveal a beautiful gold pendant with a lovely miniature portrait of Ann. Her tears flowed freely from her eyes as she clasped the chain around her neck and pressed the pendant to her chest. With great sadness bearing down on her, she slowly walked up the stairway inside her beloved home, Whitestone.

THOMAS ANNELY

# CHAPTER
## 40

On this warm and hazy August morning, one could barely make out the silhouette of Whitestone perched high upon the hill. Elizabeth stood outside on her veranda, gazing out at the tranquil setting of the grounds surrounding her home. A calm feeling came over her, knowing that she was well prepared for any danger that may occur from the war that was surely coming in her direction.

Elizabeth was startled when she heard Patty shouting that men were walking towards the house. She ran back into the house, grabbed her musket, and rushed to the front window. She watched as the men came clearly into view out of the fog. A flush of relief came over her when she saw that the five men were Continental soldiers.

Kingsley rushed into the room. "Please, let these men in; they are Americans," Elizabeth ordered. Kingsley opened the door wide and stood ramrod straight, facing the soldiers. The men stopped in their tracks, intimidated by the imposing negro man standing before them. The Colonel came forward and introduced himself, "Good day, my name is Colonel William Taylor of the Continental Army, assigned to the Long Island regiment. May I speak with the Master of the house?"

Elizabeth put down her musket, left her watch at the window, and went to stand beside Kingsley at her doorway. "Good day, Colonel Taylor, I am Mrs. Elizabeth Lewis. I am in charge of this house while my husband is away."

"Good day, Mrs. Lewis. We have come here to warn you and your husband to vacate the premises. You may be in grave danger. A conflict has ensued, and your home is too close to the battlegrounds."

"Colonel Taylor, I appreciate your concern. However, I will not be leaving my home. My family and I have taken all the precautions and are prepared if a problem arises."

The Colonel replied somberly, "Mrs. Lewis, I commend your bravery, and I can understand why you would not want to leave this magnificent home. However, my dear lady, you will not be able to fight off the might of the British Army yourself."

"We thank you for your concern, Sir, but we have made our decision, and we will not be leaving. My husband is a member of the Continental Congress, and he fully understands that I intend to stay and protect our home."

"Madam, I suppose there is nothing more I can say to convince you to leave. I wish you good luck, Mrs. Lewis", he said, turning to take his leave.

"Colonel, before you go, may I offer you and your men some food and drink? "

"Thank you kindly, but we have several other homes that we have to alert. Godspeed to you," he said as he tipped his hat, turned, and marched off.

Elizabeth watched them walk away with a heavy heart. "Look at them, Kingsley, so young, yet so brave. May God keep them safe," she prayed out loud.

A few days later, as the Colonel had warned, Elizabeth heard the sounds of gunfire in the distance. "'Tis happening, Kingsley," said Elizabeth, looking out upon the water at all the frigates with British flags waving in the breeze.

Kingsley looked over at his Mistress. Her steady calm did not surprise him, for she was the bravest woman he knew. "Mrs., we should be leaving now," said Kingsley nervously. "We will do nothing of the sort, Kingsley. This is my home, and those blokes will have to drag me by my ears to make me leave!" she said firmly.

That evening, a heavy rainstorm swept across the East River, bringing the smell of gunpowder into the air. Elizabeth sat under her veranda, enjoying the cooler air the rain brought in. The sounds of muskets firing and the pungent smells of war were all around her. She prayed the rains would halt the gunfire for the night so she could sleep a little easier.

The next morning, a thick fog covered the river, and all the surrounding islands and the sounds of gunfire ceased.

Elizabeth clasped her hands and smiled, "Will you look at this fog, Kingsley, 'tis as if God's hand has come down from the heavens, covering all the land. It will keep the Brits at bay."

Finally, all was quiet, and the smells of gunpowder no longer lingered in the air. Elizabeth took a deep breath of the fresh air, feeling thankful Whitestone had been spared.

Some days passed, and all was well until Elizabeth heard what sounded like cannon fire in the distance. She stood to look out the window when a loud, crashing sound suddenly startled them all.

Patty dropped her spoon and came running, "Mrs. Elizabeth, what was that?" she asked, shaking. Elizabeth walked out to the veranda, her hand above her eyes, squinting to see where the noise was coming from.

"Get down!' Kingsley yelled as a cannonball whizzed by his head, hitting the side of the house.

Another cannonball came spiraling through the air, crashing on the stone patio where Elizabeth was standing, barely missing her.

"Run, Mistress, Run. Get away before you get killed!" screamed Patty.

"Another strike is not likely to hit the same place," Elizabeth replied calmly, holding her post.

No sooner had the dust of the cannons settled than a small troop of British soldiers ran towards the house and burst through the front door. Frightened out of her head, Patty ran away, screaming towards the woods.

Kingsley grabbed a musket and stood by his Mistress's side as they watched the soldiers destroy everything in their path. An angry soldier ripped the musket from Kingsley's arms and cracked it against the fireplace, "Try that again, old man, and I will stick a bayonet through your heart!" he warned.

The soldiers went madly through each room, taking an ax to Elizabeth's elegant furniture. The china cabinet, filled with her fine imported dinnerware, was knocked over, smashing everything inside.

They stormed Francis's library, seeming to take the greatest pleasure in tearing up all his books and slashing his fine paintings.

Still, Elizabeth remained stoic, with only a single tear cascading down her cheek. One of the soldiers, in his boldness, crouched down and tore off the gold-colored buckles from her shoes. "All is not gold that glitters," she told the disgruntled soldier, who threw the worthless buckles aside and shouted, "You're not so rich after all, are you, Lady."

The plundering continued as the men went down into the wine cellar and cracked open bottles of Francis's aged wine, guzzling it down. Spitting it onto the floor, a soldier cried out, "Sour as vinegar, these bloody traitors have no taste!"

They came up from the basement with boxes of Francis's imported cigars and bottles of brandy stuffed inside their sacks. She was relieved they did not notice the vault door hidden behind the wine shelves.

The British Officer approached Elizabeth, "I am Lt. Colonel Samuel Birch of the 17th Light Dragoons. I have been sent to destroy this home and take you and your husband into custody."

"My husband is not here," Elizabeth boldly answered. "I am not certain if I believe you, Ma'am. Men, take this woman out front and search everywhere, inside and out, for her husband!" he commanded.

Grabbing Elizabeth by the arm, the soldier dragged her out to where the wagon was waiting, already filled with their spoils. "What is the meaning of this? I demand you let me go!" she shouted.

"Produce your husband, and maybe I will be lenient with you," he gruffly replied. "As I told you, Colonel Birch, my husband is not here," Elizabeth said boldly. "Leave her be!" Kingsley shouted, running outside towards them, attempting to free Elizabeth from his grasp.

Colonel Birch pushed Kingsley aside, "Run away, old man, to your freedom while you have the chance!" he shouted.

"Don't you dare hurt him, you bastard!" Elizabeth shouted as a soldier shoved her into the back of the wagon, binding her hands so she could not move.

"It's you and your traitor husband we want, Mrs. Lewis; I have no reason to harm your unfortunate slaves," said Colonel Birch.

"Where are you taking me?" she yelled. "Where all traitors belong, in prison!" the Colonel replied as the soldiers threw lit torches into the house, setting it ablaze.

Elizabeth, in shock, could not believe what was happening. She prayed Kingsley was not injured and was able to run away.

The soldiers threw their sacks into the wagon and jumped inside. Elizabeth glared at them with hate in her eyes. "You scoundrels should be ashamed of yourselves, treating a woman like this," she said with anger. "Keep quiet back there," shouted the Colonel, seated up front next to the driver.

Elizabeth winced with pain as they rode off down the rugged road. She sat rigid and brave, determined not to let them see her cry. Glancing behind, she saw her beloved Whitestone engulfed in flames.

In the distance, she heard the squealing and grunts from her poor horses and farm animals as the soldiers yanked them from the safety of their stalls and stole them away.

Kingsley, feeling helpless, watched the wagon moving full speed ahead. Remembering the box of valuables Elizabeth put inside the vault, he covered his face with his neckerchief and ran blindly through the smoke down to the cellar. He felt his way around until he found the door of the vault. Pulling it open, he reached inside and grabbed the small box sitting on the shelf. Slamming the vault door shut, he prayed the fire would not find its way inside. Up the stairs, he ran, clutching the box to his chest through the smoke, falling onto the ground outside.

He lay there, coughing, trying to catch his breath before he rose again, running after the wagon and following its trail of dust.

When he approached the river, there was no sight of the British wagon. He was certain they were long gone, most likely on their way to the British headquarters in the city. He made up his mind that he would go to Master Francis and alert him of what had happened to his mother.

The Colonel urged the driver to hurry along, paying no mind to the gentle lady he had tied up in the back. He rode the horses hard, taking sharp turns, which made her feel sick to her stomach. Finally, the driver slowed and came to an abrupt stop at an old large house in a part of town Elizabeth had never seen.

The soldiers jumped off and started unloading the wagon of all they stole from Whitestone. Colonel Birch ordered his men to untie the ropes that bound her and to bring the lady into the house. "I demand to speak to whoever is in charge here!" Elizabeth shouted out, to no avail. The soldier, not saying a word in response, carried on with his duties. He locked iron shackles upon her delicate wrists and forced Elizabeth down into the dismal cellar. "There ya go, lady. If you got any grievances, take 'em up with them," he said, locking the heavy, barred door behind her.

Elizabeth looked around at the slumped-over figures of shackled men and women sitting on the damp, cold floor. Not one of them spoke, nor did they even look up to acknowledge Elizabeth. One small window, barred with rod iron, let little air into the stale, foul-smelling room. A rat shimmied up the wall and slipped out of the bars, sending a chill up Elizabeth's spine. Her body shivered from the cold as she leaned against the hard cement wall. She stood until her legs could not hold out any longer and collapsed onto the floor.

The room grew darker as the sun was going down. Fear clutched her heart at the thought of spending a night in the dismal room, surrounded by strangers. She fell into a fitful sleep, waking suddenly at the sounds of people moaning and rats scratching upon the walls. Her stomach growled with hunger, yet the thought of food sickened her. She prayed this nightmare would end and someone would come to her rescue soon.

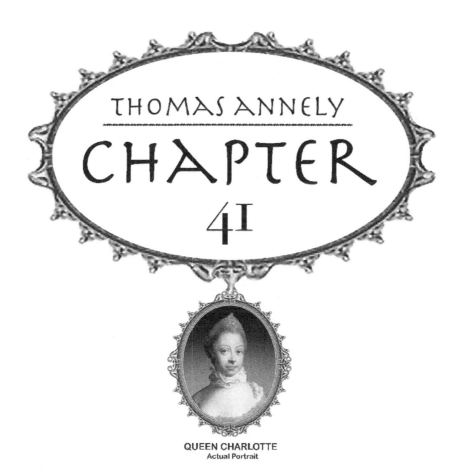

THOMAS ANNELY

# CHAPTER 41

**QUEEN CHARLOTTE**
Actual Portrait

T he ferry over the East River provided some relief for Kingsley's weary legs, and the breeze blowing off the bay awoke his senses. When he arrived at the landing in the city, he rushed along the busy streets, searching every store along the way.

The afternoon sun bore heavy on his back as sweat poured down from his face. After searching many brick storefronts, he was relieved to see the sign "Francis Lewis and Son" hanging over the doorway. He slumped against the building and peered inside the glass window. He could see Master Francis at the front counter, waiting on a customer. Francis Jr. looked up and was shocked to see old Kingsley outside the window, clutching a small box in his arms.

He quickly finished with his customer, who, as he left, turned and gave an odd glance at the negro man leaning by the door. Francis Jr. rushed over, opened the door, and ushered Kingsley inside. "Kingsley, what brings you here today?" he anxiously inquired.

Kingsley, wiping the sweat dripping off his forehead with his sleeve, spoke with labored breath. "Master Francis, 'tis your mother, British soldiers came and took Mrs. Elizabeth away."

Francis Jr. led Kingsley to the back room, "Sit down, Kingsley," he said while fetching a drink of cool water for the weary old man.

"I tried, but I couldn't stop them. They busted up everything and set Whitestone on fire, and they took your mother with them!" exclaimed Kingsley, with tears brimming in his eyes.

Francis Jr., stunned by Kingsley's words, placed his hand on his forehead, rubbing his temples. "Thank you, Kingsley. It was very brave of you to come here. Lie down and rest," he said calmly.

"Thank you kindly, Sir, but what about Mrs. Elizabeth? We got to go help her!" he cried out.

"Yes, Kingsley, do not worry; I will find her," he replied.

"I got to go see Mr. Francis and your Uncle Thomas. I promised I would tell them if something happened," blurted out Kingsley.

"Yes, Kingsley, I'm going to send word to my father and Uncle Thomas and try to find out where they brought Mother. You rest now and I will be back as quickly as possible," he promised.

Closing up the shop, Francis Jr. rushed around the block to his father-in-law's law office, which had the name Gabriel Ludlow, Esq. etched on the glass door.

He entered the imposing office, and sat in one of the high-back leather chairs, waiting for his father-in-law to arrive from his day in court. He felt confident that he, a prominent lawyer, would have the connections to help get his mother out of this situation.

His father-in-law came into his office, surprised to see his son-in-law sitting there. "Francis, what brings you here this late in the day?" he asked. "Good day, Sir. I apologize for coming in unannounced, but I have an urgent matter to discuss with you."

Mr. Ludlow sat behind his solid mahogany desk, lit up his pipe and leaned back in his leather chair, "How can I be of help, son?" he asked.

"'Tis my mother, Sir. Her manservant came to see me today and informed me that the British soldiers arrested her and took her somewhere here in the city. And they ransacked Whitestone and set it on fire!"

He sat erect and placed his pipe aside, "Francis, that is terrible news, but I am not certain I can be of any help to you. When your father signed that dreaded declaration, he set himself and his family up for this kind of trouble. Nevertheless, I will see what I can do. In the meantime, find out as much as you can from the manservant, and I will speak to my contacts."

"Thank you, Sir. I appreciate whatever you can do," Francis Jr. stood, shook his hand, and left quickly.

The days dragged by as Elizabeth forced herself to eat the disgusting gruel they called food. They would not allow her any communication with family or friends. Nor was she allowed a change of clothing or a blanket to stave off the dampness. The smells of bodily excrement and sweat permeated the air, adding to the musty smell of the cold cellar. Feeling despair that she would never be released, she finally let the tears flow; her cries filled the room.

Francis Jr. felt helpless as the days passed by and he was beside himself with worry. Finally, he received word from his father-in-law, but it was not the good news he had hoped for. "I am sorry, Francis. I went to speak with the British authorities, and they are refusing to release your mother at this time. Apparently, they are using her as an example to deter other disgruntled colonists."

Francis Jr. lashed out angrily, "This is absurd; my mother is a good woman and does not deserve this treatment! Did they at least tell you where they are keeping her?"

"Yes, but you must not tell anyone you heard this from me. I believe your mother is being held at 121 Wilson Street. It is one of the old sugar houses that the British have converted to temporary holding jails."

"Thank you, Sir," Francis meekly replied as he rose to leave.

"Watch yourself, son; these British soldiers do not take kindly to rebel sympathizers," he warned. "Yes, Sir, I understand," replied Francis Jr., even though he couldn't care less what they thought. He was sick and tired of these bloody loyalists and their pompous ways.

Francis shook his father-in-law's hand and left to tell Kingsley. With no place to go, Kingsley slept on a makeshift bed in the back of the store while he spent his days roaming the streets, trying to find Elizabeth.

"Kingsley!" he shouted as he entered his shop. Kingsley came out front, anxious to hear the news from Francis Jr. "I am sorry, Kingsley, but I have no good news. My mother is not to be freed, but I do have an address where they believe she is being imprisoned."

Feeling worthless, Francis Jr. expressed, "I don't think they will allow me to take her home. I'm certain they won't even let me talk to her."

Kingsley bravely said, "I will go, Master, and I will find a way to get to her."

Francis Jr. pondered over Kingsley's suggestion, "Alright, Kingsley, it might work. They won't suspect you and will leave you be." Francis Jr. looked around his shop for whatever he could find suitable for his mother. He wrapped a blanket, food, and even a fancy dress in a sack for Kingsley to carry. He penned a quick letter to his mother, promising to help her however he could. "Kingsley, take a good amount of the money from the box and hide it on yourself. You might be able to buy off one of the guards to see her. These things should bring her some relief for a little while," said Francis Jr, handing over the sack of goods to him, with the letter from himself tucked inside the rolled-up blanket. "In the meantime, I will try to talk to the officials and plead for her release."

Placing both his hands on Kingsley's shoulders, looking him squarely in his eyes, he said, "Godspeed, my brave and loyal man."

Kingsley set off on his way to find the street with the sack of goods slung over his back. When he came upon 121 Wilson, he hurried and hid behind the row of overgrown bushes, scanning the house for entryways. All he saw was the solid wooden door of the entryway and a small cellar window with rod iron bars on the side of the house. He suspected that was where they were holding her.

He dashed, crouched over to stay hidden, and looked between the iron bars to the darkened room below. The sight frightened him of the room full of shackled, dismal-looking men and women. "Elizabeth," he whispered through the bars. Elizabeth looked up, hardly believing her ears. She rose slowly, barely strong enough to stand. "Kingsley?" she whispered.

"'Tis I, Mistress; come to the window," he said softly. Elizabeth walked over while one of the others moved the only chair in the room for her to stand on. "Kingsley, you are here," she replied, reaching through the bars to grasp his hand. "I went to see Master Francis, just like you told me to, Mistress," he said as he emptied the sack, squeezing whatever he could through the narrow opening. The others circled her as she passed the goods down to them. "The Master is gonna get you out of here, Ma'am, you will see," he whispered. "God bless you, Kingsley. Give my love to them all," she said, trembling.

"I got to go now, but I'll be back," he said, squeezing her hand before releasing it and running off.

The others helped Elizabeth down as she fell to the floor, weeping. Remarkably, none of them touched her parcels, for they had the utmost respect for her.

Elizabeth wiped her eyes on her filthy dress as she eagerly opened each package. She found paper and writing tools, foodstuffs, undergarments, and even a dress wrapped in a thick blanket. She threw the blanket over her shoulders, and the letter from Francis Jr. slipped onto the floor. She grabbed it, quickly opened it, and rubbed her fingers along the words.

The others looked on, their mouths watering, smelling the salted beef. Elizabeth folded up the letter and stuffed it into her dress pocket. She handed each person a biscuit and a piece of meat. Gobbling it up quickly, they nodded their heads in appreciation to this kind lady.

Elizabeth was eager to change into the fresh clothing that Kingsley brought, but the chains that bound her hands would not allow it. She held the new dress to her face and sniffed the scent of the fresh linen. The thought of a bath and clean clothes against her body bolstered her spirits. She would have to wait, though, until she could try to convince a young guard to remove her restraints.

"We need to hide all this as best as we can. We don't want the guards knowing we have any of this," she told the others. "Or the rats," one of them piped up as they shared a rare laugh amongst themselves.

After everything was safely hidden away, Elizabeth took out the letter from her son to read.

Thomas Annely

*Dearest Mother,*

*I pray that this letter finds you in good health despite the awful situation that has been put upon you. I have sent word to Father and Uncle Thomas, and we will all work diligently to end this nightmare.*

*Your faithful servant, Kingsley, has been a Godsend. We are very grateful to him. This man loves you very much.*

*You are the best of mothers, and I pray that knowing you are deeply loved will carry you through this terrible ordeal. Mother, hold fast to your fighting spirit, and may your faith in the Good Lord keep you strong. I will pray every day to Saint Christopher to watch over you.*

*Rest assured that we are doing all we can to ensure your release, and we will not quit until we are all together again.*

*Your loving son, Francis*

Elizabeth folded the letter and hid it under her dress for safekeeping. Hope filled her heart, taking away her feelings of desperation. Her children loved her despite her political beliefs, giving her a renewed sense of spirit. Even the mighty British army could not conquer the power of love.

THOMAS ANNELY

# CHAPTER

## 42

Sarah and I enjoyed a quiet morning meal while Phoebe kept young Gifford amused. It had been a little over a month since the baptism, and already, my son had grown so much. Recalling that day, I realized I had not heard a word from Elizabeth or Kingsley.

I swallowed my last sip of tea and hurried along, for I had a full day of work ahead of me. I told myself to go to Whitestone as soon as possible to check on Elizabeth.

The next few days were busier than ever as the men struggled to meet the daily quota. My head was buried in paperwork when a messenger came to my door with a letter from my nephew, Francis Jr.

Pushing my paperwork aside, I was anxious to read this unexpected letter from my nephew. Ripping it open at once, the words I read took my breath away as my heart began to beat rapidly.

*Dear Uncle Thomas,*

*'Tis with great despair that I write this letter to you. British soldiers have destroyed Whitestone and arrested Mother, putting her in a prison in New York City. I am at my wit's end; all of my efforts to free my mother have fallen on deaf ears. All I managed to get was the location where they are keeping her: 121 Wilson Street. The British are treating her in a most inhumane way: in a filthy, cold cellar with no bedding or any proper food to eat. No amount of pleading on my part has done any good; the British are determined to make an example out of her.*

*Thank God for her manservant, Kingsley. If not for him, my mother would not be getting any help at all. He managed to smuggle some food and clothing to her, which bolstered her spirits a bit. Uncle, she is not doing well. The rat-infested and horrid conditions they are keeping her in will surely make her ill.*

*I sent word to my father; I hope he will receive my message quickly. I need to find out where my brother Morgan is stationed so I may alert him to Mother's plight. I pray you and Father will find a way to release her soon. Kingsley and I will not quit until Mother is free! I will do my very best and will not stop until we have Mother back.*

*Your loving nephew, Francis Lewis Jr.*

Angered beyond words, I slammed my fist upon my desk. "How dare those bastard British cowards!" I yelled out loud. Grabbing the letter, I rushed upstairs and found Sarah, tending to her cooking with young Gifford, sitting upon her hip. "Sarah, please sit down, love."

I took Gifford from Sarah's arms and handed him over to Phoebe, "Please take Gifford for a nap." I asked. "Yes, Master Thomas," Phoebe replied, cradling our son.

"What is it, Thomas?" Sarah asked, with a concerned look on her face.

My jaw was tense with anger as I handed the letter to Sarah, "I just received this letter from Francis Jr."

I could see the pain in her eyes as she read the letter. "Oh dear God, you feared this would happen. Not our dear Elizabeth! How can they do this to her? Oh, Thomas, what will we do? You must go to Francis at once!" she anxiously replied.

"Sarah, I only wish I could go to Francis. He and many members of Congress have gone into hiding in fear of retaliation for the signing of the Declaration of Independence. I have only one choice: to go to the one man who can truly help."

"And who would that be, Thomas?"

"General George Washington. Rumors have it he is right here, in northern New Jersey, at his headquarters at Fort Lee. I will go to him and plead Elizabeth's case. He's a good man, he will help us. I am sure of it."

"Thomas, do you think they will allow you to see the General?"

"They will have to. I cannot stand by while my sister needs my help. I have to find a way to talk to General Washington," I said confidently.

"Oh, Thomas, I fear for you," she said, reaching for my hand. I squeezed her hand tightly and replied, "I have no choice. I must do all I can for her. Please pack some things for me while I go downstairs and tell Ward what has happened. I will be fine, love, do not worry."

Ward was shocked and saddened to hear about his aunt's imprisonment. "Poor Aunt Elizabeth, those bloody Brits will stop at nothing!"

Ward roared, expressing his anger. His voice softened, and he said, "I wish I could go with you."

Placing my hand on Ward's shoulder, I replied, "I wish that too, but I need you here. I will do all I can for your aunt; I promise you that."

My blood was rushing through my veins as I dashed up the stairs to my home, grabbed my sack, and kissed Sarah goodbye, with a promise to return in a few days. I ran down to the stables, leaped on my horse, and rode to Fort Lee as fast as my horse would take me.

It was nearly dusk when I arrived at the imposing gate at Fort Lee. I knew I was at the right place when I saw General Washington's light blue flag with thirteen white stars waving in the breeze. Two uniformed soldiers stood by the large gate, with muskets by their side, standing guard. I dismounted from my horse and walked up slowly, recognizing one of the soldiers.

"Joe, 'tis me, Thomas Annely," I called out. "Aye, Mr. Annely, what brings you here?" he questioned as he introduced me to the other guard.

"Robert, I would like you to meet Mr. Thomas Annely. He is the finest gunsmith in all the colonies."

"You don't say, pleased to meet you, Mr. Annely. Are you as good a gunsmith as Joseph says you are?" he inquired.

"You should know, Robert. You are carrying one of my muskets."

"Is that a fact? Well, I must say, this musket has been a true shot to me," he replied.

"Take care of her, and she will take care of you, son," I replied.

I returned to my urgent need, "Joe, I need to speak with General Washington about a most important matter. I would be forever in your debt if you could get me an audience with the General."

Joe scratched his head, contemplating my request, "Aye, Mr. Annely, 'tis a tall order, but I will do my best to get you a meeting. 'Tis too late now, but come back early in the morning. I will make sure you get to see at least one of the Generals, if not the man himself. There is a tavern up the road, with fine rooms, where you can stable your horse and bunk down for the night."

"Much obliged, Joe; I will do that, but I have another request before leaving for the evening. My son Chip joined the army last year, and I have not heard from him since. Can either of you tell me any information about him? He goes under the name of Charles "Chip" Annely."

The soldiers paused and looked at each other, shaking their heads. "Sorry, Sir. Neither of us knows of him, but we will look into his whereabouts and relay any information to you," replied Joe. "'Tis good of you both to help me. I will see you bright and early in the morning," I replied, mounting my horse and heading to the Inn.

The bed at the Inn was comfortable enough, but sleep did not come easy. Wide awake, I rehearsed the words I would say to the General in my head over and over again. I had finally drifted off, only to be woken a few hours later by the morning sun beaming through the window. I dressed quickly, gulped down my tea and biscuits, and retrieved my horse. "Well, my boy, at least one of us slept," I said, patting the head of my trusted horse.

I arrived at the Fort, early as planned, and saw Robert standing guard. "Come in, Mr. Annely. You must be an important man because when I gave the General your name, he said he would be glad to see you," said Robert. I patted him on his back, thanking him as I followed him to the headquarters, with my horse in tow behind me.

I sat in the foyer of the grand home on one of the elegant, high-backed chairs lined up in the entryway. I watched soldiers of all ranks walk in and out of the General's office. I was growing weary when, finally, a soldier approached me and said, "General Washington will see you now, Sir."

I enthusiastically jumped up and followed the young soldier to the General's office.

I walked in to find General Washington standing with his hands clasped behind his back, gazing out the window. I could not help but feel in awe of this man, who was well over six feet tall. He had broad shoulders and a head of reddish-brown hair tied back in a neat tail at the base of his neck. As he turned to face me, his blue grey eyes, strong chin, and prominent nose commanded attention before he even spoke.

I bravely walked toward him, held out my hand, and humbly said, "General Washington, I am deeply grateful that you have taken the time to see me, Sir."

"Good morning, Mr. Annely; it is my pleasure to meet you. Your name is not foreign to me. I am well aware of all you have done for our cause. I thank you, Sir, for your service," he expressed with a sincerity I had not expected as he shook my hand.

"Thank you kindly, Sir; I am your humble servant and will continue to serve you as long as you need me," I said proudly. "General Washington, I have an urgent matter that I pray you can help me with."

General Washington raised his hand to halt my speech, "Before you begin, Mr. Annely, the issue of your sister's plight has already been brought to my attention. Your good brother-in-law, Francis Lewis, alerted the Board of War, who, in turn, informed me of this matter. I immediately wrote to General Howe of the British Army and demanded your sister Elizabeth Lewis's release. I informed him that the atrocities the British army had put upon her were unthinkable. Rest assured, I have turned over this matter to the capable hands of General Greene. He will be in charge of negotiations for her release as quickly as possible," he said assuringly.

General Washington continued, "I think very highly of your brother-in-law Francis. He has fought as hard as any soldier for this country's freedom in Congress. From what I have been told, your sister is no less brave and should be commended for her devotion to our cause. It seems that all of the Annelys are brave Patriots. Trust me when I say I will not give up until your sister is free."

The General then walked around his desk and placed his arm around my shoulder, "General Greene will send word to you as soon as he starts the negotiations with the British involved in this matter and will keep you informed of his progress. Mrs. Washington and I will keep your brave sister in our prayers," he expressed, walking me out to the foyer.

I shook his hand again and said, "May God bless you and your troops and keep you safe, Sir." General Washington smiled and wished me a safe journey home. "I could never repay you enough, Sir," I replied. The General answered, "Mr. Annely, no repayment is necessary; just continue with the good work you have been doing for my troops."

I rode home to Elizabethtown, feeling more confident after I met with the good General. Yet, I will not rest easy until my sister Elizabeth is free and out of harm's way.

THOMAS ANNELY

# CHAPTER

## 43

**FRANCIS LEWIS II**
Actual Portrait

The months were moving along, and winter was now upon us. We were working diligently to keep producing arms, but the war was not going well for General Washington. After his defeat in New York, he fled to New Jersey, only to be forced to retreat to Pennsylvania. The highly experienced British Army seemed too much for our inexperienced soldiers, yet General Washington had no intentions of considering defeat.

I became increasingly aggravated, worrying about my sister, Elizabeth, suffering in that cold, dingy cellar. What made the matter worse was that neither Francis nor I could go anywhere near the city, lest we would surely be captured. If not for Kingsley risking his life sneaking food and letters to her, I am sure she would have lost all hope. As brave as my sister is, how much can one woman endure?

It was the eve before Christmas, and I was looking forward to a peaceful night of celebrating with just a few of us. It was difficult to welcome the holiday cheer, with Elizabeth suffering in that terrible jail and Chip away, fighting for his country.

Sarah did her best to keep Christmas in our hearts, warmly decorating the home and cooking all our Christmas favorites. The aroma of the savory ham roasting on the spit filled the entire house. The snow had begun to fall heavily, promising a White Christmas.

Ward struggled up the snow-filled stairs, carrying gifts in one arm while helping Sally with his other. "Happy Christmas to you both. Let me help you there, son," I shouted, meeting them halfway.

Sarah rushed to greet our guests as they stood at the door, shaking the snow off their coats. "Brrrr! It's freezing out there," said Sarah, ushering them inside.

"Uncle Thomas and Aunt Sarah, I want you to meet Sally Sullivan. She and her family own and operate Buckheads Tavern," said Ward, proudly introducing his lovely girlfriend.

"Merry Christmas, Mr. and Mrs. Annely. It is a pleasure meeting you." Sally handed Sarah a nicely wrapped bottle of wine from her father's wine cellar. "Oh, this is lovely, dear. It will go well with our dinner." Sarah smiled at the pretty young girl and nodded her approval at Ward. "My father chose this particular wine from his collection for you both. He sends his regards to you, Mr. Annely," said Sally. "Please be sure to give him my thanks. It has been a while since I have seen him. How is your father?"

Sally lowered her eyes, "He has not been well, Mr. Annely. My brother William and I have been overseeing all his properties and tending to the tavern in his absence."

Sarah placed her hand on Sally's shoulder, "We will be sure to keep him in our prayers, dear."

"Tonight, we will enjoy his fine wine and toast to his health," I said, holding up the bottle of wine.

Sally smiled sweetly, "Thank you both for your kind words," she expressed.

Sally gazed upon the room, admiring the tall pine tree decorated with brightly colored ornaments and candles flickering on the branches. The fireplace was equally festive with its drape of fresh garland of holly leaves and red berries. She held back the tears, for she had not seen such a festive home since her dear mother had passed. "Your home is lovely and so nicely decorated," Sally remarked.

"Thank you, dear; come warm yourselves by the fire and enjoy some of Thomas's special punch," Sarah said, winking at Sally.

"'Tis only a fruit drink with a tinge of rum," I chuckled as I filled a glass for each of us.

"Where is that little cousin of mine? Sally is eager to meet the lad," smiled Ward.

Phoebe entered the room, carrying Gifford, dressed befittingly for the holiday in a knitted red sweater and matching cap upon his head. Sally fell instantly in love with our boy and could not stop coddling him. Watching the young couple, clearly in love, I felt it would not be long before Ward would have his own son bouncing upon his knee.

"Sally, I want you to meet Phoebe; she will join us tonight for Christmas Eve dinner. My sister-in-law, Elizabeth, was kind enough to allow her to stay with me to help with Gifford. I would be lost without her," said Sarah, making Phoebe's face flush red. "Thank you kindly, Mrs. Sarah," she replied timidly.

The mood was light and cheery as everyone overindulged with wine and extra helpings of the delicious meal Sarah had prepared.

"I hope you all saved room for dessert," announced Sarah, tempting them with a warm apple pie, its aroma filling the room. "Oh my, I cannot eat another bite," said Sally, placing her hand on her stomach. "Well, I will eat her share!" said Ward, reaching over and taking a large slice. "That goes for me too!" I said as Sarah served me a slice.

We were giddy with laughter from too much wine when, suddenly, a loud knock came upon the door. I glanced at Sarah with a puzzled expression, wondering who could be at the door on this stormy night. I walked over to the stairway, with Ward following closely behind me. I opened the door slowly, squinting my eyes through the blustery snow. There stood a young man wearing a ragged Continental uniform, his hat and cloak covered in snow, looking downward to shield himself from the cold.

The lad lifted his chin and looked directly at me. "Good evening, Sir. My name is James Dolan. I am a soldier in the Continental Army. Would you be Thomas Annely?"

"Yes, lad, I am Thomas Annely."

Ward came forward and instantly recognized him, "Why, you're Chip's friend. Sally, 'tis Jimmy Dolan!" he shouted excitedly across the room. Sally rushed over as Ward and I helped the young soldier into the house. "Jimmy, you are freezing," she expressed, removing his wet cloak and hat.

The young man's eyes brightened at the sight of Sally, yet his somber expression remained. He stood there shivering, holding something rather large, wrapped in a burlap bag close to his chest.

I led him over to the fire, "Have a seat and warm yourself, son." Sarah brought over a glass of brandy. "Here, drink this, young man. It will help warm you," she said softly.

The holiday cheer turned to an awkward silence as we all sat, staring at the young man, anxiously awaiting him to speak.

Jimmy looked at us and said, "I have something to say that is important to me, and I know it will be important to you all."

"It all started when Chip and I joined General Washington's army in '75. All of us lads from Buckheads Tavern were eager to help the General win the war. With very little training, we were told we were ready for action. For months on end, we fought together all along the countryside. It did not take us long to discover what war was truly about. All this time, our officers told us not to write to our families for fear that the British would find out where we were."

"The nights were cold and lonely, but Chip kept us all amused with his stories. We would sit around the campfire as he told his tales, mostly about you, Mr. Annely. He told us how you taught him all about gunsmithing, and how to shoot accurately. He also told us about the duel and what a great shot you are." The lad paused and smiled. "Because of you, Sir, Chip was the best shooter in our regiment."

Jimmy lowered his voice, speaking softly, "At one of the battles, Chip and I were hiding behind an old stone wall, crouching down to stay out of sight. We could hear cannonballs exploding in the distance, striking closer and closer. Chip peeked from behind the wall to see where the cannonballs were coming from. Suddenly, he leaped on top of me and pushed me to the ground. A tremendous explosion struck the stone wall we were hiding behind, and pieces of rock flew all over us."

Jimmy's voice choked with emotion. He paused to clear his throat before continuing.

"When the dust and debris settled, Chip's bruised body was lying flat on top of me. I gently rolled him over; his broken musket was still in his hand. We looked into each other's eyes, and Chip whispered, "Don't forget your promise, Jimmy.""

"He closed his eyes, took a last breath, and died in my arms," Jimmy said, weeping.

My heart sank, not wanting to believe what I was hearing, that my boy Chip was dead. We all stood up and hugged each other, sharing the pain.

Jimmy stood up, soldierlike, as he addressed me directly. "Mr. Anely, Chip sacrificed himself to protect me. I am here to fulfill my promise. It is the least I could do for my friend, who saved my life."

Jimmy laid the bundle he was carrying on the table, slowly unveiling it. There it was, lying in front of me, my favorite musket. Chip had kept his promise to return my musket to me.

Filled with emotion, I reached for the broken musket and held it in my arms, letting my tears fall freely.

"I am sorry for bringing you such bad news, but I am honored I was able to fulfill Chip's wishes," Jimmy said sadly.

I gently placed my musket on the table and wrapped my arms around the lad. "Thank you, son. It took great courage to come here. Your words have brought us much comfort, knowing my son, Chip, died so valiantly," I said, firmly embracing the young man.

"I must take my leave now, Sir, and get back to my regiment immediately," Jimmy said, despite our pleas for him to stay until the storm passed.

I stood at the door, watching him leave as he trudged through the heavy snow. Silence filled the room, for no amount of words could ease our pain. I walked over to my young son Gifford, sitting on Sarah's lap. I touched his soft cheek, gazing at him with sadness, for he would never know what a wonderful big brother he had.

I looked over at the spot above my fireplace that had been empty for over a year. Picking up my musket, I lifted it above my head and gently placed it back where it belonged on the two wooden pegs.

The others watched me, their eyes filled with tears, as I stared at my musket. Yet, I was not seeing my musket; I was seeing my son Chip's face.

That evening, lying in our bed, Sarah softly wept while I held her in my arms. "Why our Chip?" she sobbed. "Chip died a hero, Sarah, something we should all be proud of. All he ever wanted was for me to be proud of him." I said, choking on my words. I held Sarah, comforting her, until she finally drifted off to sleep.

The visions of Chip lying there, with my musket grasped in his hand, kept me from sleeping. I quietly slid out of bed and gently took down my musket from above the fireplace. Lighting a lantern, I walked softly downstairs to my shop and placed my musket on the workbench.

Amongst my scraps of wood, I found a matching piece of butternut walnut. I cut it down and shaped it to the proper size to replace the broken stock. Sanding the wood to a smooth finish, I attached it firmly into place and rubbed warm oil all over the new wood. I could not rest until my musket was whole again and my hands healed its wounds.

As I raised my musket to my shoulder and took aim, I could feel Chip's presence around me. It brought me comfort, making me feel like my boy, Chip, was standing beside me.

I slowly walked back upstairs and placed my musket back over the fireplace, where it belonged. I reached up, put my hand upon it, and whispered, "Chip, wherever you are, know that I am very proud of you. I love you, son." I slumped into my chair, staring at my musket until I fell fast asleep.

THOMAS ANNELY

# CHAPTER
## 44

Despite the bitterly cold air, the snow had turned to rain, pouring down on the city of New York. Elizabeth sat upon the hard stone floor; her body ached from the constant cold that permeated her bones. How she yearned to sit by a burning hearth, sipping a warm cup of tea.

She was becoming too weak to lift herself up, yet she still took time to aid her fellow prisoners. One of the men, Henry, had developed a chronic cough, which kept them all from sleeping at night. With no fear of catching the dreaded cough, Elizabeth would tend to the man, gently pounding on his back to release the fluids trapped in his lungs.

Of all her prison mates, Elizabeth felt most endeared to poor Henry. His crime did not suit his cruel punishment. He was only a hungry peasant man caught stealing food from a British army camp. She could see he was weakening and feared he would not live for very long. She wrapped her blanket around the old man's shivering shoulders, leaving herself vulnerable to the cold, blustering wind that blew through the barred window.

Elizabeth grabbed her sack of clothes, which she had hidden out of the guard's sight. With her hands still shackled, she gave up all hope of changing into the fresh new dress packed inside.

Margaret, the youngest of the prisoners, watched as Elizabeth struggled to pull the dress from the sack. "May I help you with that, Ma'am?" she questioned softly. "Yes, dear; if I rip up this long dress, each of us could have a piece to lay upon," replied Elizabeth. "It is quite kind of you, Ma'am, but you mustn't ruin your beautiful dress."

Elizabeth smiled at the sweet girl, who was no older than seventeen. No one knew why she was here, and the young lass rarely spoke unless spoken to. Elizabeth imagined this pretty young girl must have refused the advances of an older British officer. The girl's long golden hair was matted all around her face, and her sapphire blue eyes appeared dull from weariness.

"You would look lovely in this dress, Margaret," Elizabeth remarked as she handed the dress to the young girl. "Hide this away, my dear, and keep it for when you are released. 'Tis much too frilly for an older lady like myself."

The girl lowered her eyes, and a single tear ran down her cheek. "God bless you, Mrs. Elizabeth. I will treasure it forever," she replied, graciously accepting the gift.

Elizabeth's heart was heavy from the injustices of these British bigwigs. The young girl did not belong here, nor did any of the other poor souls locked up in this dungeon. 'Tis the price they were all paying for refusing to be loyal to the King.

Elizabeth reached into her sack and took out the letter Kingsley had brought from her beloved husband. Bringing it to her lips, she whispered, "Soon, my love, we will be together again." The words she read of Francis's love brought her peace in this unholy place.

> *My dearest Lizzy,*
>
> *How I long for you and me to be together again and away from this bondage of war. I am doing all in my power to demand your release. Each day that passes, I feel your suffering as if it were my own. Hold on to your faith, for the Good Lord is the great protector of the brave. And you, my love, are the most courageous woman I know.*
>
> *May my love for you bring you warmth in the coldest of days. I will not rest until you are released.*
>
> *Your loving husband, Francis*

Elizabeth drifted off to sleep when Margaret tapped her shoulder, "Mrs. Elizabeth, your man Kingsley is here by the window." Her heart quickened as the young girl helped her stand on the chair to greet him. "Dearest Kingsley, you have come again," she expressed barely audible.

Kingsley felt distressed. Seeing the weakness in his brave Mistress was too much for him to bear. He reached in, touching her hand. "Be strong, Mistress. The Master is gonna get you out of here soon," he said reassuringly.

Elizabeth leaned in closer, whispering, "Kingsley, I beg of you, please tell Thomas about the hiding place at Whitestone. If all is still there, you have my permission to retrieve my valuables and store them safely until I get out of this horrid place."

"Yes, Mistress," Kingsley dutifully replied, although he had strong doubts anything could have survived the fire.

Kingsley would get word to Thomas as quickly as possible about Elizabeth's request, but he was more concerned for his poor Mistress. What hid amongst the ashes at Whitestone was not as important to him as his Mistress's wellbeing. Kingsley had to find a way to get to Thomas so they could try to retrieve any of Elizabeth's belongings. More importantly, they needed to get his Mistress out of this horrible prison.

# THOMAS ANNELY
## CHAPTER
## 45

**CHANCELLOR ROBERT R. LIVINGSTON**
Actual Portrait

One day, while working in my gunshop, I heard loud hoof-beats hitting the hardened ground nearby. I gazed out my window and was surprised to see a soldier come to a sudden stop. He dismounted, hitched his horse, and banged loudly on my door. I got up quickly, went over, and opened the door to find an impressive young officer dressed in full Continental Army blues. He wore a handsome black hat with a red cockade, gold epaulets on each shoulder, and a red sash around his waist. A brass hilt sword hung from his hip.

Stunned by his presence, I let the young Officer speak first. "I am looking for a Mr. Thomas Annely?" he inquired.

"I am Thomas Annely. How can I help you, Officer?" I replied, ushering him inside.

"Good day, Mr. Annely, I am Colonel Richard Barker. I have an important message from General Nathanael Greene. Do you have a private area where we may speak?"

"Yes, please come inside my office," I replied, anxious to hear what he had to say.

Standing rigid with a reserved expression, the young Colonel took a letter from his breast pocket and began to read, "What I am about to tell you must be kept strictly between us." I nodded as he read on:

General Greene has written:

> "After exhausting all diplomatic ways of obtaining the release of Mrs. Lewis, the board has chosen a different strategy. General Washington will be ordering the house arrest of the wives of two prominent British loyalists: Mrs. Barren, wife of the British Paymaster General, and Mrs. Kempe, wife of the Attorney General of Pennsylvania. The ladies will be kept in their homes until Mrs. Lewis is released. If they do not agree to the exchange, their wives will suffer the same ill-treatment Mrs. Lewis has been subjected to. This plan will be put into action immediately, and we are confident it will be successful."

"Thank the Lord, 'tis great news. Please give my deepest gratitude to General Greene and General Washington," I replied, vigorously shaking the young Officer's hand.

"Sir, I will be sure to give your message to both Generals. I hope to return soon to report the results of General Greene's plan. I will be taking my leave now," he said, folding the letter and placing it back in his pocket. I thanked the Officer as I walked him to the door.

'Twas good news for sure, yet it was difficult for me to have much faith that these bloody British officials would take heed of it. I desperately hope that General Greene's plan works; otherwise, I'll have to break Elizabeth out of that wretched prison myself.

As I walked out back to my gunshop, I heard clapping and cheering coming from the men. Ward handed me the front page of the latest edition of the New Jersey Gazette, which read:

> *December 27, 1776*
> *WASHINGTON'S CHRISTMAS SURPRISE*
> *On Christmas night, amidst the bitter cold winds of an icy blizzard storm, General George Washington, in a daringly bold move, ordered his troops of 2300 men onto longboats and crossed the half-frozen Delaware River. Once again, Thomas Paine's rousing words surged through the men of the Continental Army, reigniting the fires ablaze that were smoldering within their souls.*
>
> *Early the next morning, he marched his tired and long-suffering troops to Trenton, to where the British allies, the Hessians, were sound asleep from too much holiday celebration.*
>
> *Washington and his troops roused the sleeping enemy, catching them completely off guard and capturing nearly 900 Hessians, suffering no casualties on the American side. The fearless Patriot soldiers, filled with a renewed sense of duty and pride, followed their fearless leader into battle, first in Trenton and then onward to Princeton!*

*Washington was victorious in both battles! General George Washington has regained the confidence of Congress and the people, thus strengthening our faith in the cause.*

After reading this article, the glorious news of Washington's triumphant battles made me proud that I had joined the Continental Army. I felt honored that we had supplied these brave men with arms. It did my heart good to know that all hope was not gone. Wholeheartedly, I knew I would never give up the fight as long as I lived. I was proud to be an American.

THOMAS ANNELY

# CHAPTER 46

Kingsley rushed to his makeshift home in the back of Francis Jr.'s merchant store. He gathered his belongings, some of the money Elizabeth had given him, and scribbled a note for young Francis. "Gone to see Master Thomas, be back soon," was all he could muster with his limited writing skills.

His back ached, and his legs were worn and tired, yet he carried on in devotion to his Mistress's wishes. Having no family of his own to speak of, the Annely's and the Lewis's were the only ones who took kindly to him. When he fled the cruelty of a southern master, he found peace and harmony, first with Richard in New York and then at Whitestone. He felt mutually respected by his new masters. He would gladly go to the ends of the earth to serve his beloved Mistress and the family he belonged to.

Kingsley's old legs would not make the journey all the way to New Jersey, so he went to see Howie at his Inn along the Hudson River. He knew he could rely on Howie to ferry him over the river and, perhaps, find him a horse to ease his travels.

Howie stood in his usual place by the river, yelling orders at the young lads tending to his ferries. "Kingsley!" Howie shouted out, surprised to see the old man.

"'Tis good to see you, Mr. Howie," Kingsley replied meekly.

"Come inside and rest. You look a wee bit weary." Kingsley sat on the padded bar stool, resting his tired legs.

Howie went behind the bar and poured two shots of brandy, placing one in front of Kingsley. "Thank you kindly, Sir, but I do not take the drink of the spirits," he replied.

Howie sat beside Kingsley and patted him on the back, "Go on and drink; it will do you good."

Kingsley gingerly sipped as the warmth of the brandy trickled down his throat. He smiled and tipped his glass to Howie, "'Tis good, Sir."

Mary, hearing voices coming from the empty tavern, came bustling out and stopped abruptly, startled to see Howie sitting at the bar with an old Negro man.

"Mary, come and meet Kingsley. He is Elizabeth and Francis's manservant," Howie called out.

Kingsley stood to greet Mary, "Please to meet you, Ma'am," he replied, extending his hand to Mary. Mary hesitated, for she rarely saw a colored man, let alone touch the hand of one. She gathered her senses, smiled, and held his hand as he gently grasped hers.

The man was rail thin and looked so tired that Mary's motherly instincts overtook her. "Come sit at this table, and I will bring you something to eat," she said as she hurried back to the kitchen.

"I am much obliged to you both," said Kingsley to Howie.

"Mary, bring something for me, too. I am famished!" Howie shouted back.

"So, Kingsley, what brings you here today?"

"Sir, my Mistress is in prison, and she ain't doing so well. I need to see Thomas," he said, his eyes downcast.

"Those bloody Brits, they will stop at nothing. When did this happen? I have not heard a word," Howie angrily replied.

"'Tis been a few months now, and they are treating her real bad," Kingsley said, with tears forming in his eyes.

Howie placed his hand on the weakened old man's shoulder, "That's awful news, for sure. How can I help you?"

"I can't walk that far, and I will need a ferry ride over the river and a horse if you got one."

"Not to worry, Kingsley, I will take care of you. My men will ferry you over and set you up with a horse from my stables across the river. Be sure to travel the back trail, away from the British checkpoints," Howie warned.

"Yes, Sir, 'tis very kind of you," Kingsley replied.

"Thomas is like a son to me; I will do anything for him and his family. I wish I could go with you, but this old man has grown too weak to travel. God bless you, Kingsley," Howie said sincerely.

Mary came out with a feast and set it before Kingsley. He smiled warmly at the elderly lady and thanked her profusely. He had not realized how hungry he was until he smelled the delicious meal.

"Mary, Kingsley will be journeying to see Thomas; fix him up with a pack of food."

Kingsley was overwhelmed with the kindness bestowed upon him and was sure the meal they served him was plenty, but there was no refusing the generosity of these kind people.

Kingsley went on his way, heeding Howie's advice to avoid the British checkpoints. The trip was longer than he remembered as he traveled along the rough trails. He feared he would not find his way. He felt relieved when he came upon a familiar road and quickened his horse to a gentle gallop. Soon, he arrived at Thomas's home. He tied up his horse and walked up the stairway, knocking gently upon the door.

Sarah and Phoebe were inside cooking dinner at the hearth when they heard the knocking on the door. "I will see who is there," Phoebe announced as she answered the door. Sarah looked on apprehensively, wondering who might be visiting at this time of day.

"'Tis Kingsley, Mrs. Sarah," she called out with excitement. A wide smile spread across her face at the sight of her old friend.

Sarah rushed to the door, helping him to the hearth. "Kingsley, sit here and warm yourself. Is Elizabeth alright?" she questioned anxiously.

"She ain't doing so well, Missus. I got to see Thomas straight away," he replied with labored breath.

"Phoebe, go and fetch Thomas," said Sarah as she served Kingsley tea.

I was startled to see Phoebe entering the workshop. She was always too shy to come inside, with all the young men working here.

"Mr. Thomas," she said, her voice quivering. "Kingsley is here and gots to see you now." I put down the musket I was working on and followed her quickly up the stairs, anxious to hear what Kingsley had to say.

As I rushed inside, Sarah grabbed my arm to stop me. "Elizabeth is alright, Thomas, but she is not doing well. Kingsley will tell you." I let out a sigh of relief, for I was fearing the worst.

Kingsley jumped up from his seat when I walked into the room. "Master Thomas, you got to get Elizabeth out of that awful place," he exclaimed excitedly.

I tried to calm the shaken old man. "'Tis alright, Kingsley. Have a seat now, and I will explain," I said as he sat back down. I pulled up the hassock and sat facing him. "A very good plan has been put in place; you need not worry. Francis and I will make sure she is out of there soon," I said, trying to ease his anxious mind.

Kingsley leaned forward and placed his bony fingers upon my shoulder, "'Tis got to be soon, Sir. She's getting mighty weak in there. She asked me to go to Whitestone," he said.

"For what, Kingsley? From what I know, the soldiers burnt it to the ground," I said with frustration.

"When the Mistress was preparing for the worst, she hid her good things deep in a hole in the cellar. She's beggin' me, Thomas, to go and get them. I'm scared as the dickens the fire has burnt it all." Kingsley said, his eyes pooling with tears.

"You are probably right, Kingsley. Whitestone is completely gone. I will get word to her, explaining this as gently as possible."

Kingsley grabbed onto my shoulder with the strength of a much younger man. "No, Thomas, I gotta go. I promised Mrs. Elizabeth I would try!"

I sat back, placed my hand under my chin, and stared directly into Kingsley's passionate black eyes.

"We will leave in the middle of the night," I replied to Kingsley's relief.

Sarah, listening intently, spoke out. "Thomas, are you sure you want to do this? You know you cannot go to New York. Those British bullies will capture you and put you away for good!" she cried, turning her back to me.

"Don't worry, Sarah; I know these woods much better than the bloody redcoats. Ward will come with me. We will take the back roads and appear as any other farmers, traveling to deliver their goods."

Sarah turned to face me, eyes red from tears, "I know nothing I say will stop you from going, but you must promise me you will be extra cautious. Do you hear me, Thomas Annely?" I wrapped my arms around her and said, "Yes, my love."

At midnight, we went down to the stables to meet Ward. He was already there, hitching up my two strongest horses and my largest wagon for the journey. "Good to see you, Ward; I appreciate you being here on time," I told my devoted nephew.

"Anything for my Aunt Elizabeth, 'tis the least I can do for all she has endured," Ward expressed.

While Ward readied the team and wagon, I loaded up three muskets and a few pistols and hid them in the crook behind the seat. Kingsley, wide awake with a new spring in his step, joined us in the stable. I was amazed by the strength of this older man as he effortlessly lifted the tools and pickaxes, hiding them in the back of the wagon. I pulled out one of the muskets and handed it to Kingsley, "Do you know how to shoot one of these?" I questioned.

"Yes, Sir, the Mistress taught me long ago," he said proudly. I smiled at the thought of my brave sister teaching this humble man how to shoot.

"Keep this behind you, and don't use it until I give the word. Do you understand?" I said sternly.

"Yes, Master Thomas," he replied, placing the musket behind the end seat.

I sprinted up the stairs to say my goodbyes to Sarah, who was waiting for me, holding a basket in her hand. "Here, Thomas, take this food and drink with you."

"'Tis not necessary, love; we won't be gone that long," I replied.

"Thomas, it's a long journey; you will take this with you," she insisted.

I took the basket and kissed her cheek, "Thank you, dear. You are too good to me."

Sarah smiled, "Never you mind flattering me, Sir Thomas. You get back here as quickly as you can."

I walked over to my son's cradle, bent down, and kissed his forehead. I paused, gazing at the peaceful babe, sleeping soundly.

THOMAS ANNELY

# CHAPTER 47

**AARON BURR**
Actual Portrait

Beneath the clear night sky we rode along to Whitestone, covering ourselves from the cold, praying the weather would remain fair for traveling. The back trails kept us away from the British lines, but it took us all the longer to reach our destination. Kingsley kept us amused by telling us daring stories about his youth. He had lived along the wild Gambia River in Africa, where he hunted crocodiles, selling their skins to the local merchants. He boasted about how he and his brother would throw rocks in the river at the mighty hippopotamus and then run like the wind when they chased after them. It sounded all so exotic and foreign to me, for I had never seen either of the creatures.

It was along that river that he was ripped from his family; whisked away in chains to a strange land and made to do manual labor. If not for the Mistress, he felt he would be dead by now. To him, Elizabeth was a gift from God.

As we came upon the Hudson River, one of Howie's men helped us board the ferry and get across. Thankfully, the river was calm today, and the ride was smooth. When we reached the other side, I saw my good friend Howie tending to his ferry boats. As we approached, he quickly came to greet us. "Thomas, good to see you, Mate. What brings you all here today?"

I grasped Howie's hand. "Good to see you as well, my friend. We are on our way to Whitestone."

"Alas, Kingsley told me all about Elizabeth and the damage at Whitestone. You know you can count on me if you need anything."

"Thank you kindly, Howie. It has been a difficult time."

"Come inside and have a drink on me," he offered. I hesitated, knowing we needed to get to our task at hand.

"Aye, Howie, we must get to Whitestone before the sun rises." Howie understood as we said our goodbyes, promising to take him up on that offer soon.

I could feel the hairs standing up on the back of my neck as we rode through the city streets of New York. I tipped my hat lower and kept the team to a slow trot, hoping not to draw attention to us. It took everything in my power to stay the course and not head my wagon over to where Elizabeth was being held in prison. Finally, we reached the East River, loaded the wagon and team on a sturdy flatboat, and floated across. I could feel my nerves settling as we reached the other side.

As we made our way to Whitestone, I barely recognized the trail I had traveled so many times before. Homes were burnt to the ground, and the trees were all cut down, their broken branches strewn all over the ravaged fields. The countryside was deserted, with only a few scavengers looting whatever they could find and throwing it in their small wagons.

Coming around the bend, Kingsley pointed to where Whitestone once stood. I pulled in on the reins and looked aghast at the piles of broken white stones amongst the burnt-out shell of what was once Elizabeth's magnificent home. Nothing could have prepared me for the sight of it. The house where I spent so many happy Sundays was now gone, ruined beyond repair. The silence was unsettling; not even the sound of birds chirping could be heard.

Kingsley jumped down, grabbed a pickaxe from the back, and rushed over to the rubble. "Kingsley, wait, you will hurt yourself!" I yelled out to no avail. With his strong arms, he smashed the stones to pieces and pushed them aside, searching frantically. Ward and I jumped off the cart and ran over to Kingsley, trying to get him to stop. Kingsley hesitated for a moment, gasping for breath. I asked him softly to calm down and try to remember the cellar's location. He slowly stood up, scanned the area with his eyes, and called out, "There, that is the place!" he said as he swiftly climbed over to the area.

Ward and I climbed over the rubble to where Kingsley was already moving the heavy stones aside. I looked downward and could see an opening between the stones. We all worked in unison, clearing the area of all the stones and making a large hole. Ward pushed his way by us and squeezed down inside until he was out of sight. "Ward, are you alright?" I yelled down inside. "I am fine; step aside; you are blocking the light!" he shouted, his voice echoing through the hole.

Ward landed in what was once the wine cellar. He blocked his nose from the overwhelming smell of fermented grapes. Broken wine bottles were strewn all around his feet. He squinted and saw a small wooden door with a pile of stones partially blocking it. He could not believe his eyes that the door was still intact. "Throw down an ax; I think I found the door!" he yelled excitedly. "Mind your head, son; here it comes!" I shouted, dropping the ax down to him.

Ward swung the ax with all his strength, breaking the rocks, and pried the door open. He crouched over and crawled inside, amazed to find all of Elizabeth's valuables covered in dust but unharmed from the fire. He let out a loud howl and shouted, "'Tis all here!"

"Good job, son. Is there enough room for us to come down?"

"Give me a little time to clear some space first!" Ward yelled.

While I waited for Ward to clear an opening, I walked over to where my brother Richard and Elizabeth's four babies were buried. I was happy to see the grave site was unharmed as I stood and paid homage. The only solace I felt was knowing that Richard never had to see his beautiful Whitestone burnt into a pile of rubble. I dreaded the day Elizabeth would have to see her home this way.

I returned to helping Kingsley clear the stones above the hole while Ward was busy below. After hours, we finally made the hole large enough to enter. Ward stacked some old wine crates that miraculously survived the fire, giving us a foothold to stand upon.

He began to empty the contents, handing them to us, one by one. We gingerly handled the portrait of Richard, carefully wrapping it in a blanket. There were treasured books, pieces of fine linen, chinaware, solid silver candelabras, and a metal locked box that had us all curious about its contents. I was overjoyed to see the musket that my father had made was in there as well.

When he handed me the portrait of Elizabeth, in her youthful beauty, it nearly brought tears to my eyes. Piece by piece, we worked together, removing the valuables and loading them into the wagon. We were all so grateful that none of the scavengers had been here before us. "That's all of it," shouted Ward as he shimmied back up the hole.

By this time, it was getting late. Kingsley had lit a fire amongst the broken-up hearth. He had brought Sarah's basket of food from the back of the wagon, along with our pistols and muskets, and placed them beside the makeshift fireplace. The sun had set, and we were all tired and hungry. Thank the Lord for Sarah's stubbornness, convincing me to bring the food and drink.

The sky turned to blackness with stars as bright as the sparks of the fire burning. In the quiet of the evening, we rested, lost in our thoughts, devouring the food Sarah had prepared. It brought back memories of when Chip and I would sleep out under the illuminated sky, enjoying the fresh night air and the moon casting shadows upon the river.

Suddenly, we heard the horses grunting and the sounds of people talking. Ward stood and said he thought he could see people standing near our wagon. I grabbed my musket in one hand and my pistol in the other and stood, ready to face the intruders. The voices became louder as the silhouettes of a petite woman and two men came into view in the light of the fire.

They stopped, and the men pointed their muskets at us. "What can I do for you all?" I asked boldly.

The man spoke gruffly, "I'll tell you what you can do. The stuff in that wagon belongs to us. This is our area to salvage, not yours! You best be getting along and leaving that wagon with us."

My blood was beginning to boil as I spoke, "Sir, I don't know who you are, but I know who I am, and this is my sister's property, and those goods in my wagon belong to her. Who might you be?" I questioned angrily.

"Mister, my name is Ben Conners; this is my wife, June, and my son, Michael. The Brits took everything, and we got nothing except for the tent we are living in down the road. We had no choice but to salvage whatever we could and sell it in town to survive. That's who we are, Sir," he replied solemnly.

Seeing the two men pointing their muskets at the three of us, Ward spoke angrily, "If I were you, I would point those muskets in a different direction because the man next to me has a musket in one hand and a pistol in the other. He is the fastest and the most accurate shooter you will ever meet. If he thinks you mean to harm us, you won't live to regret it."

The two men quickly pointed their muskets to the ground, heeding Ward's warning.

I was proud of my nephew's show of bravado as I walked over to the man. "I see you are a smart man, Ben. Why don't you and your family come by the fire and share some food with us?"

The man and his wife sat down beside their son and graciously accepted the food we offered. He went on to tell us the story of how the British took all their livestock, ransacked their home, and burnt it to the ground. "Those bloody sons of bitches took everything we owned and didn't leave us with anything to live upon," he ranted while his wife remained silent, nodding her head.

As we sat around the fire, sharing our stories, I felt compassion for them. Like so many, they were hard-working folks who had to resort to stealing to survive during these most difficult times.

Taking pity on the family, I reached into my leather pouch and pulled out a handful of shillings. I took the man aside and handed the coins to him, "Take these, please, and go buy your family some food."

The man refused the coins, "No Sir, you have given us so much already."

I reached for his hand and folded the coins within it, "It will make me feel good to do something for you and your family," I said sincerely.

The man grasped my hand, thanking me profusely for the coins as he gathered his family to leave. We said our goodbyes and watched them walk back to their makeshift home.

"Time to get a move on fellas. Remember, the night is on our side," I said to Ward and Kingsley. It had grown so late, which was just as well, for it was best to travel in the dark, especially going into the city. I decided we would bring Elizabeth's valuables to my townhouse and hide them in the basement. Despite how weary we felt, we still had our work cut out for us.

We snuffed out the fire, secured the goods in the back, and headed for my townhouse.

As we crossed the East River, the city streets were quiet, except for a few drunken soldiers coming from the shady part of town. We managed to get to my townhouse without being stopped, a miracle unto itself. Ward and I unloaded the wagon while Kingsley watched for curious British soldiers. The poor man had pushed himself too much and was quite tired.

I was pleased to find my townhouse was in good order. It had been a while since anyone had been here. I could see how weary Ward and Kingsley were, so I knew it would be too much to travel all the way back to New Jersey. "We will stay here tonight and leave before the dawn breaks."

Kingsley barely reached the chair when he fell fast asleep, sitting upright. I gently woke him and led him to the small bed in the spare room. Much obliged, he plopped down, falling back asleep as soon as his head hit the bed.

After Ward retired for the night, I sat gazing at the fire, with memories flooding my mind. I could still see Chip tending to the fire and preparing our morning meal. It was not long ago when it was just the two of us, living here and working together at Edward's workshop. That chapter of my life is closed now, yet the memories will always be vivid in my mind. I lowered the fire and went to bed, falling asleep soundly.

I rose long before dawn and woke the men up as well. "Time to go," I said as they stood, still groggy, wiping the sleep from their eyes.

"Would you kindly bring me to Master Francis's store?" questioned Kingsley.

I sat down beside him. "Kingsley, if it is agreeable with you, I would like you to stay here. You could keep an eye on the place for me and watch over Elizabeth's valuables. This is not Whitestone, but I think you will find it much more comfortable than sleeping in the back of Francis's store," I expressed.

He smiled, his dark eyes softening with gratitude, "'Tis my pleasure, Sir. I am much obliged and will watch over your home like it was mine."

It was gratifying to know that Kingsley was a man I could trust and he was always eager to help in any way.

Ward had fetched the team, and soon, we reached the river's edge, where one of Howie's men guided us onto the flatboat to cross the Hudson. The horses grew restless, standing aboard the flatboat as the waters grew rougher. I stood ahead of them, holding their bridles to calm them and keep them still. It was a relief to finally get across the wide river and be back in Jersey.

Not letting our guard down, we followed the same rough path to Elizabethtown. Along the way, we passed a few Continental troops marching, reminding us of the ever-raging war.

When we reached the workshop, Ward let me off at the base of my stairs as he rode the team to the stables out back. I flew up the stairs to find Sarah with young Gifford on her lap at the dining table. She rushed to me, welcoming my embrace, with little Gifford pressed between us.

"I am so glad you are home, Thomas," she expressed softly.

I kissed them both, happy to be back in my own home, away from the ruins that were once our beloved Whitestone.

# CHAPTER
## 48

**M**y shop in Elizabethtown, New Jersey, with Ward at my side, has been very successful. Ward now has the confidence and ability to run my workshop as well, if not better, than I do. Not only has he progressed with his gunmaking skills, but he has also proven to be a good business manager. A much-needed meeting was necessary to discuss my future plans with him.

As the day came to a close, I called him into my office, "Ward, I have much to discuss with you. Is now a good time?" I questioned.

"Of course, Uncle, let me finish up with the lads, and I will be back straight away," he replied, rushing out back to the workshop.

Ward returned quicker than I had anticipated, knocking before entering my office door. "Come in, Ward. Have a seat, son. I suppose you are wondering why I wanted to speak to you?"

"Why yes, I am curious, Sir. I hope everything is alright?" he questioned.

"'Tis more than alright, Ward. You have become invaluable to me and are a good role model to all the lads. I can see how much they respect you."

"Uncle, 'tis because of you that I was able to turn my life around."

"Ward, many men have blundered away their second chances. You, on the other hand, learned from your hard lessons and bettered yourself because of it. You should be as proud of yourself as I am of you. Your mother and father will feel the same when they hear how much you have accomplished."

Ward's face flushed with pride upon hearing my words. "I thank you, Uncle. It means so much to me coming from you."

"Now, I need to tell you why I called you here. With this war raging on, I will be relying on you even more. The troops are having problems with the muskets they are getting from other sources. The muskets the French have been supplying are not performing well. I am needed out in the field to prove and repair these muskets, and I need you to take over for me here while I am gone."

"You can rely on me," he replied.

"Thank you, Ward. You have put my mind at ease. Understand, this will also be a financial gain for you."

"Actually, Uncle, the extra money cannot come at a better time. Sally and I, um, we need to marry straight away. She is with child," he said timidly, his eyes looking up to see my expression.

I hesitated to reply, taking in this sudden news. "I see Ward. Is this happy news?"

"Oh yes, Uncle. We are very happy and love each other deeply," he expressed, hoping for my approval.

"'Tis sudden, for sure, but I am very happy for you both. Sally is a wonderful girl."

I could see the relief washing over my nephew's face as he spoke, "I have been looking for a home near here for Sally and me. We want to be closer to you and Sarah. She has no female relations except Sarah, and when her time comes, she will need help."

"That is wise of you both; Sally should not be alone. You both can come to stay with us; we have more than enough room."

"Are you sure, Uncle? We would not want to be a burden to you both."

"Son, we are family. We must take care of each other, especially during these times. It will be a comfort to Sarah, for Phoebe will be leaving to stay with Kingsley at my townhouse. I would rather she and Gifford not be alone when I travel."

A broad smile swept across Ward's face, "I am certain Sally will be overjoyed to stay at your home. Sarah is like a sister to her, and she adores little Gifford."

"Well, soon she'll have one of her own," I winked.

As Ward went to work, I sat there contemplating all that was happening so quickly around me. I realized I wanted Ward and Sally to live with us not only for Sarah's sake but for my own. The emptiness I felt, with Chip gone, left a hole in my heart. I hoped having the house filled again would help me heal.

Ward and Sally were married in a small ceremony with Sarah and I as their witnesses. Sally's brother Billy proudly walked his sister down the church aisle, for her father was too ill to attend.

"You're getting a fine girl here, Ward," expressed Billy.

"She's more than fine, Billy; she's perfection," replied Ward, smiling at his new bride.

Sarah and I looked on affectionately at the handsome young couple, remembering how joyous we felt on our wedding day.

Phoebe was sitting in the back pew of the church, holding the sleeping Gifford in her arms, crying softly. She had grown quite fond of her newfound family, and the thought of leaving us, especially young Gifford, made her melancholy. But she did miss Kingsley, for he was like a father to her, so she gladly agreed to go live with him in my townhouse.

Ward and Sally were kind enough to bring Phoebe back to my townhouse in New York City before taking a few days' holiday for themselves. Sarah already missed Phoebe, for she was a tremendous help around the home and a most delightful companion. As much as we were sorry to see her leave, we all felt that good old Kingsley should not be alone to fend for himself.

With Ward away, I needed to get to work early, for I had Ward's duties to tend to as well as my own. I had almost forgotten how good it felt to work with my hands, doing what I love: building muskets.

# THOMAS ANNELY

# CHAPTER 49

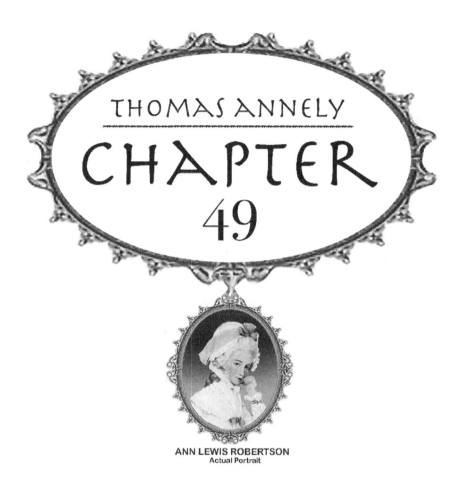

**ANN LEWIS ROBERTSON**
Actual Portrait

I was assembling one of my muskets when one of my workers approached me anxiously, "Excuse me, Sir; there is a messenger here who says he has an urgent letter for you."

I cleaned off my hands with my rag hanging from my hip and rushed over to greet the young messenger standing by the entryway. "Good day, I am Thomas Annely. I understand you have a message for me?"

"Sir, is there somewhere we can speak privately?"

"Yes, of course, right this way." I closed the door to my office behind us as he unfolded the letter.

"Sir, your brother-in-law, Mr. Francis Lewis, has requested your presence at once. The information I will be giving you must be kept secret," he said, waiting for my nod.

"Yes, I understand, of course you have my word."

The young man began reading the letter. "Mr. Lewis and the members of Congress need you to attend a meeting as soon as possible at this location," he said, handing me a rough-drawn map. "You must keep this on your person at all times and destroy it when you reach your destination. It is a two-day journey from here, so plan accordingly. How soon will you be able to leave, Sir?" he inquired urgently.

I had to think quickly. Ward was not due until tomorrow, and I needed him here to run things. "I will do my best to get there within a week."

"Fine, Mr. Annely, I will notify the congressmen to expect you then. The map I supplied you with will take you the safest route. I suggest you travel at night for your safety," he advised as he turned on his heel and took his leave.

I went upstairs and found Sarah preparing our mid-day meal, "Thomas, what brings you home this time of day?"

"Sarah, I received an urgent letter from Fran requesting that I come to meet with Congress at once."

Sarah looked perplexed, "How can you see Francis or the members of Congress? I thought they were at an obscure location that no one could know about?"

"Yes, that is true, Sarah, but I have been ordered to attend and was told not to divulge the location to anyone."

"Thomas, I would like to know where my husband is going," she said demandingly.

"Sarah, please understand. If the British come looking for me, you can honestly say you have no idea where I have gone."

With eyes cast down, Sarah spoke softly, "I understand completely, but it doesn't stop me from being concerned for your welfare, Thomas."

I walked over to her and kissed the top of her head. "You are the best of wives, my love," I expressed.

Sarah sat silently, contemplating all that I had told her. "Sarah, I won't go until Ward and Sally come back. I would never leave you and Gifford alone."

Sarah reached up and grasped my hand, "That is kind of you, dear, but my bed will be lonely without you," she expressed as she stood and wrapped her arms around me.

"Well, it shan't be lonely tonight," I said, welcoming her warm embrace.

Reluctantly, I pulled myself away from her tender arms, "I'm sorry, love, but I must get back to the workshop. I'll be home early tonight to fill your lonely bed."

Sarah smiled coyly, her voice raspy with passion, "I will be holding you to that, Thomas Annely." I hurried off before passion took me over.

Ward and Sally returned a day late, causing me concern for their welfare and fearing I would arrive late for Francis. I had to leave immediately, giving me little time to speak with Ward. Thankfully, Ward did not need much instruction because he knew the work schedule better than me. I saddled up my strongest horse, packed my goods in the saddle bags, sped off just as the sun had set low, and continued to ride for hours.

After a much-needed rest at a nearby inn, I continued with my journey, reaching the destination as planned. I arrived at a massive three-story red brick building with white wood trim that bordered the entire block. I was greeted by a finely-dressed Negro man who took my horse to the large stable out back.

As I entered the impressive foyer adorned with ornate art and portraits, Francis came rushing down the long hallway, "Thomas, 'tis so good of you to come. I don't mean to rush you, but the men are wait-ing." He ushered me into a grand room filled with Francis's fellow del-egates.

I was humbled to be in the presence of such great men. Immediately, I recognized John and Sam Adams, John Hancock, and other distin-guished men. I acknowledged them all with a courteous nod as I sat to the side.

Francis went to the podium to address the room. "Gentlemen, be-fore we commence, I am pleased to tell you we have one of the finest master gunsmiths of our time with us today. He is an Englishman by birth, a gunsmith by trade, and a Patriot by choice. He enlisted in Gen-eral Washington's army and is as devoted to our cause as we are. He has tirelessly given his time and talents to keep our men supplied with some of the finest muskets ever made. I am sure many of you are already aware of his capabilities. And, may I say, he's an excellent marksman as well. Allow me to introduce our honored guest, Mr. Thomas Annely, of New Jersey. Please stand and be seen."

The unexpected reception left me speechless as the men applauded and stamped their canes upon the floor. I swelled with pride from Fran-cis's kind words. Never have I felt so honored to be appreciated by these fine men, who are far superior to me.

Francis went on to discuss some distressing news: "Gentlemen, there is a matter that I regret having to discuss, but it must be said. Congress is having difficulties acquiring funds and is delinquent with its payments to the army and many of our trusted suppliers. I have given much of my own money, which will get us by for a while, but we need money from all of you and your states to support this war."

The men remained silent. Only the sound of throats clearing and muffled coughs could be heard throughout the room.

I listened intently, my weary mind struggling to absorb what Francis was saying. I knew I could manage for a while, but I had just promised Ward more wages.

Francis continued, "Gentlemen, we must address this matter soon; otherwise, there will be no more Continental army. Our good General Washington has contributed far too much of his own money. Good Lord, 'tis enough he has pledged his life to this cause; we cannot expect him to bleed his bank account as well. We must give more if we want to win this war! Need I remind you all of the grave sacrifices these young soldiers are making for our freedom? And our gunsmiths, like Mr. Annely here, are as devoted to the cause as our soldiers. They work night and day for little compensation to meet our never-ending need for arms. 'Tis time, my good men, we make great sacrifices as well. Brothers-in-arms we all are, and brothers-in-arms we will remain until our dying day!" he spoke out boldly.

The men stamped on the floor and cheered, "Hear! Hear!"

I could not have been prouder of my brother-in-law than at this very moment. Even when all seemed lost, he managed to bolster our spirits to carry on.

Francis sat beside me, "Thomas, I hope my introduction was not uncomfortable for you. I know how private you are, but 'tis high time you received the praise you deserve. Two of my fellow delegates are very eager to speak with you," he said, leading me over to where they were seated.

"Thomas, I would like you to meet Mr. William Paca and Mr. Samuel Chase of Maryland," said Francis.

"Pleased to meet you both," I said as they stood to shake my hand. "How can I be of service to you?" I inquired.

Mr. Paca spoke first. "Mr. Annely, firstly, I want you to know we all appreciate your dedication to the cause. Your reputation as a fine gunsmith and marksman is well-known throughout the colonies. Maryland is in desperate need of your extended services." he replied.

Mr. Chase, speaking his turn, said, "Mr. Annely, in our desperation for more guns, we have been purchasing muskets from other sources. I received nothing but complaints from the troops that the quality was inferior. We need someone with your high standards to prove these muskets and pistols before they go to our troops and make sure they are performing correctly," he said.

"Yes, Sir. I am already addressing this issue with other states," I replied.

Mr. Paca, speaking with determination, said, "To put it simply, Mr. Annely, our troops need good, working guns, and lots of them."

I hesitated before I replied, choosing my words cautiously to avoid insulting these fine men. "I understand, Sirs. I may have to employ more workmen, but I will do whatever I must do to meet your needs."

Mr. Paca, seeing my concern, said, "You need not worry about finances. We will heed Mr. Lewis's advice and see that you are paid promptly for all your services."

Francis said, "If Thomas says he will do it, you can rely on him to get it done!"

As we bid each other good day, the men gave me an appreciative smile, confident I would do what they asked of me.

When we left the men, Francis addressed me straight on, "Thomas, I know this is a lot to ask of you, but it will be all worthwhile when we win this bloody war. Rest easy, my friend; Paca and Chase may be lawyers, but they are very honorable men and will abide by their word to you," he said, relieving some of the anxiety that was building inside me.

"I thank you deeply, brother, for all you said and have done for me. You certainly ignited some spirit in your fellow congressmen. I don't know how I would have paid Ward and the men if you had not introduced me to those fine gentlemen," I replied.

Francis touched my shoulder, "Thomas, men like you need never worry, for Providence will always be by your side."

Francis led me upstairs to an unoccupied sitting area. "Have a seat, Thomas," he offered, pouring us both a generous snifter of brandy. He pulled his chair to face me, leaned in, and whispered, "Thomas, tell me what you know of my beloved Elizabeth," he asked with grave concern. "Aye, Fran, she is not faring so well, yet she is still the brave woman we both love."

I told him about when I received the letter from young Francis and learned the shocking news of Elizabeth's imprisonment. "Fran, I was frantic with worry, and with you in seclusion, I felt helpless. I went to General Washington, the only man I knew who could help us. He was not too far from me at Fort Lee, so I rode there like the dickens to plead Elizabeth's case with him. When I arrived at Fort Lee, I was surprised that I had managed to get a meeting with the general. The man is everything I imagined he would be, and he has the highest esteem for you!"

Francis smiled, "The feeling is mutual; George is a remarkable man. He knows very well the admiration I have for him," he replied.

"Fran, I was so grateful when General Washington informed me that you had already alerted the Board of War and that he had put General Greene in charge of Elizabeth's release. I recently received a message saying that General Greene's plan has been executed. I have been praying ever since that it is successful."

Francis stood up, tears forming as he gulped down the last drop of his brandy. Standing with his back to me, he poured himself another brandy as he spoke, "My poor Elizabeth. I can barely get any comforting messages to her while she suffers in that wretched dungeon. What those bloody bastards did to her beloved Whitestone was horrible!"

I stood and put my hand on Francis's shoulder, "'Tis a terrible thing that has happened, but we will persevere. I must tell you one bit of good news: Elizabeth had asked Kingsley and me to go to Whitestone to see if we could salvage any of her valuables. She hid some of your belongings in an old vault in the wine cellar."

Hearing this, Francis smiled through his grieving face, "Aye, my Lizzy, I should have known she would be smart enough to use that hideaway Richard built so long ago," he remarked.

"I thought it was an impossible task, but the devoted Kingsley insisted we go and try. Ward and Kingsley came with me that day. I don't need to tell you how devastated we all felt seeing your home in ruins. Digging through the rubble, we found a way into the cellar, and lo and behold, nothing inside was damaged! We were able to retrieve all the valuables that Elizabeth had hidden and brought them to my townhouse in the city, where we stored them safely away."

Francis replied, "Oh, Thomas, you don't know how relieved I am by what you just told me. 'Tis remarkable what you all did for Elizabeth and me. Tell me, Thomas, did you happen to come upon a strong box with the other belongings?" he asked curiously.

"Why yes, Fran, we did; 'tis safe and secure with the other belongings."

Francis's expression of concern turned to relief, "That is good to hear, Thomas, because what is in that box is very important to me, especially at this time."

"You need not worry, Fran. Your good man Kingsley is living at my townhouse and keeping a sharp eye on the place. Phoebe has gone to stay with him as well."

"Thank you, Thomas. You have greatly eased my mind. I am for-ever grateful to you for all you have done. I don't need to tell you how much I love and miss your sister."

I smiled at him and replied, "I understand completely, my brother, for I feel the same way."

The following day, I joined Fran for breakfast before returning to Elizabethtown. As we bid each other a fond farewell, Francis left me with these parting words: "Thomas, your presence here was just what the congressmen needed. Now they understand how dire the situation is and how much you men in the field need their monetary support. This bloody war stops for no one, and you, my brother, are needed now more than ever."

THOMAS ANNELY

# CHAPTER 50

I remember my journey across the Atlantic to the welcoming shores of New York City so clearly. I was filled with the promise of freedom and determination to forge a new beginning in a city so rich with opportunities. But now that the British troops have infiltrated the city, it has become far too dangerous. Anyone who is found not to be loyal to the crown is considered a traitor.

Kingsley and Phoebe, living in the city, would fare well with the British, provided they pledge allegiance to the King. They would have to wear two faces to ensure their safety.

I finally received the good news from Colonel Barker. General Greene's plan for Elizabeth's release from that dungeon of a prison was successful. However, she would have to stay somewhere in New York City for the duration of her sentence. It was disheartening. We had all hoped she could go to Philadelphia with Francis. However, we were overjoyed that she would finally leave that horrible cell.

We decided that the best place for her to stay was with Kingsley and Phoebe at my townhouse in New York City. I immediately sent word to Kingsley with this great news and instructed him and Phoebe to prepare for Elizabeth's arrival.

Despite feeling miserably depressed in the cold, dark cell, Elizabeth tried her best to keep up the morale of her fellow prison mates. Peter, a young man who left behind a wife and two small children, became especially close to Elizabeth. Her consolation brought him great comfort when he told her about how the British ransacked his home and molested his wife in front of their two young children. It was too much for any man to bear, and when he attacked the British officer, they beat him and brought him here in chains. Often, she heard Peter weeping in the middle of the night.

Elizabeth thought of a way to help herself and the other prisoners stay mentally strong. She assigned each of them a daily chore, giving them a sense of accomplishment over their dreadful situation. "Peter, you are the head of the rat patrol. Make sure those mange-riddled scavengers do not eat better than we do," she said, citing laughter amongst the group of weary prisoners.

Great sadness was felt amongst them all when the kindly old Henry passed on. The stench of his body decomposing had become unbearable. Elizabeth banged on the heavily barred door endlessly until the guards finally came and removed the poor man's body. They watched in horror as the guards dragged his body up the stairs, "No need to break your back on this old bugger, mate; he can't feel a thing," said one of the guards cold-heartedly.

As the days passed, the routine chores broke up the boredom that was dulling their senses. One day, the sounds of the lock clanging and the heavy wooden door creaking open brought them all to their feet. Before them stood two British guards with keys dangling from their waistcoats.

"Which of you is Elizabeth Lewis?" one of the guards called out. Elizabeth walked towards them, "'Tis I, Sir," she replied. "Gather all your belongings, and come with me," he replied gruffly.

"Sir, where are you taking me?" she exclaimed.

"Never you mind where. Come with us peacefully; you'll find out soon enough!"

Elizabeth was frightened, not knowing where they were taking her. As she hastily grabbed her belongings, she glanced back at her cellmates, who looked just as scared as she.

Taking her outside, the guards trudged her through the cold, muddy grounds with no regard for her unsuitable clothing and shoeless feet.

Elizabeth was taken to a small building and escorted inside. She stood there with two British guards at her side, waiting for what seemed like hours. The two guards held onto her tightly so she would not fall.

Finally, the door opened, and a short, plump officer walked in and sat down at the desk before her. He looked up at Elizabeth and said, "My name is Lieutenant John Barker, and I am the warden of this prison. You must be Elizabeth Lewis, the so-called wealthy, privileged woman we have incarcerated here in my prison. All I see is a raggedy, old woman," he said with a snarky tone. "Unfortunately, I have strict orders to release you. My guards will escort you to a relative's home in New York City. You will be under house arrest for the remainder of your sentence."

Elizabeth felt her heart pounding, realizing she would soon be free from that dreadful prison.

He placed a document in front of Elizabeth and said, "You must sign this document before I can release you," he demanded as he handed her a pen.

Elizabeth looked down at him and said, "Sir, I believe I have the right to read this first."

"If you want to get out of here, I advise you just to sign it!"

She angrily grasped onto the pen with her shackled hands, dipped it into the inkwell, and scribbled her name. Then, she aggressively threw the pen down, causing ink to splatter on the desk and the document. Lt. Barker bolted from his chair and put his fists on the desk.

He glared at Elizabeth with deadly rage in his eyes and yelled to his guards, "Remove this bloody woman from my office before I disobey my orders and throw her back in prison!"

The guards lifted her and took her outside. As they dragged her to the wagon, Elizabeth could not help but smile. She knew she had lost her temper, but it was worth seeing that little fat lieutenant so angry.

They shoved her onto the hard bench in the back of the wagon and threw her meager belongings beside her. Elizabeth looked down upon her chained hands as her body itched with filth. She felt like an ordinary, downtrodden criminal rather than the respectable woman she once was.

Bewildered as the wagon sped ahead, she yelled to the guard, "Will you be taking me back to my home at Whitestone?"

The guard looked back at Elizabeth and laughed. "Have you forgotten, my dear, that your home was burnt to the ground? I highly doubt you will be returning there any time soon, if ever," he cruelly replied.

Elizabeth let out a sigh, fighting to hold back the emotions that were building inside of her. She prayed this despicable man was mistaken and that her beloved Whitestone could be restored.

Elizabeth winced with pain as the wagon bumped along the city streets. As they drew closer to their destination, she could see dear old Kingsley waiting for her at the bottom of the stairs.

As weak as she was, Elizabeth's blood rushed through her body, and she fought back the tears. The driver brought the horses to an abrupt stop, causing Elizabeth to slide off the bench onto the floor of the wagon. He jumped down and lifted her roughly out of the wagon, placing her bare feet upon the hardened ground. The other guard unlocked the shackles from her wrists and flung them into the back of the wagon, startling Elizabeth with the loud, clanging sound.

She squinted her eyes from the bright noon sun and rubbed her wrists where the chains had left their indelible impression. Weak from the whole ordeal, she nearly fell over until Kingsley rushed to her side and held her steady.

She appeared so thin, almost angelic, with her pale complexion. Her once soft, brown eyes were now dull and gray. She paused, took a deep breath of the fresh, crisp air, and smiled weakly, "Oh, is it really you, Kingsley?" He nodded as he gently carried her up the stairs.

The guards impatiently followed behind. "Sirs, leave her to me," Kingsley said boldly.

"Well, listen to him, a slave telling us what to do? Watch yourself, old man," the guard replied sarcastically. "We ain't going nowhere till we read her the rules she must follow for the duration of her sentence."

Kingsley remained silent while fuming under his skin. He knew he better keep quiet. He did not want to cause his poor mistress any more discomfort. Phoebe, too frightened by the British uniforms, remained inside, waiting anxiously behind the door. As Phoebe watched Kingsley carrying Elizabeth inside, she was shocked by the sight of her beloved mistress.

Kingsley sat Elizabeth down by the fireplace, with the warm blaze burning brightly, while Phoebe wrapped a blanket around her shoulders. Elizabeth smiled in gratitude to her devoted servants for the comfort they provided. She stared aimlessly into the fire as the guard repeated the words she had already heard before and did not want to hear again. Before they left, one of the guards turned and winked at Elizabeth, making her stomach churn with disgust.

When they finally left, Elizabeth sighed, and tears of relief flowed freely from her eyes. Kingsley sat beside her, holding her hand to console her, "'Tis alright, Mrs. Elizabeth, you are safe now."

Elizabeth placed her frail hand upon his strong shoulder and spoke softly, "Kingsley, you have been so good and brave. I don't know if I would have survived in that prison without your help." Kingsley smiled at his Mistress. "Now you rest, Ma'am; Phoebe will tend to you," he replied as he stood and left them alone.

The savory scent of a whole chicken and root vegetables simmering over the fire filled the room. Phoebe scooped up some of the briny broth in a small bowl and handed it to her mistress. Elizabeth wrapped her hands around the warm bowl, slowly sipping the flavorful broth. Mindful of her stomach, Elizabeth reluctantly placed the bowl aside. Phoebe gave Elizabeth a disappointing glance, "'Tis delicious, Phoebe; I will eat more once I've had my bath."

Upstairs, Elizabeth undressed out of her filthy clothes while Phoebe helped her climb into the warm tub of salted water that Kingsley had prepared. Elizabeth took a relaxing deep breath, welcoming the heat against her chilled body. She lay there, letting the soothing waters soak off the grime that had built up on her skin. The scent of lavender filled the air as Phoebe gently washed her with the scented soap. Phoebe poured the soapy water through her hair while gingerly combing out the thick knots. She added more warm water to the bath as she covered

Elizabeth with a thin shift. Elizabeth, with a blissful look on her face, smiled up at Phoebe. "My dear, this feels wonderful," she sighed. Phoebe's eyes filled with tears; she would do anything to ease her dear, sweet mistress's pain.

Elizabeth felt clean and fresh for the first time in months. Phoebe dressed her in her warmest nightgown. She rubbed a creamy balm upon her bruised wrists and calloused feet and helped her to bed. Elizabeth, too tired from the long day, closed her eyes and fell fast asleep on the soft, feathered bed to the soothing sounds of the crackling, warm fire.

Morning came, and Elizabeth jolted awake, confused by her surroundings as she looked around the unfamiliar room. A wide smile spread across her face when she realized she was no longer in that grungy cell.

Phoebe helped Elizabeth to the dining table and poured her some tea as she hurried along, preparing the morning meal. "Where is Kingsley?" Elizabeth inquired as she drank down the sweetened brew.

"He went to see young Francis to tell him you are here. Your son has been real good to us, bringing us whatever we need. He's been plenty worried about you, Mistress," Phoebe expressed.

Elizabeth smiled as she went to sit by the fireplace. She could not get enough of the warmth from the roaring fire. Her hands, crippled with pain, made it difficult for her to write or do any of the things she loved to do.

Later that afternoon, young Francis finally arrived with Kingsley in tow, carrying several sacks of clothing and foodstuffs. "Mother!" he shouted as he knelt beside her and rested his head upon her lap. "I thought I would never see you again," he uttered, his words choked with emotion.

"'Tis alright, son. I am here," Elizabeth whispered, running her hands through her son's hair.

He looked up at his mother's worn face as he sat beside her. "What have they done to you, Mother? How could they treat you so cruelly?" he lamented.

"Son, what is done is done. We must move on now. They have worn me down physically, but they have not broken my will," she replied with labored breath.

Francis Jr., mindful of his mother's weakened state, reached over and embraced her gently. "Mother, I would have brought you to my home, but you know how my wife's family feel about Father's politics. You would not have been comfortable there."

Elizabeth placed her hand upon his forearm, "I understand, son, don't concern yourself with those thoughts; besides, Kingsley and Phoebe are taking wonderful care of me." she replied, smiling up at her two devoted servants.

Elizabeth despised that her son married into a family of British loyalists, but she would put that behind her for now. She was just so pleased to have her son back into her life. Young Francis reluctantly stood up to leave, "I apologize, Mother, but I need to get back to the store now. I will come by as often as possible, and if there is anything you need, just send Kingsley. I love you, Mother," he replied affectionately, kissing his mother's cheek. "Thank you, son. I love you too," she said, smiling up at him.

Phoebe filled Elizabeth's cup with more sweetened tea and placed buttered bread and boiled eggs before her. "Eat Mistress, it will do you good," she pleaded. Elizabeth's appetite had waned from the dull gruel she had grown accustomed to eating. "Give me time, Phoebe. I'll be eating soon enough. Now, both of you, come sit with me," she instructed Phoebe and Kingsley.

As they sat opposite each other, Elizabeth grasped each of their hands. "You have both been so wonderful to me. I cannot tell you how much I appreciate all you have done," she expressed sincerely.

"Tell me, Kingsley, what has become of Whitestone?" Elizabeth inquired.

With eyes cast down, Kingsley shook his head, "'Tis all gone, Mrs. Elizabeth, burnt right down to the ground," he said solemnly.

Elizabeth let go of her grasp and placed her head in her hands, "Oh dear God," she exclaimed.

Kingsley could not bear seeing his mistress so upset, "I got some good news for you, Mrs. Elizabeth. I went to Whitestone with Thomas and Ward, just like you asked me to. That nephew of yours, he's a strong young fellow; he plowed right through all that rubble and shimmied straight down into the dusty wine cellar. Would you believe all your valuables were there, just as you left them? He dug up every one of your belongings, and we brought them here and hid them real good," he said excitedly.

Elizabeth removed her hands from her face, "Where, Kingsley? I want to see it all!" she exclaimed, attempting to rise from her chair.

Kingsley stood up and placed his hand on her shoulder. "Not now, Mrs. Do not worry; they are safe. I will take you down into the cellar when you get your strength back."

Deflated, Elizabeth sighed, "Yes, Kingsley, you are right. Thank you for retrieving my valuables. It could not have been easy for any of you. 'Tis wonderful news," she replied, exhausted from all the excitement.

"Come now, Mistress, best you get some rest," Kingsley said as he and Phoebe helped her to bed.

Lying under the warm blanket, Elizabeth grasped Kingsley's hand, "Tell me, Kingsley, did you find my brother Richard's portrait?"

"Yes, Mistress, we did," replied Kingsley proudly.

"If you would be so kind, please hang it over the mantel for me," she said softly as she drifted off to sleep.

When Elizabeth woke the next morning, she was happy to see her beloved brother Richard's portrait hanging over the bedroom fireplace. His warm eyes greeted her as she looked up at him fondly. "Aye, dear brother, the British have taken our beautiful Whitestone, but I am still here and will not give up, now or ever."

As time went by, Elizabeth began to feel a little bit better, although she could not rid herself of the irritating cough she had developed. She didn't pay much mind to it, for she was just so happy not to be in that awful prison cell, suffering those dreadful conditions. Her only regret was knowing that her fellow prisoners were still in that filthy cell, and she wished she could find a way to get them released.

Kingsley was out back, fetching some fresh water from the well. Phoebe was busy tending to everyday chores when suddenly, a loud knock came upon the door. Phoebe stopped what she was doing, peeked out the side window, and saw a British guard standing there, swaying back and forth. She recognized him as one of the men who brought Elizabeth there. He started banging loudly on the door with his fists, yelling for them to let him in. Phoebe reluctantly opened the door when he pushed her out of the way and demanded to see Elizabeth.

Hearing the ruckus, Elizabeth walked over to the foyer and faced the guard straight on, "I am here. I have not gone anywhere," she said bluntly. He stumbled over to her, slurring his words, "There is the feisty lady I remember. I have missed you, Mrs. Lewis, and I had to see you again." He grabbed Elizabeth and placed his arms around her waist, forcing his lips hard upon hers. Elizabeth struggled to push him away but was too weak to fight him off. She felt nauseous from the strong stench of liquor upon him. Phoebe pulled on his arm as she yelled for him to let her go, but the guard shoved her to the floor and would not stop. Phoebe screamed as the man clung to Elizabeth, ripping the top of her dress off.

Hearing Phoebe's loud shriek, Kingsley dropped the water bucket and flew to the opened door. He rushed into the room, put his hands around the guard's neck, and squeezed hard. The guard released his grip on Elizabeth as he fought to pull Kingsley's strong hands off of his throat. He was choking and struggling to breathe, but Kingsley would not let go.

Phoebe yelled for Kingsley to stop, fearing he would kill the man, yet Kingsley fought on with the strength of a lion. He yanked the guard down to the floor, put his knee to his neck, and shouted, "You cannot do this to my Mistress; I will kill you first!" The man froze in fear, looking up at the fierce black eyes glaring down at him. Kingsley grabbed the guard's gun from his holster, pointed it at him, and said, "Get out of this house now, and if you ever come back, I will kill you with your own pistol!" He released his knee from his throat, and the guard stood up. Unable to speak, he stumbled to the door and fell down the stairs before he ran off. Kingsley followed him and shouted, "Remember, I got your pistol!" knowing that the British guard would have to explain to his superior officer how he lost his pistol to a servant in the home of a woman prisoner.

Elizabeth stood there in shock as Phoebe rushed to cover her up. Kingsley went by her side, "Are you alright, Mistress?"

Elizabeth, shaking, clutched onto Kingsley and buried her face on his shoulder. "Oh, Kingsley, thank God you were here!" she cried.

Elizabeth, as strong a woman as she was, felt so vulnerable at that moment. She shuddered to think what would have happened if Kingsley was not there. She slumped into a chair, her legs buckling beneath her, and told them both, "Do not mention this to anyone, especially young Francis. It will be our secret."

After what Kingsley had said to the bastard, they were confident the drunken fool would never return there again.

While Elizabeth struggled to regain her health, one day, she noticed that her faithful friend Kingsley was not feeling well. She would nurse him the best she could, but he seemed to be getting worse by the day. He was burning with fever, and she feared he had come down with consumption. Elizabeth and Phoebe spent their days by his side, comforting him with a cold cloth on his head.

The next day, Phoebe came to Elizabeth with tears in her eyes. "Mrs. Elizabeth, Kingsley wants me to fetch him a priest. He needs to confess his sins," she said, her voice trembling with emotion. Elizabeth, distraught, asked Phoebe to go to town and find a priest. "No, Mistress, there ain't no Catholic priests in this town anymore," she said.

Elizabeth had been in denial, but she realized now that Kingsley's time was approaching. She would honor his wishes if it were the last thing she ever did, for he had been the most faithful of servants, and she loved him deeply.

Phoebe was right. Since the British took control, it was doubtful any Catholic priests were in the city. She took her pen and paper and wrote an urgent message to her husband Francis, pleading to send a Catholic priest from Pennsylvania. "Phoebe, go down and post this message immediately; see to it that it gets there by personal messenger as quickly as it can," she instructed the distraught girl, handing her ample money for the cost.

A fortnight passed, and Elizabeth feared it would be too late, but then she heard the knock on her door. She opened the door and looked upon a slightly built negro man with a bible in his hand, dressed in a simple black cloak and white collar. By his side, carrying a small leather bag, was a petite white woman. Her pale complexion was in sharp contrast to the black veil and long black dress covering her tiny frame. Elizabeth said a silent thank you to Francis, who, with his influence, managed to smuggle a priest from Philadelphia behind the British lines into the city.

Their pleasant demeanor put Elizabeth at ease as she brought them to where Kingsley was lying. He looked up and whispered in a raspy, weak voice, "Thank you, Mrs. Elizabeth."

She could see his face relax as the woman dotted his forehead and wrists with the waters the priest had blessed. "Please leave us be," the priest said softly.

After a short while, the priest walked out of the dark bedroom. "I have heard his confession and given him his last rites. It will not be long now," he expressed solemnly. He instructed Phoebe and Elizabeth to go sit with Kingsley. "Soon, he will be at peace and one with our Lord," the priest said reassuringly.

Elizabeth sat on the bed and placed her hand behind Kingsley's head. Kingsley looked at her lovingly and whispered to Elizabeth, "My Mistress, you will be in my dreams forever." He then passed away peacefully, with a serene look upon his face.

Though saddened beyond words, Elizabeth knew she had given this most humble, deserving man the greatest gift. For many years, this man had done whatever she asked of him. She felt good that she could fulfill the one thing her faithful servant had ever asked of her.

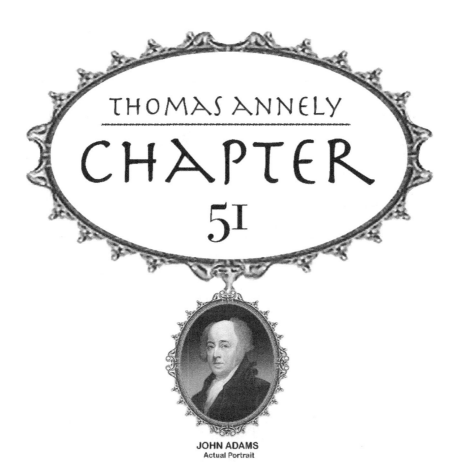

## THOMAS ANNELY

# CHAPTER 51

**JOHN ADAMS**
Actual Portrait

Elizabeth did not realize how insecure she would feel without Kingsley's strong presence, always there, watching over her. She felt angry for letting her weakness control the best of her. Fear gripped her heart with the thought that she would never regain the strength she once had.

She quickly shrugged off her feelings of insecurity and set about finding a suitable manservant. No one could ever replace Kingsley, but it would be unreasonable of her to think that she and Phoebe could handle all that needed to be done.

"Phoebe, can you please come in here, dear?" called out Elizabeth. Phoebe came rushing in, holding a wet dishrag in her hand. "Yes, Mistress?" she replied, wiping her hands on her apron.

"Phoebe, sit down, please. I know it has not been easy for you without Kingsley here. You have been doing his work as well as your own. As capable as you are, dear, I cannot expect you to be chopping wood and all those other chores that are more suited for a man."

Phoebe meekly replied, "I am sorry if I ain't as good as Kingsley, but I've been trying."

Elizabeth smiled at her fondly; she was still the shy and humble girl who came to Whitestone nearly twenty years ago. "No, Phoebe, you are doing wonderfully, as always," Elizabeth said reassuringly. "'Tis time I put an ad into the gazette for a new manservant," she announced.

Phoebe smiled to herself, for she had just the right man in mind for the job.

In the early afternoon, Phoebe went to the Fly Market near the East River. The fisherman had all their fresh fish stacked after their morning runs. "Fish, fresh fish," yelled out the burly fisherman. She held her nose tightly, doubting the fish was as fresh as the man said.

She pulled her coat around tightly to protect herself from the cold wind whipping off the water. Finding fresh fruit or vegetables this time of year was difficult, so she settled on buying preserves.

"Good afternoon, Miss Phoebe. What can I get you today, love," said the kindly old woman.

"Good day, Miss Mary. Do you have any peaches or vegetables?" Phoebe inquired. "Sorry, love. Only potatoes today, but they are fresh," old Mary replied with a toothless grin. "I ain't seen Kingsley around; I hope he ain't under the weather?" she asked, in her cockney accent.

Phoebe lowered her eyes, "'Tis sad to say, Miss Mary, but some weeks back, poor Kingsley got the fever and died," she replied solemnly.

"Oh dear, a nice man, was he," replied the old woman. Phoebe shook her head in agreement, trying to hold back her tears. "Take these; this will cheer you up," said Mary, handing Phoebe a bag of chestnuts.

"Thank you, 'tis awfully kind of you; Kingsley loved these," Phoebe replied gratefully.

"I know, he was my best customer for chestnuts," boasted Miss Mary.

"Phoebe, there you are," came a familiar voice, making her heart skip a beat. "I hoped you would be here today. I got the new fabric you'd be wanting."

Phoebe turned to face him, his soft golden eyes captivating her as she fought to catch her breath. "Are you feeling alright, Phoebe? You look a wee bit pale," he said, taking hold of her elbow. Gazing up, she thought she would faint at the very sight of him. "Good day, William, I am fine; just a bit hungry is all," she said, knowing full well that it was William Jones who made her feel weak at the knees.

Never before, in all of her years, had she seen such a good-looking man. His skin was the tone of rich mahogany, and his eyes were yellow with golden flecks that shone brightly in the mid-day sun.

"Come with me; I will get you something proper to eat," he said, with Phoebe following like a little lamb beside him. She would follow this man to the ends of the world if he asked her to.

As she nibbled on the bread and cheese he placed before her, he never took his eyes off her face. This made Phoebe uncomfortable but in a most enjoyable way. "Feel better now?" he questioned. Phoebe nodded yes as she gobbled up the rest of the cheese. "Thank you kindly, William, 'tis lovely," she remarked. "And so are you," he replied, making Phoebe feel flush once more.

He reached over and placed his hand over hers. "I was real sorry to hear about old Kingsley. He was a good man," he said sincerely. Phoebe's expression turned solemn as she looked downward. William placed his strong hand upon her chin, lifting it to face him. "Do not worry, Phoebe. I will watch over you," he said, causing a tear to drop down her cheek.

"'Tis too kind of you, William," she replied shyly. "Kingsley liked you too, but he told me to be wary of your sweet words," she said bluntly, regretting her words as quickly as she said them.

William laughed out loud, "Old Kingsley, minding his baby hen. He was plum wrong, Phoebe; every word I say is true. You must know how I feel about you by now?"

Phoebe looked away, disbelieving that this remarkable man, who all the women had been fawning over, would want her. She quickly changed the subject before he could go on any further.

"William, with Kingsley gone now, my mistress needs a new man-servant. I feel awkward asking you about this, but would you be needing work?"

"Me a servant, ha ha," he laughed, and then his tone softened, "Only if she lets me marry you." Phoebe was speechless, feeling as if she was in a dream.

"I mean it, Phoebe. I have loved you since the day I first laid eyes upon you. I would be humbled to take you as my wife," he said, bringing more tears to Phoebe's eyes. She, too, loved this man from the moment she laid eyes upon him.

William helped Phoebe from the chair, wrapping his strong arms around her. "Let's go meet this Mistress of yours," he said confidently.

"William, don't you be saying anything about marrying me to my Mistress."

Elizabeth heard a soft knock upon her door. She knew it could not be Phoebe, for she would come in through the back entry with her own key. She approached the door cautiously, peered out the side window, and was surprised to see her son Francis's wife, Beth, standing there.

She immediately unlocked the bolt and greeted her warmly: "Beth, 'tis good to see you, my dear. Please come in."

As Beth entered the front foyer, she was taken aback by the weakened state of her once vibrant mother-in-law. She gave her a rather awkward embrace as Elizabeth smiled weakly. "Come and warm yourself by the fire," Elizabeth said, inviting her into the sitting room.

Beth unwrapped herself from her luxurious fur cloak and laid it across the chair beside her. Elizabeth observed her plain-looking daughter-in-law, wondering what young Francis found attractive. Elizabeth was certain it was the promise of prestige and wealth she brought to the marriage that enticed her oldest son. "Mother Elizabeth, I sincerely apologize for not getting here sooner, but Frannie insisted you needed to rest. It was so horrible how they treated you!"

"Yes, it was, dear, but I am feeling stronger each day," Elizabeth replied.

"That is good news, Mother. I am glad to hear you are feeling better."

An awkward pause came between them as Beth gazed about the room.

"Uncle Thomas's home is lovely. Don't you think? I hope you are comfortable here."

"Why yes, dear. I am very fortunate to have such a generous, wonderful brother."

Beth squirmed in her seat, clearly knowing what her mother-in-law was implying. "You know Fran and I wanted you to come live with us."

Elizabeth raised her hand, "There's no need to speak of that, Beth. I know what your family thinks of me and my husband," Elizabeth said boldly.

"No, Mother dear, you are mistaken. It is your husband with whom we are angry. Imagine him leaving you in harm's way, all for signing a worthless piece of parchment," she ranted.

Elizabeth's blood was beginning to boil at the ignorant words of her daughter-in-law. "Dear Beth, if you are referring to our Declaration of Independence, I assure you 'tis much more than a measly piece of parchment. As for my husband leaving me in the fray of things, it was entirely my choice to join this fight for our freedom."

"Come now, Mother, you cannot be serious; a woman of your means has no need to meddle with men's affairs. You cannot truly believe that these rebels will win over the King's mighty British army. Why would you go against your mother country? You and your husband Francis were born in England; one would think, at the very least, you would be neutral in these matters," she spoke out brazenly.

Anger was building inside Elizabeth as she looked sternly at her. She took a huge breath to steel her nerves, "Beth, perhaps 'tis you who should not speak of what does not concern you. After all, a woman of your means is not affected by what this King has put upon the colonies."

"Oh dear mother, I did not come here to quarrel with you," said Beth, placing her hand upon Elizabeth's hand.

"I know that, dear; please, help yourself to some tea and the wonderful scones Phoebe has made," Elizabeth said, attempting to calm the storm brewing inside her.

The two Elizabeths sat silently, sipping their tea, carefully contemplating their next words. Beth addressed Elizabeth; "Mother, I will leave you to rest now. Fran and I are here for you if you need us."

Elizabeth rose, relieved that her daughter-in-law was leaving before any more hurtful words could be said. "I am most grateful, daughter. Give my love to my son, Francis," she replied.

After she left, Elizabeth immediately went to her desk to pen a letter to her husband, Francis, to expel some of the anger that was festering inside her.

> *Dearest Francis,*
>
> *I hope this letter finds you well. I had a visit from our daughter-in-law, the other Elizabeth, today. What possessed our son to marry this woman is beyond my imagination. Her ignorance surpasses her homely appearance; she clearly is her father's daughter. Her father's influence upon her is evident in every word she says. If I had my way, I would wrench our dear son away from this woman and find him a more suitable bride. Are we to blame for his desire for wealth and prominence amongst these arrogant snobs who call themselves Englishmen?*
>
> *I'm sorry, my love, for going on as such, but I could no longer hold in my frustrations.*
>
> *I shall imagine you are here, with your loving arms around me, to calm my rattled nerves.*
>
> *Your loving wife forever, Elizabeth*

Elizabeth placed down her pen, crumbled up the letter, and threw it into the fire. She would not burden Francis with any of this family drama. It felt wonderful to write her words down and watch the fire crackle, turning the paper to ash.

Upon hearing Phoebe returning inside the back door, Elizabeth rose to greet her. She was alarmed to see a tall, rugged negro man standing beside her. Phoebe stumbled with her words as she introduced him. "Mrs. Elizabeth, this is Mr. William Jones. He works at the Fly Market and is looking for new work." William nodded respectfully before speaking, "'Tis nice to meet you, Ma-am."

Elizabeth sensed an uneasy tension between them and was concerned about this stranger's motives. "Mr. Jones, I have not yet posted my ad. Once I do, perhaps you could return for a formal interview," Elizabeth replied curtly.

"Yes, Ma-am," he replied, intimidated by Elizabeth's boldness. "I'll be takin' my leave now. 'Tis nice seeing you today, Miss Phoebe," he said, leaving quickly out the back door.

Phoebe's heart sank as her face flushed with anger. She could not understand why he did not speak up.

"Phoebe, do you know this man?" Elizabeth asked quizzingly.

"Yes, Mistress. I met him at the Fly Market with Kingsley when we first arrived here. He's been very nice to me," she replied solemnly.

"Phoebe, perhaps 'tis none of my business, but are you keen on this man?"

Phoebe was stunned at Elizabeth's directness, her eyes filled with tears. "I believe I might love him, and he says he loves me," she said shyly, ashamed of her words. "I don't know much about men, but I know what my heart says," Phoebe replied.

"I suppose you will leave to be with this man you love?" Elizabeth asked softly.

"Oh no, Mistress, I would never leave you."

"Well, you realize you cannot marry anyone without my permission. Now that I know how you feel about this man, I must meet him again to be sure his intentions are real."

Phoebe bowed her head. "Yes, Mistress, I will be getting back to my chores now," she replied in her usual humble fashion.

A week had passed since Elizabeth placed the ad in the Gazette for a new manservant. She had not received any interest as of yet, so she decided, against her better judgment, to meet with Phoebe's fellow. Elizabeth was concerned not only about him being suitable for Phoebe but also about whether he was right for her household. The man must know how important discretion is regarding her personal affairs.

"Phoebe, I would like to meet with your friend William; the next time you go to the market, ask him to come to see me so I may talk with him."

Phoebe answered a polite yes, while deep inside her heart was all a flutter.

Later that week, William arrived early in the day, "Morning, Mrs. Lewis. "'Tis good to see you again," he said as Phoebe brought him inside the foyer.

"Good morning to you, William. Come inside and be seated, please," said Elizabeth sternly. "Phoebe has told me that you are interested in the position as my manservant. Have you any experience as such?" she inquired.

"No, ma'am, I mostly work at the Fly Market, selling goods I buy from the merchant ships," he replied.

"May I ask how you acquired money to purchase goods?" Elizabeth asked boldly.

"Ma'am, in the warmer months, I worked in Jersey for a kindly old farmer. He gave me a room and was paying me some until the British took it all away from him," he said, lowering his head to his chin. "I was sorry to hear about your man Kingsley; he was real kind to me. I ain't never had a job as a manservant, but I am strong and real good at fixin' things," he boasted.

Elizabeth took a deep breath before responding, "William, you may find me too bold, but I must ask, what are your intentions with my Phoebe?"

William's eyes softened, "I am very fond of her; she's a fine woman, Ma'am," he replied.

"She has told me this, William, and it is clear that she is very fond of you as well. If I employ you, it has to be understood that Phoebe is not to be taken advantage of. You are free to socialize on Sundays but not during your work time. You will address me as Mistress or Mrs., and you will be expected to act in a gentlemanly way at all times. You must not discuss my private affairs with anyone outside of this household," said Elizabeth sternly.

"Yes, Mrs., I understand," William replied.

"I will have you work each day of this week, and if your work is satisfactory, I will have you continue on. We can discuss your wages at that time. Understand that if at any time I find your behavior or work unsatisfactory, you will be released from your service," Elizabeth said firmly.

"Yes, Mrs., I am much obliged," he replied gratefully.

"Very well then, be here every day at this time. Sunday is a day for yourself, but I will need you the rest of the week."

"Thank you kindly, Mrs. Lewis. You will have no trouble with me," he said as Elizabeth escorted him out.

Elizabeth locked the entryway door and went to sit by the fire. It made her weary, wondering if she had made the right choice in hiring this man.

Phoebe silently entered the room and placed a tray with tea in front of her Mistress. "Oh, Phoebe, you startled me," exclaimed Elizabeth.

Phoebe curtsied, "Beg your pardon, Mrs.," she replied timidly.

"'Tis alright, Phoebe. Please sit. I need to discuss a few things with you," replied Elizabeth.

Elizabeth told Phoebe that she had agreed to employ William for one week to see if he was suitable for the job. "'Tis very important that he knows I value trust and loyalty, above all other things. For my safety, as well as your own, he must not discuss the goings on of myself or my family with anyone. I expect you to make sure he abides by the rules of my household. I have faith that you won't let your feelings for each other get in the way of your duties. Phoebe, you have become like a daughter to me, and because of this, I will be firm in my convictions towards you. Do you understand all I have said, dear?" Elizabeth questioned.

"Yes, Mistress. I will make sure William understands, too," Phoebe replied respectfully.

Any doubts Elizabeth had about William were quickly relieved when he proved capable of handling all the chores around the home. Although he was rough around the edges, she felt that with a bit of polishing, he could become a fine manservant. Phoebe went about her duties as usual, except now, her face glowed with young love. Happiness filled the home with the forthcoming of a new season and the love that was blossoming within.

THOMAS ANNELY

# CHAPTER
## 52

I received word from my sister Elizabeth that my friend Kingsley had passed away. The man who was as mighty as an oak tree had fallen. The bloody fever spared no one; even a strong man like Kingsley was not immune to it. How Elizabeth and Phoebe would get on without him concerned me greatly. As much as I was needed here, Elizabeth's welfare was far more important. I knew I had to take the risk to go see her at once.

After settling things at the workshop, Sarah, Gifford, and I left for New York City, taking the backroads away from the enemy lines. I had to ensure my precious cargo made it safe and sound to the city where I was no longer welcome.

While we ferried over the Hudson, I saw Howie standing alongside the riverbank. As we disembarked, I embraced my old friend, feeling his bony frame beneath his baggy clothing. It pained me to see how much he had aged but he was as sharp and spry as ever.

His face broke out in a wide grin at seeing our son sleeping soundly in Sarah's arms. "Aye, would you look at this little lad, spittin' image of his old man."

After we exchanged pleasantries, Howie warned that it would be best if he traveled with us to my townhouse. "I know most of these bloody redcoats, and they won't be messing with me, not if they want their steady supply of rum."

I had forgotten how much I enjoyed Howie's company. He put our minds at ease as we rode through the crowded city to see Elizabeth. When we arrived at my townhouse, Howie took our carriage back to his Inn, planning to return for us on Monday morning.

Climbing up the stairs, I caught a glimpse of Phoebe peeking nervously out of the side window. When she recognized our faces, a look of relief crossed her face, and she quickly opened the door. "'Tis Master Thomas and Mrs. Sarah with little Gifford!" she called out excitedly to Elizabeth.

Surprised at our arrival, Elizabeth rushed to the doorway to greet us. "Thomas, Sarah, you have come! And look how much my godson has grown."

My eyes could plainly see how Elizabeth's imprisonment had affected her. Her face, lined and weary-looking, made her appear ten years older. The sparkle in her soft brown eyes had dulled, yet the broad smile on her face was most welcoming.

Sarah placed Gifford in Phoebe's waiting arms, embracing Elizabeth, "Oh my dear sister, we have missed you so!"

I went over to my sister, afraid I would crush her delicate frame, and gently wrapped my arms around her. "Sister, 'tis so wonderful to be here with you."

"'Tis so good to see you, brother. You have risked everything to come here. I am most grateful to you both!" Elizabeth exclaimed.

We sat and talked for what seemed like hours. Elizabeth was delighted when we told her that Ward and Sally were married with a baby on the way. Elizabeth, nearly in tears, reminisced about dear Kingsley. She expressed how sad she was to hear about Chip's passing and how much she would miss him.

With little Gifford in her arms, Sarah retired to bed, leaving Elizabeth and me alone. We sat, enjoying the warmth of the fire, when, through the silence, I spoke, "Elizabeth, had you heard that I attended an important meeting with Francis, along with his fellow congressmen?"

A smile broke across Elizabeth's face, "No, I was not aware of that, Thomas, but I am so relieved, for I rarely hear from Francis. 'Tis so difficult to get letters in and out of the city. How is my dear husband?"

"Aye, Elizabeth, his hair has gone all gray, and he has developed a bit of paunch, but he is still as lively as ever. You should have heard the speech he gave. I was bursting with pride at the boldness of his words. Yet, I could see the sadness in his eyes; he misses you greatly. 'Tis plain to see he is carrying a great burden upon his shoulders for not being here for you."

"Oh no, Thomas, he mustn't feel that way; what he is doing is much more important than the two of us! When we pledged ourselves to this cause, it was a promise we took as seriously as our marriage vows. We knew full well what the consequences could be, even if it meant our lives."

"You did not deserve to be treated as you were. I suppose 'tis the price we are all paying for this fight for our liberty."

"Yes, you are right, dear brother," replied Elizabeth solemnly.

"How are you and Phoebe carrying on without Kingsley?"

"'Tis not easy, Thomas, but I have hired a new hand, a friend of Phoebe. No one can replace our dear Kingsley, but he has been a great help to us both. It seems our Phoebe has found a gentleman admirer. He is quite smitten with our girl."

I looked at my sister with concern, "Elizabeth, can you trust this man? Does he know about our involvement with the cause?"

"Do not worry yourself, Thomas. I made it clear to him not to discuss my personal affairs with anyone. He dislikes what the British are doing as much as we do. I believe I have made a wise decision in hiring this man."

I reached over and touched Elizabeth's hand, "Dear sister, I will repeat the words our late Mum told me: I trust your judgment." Elizabeth's face relaxed upon hearing our sweet Mother's encouraging words.

I let out a soft yawn. "I think a rest would do us both good; it has been a long day."

Elizabeth grasped my hand, "Good night, dear brother; I will sleep well having you and Sarah here with me. God bless you."

The next morning, I woke to the sound of church bells ringing, calling out to all the faithful. The peaceful dawn reminded me of how New York City once was before the British took reign.

Sarah turned and faced me, her green eyes gazing at me seductively, "Good Morning, Thomas. How does it feel to be back in your old bed?" she said sweetly. I pulled her close, holding her in a warm embrace. "'Tis wonderful, my love, especially with such a beautiful woman beside me," I replied, tightening my embrace around her.

The soft cry from our son Gifford ended our quiet moment together. Sarah released herself from my grasp and rose out of bed as I reluctantly let her go. "Sorry, Thomas. Your son is calling," she said, putting on her robe to tend to him.

After I finished my morning ritual, I found Elizabeth in the dining room, enjoying her morning tea. The quietness gave us time to talk, "Good Morning, Thomas. I have not had the chance to thank you for going to retrieve my valuables at Whitestone. Kingsley told me all about you and Ward digging them out of the rubble."

"'Twas Kingsley's determination that kept us all going. That man had the strength of a lion," I remarked fondly.

Elizabeth's warm expression turned solemn when she inquired about her precious home, "Tell me, Thomas, how bad is the damage at Whitestone?"

I looked at her sorrowfully, "Elizabeth, all that is left is the white stone from which it was built. 'Twas a sad sight to see, but 'tis a miracle from God that the graves were not damaged. It brought me peace to pay my respects to our dear brother and your children."

Elizabeth smiled and softly replied, "Thank you, dear brother."

In true Elizabeth fashion, she quickly shook off her feelings of despair and changed to the matters of the day. "Thomas, would you believe I have not been down to see my belongings yet?"

"Sarah and I would be happy to take you down there, Elizabeth," I replied. "Oh, that would be lovely, Thomas," exclaimed Elizabeth, excited to see her belongings again.

While Gifford slept, the three of us went down to the cellar, where we had safely stored Elizabeth's valuables. As we entered, the first thing we saw were the portraits of Francis and Elizabeth, side by side, leaning against the brick wall. Elizabeth paused, her eyes fixed upon the portraits, as her mind wandered back to her younger days. "I was so young and naive then; I looked out at the world with such optimism," she commented.

Elizabeth sat on the floor and took out one of her fine linen tablecloths. She placed it upon her cheek to feel its softness. "Remember those lovely dinner parties? Oh, how we all enjoyed ourselves." Standing beside her, I placed my hand on her thin shoulder, "I remember them well, dear sister, and we shall have them again," I said reassuringly.

Sarah fawned over all the fine chinaware and recalled how beautifully Elizabeth displayed her tables. "I remember all the flowers; you always had such wonderful, fragrant flower settings," Sarah recalled.

"Ahh yes, those lovely flowers, but it was Kingsley who had the green thumb," Elizabeth recalled fondly.

"Sarah, you must help me bring up some of this lovely china so we can enjoy it now!" Elizabeth exclaimed. "Of course, Elizabeth, that is a wonderful idea," Sarah replied.

Elizabeth let out a sigh, holding open a gold pendant with a miniature portrait of her daughter Ann enclosed. Sarah gazed at Ann's portrait. "Such a beautiful girl. Does she write to you, Elizabeth?" Sarah inquired softly.

"Yes, Sarah, she does, as often as she can. It pains me to hear that she has become quite close with King George and Queen Charlotte. The Royals think highly of her husband's gallantry at sea, and Ann has become a confidant to the Queen. The poor Queen is awaiting the birth of her eleventh child. Can you imagine that? Ann loves minding the Queen's children and anxiously awaits her own. With that husband of hers off at sea most of the time, she shan't have much time for that," Elizabeth said with a chuckle.

Sarah laughed and remarked, "She's a smart girl; being friendly with the royal family will do her no harm. As for her own children, I am sure she will be blessed soon."

Elizabeth reached into one of the boxes, lifting a crystal champagne flute as if to salute. "Here's to you both. This has been the most joyful of moments, seeing you all and my precious belongings," she exclaimed, her smile lighting up her face. "I can hardly wait to be together, enjoying those wonderful times again."

"Hear! Hear!" Sarah and I said in unison, smiling at the thought of it.

I dragged over the heavy strongbox, "Francis asked me about a strongbox with his valuables. Is this the one?" I asked Elizabeth.

"Why yes, Thomas," she replied.

"He was very pleased when I told him it was here and was concerned if it was in a safe place. Perhaps I should move it somewhere more secure?" I questioned.

"Do not concern yourself, Thomas; 'tis securely locked, and only Francis has the key. I will be sure to keep the cellar door properly locked at all times, as well."

Elizabeth began to cough, and Sarah went over to tend to her, "We should take you upstairs now, Elizabeth," Sarah said, gently taking Elizabeth's arm while I carried up a box of her china and linens.

Later that day, we heard knocking at the door. I instinctively headed to answer the door when Elizabeth lifted her hand to halt me.

She lowered her voice and spoke softly, "Thomas, wait. Go upstairs into the bedroom with Sarah and keep yourselves unseen. I will see who is at the door and call you out if I need you."

I reluctantly heeded her word and followed Sarah upstairs to the bedroom, closing the door behind me. "Thomas, who do you think is there?" Sarah asked with concern. I placed my finger to my lips. "Quiet, Sarah, please," I whispered as I reached for my pistol, keeping my ear to the door.

Elizabeth slowly opened the entryway door to see two British soldiers standing there with stern expressions on their faces. She stood blocking the entrance, not offering them entry. "Good day, sirs. How can I help you?" she asked calmly.

The men pushed their way into the foyer, looking around the room. "Mrs. Lewis, I presume?" the taller one asked.

"Yes, Sir, 'tis I," she replied. "Our superiors have sent us here to check your status and ensure you have not left the premises," he said gruffly. "As you can see, Sir, I am here," she replied smartly.

"Mrs. Lewis, we need you to answer some questions. My name is Officer Pendleton, and my partner is Officer Bennet. May we please sit down?"

Elizabeth reluctantly led the officers to sit by the fireplace. "May I offer you gentlemen some tea?" she asked politely.

"No, ma'am. We are not here on a social visit," Pendleton replied rudely. "Mrs. Lewis, who owns this home, and is there anyone staying here with you?"

"'Twas my brother Richard Annely's home, who has since passed. He bequeathed this home to our family. My maid stays with me, but this is her day off," she answered bluntly.

"Your husband is Francis Lewis, a known sympathizer with the rebels. Is that correct, Ma'am?"

"Francis Lewis is my husband, but I know nothing of him being a rebel sympathizer."

The officer paused and looked at Elizabeth doubtfully. "Come now, Mrs. Lewis. You cannot expect me to believe you know nothing about your own husband's treasonous ways?"

Elizabeth, growing angry, replied, "Sir, all I know is my husband is a successful businessman, and you, Sir, will not speak ill of him in front of me."

"Mrs. Lewis, do I need to remind you that you are still a prisoner of the British court?"

"Officer Pendleton, I am reminded of that every day, how I was unfairly taken away from my home that your fellow officers burnt to the ground. And what they did not break, they stole."

"Ma'am, your husband, who you are clearly protecting, is the one to blame for your misfortune. Tell us where he is, or you will suffer dire circumstances."

Elizabeth sat stiffly, her jaw tense with anger, "Officer Pendleton, I don't know where my husband is. He had left for Boston several months ago to purchase merchandise for his store. That is all that I know of his whereabouts."

Officer Pendleton let out a long, frustrated breath. "It seems you have chosen not to cooperate with us. I will report your answers to our superiors. If I were you, I would seriously consider changing your words."

Elizabeth could hear little Gifford's soft whimpers, which caused her concern. "I thought you said you were alone, Mrs. Lewis?" he questioned. "Why yes, I am alone, Sir," she replied.

The officer looked on with a puzzled expression. "I heard a noise coming from somewhere. Are you sure no one is here with you?" he said, staring straight into her eyes. "We may have to search your home."

"Sir, I heard nothing, but if you feel you must search the house, go ahead and damn well do it. You have my permission."

"We don't need your permission, Mrs. Lewis. If we see fit to search your home, 'tis our duty to do so," he replied sternly.

The other officer whispered, "Sir, if this woman is so anxious to allow us to search her home, then she must be alone. Besides, we are late for our next assignment."

Pendleton paused, contemplating the situation, "Alright, we will not search today, but we will be back to check up on you periodically," he said boldly.

The Officers rushed out the door and down the stairs, mounted their horses, and galloped off.

Elizabeth locked the door behind them. She released a long breath and slumped onto her living room chair. I came down from the bedroom and rushed to her side. "Elizabeth, you amaze me the way you spoke to those men. Somehow, you convinced them not to search the house."

"Thomas, I did not leave anything to chance; I had this." Elizabeth pulled a small pistol from her pocket. "When we were going through my belongings in the cellar, I found the pistol and slipped it under my dress into my pocket," Elizabeth said, handing it over to me.

"I remember this pistol; years ago, Fran had me make it for you for your safety. But, Elizabeth, 'tis not even loaded!" I exclaimed.

"Yes, I know Thomas, but they wouldn't have known," Elizabeth remarked with a sly smile.

"Elizabeth, you are the bravest woman I know."

I poured each of us a glass of brandy to calm our nerves. "Sister, I realize now that I took a big risk coming here. If they found me here, they may have hauled us both to jail. I was warned not to return to New York, but Sarah and I could not stay away."

Elizabeth replied confidently, "Thomas, do not think that way. I am so grateful you both came to see me."

The following day, we ate our breakfast in silence. The mood in the house shifted from joy to sadness, knowing we had to leave Elizabeth this way. "Thomas, before you leave, I want you to meet William. He should be arriving shortly," said Elizabeth.

As expected, William arrived on time, eager to start the day's work. "William, come in, please; I would like you to meet my brother, Thomas Annely, and his wife, Sarah," said Elizabeth proudly.

"Please to meet you, Mr. and Mrs. Annely," he greeted us humbly.

I was immediately impressed by his pleasant manner and how attentive he was to Elizabeth. From the look of him, with his solid build, it was obvious he could handle the heavy work around the home. "Nice to meet you as well, William. I am sure you are a great help to my sister," I said, looking him directly in the eye.

"Yes, Sir, you can trust me to take good care of her," he replied as he left to attend to his chores.

As planned, Howie arrived to escort us back to the river. I embraced Elizabeth and promised to see her again soon. She smiled, knowing full well that it may be a promise I could not keep.

Little Gifford wiggled in Sarah's arms, "Well, the little Prince does not want to leave his Godmother," I said to Elizabeth's delight. "I would love nothing more than to keep you here, my little love, but your Mama and Papa would miss you so," she said, kissing his cheek.

I could see the sadness in Phoebe's eyes as she had to say goodbye to our little lad, whom she had grown to love. Sarah held back the tears as she embraced Elizabeth goodbye.

I whispered in Elizabeth's ear, "Do not worry, I will get word to Fran straight away. He will find a way to get you to Philadelphia so you can be together again."

With tears in her eyes, Elizabeth replied, "Thank you, Thomas. Your visit has lifted my spirits and made me feel much better."

Howie, waiting patiently in our carriage at the bottom of the stairs, waved hello to Elizabeth. When we boarded the carriage, I let out a long breath, "Thank you kindly, Howie, for your patience. 'Tis so hard to leave her here."

"Aye, Thomas, your visit must have been like a ray of sunshine to her. 'Tis sad to leave for sure, but we'll get her out of this bloody city soon enough," Howie said with his usual bravado.

I placed my hand on his shoulder, "'Tis words I needed to hear, my friend. The bloody Brits paid her a nasty visit yesterday. I won't rest easy until she is back with Fran."

Redcoats were standing guard all along the city streets. They tipped their hats to Howie as we rode past them to the river's edge. I laughed and remarked, "'Tis good to have friends in high places." Howie smiled and said, "You'd be surprised what a wee bit of rum can get you in this town."

We crossed over the Hudson and landed safely on the Jersey shoreline. The gentle rocking of the flatboat lulled little Gifford to sleep as Sarah leaned her head against my shoulder. "Oh, Thomas, Elizabeth seems so weak to me," she remarked sadly. "Don't you worry, love; she just needs some time to regain her strength," I said, wanting to believe my own words.

When we arrived home, Ward and Sally were anxious to hear all about Elizabeth. I took Ward aside, leaving the ladies to fuss over my coddled little boy. "How is Aunt Elizabeth?" Ward asked anxiously.

"'Tis no doubt her ordeal has weakened her greatly, but her will is very strong. In time, she will be back to her old self. Don't you worry, son. I have all the confidence in the world that Elizabeth will get well."

That evening, my mind would not rest until I penned a letter to Francis, pleading with him to do everything in his power to get Elizabeth out of that Tory City, once and for all.

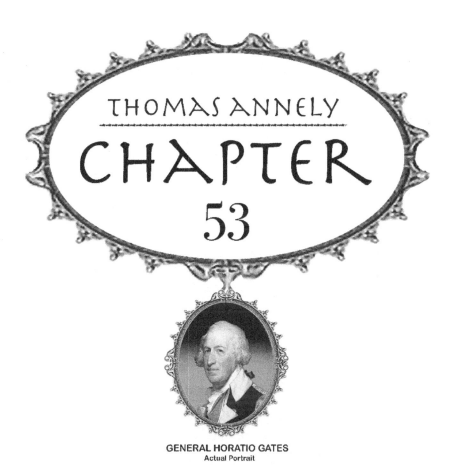

# THOMAS ANNELY

## CHAPTER 53

**GENERAL HORATIO GATES**
Actual Portrait

It was a rainy, dreary day in Elizabethtown, and I had the unpleasant task of delivering some weapons through unfriendly territory. Not one of the men would volunteer to make this dangerous delivery, except my nephew Ward, but I needed him to stay behind to mind the shop.

The lads loaded up my wagon with four crates of muskets and covered them completely with hay. I tucked some bottles of rum and boxes of cigars in the back to bribe any British troops that may harass me along the way. As I steered my horses to Maryland, with my trusted musket by my side, I kept myself acutely aware of my surroundings.

Monday was always the busiest day in the workshop. This was particularly challenging for Ward, who, while I was gone, would have to oversee the men and attend to the recordkeeping out front.

"Excuse me, Ward. There's a British officer here asking for the owner of the shop?" said one of the men, startling Ward at his desk.

Attempting to hide his concern, Ward replied calmly, "Take him into Thomas's office to have a seat. I will be right with him," he replied, looking for anything he should hide.

The visit that Ward was dreading came without any warning. He wiped the sweat off his brow, took a deep breath to calm his composure, and walked over to meet him. The officer was sitting down in a chair, making himself comfortable with his boots resting up on the desk. Upon seeing Ward, the British officer stood up straight; his shoulders arched back with a self-assured look. Holding a Brown Bess musket by his side, he spoke boldly, "Good day, Sir, my name is Lieutenant Jason Briggs. I would like to speak to the proprietor of this establishment."

Ward thought quickly, knowing he would have to lie. "My name is Ward Annely. My father is the owner, but I am in charge while he is away. He is presently in England, visiting our hometown of Bristol. How can I be of service to you, Sir?"

"Young man, my superiors sent me here to inquire who your patrons are. We must be sure that the arms and powder you sell are not getting into the rebels' hands."

Ward replied, attempting to sound humble, "Lieutenant Briggs, you can rest assured, anyone who is not loyal to our King George is not welcome here. Our patrons are fellow, loyal Englishmen. We keep their guns in good working order for hunting. And for their protection from these damn rebels causing havoc through the colonies."

The Lieutenant smiled, pleased with Ward's response. "This is very good to hear, Mr. Annely. My superiors will be glad to know your loyalties are with your fellow Englishmen and our King."

Ward followed the Lieutenant as he walked out into the front room. His eyes scanned the room, taking a mental inventory of all we had on display. "May I ask, what is behind that door in the back?"

Ward swallowed hard. Several muskets and pistols were stored behind that door. He thought fast and lied again, "That is where we assemble paper cartridges and do most of our repair work."

Attempting to distract the Lieutenant, Ward said, "I see you have a beautiful brown bess. It would be my pleasure to fix it for you."

The officer held up his musket and smiled smugly, "Thank you kindly, but 'tis not necessary; my musket is in fine working order. However, I would gladly accept some cartridges."

Ward reached under the counter, grabbed two boxes of paper cartridges, and handed them to the Officer. "These will fit your brown bess perfectly. You will find they will make for superior shooting."

The Lieutenant shook Ward's hand, gladly accepting the cartridges. "Why, thank you kindly. I trust you understand that we must be suspicious of everyone during these times."

"Yes, I understand and agree with you wholeheartedly, Sir."

"I must say, Mr. Annely, I am pleased to see you are a true Englishman. Carry on with your good work, and I shall only be bothering you in the future if I require some of your superior cartridges."

Ward watched him as he mounted his horse and swiftly rode down the road. He sighed in relief and thought to himself; it was worth a few boxes of cartridges if it keeps this bastard away from our shop.

When I returned, Ward told me of his unfortunate encounter with the suspicious British Officer. It was impressive how my nephew was able to fool the Officer into believing he was a loyalist. Truth be known, no matter how much convincing Ward did, the British now have us on their watchlist, and that was not good.

"Uncle, I felt like kicking his pompous ass out the door. The bloke made himself at home in your office, putting his feet up on your desk like he was the bloody King himself. 'Twas humiliating for me to have to put on an act and pretend I was one of those Tory bastards," Ward said with frustration.

"Aye, nephew, you did good, son; I know how hard it had to be for you. How do you feel in your gut? Do you think he was truly sent by his superiors?" I inquired with genuine concern.

Feeling confident in his judgment, Ward replied, "Initially, he had me convinced with his commanding presence. On the other hand, the way he readily accepted my handout made it clear he just wanted something for nothing. I don't think he will return, but I do not trust the British. I suggest we be extra cautious from here on in."

"I agree, Ward, we need to take precautions and be more discreet than we have ever been. Our storefront should be the only area accessible to our patrons, with minimal guns and parts on display. We must secure the back workshop doors and put bars on all the windows. Our finished arms must be packed away in crates, ready for me to deliver as quickly as possible. We must maintain the look of a small gun shop and not have too much inventory stocked up, thus raising suspicion if the Brits come calling again," I stated firmly.

It bothered me that we had to take these precautions, but it was the only way to keep us from being discovered for what we truly are: American Patriots.

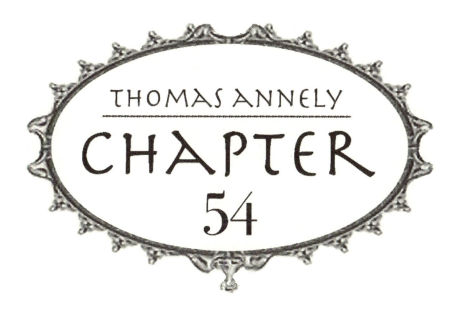

# CHAPTER 54

The warm breeze wafting through the window beckoned Elizabeth to go outside. She yearned to feel the warm sun upon her face and breathe in the fresh air of spring.

"Phoebe, please fetch my cape for me. I want to go down to the Fly Market." Concerned about her mistress's wellbeing, Phoebe questioned her, "Mistress, should I have William bring the wagon up front?"

"No, Phoebe, I prefer to go by myself. 'Tis only a short walk, and it will do me good to get out and stretch my legs," Elizabeth replied, longing for freedom from her confinement.

Elizabeth found the streets pleasantly quiet, allowing her to enjoy her leisurely walk. When her breath became labored, she would sit wherever she saw a bench along the way. The beautiful day was just the remedy to help ease her feelings of loneliness.

When she reached the Fly Market, she recalled her days with her brother Richard, selling the wares he brought back from faraway lands. Those were some of her fondest memories, which she held dear to her heart and reflected upon often. The market was not nearly as stocked as it was during those days, yet she was pleased to find some fresh fish and jars of lovely preserved fruits and vegetables.

Elizabeth chose the items sparingly, making her sack manageable for her walk home. As much as she enjoyed the walk, she felt winded, for she was no longer accustomed to daily exercise.

As she approached the townhouse, she saw a rundown wooden wagon with a team of slump-backed horses out front. At the top of the stairs stood an old, hunched-over man wearing a long brown coat and a dusty wool hat upon his head. A long tail of scraggly gray hair hung down past his shoulders. The man was speaking through the door, to no avail, trying to get Phoebe to open it.

Elizabeth quickened her pace, curious to see who this man was. She hurried up the stairs, and breathlessly, she boldly spoke out, "May I help you, old man?"

The peddler turned around to face Elizabeth, revealing the face of a man much younger than he appeared from behind. "Morgan?" she exclaimed with excitement. "Phoebe, open the door and let my wonderful son in."

Phoebe opened the door slowly, barely recognizing the young man she had cared for all his life. Her face broke out in a wide grin as she welcomed him inside.

Morgan took the sack from his mother's arms, "Let me carry that, Mother; 'tis far too heavy for you," he said. Morgan straightened his posture as Elizabeth wrapped her arms around her youngest son.

"I am sorry to frighten you, Mother, but I had to see you. This disguise was the only way I could be sure the Brits would not recognize me," he said, welcoming her warm embrace.

Elizabeth led Morgan over to the fireplace, "Son, we must get you out of your dusty clothes, and where on heaven's earth did you get that long gray hair?" Morgan laughed, overjoyed to be in his mother's company once more. "One of my men made it for me from a horse's tail," he replied as their faces lit up with laughter.

Elizabeth's face turned to a somber expression, "Morgan, my love, you should not have put yourself in danger like this. There is no telling what would have happened if a British soldier found you here."

Morgan reached over and grasped her hands, "Mother, I waited far too long. I had to take the chance to be certain that you were alright. Frannie had me worried about your well-being."

"Hogwash, Morgan. I am a wee bit weak from my ordeal, that is all. I will be fit as a fiddle once I return to your father. Don't you worry about me, son," she said confidently.

Morgan smiled at her remark, but the weariness across his mother's once serene face made him understand his brother's concern.

"Mother, I heard what the British did to our beloved Whitestone. I will rebuild it for you as soon as we win this war."

"Aye, son, 'tis a pleasant dream, but I am afraid your father's finances have suffered deeply in his support of this war," Elizabeth said somberly. "I don't think there will ever be another Whitestone."

"Do not worry, Mother. I will be a grand lawyer someday. I will take care of you and Father," he said with youthful optimism, gently squeezing her thin hands.

"Never mind all this talk; you must be famished from your journey." Elizabeth poured a brandy for her son as Phoebe prepared their supper. Elizabeth could see how the war had aged her youngest son, who was now a man. She prayed silently to the good Lord to keep her brave son safe.

After a delicious supper, they retired to the sitting room in front of the roaring fire. Elizabeth was elated that Morgan did not have to return until tomorrow. Having her son here filled her with happiness and relieved her loneliness.

Morgan made her heart swell with pride as he spoke of being Chief of Staff to General Horatio Gates and having the opportunity to be in the company of the honorable General George Washington.

"Mother, I had the rare opportunity to stay in the home that General Washington was using for his headquarters. Occasionally, I would speak with him about the matters of war. I swear the man does not sleep. He would still be up when I retired and awake when I would rise. Never have I witnessed a man so devoted to the task placed upon him. The soldiers have the highest esteem for General Washington. We cannot afford to lose this great man if we intend to win this war."

Morgan intentionally left out the horrors of the war he had witnessed, even though he knew his mother was well aware of what was happening. "I was so saddened to hear about Kingsley's passing," said Morgan, slumping his head to his shoulders.

Elizabeth stood up and put her hand on her son's muscular shoulder, "I know, son; I remember how close you were to Kingsley growing up. He was a brave man. If not for him, I am certain I would not have survived that awful prison."

"Aye, Mother, knowing you as I do, I am sure your inner fortitude aided you as well," he replied, smiling.

Morning came too quickly for Morgan. As he ate his breakfast, he gazed across at his mother. He was astounded by her strength and resilience, even after all she had been through.

William arrived early, in time for Elizabeth to introduce him to Morgan. He was impressed with William's polite manner and pleased to see his mother had found a new manservant who seemed perfectly capable for the job.

He put on the old peasant disguise and readied himself for his journey up North.

Morgan held his mother in a long embrace, "Take good care of yourself, Mother. I promise to write to you soon," he said, his heart aching from having to leave his dear mother.

Elizabeth smiled as she waved goodbye at the ragged stranger riding away. She thought about her dreadful days in prison and how she thought she would never see her children again.

Morgan's visit gave her a new-found strength to go on. She was determined to regain her health and be the wife and mother she once was.

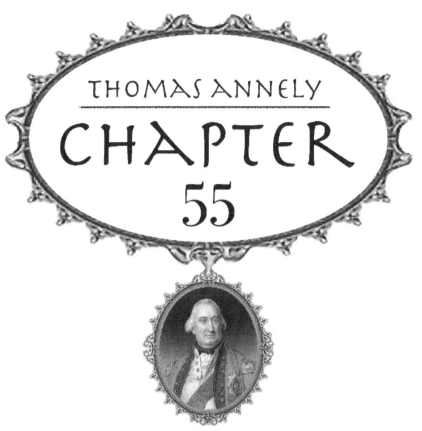

# THOMAS ANNELY

# CHAPTER
# 55

**GENERAL CHARLES CORNWALLIS**
Actual Portrait

This morning, I received a long-awaited letter from my brother Edward. Eager to read what my brother had to say, I sat in my most comfortable chair and ripped it open straight away.

*Dearest Thomas,*

*It seems bad times have surrounded you this past year. I regret not being there to offer my support.*

*Eva and I are beside ourselves with grief upon hearing of Chip's passing. I hope you find peace knowing he was a gallant young man who was loved by us all.*

*I was horrified to hear about what happened to Eliza-beth. We had all warned her this could happen, but one can-not help but be proud of our brave sister and her strength in her convictions. I have sent word to my business acquaintances in New York to lobby for our sister's release. Being so far away, I cannot make any promises, but I will do whatever I can.*

*Eva sends her love to you all. She has become a most attentive wife and seems quite content being back in her mother country. After hearing of Elizabeth's imprisonment, Eva immediately went to London to console our niece, Ann. Naturally, Ann is beside herself with worry for her mother, our dear Elizabeth. We have assured her we are all doing our best to get her mother released.*

*I truly miss our blissful days working together before this bloody war tore us apart. I regret letting that one man, whose name I care not to mention, come into our lives and ruin eve-rything.*

*Eva and I are forever thankful to you for coming to Ward's rescue against that monster of a man. She told me about what you had to do that dreadful day to protect our son. I may be the older brother, Thomas, but you have proven to be much wiser and braver than I. Because of you, our son, Ward, is alive today and has become a fine young man. For this, dear brother, you have my utmost respect and gratitude.*

*By coming back to Bristol, I had hoped I would be away from this business of war. However, that has not been the case. Our fellow Englishmen are not taking too kindly to the hap-penings in America. The morale is low for all the British people. They thought the war would be over by now, and they would be victorious. It seems your man Washington has proven to be a formidable foe and is determined not to give up the fight.*

*Since I voyaged to England, my heart and my stomach have been in constant distress. I have tried many remedies, and nothing seems to rid me of my ailments. I am much thinner now, and I'm afraid you would not recognize your once robust brother.*

*On a more cheerful note, our brother Bernard finally married the schoolmarm he had been courting for the last eleven years. Bernard and his wife have been tutoring Joseph, who has proven, like his older brother, to be a quick learner. Unlike Ward, he has no desire to be a gunmaker. It seems he will follow in Bernard's footsteps and become a great scholar.*

*We are all anxious to meet Ward's new bride and had hoped to return for the birth of our first grandchild, but I am afraid it will not be possible. My poor health and the ongoing war have squashed any thoughts of returning to America at this time. When this war is over, we hope to return to live in the city we all once loved.*

*I am afraid, dear Thomas, I have painted the bleakest of pictures of what my life has become. Fear not, my good brother, for I will soon be healed of my afflictions and be strong again.*

*As with the tides of the ocean, all things rise and fall, and so shall our lives as we pass through this world. I look forward to the days when we will all be together again.*

*I remain your humble brother,*

*Edward*

Watching from the door, Sarah came over and knelt before me. I looked up at her soft, green eyes. "Is everything alright, dear?" she questioned softly.

I stared into her eyes. "Sarah, I am useless. My brother Edward is not well, and my sister Elizabeth is still in confinement, and there is nothing I can do for either one of them," I said with despair.

"Thomas, do not feel that way; you have been the steady rock for all of us. Do I need to remind you of all you have done? Edward would have lost a son that day of the duel if not for you. What about all those Sundays spent with Elizabeth and the children? And those are just a few of the wonderful things you have done. You are the finest husband, brother, father, and patriot. Don't you ever forget that, Thomas Anely!" she exclaimed, wrapping her arms around my neck.

As I held Sarah tightly, her words lifted me out of my self-doubt and made me realize that all I needed in this world was right here in my arms.

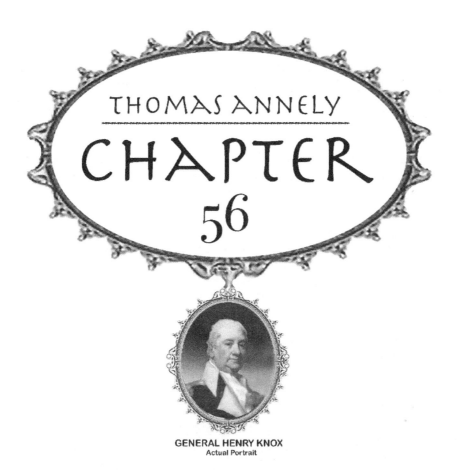

# THOMAS ANNELY

## CHAPTER
### 56

**GENERAL HENRY KNOX**
Actual Portrait

S ummer was upon us and the fields were golden yellow, filled with wheat. The farmers would have to work swiftly to harvest the much-needed grain, or they would lose it all to the armies. They had suffered over the winter months as the British and the Continentals foraged their fields and slaughtered their livestock. It was a shame how the soldiers, in their time of hunger, left very little for the farmers to live upon.

These times bring to mind the words of my brother Edward; our lives truly replicate the tides, ebbing and flowing, forever changing, for better or worse.

My workers secured the workshop and ensured all the finished muskets were safely stored. We separated the work area from the storefront so only my workers could enter the back of the workshop. I was pleased with the results, even though I preferred the open floor plan we had before. I pray that life will return as it was before the war.

Several minor battles waged on throughout the colonies. Unfortunately, most of them were British victories. Despite the disappointing news of the war, we did not lose our confidence in our Commander-in-Chief, General Washington. The local gazettes boasted the glory of how, through his uncanny abilities, Washington managed to outwit the British forces. The British General Cornwallis was hoodwinked over and over again by General Washington's cleverness on the battlefield. To quote Cornwallis's description of Washington, "The Old Fox Fools the Hounds."

As I pondered over the morning paper, a messenger came to my door with a letter from Francis.

> *Dear Thomas,*
>
> *Today, I received the joyous news from General Greene that our beloved Elizabeth will be home within the week!*
>
> *Two Continental soldiers will escort Elizabeth, Phoebe and William and all our belongings from New York to our home in Philadelphia.*
>
> *Thomas, I cannot thank you enough for all you have done for Elizabeth. Never have I known a more faithful brother than you. I know it will be difficult for you not to go to her aid, but I assure you, she will be in good hands and guarded well. Francis Jr. will see to it that your townhouse is left secure.*
>
> *I will send word when Elizabeth has arrived safely, and I look forward to celebrating her homecoming with all!*
>
> *Your devoted brother-in-law, Fran*

I could hardly believe what I was reading. Finally, Elizabeth's suffering would end, and she would return to her loved ones. The lingering heaviness that had weighed down on my chest for so long was now lifting away.

I told Ward the great news, and we ran up the stairs, surprising our poor wives, Sarah and Sally. "Ladies, I have wonderful news," I boasted out loud, waving Francis's letter in the air. "Elizabeth is finally free to go home!" Sarah rushed over and wrapped her arms around me. "Oh, Thomas, thank the Lord!"

"This is wonderful news!" Sally cried out, hugging Ward.

"Ladies, I hope you are preparing a feast, for tonight we shall celebrate," I exclaimed.

We had the most joyous of evenings, celebrating our happiness at knowing Elizabeth would finally be back with Francis. We held each other's hands and prayed for Elizabeth's safe journey and to restore her to good health.

That evening, I slept more soundly than I had in months. It was one of those moments when the tide was in our favor. I relished the moment, for I knew too well how quickly it could change.

THOMAS ANNELY

# CHAPTER
## 57

Today was "Shooter's Day" at the workshop. Each year, the men eagerly await this day to display their shooting skills and see who is the best shooter amongst them. They seem more interested in trying to outshoot me, for they insist I participate every year.

The day has bittersweet memories for me. It began when Chip was alive, working alongside Ward. The two would go out back and prove their newly made muskets to ensure they could hit a target square on. Chip would always challenge Ward and wager that he was the best shot. And true to his word, he would hit that bloody target every time.

Chip had the grand idea of making it an annual event for all the men to participate in. I made a plaque from maple wood with a miniature musket mounted on top. I carved the words "Shooter's Day Champion" into the hardened wood. Each man would boast every year that they would be the one to win the trophy. So far, not one of them has succeeded in taking it home.

I had to admit I looked forward to the event as much as the men. After a restless night with our son, Sarah was finally asleep. I tiptoed over to see my little boy sleeping soundly, clutching the little wooden pistol I had carved for him. I thought that maybe someday, he'll be participating in our Shooter's Day event as I watched him sleep.

As I walked by the fireplace, I could not help but look up at my favorite musket displayed proudly above it. I would use that very musket to win the event every year.

After Chip died in the war, I could never bring myself to use it again. As I stared at my musket, I could almost hear Chip saying, now is the time. So, I took down my musket, wiped the dust off with my sleeve, and brought it downstairs.

It was early, and I was alone in my workshop with only my musket for company. Holding it in my arms, a flood of memories came back to me of Chip and the closeness we shared. "How I miss you, son," I said out loud, breaking the silence in the room.

The morning sun was slowly rising, and the men filed in. Ward rushed over to greet me. "Good morning, Uncle. Are you ready for the big shootout?" he asked, brimming with excitement.

"Yes, I am, Ward. 'Tis Chip's musket I will be using today." I said to Ward's delight and astonishment. "Oh, Uncle; Chip would be proud," he replied, smiling.

As the time drew closer to start the event, the men yelled, "Where is our Champion who refuses to give up the trophy? It's time to start the match!" I walked out back as they cheered, "Here comes our Champion, now!"

John, one of my apprentices, spoke, "I have been practicing, Sir. I hope you brought your trophy, for I will be taking it from you today," he boasted. "We will see, John," I replied, smiling at his bravado.

Finally, it was time to begin. We loaded our muskets, and with the targets in their ready positions, we fired away. After many lead balls had been fired, Ward halted the shooting. He gathered all the targets and evaluated the results. Ward ran to me and exclaimed, "Uncle, you and John made the finals! You are both even, with the most targets hit."

Ward and the men put up two new targets, side by side, this time seventy-five yards away. John took a lead ball from his pouch and hid both hands behind his back. He brought his two-fisted hands before me and asked me to choose which hand held the musket ball. I went along with his game and pointed to his left hand. "Sorry, Sir; I'll be shooting first," he said, opening his right hand to reveal the ball.

As John and I loaded up our muskets, the men placed wagers on who would win. Ward recited the rules: "Each man will shoot three rounds attempting to make a small triangle within the target. If any one of your shots misses the target, it will result in your automatic disqualification." We shook hands and wished each other good luck.

I watched John get into his stance and take aim. With his confident manner, it was unlikely he would miss. When he finished firing, he looked at me and winked sarcastically, confident he would win. Ward, down range, waved the white flag, signaling John hit the target with all three shots.

I nodded to John, acknowledging his fine shooting. It reminded me of when I would target shoot with Chip and how badly he wanted to outshoot me. I could have let Chip win, but I knew the lad would never better himself if I did. With that thought in mind, I decided to try my best to get the three balls in the bullseye.

I proceeded to load my musket. Using my powder horn, I poured the right amount of powder into the barrel, followed by a ball and patch, and rammed it home. I replaced the ramrod, put a small amount of powder into the pan, and closed the frizzen tight. Placing the butt of my musket into my right shoulder, I wrapped my left hand around the stock. I pulled the cock back with my thumb while putting my right-hand index finger on the trigger. I aimed the barrel through the site to the target, held my breath while slowly pulling the trigger, and fired. The burst of the powder exploding sent the ball to its final destination.

After I finished shooting, Ward enthusiastically waved the white flag, alerting us that all three shots had hit the target. The men, watching from behind, ran down to examine the targets to see the final results. They encircled me, shouting, "He did it again; he is still our Champion!"

Ward carried the targets over, showing John had impressively hit three close shots, making a perfect, tight triangle. Then he showed me my target, which had one large hole in the center where the three shots had hit directly in the bullseye. It was the smallest triangle the men had ever witnessed.

John congratulated me, "Sir, the men told me how good a shot you are, but that was an understatement. You are the greatest shooter I have ever seen." he said, walking back to the shop, his head hung low. I called him to hold up, "John, when you get inside, tell Ward I want you to be in charge of proving all the muskets and pistols. You are too good of a marksman to let your talents go to waste. You will be compensated for your extra work." John's expression changed to a proud smile as he replied, "I will do that, Sir. Thank you very much!"

Like my boy Chip, my musket was always faithful to me. At the end of the day, I placed the trophy back on the wall and hung my favorite musket over the fireplace. All in memory of Chip.

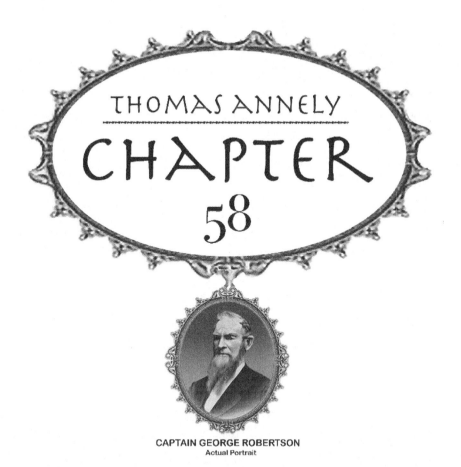

# THOMAS ANNELY

## CHAPTER 58

**CAPTAIN GEORGE ROBERTSON**
Actual Portrait

Elizabeth had only been home for a few months when Francis had to leave again. The British had taken over Philadelphia and now controlled the city. Francis and the members of Congress had to flee once more. He regretted leaving Elizabeth but was relieved when I wrote that we would visit while he was away.

I had my concerns about traveling there. Even though Fran's house was in a secluded part of town, I knew British regulars would be everywhere.

Despite the baby on the way, Ward and Sally decided to join us, for Sally was not due for some time. I arranged to put John Sayles in charge while we were away. John had become a reliable and trustworthy apprentice, and his loyalty to the American cause put Ward and me at ease.

We loaded the wagon full of extra blankets and foodstuffs for the journey. Thankfully, the autumn weather brought cooler air, which was most welcoming after the heat of the summer. We traveled down the backroads to Trenton, crossed over the Delaware, and, after one night of rest at an Inn, continued on.

I traveled the backroads, avoiding the occupied city of Philadelphia, to get to their home in the peaceful countryside. On the verge of turning their vibrant fall colors, a row of maple trees complemented the handsome homes we rode by in what was clearly the affluent part of town.

We finally arrived at Francis's stately home and drove up the brick pathway lined with boxwood hedges. Although the house was not as majestic as Whitestone, we were all quite impressed.

The red brick, two-story home with white-trimmed paned glass windows and green shutters seemed ideally suited for a gentleman of Fran's status. Two stately white columns stood aside the matching green entryway door.

Phoebe and her new spouse, William, greeted us at the grand entrance. Elizabeth had insisted the pair be married if they were to live under her roof.

As we walked down the long hallway, our footsteps echoed off the vaulted ceiling. We followed Phoebe into the sitting room, where Elizabeth was waiting. It was wonderful to see her looking much healthier, her skin glowing from the time she spent in the sunshine.

Elizabeth rose, happy to see us, "'Tis so very good to see you all!" she exclaimed as we all took turns embracing her.

"Aunt Elizabeth, this is my wife, Sally," said Ward. "Oh my, she is a lovely girl, Ward," she expressed. Sally blushed, "Thank you, Mrs. Lewis. It is a pleasure to finally meet you," she said, extending her hand.

"Come, everyone, let's go sit outside; 'tis too lovely a day to be inside," Elizabeth said.

We relaxed in the warmth of the fading sun while the ladies fawned over Gifford, watching him take his first steps. Seeing the happiness on Elizabeth's face made the long journey worthwhile.

After a light dinner, Elizabeth gave us a tour of her grand home. Fran's influence was evident throughout; each room was masculinely decorated, with richly-colored walls, dark leather furniture, and mahogany wood.

As we entered Fran's library, I took a deep breath and looked about, envious of the room every man dreams of having. Upon the dark paneled walls were shelves lined with books. A glass cabinet housed crystal-cut snifters and a matching decanter filled with brandy. The portraits we had rescued at Whitestone of Francis and Elizabeth were hung handsomely over the fireplace. Silver candelabras in each corner filled the room with warm candlelight. In the center of the room sat a nine-foot billiards table. "Now, this is my kind of room; I look forward to challenging Fran to a game of billiards," I remarked. Ward nodded in agreement.

Ward and I stayed up, sitting out on the veranda, gazing at the night sky, enjoying our brandy and Fran's fine cigars. It was not the same without my boisterous brother-in-law here, but we enjoyed ourselves just the same.

The ladies had already retired upstairs to the bedrooms that Phoebe had prepared. I tiptoed into the bedroom, not wanting to wake Sarah or my boy, and plopped down onto the feathery, soft bed.

Sarah woke briefly to kiss my cheek goodnight as she turned and quickly fell back asleep. It was a long day, so I could not blame her for being weary. I silently prayed to our good Lord for how grateful I was to see Elizabeth looking much healthier. I soon drifted off into a deep slumber.

Suddenly, I woke to the loud sounds of a woman crying out in pain. Groggy from sleep I saw Sarah sitting up in bed, her face pale with fright. "Who is that, Thomas? Is it Elizabeth?" she asked, her voice quivering.

"Stay here, dear; I will go see." I slipped out of bed, threw on my breeches, and went out into the hallway. Elizabeth was racing up the stairs with Phoebe and William behind her. Oh dear God, it must be Sally, I thought as I watched them rush into the bedroom where they were staying.

I stood there frozen, unsure what to do, when I overheard Elizabeth shouting out orders, "Phoebe, gather as many clean linens as you can find. William, fetch some buckets of clean water and put them to the fire to boil," she said firmly.

Ward came rushing out of the room, his face as pale as snow, "Uncle, Sally's bleeding; I need to fetch some water!" he shouted as he flew down the stairs. Standing in the doorway, Sarah sprang into action and assisted Elizabeth.

Elizabeth yelled, "William, go fetch the doctor!" I could hear the horse's hoofbeats galloping off as I went downstairs to help Ward.

Carrying a bucket of water into the bedroom, I was shocked to see Sally, half-conscious, lying on the blood-soaked bed linens. She mumbled out in pain, delirious with fever, as Sarah and Elizabeth tended to her.

I could not bear to stay in the room any longer, so I rushed down for more water. "Ward, go to your wife; I will take over here," I told the distraught lad.

A moment later, an ear-piercing shriek came out of Sally, sending Ward flying back up the stairs.

I felt so helpless, but this was women's work, and Sally's fate was in the Lord's hands now. I carried up two more buckets of hot water and saw Elizabeth crouched over Sally, calmly speaking to the young woman, "Sally, dear, your baby is breached. Do not worry, it will be alright, love. You hold on to Ward, now."

Sarah and Ward held Sally still as Elizabeth positioned her hands against her swelling belly, feeling the head and feet of the babe inside the womb. She pressed firmly, turning the infant, as Sally screamed in pain. Elizabeth gently coaxed Sally, "Now push Sally, that's it dear, keep pushing." Finally, the head appeared, and Elizabeth gently guided the babe into her arms.

Phoebe rushed to Elizabeth's side and wiped the baby with the clean linens as Elizabeth cut and tied off the cord. She held him up and slapped his backside as he miraculously let out a loud wail, taking in his first breath of air. As weak as she was, Sally smiled at the sound of her babe's cry as tears streamed down her face.

Elizabeth swaddled the babe and gently placed him in Ward's arms. "You have a beautiful baby boy," she announced, smiling at the young couple. Sally reached over with a shaky hand and grasped onto Elizabeth's forearm.

"Thank you, Elizabeth. You saved our baby's life," she expressed, her voice weak from exhaustion. "'Twas the lot of us, dear, and you as well. You were very brave through it all," Elizabeth replied softly, wiping her brow with her sleeve.

The room turned eerily silent as Sally fell unconscious from the constant loss of blood. All the attempts from the women to stop the bleeding were futile. Finally, William returned, rushing up the stairs with the doctor following.

The elderly doctor, carrying a worn-out black leather bag, went in and immediately took control. He walked over and quickly looked at the babe before tending to Sally. "I need the assistance of two women, so that I may tend to the mother," he instructed. "I will stay with my maid," Elizabeth spoke up boldly. "Very well, thank you, Mrs. Lewis, and you men, please, get the hell out of here. There is nothing you can do," he said sternly and swiftly went to work. Ward reluctantly left the room with his newborn son, wailing in his arms.

"She's in good hands, Ward," Sarah said, attempting to ease his worried mind. "Come sit in our room, son. I will take your boy to get him cleaned up."

Ward looked on in shock, hesitant to release his son, clutched in his arms. "It will be alright, Ward. I will take good care of him and bring him right back to you," Sarah said softly.

After almost an hour, the doctor came out of the room, wiping the sweat from his brow. Ward stood there speechless, waiting for the doctor to speak. "She is awake now. I managed to stop the bleeding, and her fever has subsided, but your wife must remain in bed for a few days. She has lost a lot of blood, so monitor her closely, son. She is a fortunate young lady. If not for Mrs. Lewis's swift action, we could have lost her and the babe."

"Thank you, Doctor," said Ward humbly, his voice weak and shaky.

"It's quite alright, son. Now you take care of that lovely wife of yours, and by the sounds of it, you have a very healthy son," he said, smiling as the baby's cries filled the house.

I led the kind doctor to the door. He turned to me and said, "You have a remarkable sister. What she did took great skill and an even greater amount of steady nerve. I could not have delivered that baby any better myself," he said.

"Yes, Sir, we are very grateful, but I am concerned for my sister's health."

The doctor scratched his head, hesitant to discuss Elizabeth's health concerns with me, "I only discuss my patients with their immediate family. But you are her brother, and I can see how much you care." he said before continuing. "Francis has me come once a month to check on her welfare. She is not recovering as quickly as we hoped, although, as you can see, she has a strong will. I am certain she will return to herself in time and with plenty of good sunshine. Rest assured, I will keep an eye on her," he said confidently.

"Thank you. 'Tis comforting to know Elizabeth has such a kind doctor watching over her," I replied. "It is also comforting to know that she has such a loving family watching over her. May God bless you all," he said before leaving.

Although the good doctor meant well, he did not completely put me at ease about Elizabeth's health.

Elizabeth came slowly out of the bedroom, holding the walls to steady herself. Ward went over and embraced her, "Aunt Elizabeth, thank you for saving Sally and my boy!" he cried, tears filling his eyes. "'Tis alright, son," Elizabeth said back weakly. Phoebe rushed to her Mistress's side, pleading for her to sit after the exhaustive ordeal she had just been through.

Ward rushed back to Sally, clutching her in his arms. Sarah went into the room with the babe sleeping soundly in her arms. "He's perfect in every way," she said, placing the babe in Sally's arms.

"I will stay and watch over them tonight," Phoebe offered, sitting beside the bed. "Thank you kindly, Phoebe. My son will be waking up soon, crying for my attention. I will be across the hall if you need me," said Sarah, grateful for Phoebe's help.

I went back to our bed, exhausted from it all. Sarah was up, tending to our little boy, who had thankfully slept throughout the whole ordeal. "Oh love, what a night this has been," I expressed, yawning, as my head hit the pillow. "Yes, dear; now let's try to get some sleep," she said lovingly, laying Gifford between us. I fell asleep peacefully, with the comfort of my two loves beside me.

After the excitement of the night, everyone woke up feeling groggy. The only cheerful voice was that of my son Gifford's giggles as he wobbled over with delight to meet his new cousin.

Cradling his newborn son in the crook of one arm, Ward sat and leaned his weary head in his hand. As I entered the room, I patted Ward on his back. "You have a fine son there, Ward. How is Sally this morning?"

"She had a fitful night's sleep but is resting well now, Uncle," he said with exasperation.

Phoebe came and took the babe from Ward's arms. "Time for a feeding now, Sir. I'll be taking him up to his Mama." Young Gifford outstretched his arms and let out a cry of disapproval. I picked up my son and swung him around, bringing a smile to his face once more.

Sipping his tea, Ward spoke first, "We never expected the little guy to come so soon," he said, with a half chuckle. Sarah walked over to Ward and placed a comforting hand on his shoulder, "Ward, we are just pleased that Sally and your boy are doing well. The bumpy ride over must have moved her along in her cycle."

"Thank the Lord we had Elizabeth here," I expressed.

Elizabeth, looking a bit worn, came to join us. "Good morning, everyone. I hope Sally and your little one are doing well?" she inquired as Sarah served her tea.

Ward's face turned red. "I am sorry, Aunt Elizabeth, for the trouble we caused in your fine home," he said remorsefully, with his chin tucked into his chest. Elizabeth piped up, "Nonsense, nephew; you and Sally are family. We are grateful we could help. Do not say another word."

Ward had barely touched his food as he excused himself and went to be with Sally.

"Thomas, please watch Gifford. I am going upstairs to relieve Phoebe so she can rest," said Sarah, leaving Elizabeth and me alone.

We sat silently, pondering over our tea, when I spoke up, "'Twas remarkable what you did last night, sister. I hope having them here for a few days will not be too much for you."

"Not to worry, Thomas. They are welcome to stay as long as they need to. It will do me good to have a wee one in the house. I understand you may need to return, so I will arrange to get them home."

"Thank you, Elizabeth. Unfortunately, with this bloody war going on, I must return to the workshop."

Elizabeth smiled, "I understand, Thomas. Having you here has been such a joy, even for only a few days."

"Aye. sister, we miss you and Fran so much. I look forward to coming back soon. I might even get a chance to beat Fran at his billiard game," I said, bringing a laugh to Elizabeth's weary face.

Ward was concerned about not returning with us to Elizabethtown, but we all agreed that he would stay here until Sally was well enough to travel.

Once again, I was leaving Elizabeth without Francis at home. My only solace was knowing that she had the help of her two trusted servants to care for her. All I could do was pray that this British siege of Philadelphia would end soon, bringing Francis back to her.

# CHAPTER 59

It had been months since I visited my sister Elizabeth in Philadelphia. The winter months were brutally cold but she managed to get a message through, letting me know she was doing well. Francis and most of the members of Congress were still away in seclusion. The thought of her being in her empty home, without any family nearby, worried me. Unfortunately, with the British still occupying Philadelphia, all my hopes of visiting Elizabeth would have to wait.

The papers were filled with discouraging news of the war, making it clear that the army was in deep trouble.

The year was not going well for General Washington, either. A group of commanding officers and some members of Congress had lost their confidence in him and wanted him out of command. General Horatio Gates, with his triumphant victory at Saratoga last autumn, was the man they believed could provide the leadership they needed to win this war.

One thing I knew for sure was that Francis did not agree with these men. He was fiercely devoted to General Washington. While the British army wintered in the comfort of stately homes in Philadelphia, General Washington's army braved the winter months at Valley Forge in cold and drafty barracks. The soldiers suffered greatly from the lack of basic supplies, such as food and proper clothing, to brace against the wintry weather. The brave men who fought gallantly throughout the year were now succumbing to the diseases that spread like wildfire throughout the camp. All of this was lowering the morale of our army. Many chose desertion to rid themselves of the hell they were enduring.

Yet, Washington ignited their Patriot souls once more with his encouraging words: "Patience and perseverance will win each soldier the admiration of the world and the love of their country."

Finally, a good headline graced the papers across the colonies: France had signed a Treaty of Alliance with America and would join us in our fight for independence. The tides were finally turning in our favor. I was elated when a messenger brought me a letter from Francis.

*Dear Thomas,*

*First and foremost, I am safe in a location I cannot divulge. I am sure you have heard the good news of France forming an alliance with our cause. I am forever grateful to my friend Ben Franklin for his sharp-witted abilities to convince the French to sign the Treaty of Alliance. Our victory at Saratoga, which I am proud to say Morgan was a part of, proved to the French that America's independence was worth fighting for.*

*The money pledged from France has come at the most favorable time for all of us, especially our poor soldiers, who have done without basic provisions for far too long. Mrs.*

*Washington has been visiting Valley Forge and doing what she can to help our troops. Her kind manner must be doing wonders for the men. Elizabeth would have been right by Mrs. Washington's side if she could.*

*You may have heard about "Conway's Cabal," the plot to relieve Washington from his command and put General Gates in charge. Good old "Granny Gates" is no match for our good General. 'Tis bad enough that Washington has to keep up the fight with the bloody British and then have this internal fighting going on. 'Tis just too much to ask of one man.*

*After much deliberation, the Congress came to its senses and finally agreed that General Washington would remain commander-in-chief. A wise decision indeed!*

*This relentless war has tested our patience, but I have faith in General Washington, our dedicated army, and our Good Lord.*

*I look forward to the day when I return to my dear Elizabeth, and we can all be together again in peace.*

*I will write to you as soon as time allows.*

*May God protect you, your humble brother, Fran*

Fran's letter and the news about France brought me much relief. Now that I know Fran is safe and Congress is pledging to send more money, I feel a renewed surge of hope.

Later that month, I was busy in my office when I heard someone entering my shop. I walked out to the front and was startled to see my nephew Morgan standing there. Sharply dressed in Continental blues, I was very impressed by the sight of him. "Morgan, I am so glad to see you! Come into my office," I said as I pulled out a chair for him and poured a glass of rum for each of us.

"'Tis so good to see you, Uncle. Much obliged, 'tis just what I needed after the long journey from up North," he said, sipping his rum.

"Ironically, I received a letter from your father a few weeks back. He is doing well and is very proud of you."

"That is good to hear, Uncle. 'Tis so difficult to get letters through during these times. I miss Mother and Father so much."

"Yes, I miss them as well. Now, tell me, Morgan, what brings you here today?"

"Uncle, I apologize for not warning you before coming here, but I did not want my message to get intercepted. My orders are to work with you directly to supply the northern division with new muskets and ammunition.

I brought with me a good many damaged muskets, which are in need of your expert repair. In turn, I will need to bring back as many new muskets as you can spare to replace them."

"Of course, nephew, I will be happy to supply you with as many guns as possible," I replied assuredly.

"'Tis good to hear, Uncle. I must stay until the order is completed. Is that alright with you and Aunt Sarah?"

"No need to ask, son, 'tis our pleasure to spend some time with you. Come with me to meet the men. They will bring your wagon out back and unload the damaged muskets." I rose and headed out to the workroom, with Morgan following behind.

The men stiffened in salute to Morgan, "May I have your attention, men? I would like you all to meet my nephew, Colonel Morgan Lewis. He is the Quartermaster General for the Northern Army," I announced proudly.

"Pleased to meet you all," Morgan replied. "'Tis an honor to meet you, Sir. We all think very highly of your father. A true Patriot, is he," said John, as the other men nodded in agreement.

Even though Morgan came on official business, Sarah and I were delighted he could stay. It was good to hear firsthand from him about what was happening within the war.

After dinner, Morgan amused us with the story of the Prussian officer, with the regal name of Baron Von Steuben, who has been at Valley Forge, training Washington's army. "From what I heard, despite his gruffness, he is making remarkable progress with the men. The Baron is turning them into bona fide soldiers to rival any army, even the mighty British forces. Not one soldier understands him, and the only words he speaks in English are quite vulgar. Hamilton and Lafayette have been translating his words to the men, even the colorful ones," Morgan said with a chuckle.

"Well, it proves what they say; a man's actions speak more than his words, even the vulgar ones," I laughed.

As Sarah left to tend to Gifford, Morgan confided in me how Chip's passing had shattered him. "Uncle, I was so devastated to hear about Chip. We were the best of friends growing up. He was just like a brother to me," he said with sadness.

"Morgan, Chip died a hero and a true Patriot. He gave up his own life to save a fellow soldier by shielding him from a cannonball explosion." Morgan looked at me with a sad smile, "It does not surprise me, for Chip always cared deeply for his fellow man."

Young Gifford came wobbling out, taking our minds off our melancholy moment, "Come here, my wee little cousin," Morgan said affectionately as he playfully lifted Gifford and swung him around. Gifford giggled with delight and begged Morgan for more. "Time to go to bed now, son," I said sternly to Gifford's disapproving face. "No, I want

Morgan!" he said, stamping his little foot. "Come along, Gifford. I will tuck you in," said Morgan, gently grabbing his hand and bringing him into the bedroom.

After lulling our son to sleep with one of his many stories, Morgan joined us back in our sitting room. "Thank you, Morgan. Our little boy will be missing you greatly. If you men will excuse me, I will be retiring as well," Sarah said, leaving me alone with my nephew.

We sat silently, enjoying a warm glass of spiked rum and the crackling sounds of the fire. "Uncle, when do you expect Ward back?" he inquired.

"Ward and Sally are attending her father's funeral service. I expect them back soon, hopefully before you leave. I know Ward will be disappointed if he doesn't get to see you," I replied.

"Unfortunately, I cannot stay too long, but once I complete my commission, I will return to Elizabethtown to finish my law studies. It will be good to be closer to all of you. Incidentally, I heard there is a good probability that the British will soon leave Philadelphia. General Howe is resigning from his post, and General Clinton will replace him. Of what they say about Clinton, he is anxious to get the British troops back to the Tory city of New York to hide away from our new French allies."

"I hope what you have heard is right, Morgan. The sooner the bloody British get out of Philadelphia, the sooner your father will be able to return to your mother," I replied.

"Yes, Uncle, we are all looking forward to them being back together again. I would have liked to visit my mother, but I would not want your fine muskets or me getting into the hands of the British soldiers."

I laughed and replied, "Smart thinking, son. I am certain your mother understands. She knows how risky travel is these days."

Our visit with Morgan ended far too soon, and unfortunately, he had to leave before Ward and Sally returned. He climbed aboard his wagon as we said our goodbyes, "Godspeed, Nephew; I hope you know how proud we all are of you."

"Thank you, Uncle; I look forward to seeing you again soon."

Morgan went on his way with a wagon full of new muskets and plenty of cartridges hidden under a thick cover of wooden planks.

When I first came to this great land, I never imagined we would be sending our young sons off to war. I suppose it is their fate in life, something we have no control over. Their legacy will be the example they set forth for all future generations.

I will continue to do my part to aid these brave young lads in winning this war and preserving our country's freedom.

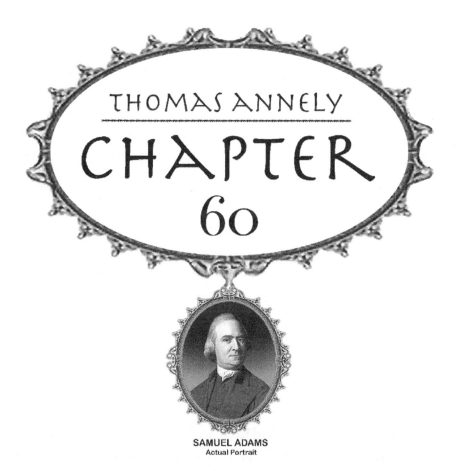

THOMAS ANNELY

# CHAPTER 60

**SAMUEL ADAMS**
Actual Portrait

The year is now 1779. Thankfully, the British have left Philadel-phia, and Francis and the members of Congress are holding their meetings there as usual. We are all grateful to have Francis home again, living with Elizabeth.

As Elizabeth relaxed on the veranda, admiring the tender sprouts shooting up from the softened ground, she felt sadness in her heart. Her favorite pastime was too much for her now. The exertion of gardening caused her to cough uncontrollably, leaving her weak for the rest of the day.

Gravely concerned for his wife's failing health, Francis took a leave of absence from his position with Congress. She was his priority now, and he was determined to get her well.

He went outside to join Elizabeth on the veranda. "Your garden is coming along well, dear," said Francis, sitting beside her. "Yes, Francis, we have William to thank, for Lord knows I don't have the strength," she said, frustrated with herself. "Give it time, love. You will be back in your garden again," he said, affectionately patting her knee.

Elizabeth reached for her husband's hand, "Frannie, you are such a kind and loving husband. 'Tis so wonderful of you to be here for me, but I don't like taking you away from your duties. The Congress still needs you and your experience to resolve this war."

"Nonsense love, the Congress has many great men and will survive without me for now. Now that winter is over, I want to enjoy this warm sunshine and lovely spring air more. It will do us both wonders," Francis said reassuringly.

Elizabeth smiled and lifted her chin to face the sun. "Yes, dear, the warmth feels so lovely, and having you here beside me gives me strength."

Elizabeth sat up straight and faced her husband, "Francis, perhaps 'tis time we invite the family here. I miss them all so much. Although, I do not want them to see me as a tired, old lady."

Francis laughed at her remark. "Lizzy, my dear, you are no such thing. You are still the lovely girl I married," he said, making her smile. "I will start writing invitations at once, and you will start barking your orders to William and Phoebe to make the preparations. I don't want you lifting a finger, my Queen," he said, reaching for her hand to kiss it.

"Oh hush, Fran, we have worked too hard to keep royalty from coming to this land. Do not be calling me your Queen," she shot back teasingly.

"That's the spirit, my dear," he said, kissing her cheek as he hurried off to the library to his desk and quill pen.

Sarah and I were so excited when we received Fran's invitation to the family gathering. It was a wondrous feeling to put aside our thoughts of the ongoing war and look forward to a joyous occasion with the whole family.

Fran mentioned that Francis Jr. and his wife Beth, who is now with child, will be there, along with Morgan and his new wife, Gertrude Livingston. Gertrude comes from a very wealthy family in New York City. Her father was a prominent politician and a leading whig until his untimely death just before the revolution began.

A week had passed, and it was time to start our journey to Philadelphia. After packing up our carriages, we were finally on our way. Ward and Sally followed behind, with two young stallions pulling their stately carriage, which they had inherited from Sally's father's estate. Now that the British are no longer occupying the city of Philadelphia, it will be much easier to get to Elizabeth's home.

Even though most battles were now in the southern colonies, we chose the less traveled pathways and kept our muskets handy. The excitement of us all being together again made the long and monotonous ride more bearable.

Sarah's parents, Mr. & Mrs. Dally, were overjoyed at receiving the invitation from Francis to join us at their home in Philadelphia. "Thomas, it is very gracious for Francis to invite us to his family gathering. It has been far too long since I have seen my good friend, Fran, and I want to tell him how proud I am of what he has done as a congressman for our country," my father-in-law expressed sincerely.

"'Tis our pleasure, Sir. I am certain you and Anne's presence will do Elizabeth a world of good," I replied.

After a long and tedious journey, we arrived at their splendid home in Philadelphia and were pleasantly surprised that we did not encounter any redcoats. Mr. and Mrs. Dally were impressed by the grandness of their home and the lush green lawn and garden surrounding it. Little Gifford was smitten when he saw the goats and sheep grazing on their lawn.

Fran and Elizabeth greeted us at the entryway, excited to see us all. I smiled warmly at Elizabeth and embraced her gently in my arms. For a moment, the warmth on her smiling face made me forget just how ill she was.

Phoebe had prepared a refreshing peach-flavored tea and a large platter of fresh fruits, nuts, and sweet treats. It was most welcoming after the exhausting journey, as we all indulged hungrily.

"Do not fill your bellies too much," Elizabeth said. "Phoebe is preparing a wonderful dinner for us all. But first, William will show you to your rooms, as I am sure you would like to freshen up before dinner. I will meet you all in the dining room promptly at 6:00," announced Elizabeth, appearing as her old self, the perfect hostess.

After a brief rest, I left Sarah and Little Gifford napping as I went downstairs, eager to speak with Francis. I found him sitting outside on his veranda, enjoying the late-day sunshine. The scent of one of his rum-flavored cigars wafting through the hallway enticed me to join him outside.

"Come have a smoke, Thomas," he said, offering me one of his fine cigars. "Why, thank you, Fran. I would like that very much," I replied, lighting my cigar as the smoke encircled my head. "Very enjoyable," I remarked, taking my first puff.

We sat quietly, enjoying our cigars, looking out upon the vast green lawn and rows of flowering shrubs. "'Tis so wonderful of you and Elizabeth to have us all here in your lovely home. It has been far too long, my brother, since we have all been together."

Francis's face turned somber as he spoke, "Thomas, I am so glad to have you here, for you are the only one I can confide in. I fear our Elizabeth may never recover from her ailments. The doctor feels she contracted a sickness in her lungs from the time she spent in prison. She will only get weaker as time goes by," he uttered, his face flushed with anger. "I cannot believe how cruelly those British bastards treated her, as if the burning of Whitestone was not enough."

My heart sank, not wanting to hear the truth about my dear sister. "Do not lose all hope, dear brother. Elizabeth is a strong woman; perhaps being with us all will renew her strength," I replied, hoping my mere words would bring him the solace he sought.

Francis rose from his chair and touched my shoulder. "You're a good brother, Thomas, to us both. We better get inside before Lizzy scolds us for being late for dinner."

I met Sarah walking down the hallway, looking as lovely as ever in the emerald green dress she had worn the first day I fell in love with her. The sight of her calmed my nerves as she held my hand and led me into the dining room. Sarah gasped at the beautiful table setting as we took our seats alongside Sarah's parents while young Gifford sat obediently between them.

In the center of the table was a large arrangement of fresh red, white, and blue flowers. The entire table was decorated lavishly with the colors of our new flag.

"My goodness, what a lovely setting, Elizabeth. You have outdone yourself!" my mother-in-law Anne expressed admiringly. "It appears as if we are expecting the General himself," quipped my father-in-law, citing laughter around the table.

Only the face of their daughter-in-law Beth remained stoic, sitting stiffly, observing her in-laws' show of patriotism. Her family were loyalists, and she would never go against their alliance with the crown.

William walked around the table, filling each glass with what Fran had told us was General Washington's favorite wine from the Portuguese island of Madeira.

After William filled all the glasses, Francis rose and spoke, "I welcome all of you to our home. Elizabeth and I are so pleased to have all of you here at this time. Let us all raise our glasses to the promise of a new America, independent from the stronghold of Britain, so our children may live free." Everyone clinked their glasses, save for one, as we shouted, "Hear! Hear!"

Phoebe and William waited on us, serving a bountiful feast, course after course, of the finest meal any of us had eaten in a long time. It had been years since we all sat around Elizabeth's grand table, and I could see the sheer joy on everyone's faces. It brought back fond memories of our Annely family gatherings at Whitestone. Even Francis Jr's wife could not deny how delicious everything was, as she complimented her mother-in-law graciously.

The wine, which flowed freely throughout the meal, loosened our lips as a robust conversation began. I stood and raised my glass to our hosts, "Here's to Elizabeth and Francis for this wonderful meal and bringing us all together again," I said gratefully. Soon, others followed, "Here's to our wonderful mother, Elizabeth, the strongest and bravest woman I know," said Morgan, beaming at his mother.

One by one, the accolades followed around the table for Elizabeth and Francis, who have shown what it truly means to live a life not for oneself but for the good of others.

Elizabeth spoke, her voice filled with emotion, "It seems only yesterday when my sons were boys. I only wish my daughter Ann could be with us today. Now here we are, with another generation of Annelys," she said, smiling at the little ones. "I can hardly wait for my new grandchild," she said, gazing at Beth and Francis Jr. with tears brimming in her eyes.

Laughter filled the air as we recollected stories of the days gone past.

"Uncle Thomas, do you remember when Chip and I dragged up that poor deer after hunting at Whitestone?" Morgan said, smiling at the memory.

"I certainly do; 'twas a 6-pointer!" I exclaimed.

"We argued about which of us brought him down," laughed Morgan.

"You both were so proud of your kill, and I also remember Kingsley's fine venison stew," I expressed with laughter.

Ward recalled fond memories of Chip. "Who could ever forget the sight of young Chip? When we first laid eyes on him, he was just a scrappy little lad, no more than ten years of age. He came into the shop every day looking for work. No matter how many times I kicked his backside out the door, he would still come back, asking for work. Uncle Thomas had the foresight to see Chip for what he would become: a brave young man and a helluva gunsmith," said Ward fondly.

I nodded in agreement as a lump began to form in the back of my throat, for the boy that I loved and considered my own flesh and blood.

"Here's to dear old Kingsley for his loyalty to Elizabeth and how he helped her when she needed him the most. We will remember him forever," said Fran, holding up his glass again.

Thankfully, my father-in-law changed the subject, shaking us out of our sad memories. "So Fran, are you officially retired from Congress now?" he inquired.

Fran paused as he sipped his last drop of wine. "I have only taken a leave of absence at this time. I dare say, an old goat like me must still have some merit, for they have not booted me out yet," he said, with his usual boisterous voice.

"What say you, Morgan? Do they see any end in sight to this war?" my father-in-law asked, turning the conversation over to Morgan.

"No, Sir, I am afraid not; the troubles down south have just begun," Morgan lamented.

"Is it true that the British have taken over Georgia? It is such a lovely state; I tremble at the thought of it in ruins," said my mother-in-law with great concern.

"Unfortunately, 'tis true that the British have captured Savannah and Augusta. Rest assured, though, our fearless troops will never give up. I am certain they will give the Brits a rough go of it," Morgan replied confidently.

I spoke boldly: "Fran, I must say, I was annoyed by some of your fellow congressmen who were considering removing our honorable General Washington from his command and possibly replacing him with General Gates."

"I was annoyed as well, Thomas. We are all aware that Washington has had his share of defeats, but he has also had some major victories. The man is driven by one desire: his allegiance to his country. I harbor no ill will against General Gates. He has proven himself to be a very competent general throughout the years. However, the only way we will win this war is with the intestinal fortitude that only our General Washington possesses. He has God on his side. Thank the Lord that Congress came to their senses and voted for General Washington to stay in command."

My father-in-law Gifford responded proudly, "You are quite right, Francis; I, like most of you here, have the greatest confidence in our brave leader. He is a master strategist, which is the only way we can defeat the mighty British army."

Elizabeth's face, though pale and worn, beamed with pride as she listened intently to all the stimulating conversations around her table.

Francis Jr. stood up and spoke, "My dear family and friends, as you all know, I am no expert on the war, for I, like Uncle Edward, have chosen to remain neutral. However, I share the same dreams that our children will grow up free Americans," he exclaimed, holding the hand of his wife Beth.

I boldly stood up, with the wine giving me the courage to say what was in my heart. I tapped on a glass with a spoon loudly and said, "May I have your attention, please? I want to share a story, especially for the younger ones at this table. It all started with our older brother Richard, the first of our Annely family to sail from England to America. Not long after, Richard brought Elizabeth and Francis to America. Richard made the wise choice of making Francis his partner; together, they were very successful in business. They all came to live in the magnificent home Richard had built, named Whitestone. Unfortunately, our dear brother Richard passed away far too soon."

I continued, "Our brother Edward and his wife Eva, with their two young sons, Ward and Joseph, soon followed them here to America. Edward built up the business to bring the Annely name to an even higher status. It was Edward who convinced me to come to this new world. All I brought was my gunmaking skills, which I had learned from our father, the first great gunsmith of the Annely family."

"My first impression of this grand, new land was how free I felt, freer than I had ever felt before. I fell in love with this country and this lovely lady seated next to me, and I knew this was where I belonged. Now that this tyrant King is threatening our liberties, I am proud to say that we,

Annelys, have chosen to stand and fight. We must hold onto our desire for freedom, no matter the cost."

"I ask that all of you stand with me and toast our General Washington, a great man who will never give up, and pray that he will be victorious in keeping the freedom we have in this country."

They all stood and tapped their glasses in unison, in appreciation for our General and everything I had said. I had never been prouder of the Annely family than I did now.

The following day, the men gathered in Francis's billiards room. None of us could match Francis's skill, so he naturally won most of the games we played.

Ward said, "Now, how about we have a shooting contest? At least I will have a fighting chance!"

"'Tis a grand idea, Ward. It will be like old times at Whitestone," replied Morgan, excited about the idea.

Francis Jr., reluctant to join in, said, "Oh yes, I remember those days fondly when Thomas would teach us all how to shoot. I recall I was quite bad at it. Perhaps I should sit this one out."

"Come now, son, 'tis only for the sport of it. I think you will enjoy yourself," replied Fran.

"Sounds like a jolly good time to me. I'll have a go at it, but I only have my pistol," piped up my father-in-law, joining in on the lad's enthusiasm.

"No worries, Gifford. I have a musket you can use and one for my son," replied Francis, walking to his gun cabinet to retrieve them.

"Well, that settles it, men; put down your pool sticks and grab your muskets!" exclaimed Francis as we followed him out back.

We loaded our muskets while William gathered old glass bottles for us to shoot. Francis yelled, "William, place one of those bottles on that large boulder over there!"

As instructed, William placed the bottle on top of the rock, ready for the first shooter. Each man would get one shot to knock the bottle off the rock. Ward went first and skillfully shot the bottle down. William quickly replaced the bottle, as Morgan shot it straight on with the eye of a sharpshooter. Fran, Francis Jr., and Mr. Dally shot their turns; unfortunately, all three missed.

"Now 'tis your turn, Uncle Thomas," said Ward, anxiously awaiting to see me shoot. I loaded up my musket and fired, hitting it straight on, leaving only the neck of the bottle lying on the rock. I reloaded my musket, quickly took aim, and fired, hitting the remaining small piece of the bottle and clearing off the rock. The men whooped and hollered while patting me on the back. "Aye, Thomas, with that sharp eye of yours, you never cease to amaze me! " exclaimed Francis as they all took turns shaking my hand.

The noise of the gunfire scared poor Phoebe out of her wits, and she ran screaming through the house, "The British are here, the British are here." Elizabeth laughed out loud, "Stop that, Phoebe. 'Tis just the men having some fun. Do you not recall the shootouts after dinner at Whitestone?" she said, calming the poor girl down. Beth held her hand to her heart while taking a large breath. "My goodness, Mother Elizabeth, that gave me quite a scare; I thought the British were invading us," she exclaimed, letting out a nervous giggle. The ladies laughed heartily at the confusion that was happening all around them. Elizabeth smiled and remarked, "Men will be boys at times."

After our shooting contest ended, we returned to the house and joined the ladies at the table. Ward excitedly said, "You should have seen Uncle Thomas. He surely has the eye of a hawk. He blasted off the bottom of the bottle, leaving only the neck lying there. Within seconds, he reloaded and shocked us all when he shot that small piece straight off the rock, right Morgan?"

"He most certainly did. He still has the knack," said Morgan proudly.

"Aye, Thomas, you are like fine wine; you keep getting better with age," Francis replied, saluting me with his wine goblet.

After witnessing my shooting abilities, Mr. Dally said, "I must say, Sarah, your man is the best shooter I have ever seen, and you know I have seen many. Thomas, where on heaven's earth did you learn to shoot like that?" he questioned.

Elizabeth replied, "'Twas our father who taught him so well," she said with pride.

"Aye Sister, 'tis true, but our dear brother Richard, God rest his soul, instilled my confidence in me. I still remember, clear as the day, when Richard and I would lay in the tall grass with our muskets loaded, waiting for the deer to come. In the clearing, about 100 yards away, stood a single buck. Richard whispered in my ear, "Take him, Thomas. You are a better shot than me, and I do not want to disappoint our family at home, waiting for their venison dinner," I said, vividly recalling the moment.

"I bet you all ate well for a week!" exclaimed Mr. Dally.

"All my husband ever brought home was a small duck," said Mrs. Dally, poking fun at her husband while everyone at the table roared with laughter.

After a delightful Sunday, relaxing and enjoying each other's company, Monday morning came too swiftly, and it was time to leave.

We said our farewells on the front lawn, where our horse-drawn carriages were waiting, ready for our journey home. As we rode off, I glanced back to see my dear sister, Elizabeth, standing on the porch, smiling while she waved goodbye.

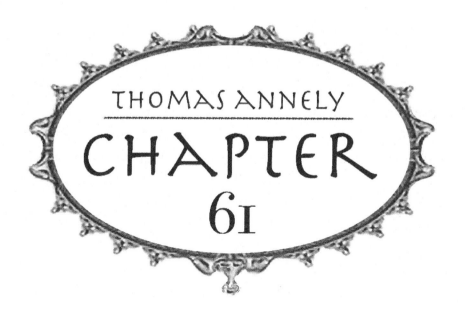

THOMAS ANNELY

# CHAPTER
## 61

It had only been two months since our joyous family reunion, when an urgent message arrived from my brother-in-law, Francis. I was apprehensive about opening the letter, as I ran my fingers over my name on the envelope. "What is it, Thomas?" Sarah asked. "'Tis a message from Fran," I replied softly. Sarah placed the pan back onto the hearth and came quickly to my side.

I slowly opened the letter and read Fran's solemn words. Since we had last seen her, Elizabeth had taken a turn for the worse and had grown much weaker. He asked us to visit as soon as possible.

"Oh, Thomas, we must go at once," replied Sarah. I nodded in agreement as my heart grew heavy with despair. Words escaped me, and all I could see in my mind was Elizabeth's face, smiling as she stood on the doorstep waving. Without a second thought, Sarah quickly packed while I prepared the horse and carriage. We left straight away, with young Gifford seated between us. Ward stayed behind to mind the workshop.

Our minds seemed lost in our thoughts as we rode along the dusty roads to Philadelphia. When we arrived at their home, William greeted us warmly, though his face bore a look of sorrow as he carried our things into the foyer. Phoebe entered the room and bent down to embrace Gifford, bringing a brief smile to her face. "'Tis good to see you, Mr. Thomas and Mrs. Sarah," she said. With her head hung low, she showed us to our room upstairs. "There's warm water in your room to freshen up. Master Francis and Mrs. Elizabeth will be down for supper at 7:00," she announced.

I anxiously paced the floor in our room while Sarah prepared Gifford for bed. Phoebe had missed our lad so much that she insisted on minding him for the evening. "Sarah, if you don't mind, I would like to go downstairs to talk with Fran before supper," I expressed. "That is fine, Thomas; you go ahead. I will be down later," she replied, struggling to get our little lad to wash. "Mind your mother, son," I said firmly as I left to find Francis.

As I looked around the house, William informed me that Fran was in his study. I knocked lightly on the door, not wanting to startle him. Fran opened the door and greeted me warmly. He appeared much more tired and worn since our last visit. The smile on his face told me how grateful he was that I was here. Yet his eyes showed the sadness he bore in his heart.

"Thomas, you're a Godsend. You are much needed here now, for Elizabeth's sake and mine," he said, grasping my hands. "Unfortunately, this bloody war stops for no one and still needs our attention. Our army is stronger now than ever before, but I am afraid I cannot say the same for our congress. I am getting bled dry and have been selling some of my possessions to help pay for this war. Before the war began, I did not realize how costly it would be. I haven't told Elizabeth the total amount of our money I have invested into it. She does not need anything more to trouble her," he said solemnly.

"I understand all too well, Fran. Congress has been very slow in paying me, but you have enough to think about right now. I do not want to add to your troubles," I said humbly.

"I thank you, Thomas, for feeling that way, but you, of all people, must be paid promptly. I will see to it straight away. They made a promise to you and I will make sure that they keep it."

"Fran, I appreciate your loyalty to me. Rest assured, I will never falter in my service to the troops and my dedication to this great country."

We both stood, locked our arms, and repeated our solemn pledge to each other, "Brothers-in-Arms, devoted to ending the tyranny that threatens our liberty."

We left the comforts of his study and walked down to the dining room. There, we found Sarah sitting there, alone. Fran embraced Sarah, thanking her for coming on such short notice.

"Lizzy will be down shortly. I ask you not to comment on her appearance. She has become quite self-conscious of how thin she is. Frannie and Morgan will be coming tomorrow with their wives. I thought it best to give you time alone with her before the children arrived," said Francis, in a weak tone.

Francis held onto Elizabeth's arm as he led her into the dining room. I embraced her with a warm smile, hiding my feelings of despair at how thin and frail she appeared. Her skin was as white as alabaster, and her hair was completely gray now. A touch of color had been applied to her lips and cheeks, giving her face the angelic appearance of a china doll. She looked like the waif, fragile girl I remembered in my youth, but her eyes were dull and tired. It took all I could muster not to show my emotions at the sight of my once strong and beautiful sister looking so weak.

Sarah stood beside me, trying to hold back the tears that were forming in her eyes. "It is so wonderful to see you again, Elizabeth," she said warmly, her voice filled with emotion. The two sisters embraced, and Elizabeth whispered in Sarah's ear, "Take good care of my favorite brother."

It was becoming too much to bear, so I turned my attention to the delicious meal before us. "My, what a feast you have prepared for us. I must say I am famished from the journey," I said enthusiastically, feigning hunger despite the pit that had formed in the bottom of my stomach.

Francis helped Elizabeth to her chair. She smiled sweetly at us, attempting to appear unchanged. Francis spoke for both of them, discussing the events of the day.

Elizabeth seemed to be enjoying the conversation when suddenly she excused herself and rose from the table, heading for the stairwell to go upstairs. Francis followed quickly behind her, apologizing as he grasped her arm and helped her to their bedroom.

Sarah and I looked at each other bewildered and were deeply concerned for Elizabeth's well-being. As we waited for Fran to return, Sarah took hold of the silver cross she wore around her neck and recited a prayer under her breath.

Francis returned, looking disheveled and worn. "I apologize for Elizabeth's speedy exit. Exhaustion took her over, and she needed to rest her head," he explained, trying to catch his breath. He sank in his chair, his head hanging low to his chest.

I walked over to Fran, with Sarah following behind me. I placed my hand inside the bend of his elbow and said, "Come along, Fran, you must be exhausted yourself. Let me help you to bed. We can finish our conversation in the morning." Sarah and I led him up to the top of the stairs. "'Tis very kind of you both; I am much obliged. I suppose I am in need of a good rest. I can't tell you how much it means to Elizabeth and me to have you and Sarah here with us at this time," he said before retreating to his bedroom.

Sarah and I felt overwhelmed as we went to our bedroom, where Gifford was sleeping soundly. As exhausted as we were, our minds would not settle, and we talked most of the night before finally drifting off, wrapped in each other's arms.

Early the next morning, we were woken by a quick knock on the door. I rushed out of bed, still groggy from not enough sleep, and threw some cool water on my face.

When I opened the door, I was pleasantly surprised to see Elizabeth standing there. "Sorry, Thomas, I hope I didn't wake you. I would like you to join me for tea on the veranda. 'Tis such a lovely morning," she expressed, looking much more lively than the night before.

"My dear sister, 'tis so good to see you bright and cheerful as usual. I would be delighted to join you; I will be down shortly," I replied, with a wide grin. "Wonderful, I will see you on the veranda," she said. I watched her walk down the stairs with a bounce in her step.

I turned with a stunned expression. Sarah sat up in the bed, puzzled at my expression, "Thomas, who was at the door?" she inquired. "You are not going to believe this: 'twas Elizabeth, looking like her old self, inviting me for tea," I said with astonishment.

Sarah leaped up from our bed and rushed over to me, wrapping her arms around my neck, "Oh Thomas, I prayed she would get well, and the Lord has answered," she replied with a fevered pitch. I held Sarah tightly, kissing her lips, as we stood together in each other's arms, relishing the moment. "You go join her for tea; I will stay with Gifford. I want you to enjoy some time with your sister alone," she said sweetly. "Thank you, dear," I replied, grateful for Sarah's caring and loving ways.

As I got myself dressed, excitement mixed with trepidation filled my mind. Nevertheless, I would enjoy my moment with my sister for however long it lasts.

I found Elizabeth sitting on the veranda, with the warmth of the morning sun beaming on her face. "Good day, dear sister, 'tis a lovely morning," I said as I sat beside her. "Thomas, thank you for joining me so early," she said as she grasped my hand. "I apologize for last evening. I was quite weary, but now I feel wonderful," she said, taking in a breath of fresh air. "What a day 'tis going to be, and to have you here with me makes it all the more delightful." I poured myself a cup of tea and held it up to salute. "Here's to you, my dear sister. May you continue to enjoy good health," I said with optimism.

I let my sister talk, baring her soul about how much she missed her days at Whitestone and how she wished we could go back there. "I would like to be buried there, Thomas, but I suppose that will not be possible," she said solemnly. "Elizabeth, do not speak of such things; you will be well soon." Elizabeth smiled, but I could see she thought otherwise.

"Thomas, I know what I am about to ask you may be an impossible task, but I need to say this. Once the war is over, I would like you to tend to the graves of Richard and my babes at Whitestone," she pleaded. "Why, of course, Elizabeth, we will both go," I replied, placing my hand upon hers. "Thank you, dear brother, 'tis a lovely sentiment, and yes, I will be with you, one way or another." I looked off to the vast green lawn in front of us, not wanting to face the realization of what was to be.

She quickly changed the subject to a more delightful conversation. "I received a lovely letter from our brother Edward the other day. I am so pleased to hear he has recovered from that awful stomach virus. I remember all too well how unpleasant those sea voyages can be. Can you believe our brother Bernard finally got married? And our nephew Joseph loves books, just like Bernard," she expressed.

I nodded in agreement, "Aye, Edward has written to me as well. I wonder how he really feels about Joseph not following in his footsteps. I remember how our father was not pleased about Bernard not becoming a gunsmith. Well, at least we have Ward, keeping the Annely tradition going," I replied.

"Oh Thomas, I am just pleased that Edward is happy after all he went through with that nasty Edmund Fox," she said.

"Aye, Elizabeth, he is a fellow I shall like to forget," I replied.

"Thomas, the man got what he asked for, plain and simple. Do not blame yourself for what happened that day. He was a menace not only to Edward, but to you and Francis as well. And, when he threatened Ward, that was the final straw. If you had not done what you were forced to do, that evil man would have surely killed our nephew," said my wise, bold sister.

William entered the veranda to alert us that our meal was ready. I lent my arm to my dear sister and escorted her into the dining room. Fran and Sarah were already seated, fussing over how much Gifford had grown. Gifford rose from his chair and rushed over, wrapping his arms around her, "Auntie Lizabeth," he shrieked excitedly to Elizabeth's delight. She bent over and gave Gifford a kiss and a warm embrace, "Oh my little love, how I have missed you!" she exclaimed while escorting him to sit beside her. "You sit right next to your old Godmother, and I will give you extra bacon," she said, pinching his smiling cheek.

Fran smiled broadly at seeing his wife so happy. He knew he had made the right decision to invite us here at this time.

"I expect the boys and their wives to arrive by early afternoon. It will give you time to rest, dear," Fran remarked, patting her knee.

"Nonsense, Francis, I want to spend every moment with my little godchild," she replied, smiling at Gifford as he gobbled up his food.

We all laughed with delight, seeing Elizabeth in her moment of happiness.

That evening, when Morgan and Francis Jr. arrived with their wives, we all joined together for another one of Elizabeth's delicious suppers. 'Twas an enjoyable time, hearing all that was happening in their lives.

We were all surprised when Francis Jr.'s wife Beth suddenly stood up to speak, with her hand upon her protruding belly. "As you all know, I come from a family of loyalists. However, I must take this moment to say that I have the utmost respect for you, Mother Elizabeth. You are such a courageous woman, standing up for your beliefs, even with all you have endured. Our wish is that our child will inherit their grandmother's strength of convictions," Beth expressed sincerely. We all raised our glasses to Elizabeth.

Elizabeth's face glowed with pride, astounded by her daughter-in-law's words of praise. She never dreamed she would hear them coming from her.

Morgan lightened the mood in the room as he recalled how, as a young lad, he would torment his mother. "Mother would never get a moment's peace with me. I was forever teasing Ann, and causing havoc about the house," he boasted.

"Oh my, is this all true, Mother Elizabeth?" piped up Morgan's wife, Gertrude. "I am afraid so, dear; perhaps you should wish for daughters," Elizabeth said in jest as laughter filled the room.

"I always felt you were Mother's favorite," said Francis Jr., winking at his mother. "Oh, come now, I loved both of you equally, even when you misbehaved," Elizabeth said, gazing fondly at her sons.

"'Tis a shame our Annie is not here, but she is always with me," Elizabeth said, lifting the locket around her neck. She opened it and exposed a beautiful miniature portrait of her daughter Ann.

"She writes to me often and sends her love to every one of you."

As the conversations continued, I could see Elizabeth growing weary. Once again, she excused herself to retire to her room. We all rose from the table and wished her a pleasant night's sleep.

Both Morgan and Francis Jr. quickly went to their mother's side. "Father, we will escort mother to bed. You sit and enjoy your brandy," Morgan said as they helped their mother upstairs. As they entered her bedroom, Morgan helped her sit in her chair next to her bed. "Shall I help you to bed, Mother?" he asked tenderly as both sons knelt beside her. "Not yet, sons," she replied.

Elizabeth gently placed her hands on their faces, gazing at them. "My sons, I am so proud of the fine young men you have become," she said affectionately. "If we are as fine of sons as you say we are, 'tis because we have the finest mother," said Francis Jr. "'Twas your love and guidance that led us down the proper paths, and 'tis how we will live for the rest of our lives," Morgan said lovingly. They held each other in a long embrace. "I love you both, dearly," she said softly. "And we love you Mother, with all our hearts," expressed Francis Jr.

Phoebe entered the room, embarrassed that she had interrupted the tender moment between mother and sons. "I beg your pardon, Mistress, I will leave you be," she said timidly. "No, Phoebe, please come in so I can relieve my sons to enjoy the rest of the evening," she said as they kissed their mother's cheek. "Have a good rest, Mother; we will see you in the morning," said Francis Jr.

She watched her sons with admiration as they walked out the door. "My sons are so handsome," she remarked to Phoebe, who nodded in agreement, helping her mistress to bed.

When morning arrived, I heard the familiar knock upon the door, but this time, Francis was standing there, looking devastated, with no life in his eyes.

"Thomas, she is gone. Our dear Lizzy is gone," he repeated as I grasped his shoulders, holding him up. I led him into our room and sat him down while Sarah stood there, stunned, with Gifford in her arms. I knelt beside him and let him speak, for no words could form in my mouth. "The Lord has been merciful and has taken her peacefully while she slept. She looked like an angel; her face showed no pain," he expressed as he dropped his head to his hands and wept.

Gifford began to cry softly at the sight of his uncle in tears. Sarah took him out into the hallway to Phoebe's welcoming arms as she held back her tears.

I had prayed the morning would bring my lovely sister back to her old self again, but it was not God's will. My heart sank with dread, for I could not believe my sister was gone. She has been such a guiding force in my life, with her unconditional love and devotion to me. I could not fathom my life without her.

I shook off my self-centered thoughts and gave my attention to my grieving brother-in-law, who will suffer the greatest from her absence. The words finally formed on my lips as I expressed my sympathy.

"'Tis a blessing she went peacefully by your side, Francis," I said, offering whatever comfort I could when I knew mere words could never ease his pain.

As Sarah consoled Francis, I went into their bedroom to see my sister once more. I found Phoebe by her bedside with her face in her hands, with William holding her as she wept. There was Elizabeth, lying there peacefully, free from her pain and suffering. I knelt beside her bed and grasped her cold, lifeless hand. I whispered the words I wished she could hear, "You will always be in my heart, dear sister" as I bent over and kissed her forehead.

We spent the next few days preparing for Elizabeth's funeral. Francis sent William out to get the local priest to speak over Elizabeth. She was laid to rest in a small clearing, surrounded by her lovely flowers. Once the war was over, Francis would see to it that her final resting place would be at Trinity Church in New York City, where he would join her when his time came.

We all stood solemnly around her grave while the priest recited his prayers. Francis spoke proudly, saying that she was heaven's gift to him and the most wonderful of mothers. Morgan spoke of how gallant she was in her love for her country and how happy he would be when they were reunited again in heaven. Young Francis expressed how she was the most remarkable of mothers and the bravest woman he knew. We all drew comfort from the tender words spoken, yet I remained silent. I could not find the words that I felt in my heart.

As we returned to their home, the silence was deafening as we all felt the loss of her presence. I walked out to the veranda, recalling my last moments alone with Elizabeth, which was all too brief.

Fran had retired to his room, and Sarah was packing and tending to Gifford to prepare for the journey home. Beth and Gertrude helped Phoebe prepare the meals, for she was beside herself with grief for the Mistress she had served since she was a young girl and had grown to love deeply.

Overcome with grief, Morgan and Francis Jr. joined me on the veranda. I spoke up, breaking the silence that surrounded us. "I hope you realize what wonderful sons you both are," I expressed.

"Uncle, I could have done so much more. Mother should have lived with me when she was in confinement, but no, I had to appease my Tory in-laws," Francis Jr. blurted out, burying his head in his hands.

"No, Frannie. Mother would not have wanted to hear you say that. She was perfectly content being with Kingsley at Uncle Thomas's home," Morgan responded, attempting to ease his brother's guilt.

"Morgan is right, Frannie. When I visited her at my townhouse in New York, she showed me the letter you had Kingsley smuggle into her. Your mother kept it close to her heart, for it meant so much that you loved her despite her beliefs. And she was so proud of how you sent Kingsley, with all those supplies, that brought such great relief to her and the other prisoners," I replied.

"Morgan, she was so delighted when you appeared in your peasant disguise. You gave her quite a laugh, but she could not stop talking about how you took such a big risk to be with her. Your mother was so pleased that you accepted her for what she believed in and always treated her with kindness and respect. She had a great love and devotion to this country, but not as great as her love for her children. Her family was always her first priority." My nephews remained silent, but I could see my words brought them comfort.

It was time to leave, and I begged Fran to come with us. He politely refused, saying he needed to be here, and assured us he would not be alone. Morgan and Gertrude would be staying on to be with him. He promised to visit when the time was right. Francis Jr. reluctantly took his leave, for their baby was due soon, and Beth needed to return to lie in wait for their child to be born. Sadness filled their hearts because Elizabeth would never have the joy of seeing her first grandchild.

As Sarah, Gifford, and I made our way back home, my heart swelled with the memories of my beloved, remarkable sister, whom I shall grieve for the rest of my life. I will respect my sister's legacy by remaining as devoted to the cause as she was.

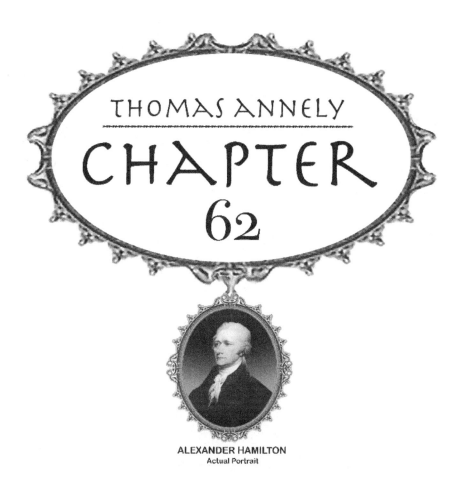

THOMAS ANNELY

# CHAPTER
# 62

**ALEXANDER HAMILTON**
Actual Portrait

The years are passing by quickly, and it is now 1780. It has been two years since the death of my dear sister, Elizabeth, and still, the war lingers on. Fran has little of his fortune left, for he lent most of his money to help support the war. He still grieves deeply for Elizabeth, but his dedication to the cause has not wavered. His love of books and the joy of spending time with his grandchildren helped him through the lonely days.

On the other hand, I continue to build arms for the Continental Army, but production has slowed considerably due to the little funds I am receiving from Congress. My nephew, Ward, now manages my entire gun shop by himself while I spend much of my time proving and supplying arms to the surrounding colonies.

Finally, the day came that would change the course of the war. Our French ally, Lieutenant General Rochambeau, met with General Washington, and they agreed on a plan to defeat General Cornwallis at Yorktown.

The plan was tremendously successful, and Cornwallis had no choice but to surrender his army at Yorktown, Virginia. Washington's victory gave us all hope that the war would end.

It is now the Autumn of 1783. I received a letter from Fran telling me that on September 3rd, the British and the Americans signed the Treaty of Paris. At last, the war was officially over. The Continental Army had defeated the most powerful army in the world with the strength of its sheer determination and devotion to the cause. Our freedom as an independent nation was now secured!

Fran filled his letter with accolades, saying I should be proud of myself.

He expressed that if dedicated men like myself had not supplied the Continental Army with the arms they needed so desperately, they would not have achieved victory. His inspiring words deeply honored and humbled me, for I was among many good men and women devoted to the cause.

To the joy of all American Patriots, on November 25th, the British army was forced to evacuate New York City. General Washington, seated high upon his grand horse, rode proudly into the newly liberated city with his troops marching alongside him. He was greeted by thousands of people cheering and scrambling to get a glimpse of this great man. Young girls and boys were laying flowers at his feet as he rode through the streets. My only wish was that my sister Elizabeth could have lived, to see the country she died for free once more.

Although the war was over, and I was no longer in the service of the Continental Army, I was still producing arms for New Jersey and other neighboring states. I felt proud to be a gunsmith who contributed to the War of Independence. I was just one of many to do so. I would like to think I have now earned the honor of calling myself an American Patriot.

Now that our country was at peace again, my brother Edward and his wife Eva had decided to return from England. They could now live in the country they once loved so much. Ward was elated to have his parents back in his life, and Edward and Eva were the most loving grandparents to their grandson, Eddy. My brother Edward spent countless hours teaching his young namesake all the parts of a musket. Edward and Eva sold their elegant home in New York and moved to Elizabethtown to be near Ward and Sally. Their youngest son, my nephew Joseph, stayed behind in England with our brother Bernard to continue his studies at Oxford. His scholarly Uncle would be an excellent example for young Joseph to follow.

It was like old times, with Ward, Edward, and I working together again, yet life can be cruel. Suddenly, without warning, my brother Edward suffered a fatal heart attack. Ward found him unconscious, slumped over at his desk. It seemed he had inherited our father's sickly heart. I was devastated. I could not believe my brother Edward, who gave me my start in this new world, had died. I had hoped we would share our golden years together. His time back in America was far too short, and we all miss him greatly. His namesake, Little Eddy Annely, asks for his Papa every day. I am certain the lad will grow to be in his grandfather's image, for one can see he is an Annely, through and through.

The years have gone by, and it is now 1789. Finally, freedom has prevailed! I received a wonderful message from Fran informing me that George Washington was to be our nation's first President. My nephew Morgan would have the honor of escorting General Washington and his entourage to the inauguration. Fran insisted that Ward and I accompany him, which we gladly accepted.

When we first arrived in the city, thousands of people stood, shoulder to shoulder, covering the streets. We had to struggle to get through the crowds before finally making our way to Wall Street. Up ahead was my nephew, Colonel Morgan Lewis, leading the procession to Federal Hall, with George Washington traveling behind in his guarded coach. A parade of over five hundred men in various military uniforms marched alongside him.

Many of the members of Congress were waiting on the balcony of Federal Hall, including a great man I have the pleasure of knowing personally. The man was John Adams, who was appointed our first Vice President.

At the entrance to Federal Hall, we could see George Washington escorted inside by his two aides. Morgan's brother-in-law, Robert Livingston, the Chancellor of New York, led the way. As they took their places on the balcony, Mr. Livingston proceeded with the swearing-in of our first President, the Honorable George Washington. With great pride, we watched the man we hailed as the *Father of our Country* take his Presidential oath of office. He was simply dressed in a brown broadcloth suit to bear resemblance to the common man, yet he appeared as dignified as ever.

Although our first President's words were difficult to hear, through the shouts and whistles of those who attended, we were in awe of this great man. When he finished reciting his pledge, he lifted his right hand from the Bible and turned to glance down at the crowd. I swear, as God is my witness, he looked directly at me and smiled.

At the end of the ceremony, the crowd exploded with cheer, throwing their hats in the air as all the church bells rang out throughout the city.

On the very top of Federal Hall, our flag was being raised up the flagpole by two Continental soldiers. There, it waved grandly in the gentle breeze. Its red, white, and blue colors were in bright contrast to the pale blue sky. Thirteen stars and thirteen stripes boldly displayed the unity of our colonies. I glanced over at Ward and Fran, their faces filled with pride, as we joined in with the hoops and hollers at the sight of our new country's flag. We were proud to witness one of the most important events of our new country, for we now have our first President of the United States of America.

Our new President, within months of his first year in office, made a proclamation declaring November 26, 1789, as the national day of Thanksgiving. This was not just a day of feasting and celebration, but a day to acknowledge the blessings bestowed upon us by the Almighty

God. Fran thought this holiday would be a wonderful time to celebrate with our whole family, and invited us all to join him in his Philadelphia home. He had already mentioned this to his son, Morgan, and he said he would be more than happy to go out back in the woods and catch a big, plump turkey for our table.

When that day in November came to pass, we were all delighted to be together again. As we sat around the massive table, filled to the brim with a feast for royalty, I gazed at all the old and new young faces. At the head of the table was Fran, looking content and proud of how his family had grown. Francis Jr. and his wife Beth sat beside him with their brood of five young children. My nephew Morgan and his wife Gertrude were on the opposite side with their ten-year-old daughter Margaret, born the year Elizabeth passed. Young Eddy Jr. and my son Gifford sat beside each other, their mouths watering for the roasted bird on the table. My nephew Ward, his wife Sally, and mother Eva, sat beside my in-laws Mr. and Mrs. Dally alongside Sarah and me.

With his glass in hand, Fran stood up and said, "'Tis with great joy that I celebrate this first official day of Thanksgiving with all of you. William and Phoebe have prepared a wonderful feast for us. Before we partake, I want us all to bow our heads and thank Almighty God. 'Twas with his Providence that we are able to be here today."

As Fran's words echoed in the room, I felt a surge of pride and joy. I stood up, raising my glass, and proclaimed, "Well said, Francis." The others joined in with a resounding "Hear, Hear!" It was a day filled with joy and inspiration, one we hope to continue through the years.

Four years later, in 1793, I was honored to receive a commission from the Secretary of War, General Henry Knox. My duty was to prove and repair all the damaged muskets and other arms stored at West Point in New York. The plans were in place for the fort to be a cadet training academy for newly enlisted soldiers. It is a formidable location, high above the west bank, with spectacular views of the Hudson River below.

Ten years had passed since General Benedict Arnold plotted to turn over West Point to the British. And he is still a topic of debate amongst the men. Those who fought under his command sympathized with Arnold, saying his treasonous wife was to blame. They say her beauty bewitched any man who passed her way. What bewitched me was how such a superior general could be so disloyal, especially after swearing his allegiance to General Washington and the Continental Army. Where would our country be today if his devious plan was successful? Providence lent a hand and saved us from ever knowing.

Three years later, my good fortune was still ahead of me. In a letter to President George Washington, Timothy Pickering, our country's Secretary of State, recommended that I produce arms for the state of Virginia. I gladly accepted this honor, for we now have our own country, and it was our duty to protect it from harm.

Our son Gifford is now twenty and attends the College of Philadelphia. Following in his cousin Morgan's footsteps, Gifford chose to study law. As much as I would have liked him to work in my trade, a young man has the right to choose his destiny. I came to America to be free to make my own way, and I want nothing less for my son.

Sarah and I agreed to move to Philadelphia to be closer to Gifford while he attends college. Before leaving, I sold my home in Elizabethtown, New Jersey, for a fair price to my nephew Ward. I gave him my workshop free and clear, simply because he deserved it. None of my men worked as hard as Ward, supplying our troops with the arms they needed to win the war. He is now the proud proprietor of his own gunsmith shop and has become well-known for building superior hunting rifles throughout the colony. I felt proud when he chose the name "Gun Endeavors" after my old gun shop in Bristol, England. It is wonderful that he is keeping our family tradition alive.

Ward and Sally have been blessed with another son. They honored me by naming him Thomas. I am pleased to know another Thomas Annely will carry on my name. With Edward gone, Ward has become more and more like a son to me. To our delight, they visit us often, and once again, our home is filled with the laughter of young children. Eva occasionally joined them and amazed us with how she had become the most pleasant of sisters-in-law.

Now that Gifford is away at school, Sarah and I spend much more time together. I must admit, I enjoy having my wife's undivided attention. We spend our Sundays leisurely strolling along the Delaware River. The city is bustling with merchants lined up along the streets, selling all sorts of delicacies. It was exciting to live the city life, enjoying all the sights and tastes of all the different foods from all over the world.

Our time alone has made me appreciate how much Sarah has fulfilled my life. She is still as lovely as ever, I thought as we rode through the crowded city streets in my carriage. We went by the Presidential Mansion on Market Street, hoping to catch a glimpse of President

Washington. Many have seen the President with his wife, Martha, enjoying the lovely gardens on the grounds.

As I glanced at Sarah's peaceful expression, I felt blessed to have such a wonderful wife. Even after all these years together, my love for her has only grown stronger. She has been my guiding light through some of the darkest days of my life. Never a discouraging word has ever passed by her sweet lips, only words of encouragement and love. God has given me this beautiful woman to spend the rest of my life with.

It is now 1797. After eight devoted years as our President, George Washington retired and returned to his home at Mt. Vernon. Although I am sad to see him leave, I am delighted that my good friend, John Adams, has been elected our second President. Thomas Jefferson, another great man, will serve as Vice President. I am confident these two fine gentlemen will govern in the same tradition as our distinguished President, General George Washington.

Later that year, the War Department bestowed upon me a great honor. I was appointed the *First Master Armorer* for the Harper's Ferry Arsenal of Virginia. George Washington had fought hard to build this arsenal in his state of Virginia, and I was proud to be a part of it.

Shortly afterward, I was appointed the *Inspector of Arms* for the state of Maryland.

After several weeks at Harpers Ferry, I was relieved to finally get home. I ran up the stairs, anxious to see Sarah. When I entered, the fireplace was cold, with barely a flame flickering. I was surprised not to find Sarah tending to the fire, preparing the evening meal as usual. I called her name and heard her faint response coming from the bedroom. I rushed in to find my lovely Sarah lying in bed, burning with fever. I immediately summoned the doctor, and after examining her, he confirmed what I had feared. Sarah was stricken with yellow fever. The doctor told me there was nothing more he could do for her. I did not want to believe the doctor's diagnosis, so I stayed by her side, trying any remedy I knew to cure her. Night and day, I wiped the beads of sweat from her forehead, hoping to comfort her. As she shook with chills, I held her close, continually telling her how much I loved her. She pleaded with me to stay away from her, but I would have rather died myself than not be by my dear Sarah's side.

After hearing of his mother's illness, Gifford rushed home to be by her side. Sarah feared he would become infected and insisted he stay with her parents. They were beside themselves with worry at the thought of losing their beloved daughter. I hoped having Gifford there would bring them some comfort.

After five days of watching my dear wife suffer, the Lord took her mercifully away from me. The love of my life, my beautiful green-eyed girl, had passed on, leaving me alone and heartbroken. The pain was so great it felt as though someone stuck a bayonet straight through my heart. My only comfort was knowing she was no longer suffering. I felt deeply for my son Gifford, who had lost the most loving of mothers. Somehow, I was spared from catching the dreaded fever and was able to remain strong for the sake of our son. Yet, my nights were filled with despair as I longed to hold my Sarah once more in my arms. Mr. and Mrs. Dally, myself, and Gifford were grateful for all our family and friends who attended her funeral to support us during this trying time. My life will never be the same without my beautiful girl. She will live on forever in my heart.

The following year has brought more terrible news. All the newspapers in the thirteen states had the bold headline, "George Washington is Dead." Our first president and our fearless leader, who had bravely fought beside his loyal soldiers and escaped the enemy bullets on so many occasions, had fallen from a mere throat infection. The whole world mourned alongside his faithful wife Martha, as he was laid to rest at his Mt. Vernon home alongside the Potomac River. It seems the good Lord decided it was time for his faithful servant to come home. His passing left the whole nation stunned and heartbroken, for he truly was the "The Father of our Country" and loved greatly by all.

My son Gifford has finished his studies and is now an apprentice at a prestigious law firm in New York City. He resides in my townhouse and lives the exciting life of a bachelor gentleman. Getting away was difficult for him, so I visited him in the city I once called home. Traveling over the Hudson, I missed seeing my old friend Howie, who retired from his business and moved away with Mary Blackinton. From last I heard, he was doing remarkably well for a man well into his nineties.

Visiting Gifford at my townhouse was bittersweet, with all the memories it held. The last time I had been there was when I visited Elizabeth with my lovely Sarah by my side.

The following year, I received a disheartening letter from Fran. His daughter Ann, who was the mother of four children and widowed for eleven years, had passed away. My dear niece was only fifty-four years of age. Fran was beside himself with grief and guilt over never having the chance to make amends with his only daughter.

After Ann's death, Fran learned that Queen Charlotte, the wife of King George III, had been sending Ann money each month. After the untimely death of Ann's husband, the Queen wrote, "*The wife of a gallant sailor like Captain Robertson ought not to suffer penury.*"

Fran, in his loneliness, decided to move to New York City to live with his son, Francis Jr. Through our many correspondences, I sensed how grief-stricken he was for losing not only his wife but also his dear daughter. I felt lonely without him nearby, so I would make the long trip to New York City as often as I could. We spent those days reminiscing, as two old gentlemen do, and enjoyed each other's company immensely.

Sadly, at the end of that very same year, I lost my dearest friend. On New Year's Eve, my beloved brother-in-law, Fran, passed away. The man, who was my closest confidant, had departed from this earth. I was devastated, having just been in his company a fortnight ago. I never imagined it would be the last time I saw him alive. He was eighty-nine years of age and had lived a good, long life, but I still yearned to have him here with me.

I attended the funeral to pay my last respects to Fran at Trinity Church in New York City. A year before, he had Elizabeth's remains moved from Philadelphia to Trinity Church so that when his time came, they would be buried alongside each other. I was glad to see how many of his fellow Congressmen and friends were there to honor this most

remarkable man. As I stood over their graves, I was comforted by knowing that my beloved brother-in-law and my loving sister were together
again, resting in peace.

In the spring of 1803, I was surprised to receive an invitation for a
private meeting with President Thomas Jefferson in Washington, D.C.

When I arrived at the impressive white stone mansion, two soldiers
immediately escorted me into the President's office. The President rose
from behind his desk, reached across and shook my hand. "Mr. Annely,
I am pleased to meet you. I asked you here because I am well aware of
your loyalty to this country."

"Mr. President, you have my deep admiration for what you have
done for our country," I replied, humbly.

"Please sit down, Mr. Annely. Your expertise is needed greatly for a
plan I have to expand this country. I am proposing an expedition which
will be led by two fine men, Captain Meriwether Lewis and Lieutenant
William Clark to explore the new territory to the West. They will need
weapons for hunting, trading and protection, and I want you, Thomas,
to build them."

"Mr. President, I will be deeply honored to supply you with whatever weapons you need."

"Thank you, Thomas. I knew I could count on you."

Suddenly, a man walked in unannounced and introduced himself as
Vice President Aaron Burr. He looked down at me and said, "I know
you Mr. Annely, your reputation precedes you. I am also well aware of
your shooting ability. I am somewhat of a marksman myself. Let me ask
you: do you still have the eye of an eagle?" he questioned.

"Well, Mr. Burr, I will surely find that out when I have to prove out the weapons I will be building." I replied.

"I am sure you will, Mr. Annely," Burr replied and swiftly exited the room.

I felt this pompous man, Aaron Burr, knew more about me than meets the eye.

President Jefferson, unfazed by our conversation, walked over to me and said, "Thank you Thomas, I will be contacting you soon."

I thanked the President, said my farewell and took my leave. With the aid of two other gunmakers, Robert McCormick and John Miles, we went on to build 320 weapons that included horseman's pistols and muskets. It was most satisfying to know that I played an important part in the Lewis and Clark expedition, which will lead to the expansion of our new country.

Two years have passed since I lost my best friend, Fran, and I am now growing too old to travel. To my delight, my good son Gifford visits me every Sunday and keeps me updated on all the political news. He informed me that my nephew, his cousin, Morgan Lewis, had won victoriously over Aaron Burr in his run for the Governorship of New York. I only wish that Elizabeth and Francis could have witnessed this proud moment.

What was remarkable to both Gifford and me was how Morgan was able to defeat the sitting Vice President, Aaron Burr. From what Gifford had learned, Alexander Hamilton, the former secretary of the treasury, helped turn the tide in Morgan's favor. Hamilton was not an admirer of Aaron Burr and made it well known to all.

During the gubernatorial campaign, Aaron Burr was so humiliated by Alexander Hamilton's accusations that he challenged him to a duel. Hamilton accepted the challenge, and the duel occurred on July 11th, 1804, at Weehawken, New Jersey. Tragically, Burr shot Hamilton, and he died two days later, with his grieving wife Elizabeth by his side.

The very mention of Weehawken always sends a shiver down my spine. It brings back the memory of when I had no choice but to accept a duel against a madman named Edmund Fox.

Despite all I have endured through the years, I've had many good fortunes as well. I truly believe that God has left me on this earth to witness the many events that took place in the building of this great country called the United States of America.

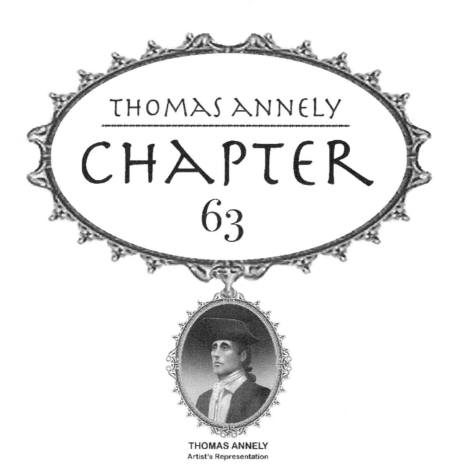

## THOMAS ANNELY

# CHAPTER

## 63

**THOMAS ANNELY**
Artist's Representation

I am old now, tired and frail, and in the winter of my life. My memories of all the people I have shared my wonderful life with keep me company during these long days. I can still see Sarah's deep green eyes, as clear as the first day I met her. I feel her presence all around me, and with my weakening heart, I know we will be reunited forever soon.

Most of my days are spent reading my favorite books in my comfortable leather chair. Glancing at my musket over the fireplace, I placed my book down and slowly stood on my unsteady legs. I gently took my musket down from its resting place and cradled it in my arms.

I felt it was time to put my thoughts to paper. I leaned my musket against the stone fireplace and walked over to my old writing desk, feeling the desk chair creak as I sat. Although my hands shook with palsy, I dipped my feathered quill pen in the inkwell and began to write.

## *My Last Will and Testament*

*To my dear son, Gifford Annely,*

*You have been the light of our lives to me and your dear late mother.*

*Upon my death, I willingly bequeath all my belongings, my home in Philadelphia, and my New York townhouse, to you, my son, Gifford Annely.*

*I also leave to you my most treasured possession, my favorite musket.*

*This great responsibility I have put upon you is not to be taken lightly, for you are now the keeper of my finest musket. 'Tis the very first musket I proudly built here in America. I inscribed "T Annely" on the lock plate, and it is one of the few I have signed. This musket also served its country during the American Revolution.*

*Do not attempt to repair it, for the imperfections are a reminder of when it fought alongside your brother Chip, who bravely gave his life for his comrade and his country.*

*My musket has been my trusted companion throughout all the years. It always shot straight and true for me. It shall be yours now, and if the need should arise, it will protect you by its mere presence.*

*Proudly display it for all to see and serve as a reminder of all that the Annely family sacrificed for the freedom of this great land, the United States of America.*

*When your time comes to an end, as mine will soon, be sure whomever you bestow my musket to will honor its legacy and protect it for the generations to come.*

*Your loving father, Thomas Annely*

I signed and dated my will, Thomas Annely, on this 20th day of December in the year 1804. I left my will on my desk, knowing my son Gifford would surely find it.

I grabbed hold of my musket, sat in my well-worn chair, and ran my fingertips along the smooth butternut wood. Reflecting on my long life, I realized I was merely a young English gunsmith who migrated to this country and proudly became an American Patriot.

A hazy ray of sunshine coming through my window showed me the faces of those I loved who had gone before me. I felt comforted as they invited me into their peaceful existence.

I held my musket tightly, closed my eyes, and all the weight on my tired shoulders faded away. A great calm came over me as my soul lifted and my last breath left my body.

*Thomas Annely died alone, yet peacefully, that day, knowing that his musket would live on to tell the true story of how this great country of ours came to be.*

*Lest we forget, my fellow Patriots!*

# ACKNOWLEDGMENTS

This novel has truly been written as a labor of love for my husband Fred. I devote this book entirely to him, who I am eternally grateful to for igniting in me a love of history and art from our many trips all around the globe, including annual trips to the old North Bridge in Concord, Ma. I have learned so much, because of him.

What started out as my desire to write a small booklet for "provenance" about the Revolutionary War musket my husband had purchased many years ago, turned into a full-page novel.

My husband Fred, through his tireless research to find information about the maker of his musket, an obscure gunmaker named Thomas Annely, sparked an even greater desire in both of us to tell this man's story. Finding information about Thomas Annely proved to be a daunting task for there was, *"scant information about him to be found"* (quoting the words of another individual who, like us, was finding it challenging to find information about Thomas). Yet my husband carried on in the typical British fashion, although he is full blooded Italian, with his research to discover all the amazing accomplishments Thomas had throughout his lifetime and how devoted he was to our country. As we delved into Thomas's life we were astounded to find interesting facts about his family members as well. My husband put together a timeline which traced Thomas's life and that of his family members from 1750 up until his death in 1804. My husband truly felt that Thomas Annely was put on this earth by God to be our witness to the building of our country.

I am grateful to the Bristol Historical Society in England who helped me trace Thomas's family tree. Although Thomas had several siblings, some who had perhaps died young, we chose to include only the ones we were able to find enough information about to make their story interesting.

As written, Richard Annely was the first brother to find success in the new land and tragically died before his time.

Thomas's sister, Elizabeth Annely Lewis, could have been a story to tell all on its own. She was a remarkable woman from a time when women were expected to be subservient to their husband's needs and support them in their endeavors. Elizabeth was far beyond just a devoted wife, who enabled her husband, Francis Lewis, to pursue his dreams to bring this country to its greatness. She was an "active participant" who was as passionate a Patriot as any soldier on the field. As quoted from Francis Lewis's great granddaughter, Julia Delafield, "*Mrs. Lewis had more than one opportunity of showing the steady purpose, the firmness of nerve that would have distinguished her had she been a man*". The society of the "Daughters of the American Revolution" tell the story of Elizabeth with great pride. I hope my depiction of Elizabeth has done this great lady justice in bringing her story to life.

Edward Annely was indeed a brother with a bone to pick, about the business of their brother Richard's will. Most of his story was based on factual information we had discovered in his handwritten letters. Edward comes across as a rather crude, stuffed shirt at times, but to me, he was like most men, simply trying to make his way in this world, in the most honorable way.

Francis Lewis's story, as with many of the brave signers of the Declaration of Independence, was downplayed and in great need of telling. He made a fortune in the early years of the 18th century, as a merchant, and yet, he was willing to give it all away so that we all could live as free Americans. I made a point to tell this man's story in the best of light, for I have nothing but the utmost respect for his unselfishness and bravery he displayed throughout his whole adult life. Not only through the years of the Revolutionary War, but during the Seven Years War, where he was held prisoner for (ironically) seven years. He displayed a strong constitution which carried him through, even after losing the love of his life, Elizabeth. He was quoted as saying she was "heaven's gift" to him. Elizabeth and Francis's story, was for me, akin to the story of John and Abigail Adams, who also shared a great love, devotion and support for each other.

Kingsley was in fact, Elizabeth's humble manservant, who came to her aid in prison as illustrated on a 1976 Franklin Mint commemorative medal (pictured within book).

Hannah Beard was their brother Richard's assistant and was very much devoted to him. She was also one of the benefactors of Richard's will.

Ann, Francis Jr, and Morgan were the children of Francis and Elizabeth and what was written about them is based on actual facts. Elizabeth did have 7 children and only the three survived.

Thomas's brother Bernard in England, was an author of a book called *The Theory of the Winds,* and was well respected amongst the academicians of the time.

All the other characters wrote themselves into the novel, as the story took on its own legs and started to write itself. We all have special people in our lives that make living worthwhile, and so was the case for Thomas, Elizabeth, Francis and Edward.

What amazed me most about writing this book was how little I knew about this very important time in our history. And how much we truly owe to these great men and women of the 18th century in securing our own freedom, that we freely take for granted these days.

The 21st century, as with every century before it, has its own set of challenges, not so unlike what our ancestors had faced. I have found that by looking into our past, we can find the answers to solve our issues of today, if we take the time to read the words of these great people who came before us. I have gone through most of life being a spectator, too busy with my own little world to get involved with what was happening to our country. By writing this book, I have awoken in myself, a pride in my country which I hope to awaken in you, the reader.

During the years preceding the revolution, the colonies were greatly divided between loyalists and patriots. It appears, as they say, history is repeating itself, and we are once again a nation greatly divided. It pains me to think that we have not evolved enough to look beyond our differences to find a common ground, and not resort to revolt. I pray that our leaders of today will see that war is not the answer and will put aside their pride and base their decisions, like our forefathers did, on preserving the basic core values this country was built upon; *of life, liberty and the pursuit of happiness*, for all the generations to come.

I wish to thank my wonderful family who has brought much fulfillment to me through the years. For the past two years they listened patiently as I spoke incessantly about writing our novel, and were always supportive. Special thanks go to our daughter Vicky for her endless hours of assisting us graphically as well as polishing up the rough edges of our story, and to our granddaughter Sofia, who listened endlessly to my self-doubts and always encouraged me to keep writing. I wish I could have shared this book with my mother Evelyn, whose wisdom and infinite knowledge I valued greatly.

I am honored to have spent this time with the wonderful Annely family and hope you enjoy their story. It should make all their descendants proud.

I remain, your humble servant, Mary Machado Marzocchi

PS. I cannot forget our trusted pet, Coffy. A descendant of King Charles himself. He has been my trusted companion and patiently stayed by my side while I wrote, even forfeiting some much-needed walks. It's all done now boy, for now.

# THESE NAMES LISTED BELOW ARE THE ANNELY FAMILY AND THE HISTORICAL PEOPLE WHO PARTICIPATED IN THOMAS' LIFE STORY

Edward Annely, Sr. (Patriarch)
Susannah Annely (Matriarch)
Richard Annely
Bernard Annely
Thomas Annely
Sarah Dally Annely
Gifford Annely
Elizabeth Annely Lewis
Francis Lewis
Francis Lewis, Jr.
Elizabeth "Beth" Ludlow Lewis
Ann Lewis Robertson
Captain George Robertson
Morgan Lewis
Gertrude Livingston Lewis
Edward Annely
Edward "Ward" Annely, Jr.
Gifford Dally
Anne Dally
Hannah Beard
Kingsley
Phoebe
William Kempe, Esq.
Chancellor Robert R. Livingston
Gabriel Ludlow, Esq.
George Washington
Martha Washington

John Adams
Samuel Adams
John Hancock
Thomas Jefferson
Timothy Pickering
General Henry Knox
Alexander Hamilton
Marquis de Lafayette
Aaron Burr
Thomas Paine
General Nathanael Greene
Benjamin Franklin
General Horatio Gates
Lt. General Rochambeau
General Charles Cornwallis
King George II
King George III
Queen Charlotte
Benedict Arnold
General Thomas Gage
Baron Von Steuben
General William Howe
Lewis & Clark
William Paca
Samuel Chase
Lt. Colonel Samuel Birch

# ABOUT the ARTIST and the AUTHOR

Through the years, Fred and Mary Marzocchi have had the pleasure of working together in the creative world of advertising. Establishing their own graphic design studio allowed them to showcase their natural talents: Fred as a creative artist and Mary as an aspiring writer. Fred's three children, talented in their own right, worked alongside them.

Inspired by the true story of the maker of Fred's 18th-century musket, Fred and Mary applied the same passion and principles they acquired in their business years to bring Thomas Annely and his family's story to life.

We sincerely hope you enjoy reading about this remarkable family who contributed to the building of our great nation.

-Fred and Mary Marzocchi

Made in United States
Orlando, FL
09 April 2025

60235103R00277